AF478163

GREEN CARD SOLDIER
©2014 Bruce Zielsdorf

Published by Hellgate Press
(An imprint of L&R Publishing, LLC)

Hellgate Press
PO Box 3531
Ashland, OR 97520
email: sales@hellgatepress.com

Editor: Harley B. Patrick
Interior design: Michael Campbell
Cover design: L. Redding

ISBN: 978-1-55571-7568

Zielsdorf, Bruce.
 Green Card Soldier / Bruce Zielsdorf. -- First edition.
      pages cm
1. Bosnians—United States—Fiction. 2. Americans—Bosnia and Hercegovina—Fiction. 3. International relief—Fiction. 4. Self-realization—Fiction. I. Title.
PS3626.I4858G74 2014
813'.6—dc23
      2013049121

Printed and bound in the United States of America
First edition 10 9 8 7 6 5 4 3 2 1

GREEN CARD SOLDIER

Bruce Zielsdorf

DEDICATION

According to the U.S. Department of Defense, there are about 30,000 non-citizens (approximately 1.6 percent of the force) currently serving on active duty in the America's Army, Marine Corps, Navy, Air Force and Coast Guard. More than 4,100 deployed to Iraq and Afghanistan from all branches of the Armed Forces. These brave men and women may be permanent legal residents, but they are not U.S. citizens. At the same time, they have voluntarily chosen to defend the very country where they now live.

Since the Revolutionary War, it's not been uncommon for refugees to take pride in America and want to show their patriotism by serving. Although newspaper, magazine and Internet coverage of "green card" troops has been extensive, little has been done to tell their stories through the heart and mind of a *Green Card Soldier*. That's what this literary voyage attempts to do.

It is an honor and a privilege for me to dedicate this book to those who routinely stand in harm's way and especially the heroes who've made the ultimate sacrifice in the name of America's freedom.

—⁂—

CONTENTS

ACKNOWLEDGMENTS

Raleigh Banks
The late, great merchant mariner who inspired everyone he touched

Robert M. Bauer
Life-long friend, protagonist, proof reader and critic

Karen Brown
The most gentle and caring artist to ever touch a keyboard

Hazel Cathers
Den Mother to the United States Armed Forces

Carol Cook
Hard-charging business woman and unqualified friend

Valerie (Voom Voom) Dowd
Loving friend, ally and elegant window dressing

David Hansen
Backstage magician, life of any party and very special friend

Chet Marcus
Cohort-in-crime, creative partner and loving father

Gary Perugini
Jeopardy enthusiast, proud Air Force veteran and one great guy

Elizabeth Ann Reddick
Friend, counsel, motivator and soul mate

Cathy Clardy Taff
Cosmic twin, creative critic and truly genuine soul

Ruth Zielsdorf
Special sister-in-law, cheerleader and listening post

FOREWORD

WHILE CHIEF OF ARMY PUBLIC AFFAIRS, I worked closely with Bruce Zielsdorf when he led the charge to revitalize the Army's public relations effort in New York City—the media capital of the world. With a limited staff and resources, Bruce was relentless in his efforts to tell the Army story through the achievements of Soldiers, veterans and family members across the country and around the globe. It's not surprising, then, his first novel would follow the exploits of a naive Bosnian teen who eventually joins the Army to earn his U.S. citizenship while coming to grips with the horrendous upheavals in his homeland.

Defense Department officials estimate there are currently 30,000-plus non-citizens (about 1.6 percent of the force) serving on active duty. More than 4,100 of these Soldier, Sailor, Airman and Marine warriors deployed to Iraq and Afghanistan. Many were wounded in the line of duty and some made the ultimate sacrifice for this great Nation.

Since the Revolutionary War, it's not been uncommon for refugees to take pride in America and want to show their patriotism by serving. Although newspaper, magazine and blog coverage of "green card" troops has been extensive, little has been done to tell the story through the heart and mind of a *Green Card Soldier*. That's what this literary voyage does. The book's theme is as fundamental as the core values of any American Soldier: Life can become richer and everyone become stronger when we look beyond stereotypes and appreciate each other for the unique individuals we are.

U.S. Army Maj. Gen. (Ret.) John G. Meyer, Jr.
CEO, J. G. Meyer & Associates

Publisher's Note: *General Meyer is a proud and dedicated Soldier with 33 years of distinguished service to his credit. He's also the author of* Company Command: The Bottom Line, *an authoritative leadership text widely used throughout the Defense Department.*

PREFACE

GREEN CARD SOLDIER marches through the exploits of a naïve Bosnian teen who joins the U.S. Army to earn his citizenship while coming to grips with the upheavals in his homeland. The tale is told by a cynical, yet self-deprecating, war correspondent who, over the years, has reported on similar pursuits in bizarre locations around the globe.

I wrote this book after years of living in Europe and falling in love with the historical magnificence of the continent. The tragedy that was the breakup of the Yugoslav Republic and the subsequent trilateral civil war only added to my personal intrigue with the area. Having seen the beauty of the Balkans during trips to the region, it was gut-wrenching to witness the horrors that tore that special place apart.

With despair, I watched the former Yugoslavia as it was battered by thunderous storms of religious and nationalistic disgust that rip apart families, villages and the Balkan countryside. It was hard to believe once-civil debate had decayed into such a degree of hate mongering, land grabbing and ethnic cleansing on all sides.

Trying to reconcile all that in my mind and commit it to paper was the genesis of this book. Hopefully, the diverse characters in this novel and their sometimes bizarre adventures challenge readers with the question: *Can life become richer, and people stronger, when we look beyond labels to appreciate one another for the unique individuals we are?*

Just as this book is dedicated to the brave men and women who voluntarily serve in defense of our Nation's values, I hope my *Green Card Soldier's* quest for citizenship and service is a morsel of motivation for the thousands upon thousands of naturalized Americans who seek much the same.

Bruce E. Zielsdorf
Author, civil servant and military veteran

A TREKKER'S TALE

Prologue to the Novel
Green Card Soldier

EVERY REPUTABLE REPORTER KEEPS A NOTEBOOK. As a proud member of the Fourth Estate, I'm constantly writing in mine. These records are so important I scribble my name, Heath Winslow, full across the cover of every spiral binder. Then I jot my New York address below my moniker. Should I misplace one of these journalistic gems, I hope a stranger will forward the grungy notepad to me.

But, if my chronicle is mailed home, am I obligated to act on it? Do I call out my inner correspondent and scurry to draft a story from those recovered remarks? Okay, I'll be the first to admit my sarcastic edge has been sharpened through decades of endless reporting on bloody conflicts large and small. That's why I bristle at the thought of interacting with dutiful strangers.

Not meaning to be a wet blanket, it's time to stop this mind game and focus on the task at hand. Let me take a moment to scan a memo dated Nov. 1, 1990. I know they're not hard-hitting, fact-based footnotes for my next article, but I find them to be critical mileposts along my wandering road to discovery.

Notebook entry: Liptauer cheese spread…

"Check!" I can state with pride as I locate item one on my shopping list. I've long realized such records are a matter of survival. Without an inventory, a diligent foodie like me would be lost trying to navigate Budapest's Great Market Hall—this country's largest indoor bazaar. The barrage of sights, sounds and smells within this massive wrought iron and stained glass food palace is relentless. My senses are bombarded from every direction. Shouldn't this place be proclaimed Europe's cornucopia of culinary delights? I've yet to see that entry in any *Michelin Guide*.

Notebook entry: Csabai Kolbász...

"Check again!" is my response as a vendor thrusts forward my second paper-wrapped purchase. When shopping here, I instinctively adopt a bloodhound's sense. I'll not be seduced by the aroma of opulent Turkish coffee, or the peppery bite of Göcseji cheese. No way... Instead, I revel in nibbling on teeny Hungarian sausages, trying to choose which ones to befriend. This is no small task, even for a self-proclaimed gourmet like me.

Notebook entry: Tokaji wine & plum Pálinka...

"Check!" I assert as a fine liquor is discovered. All gastronomic goodies should be balanced by a sweet vino or fruity brandy. Tokaji wine is heralded in Hungary's national anthem. So, I feel obligated to buy it; should I not?

Notebook entry: Paprika & caviar...

A final "Check!" and I pronounce my excursion complete. Exploring the corridors of this red brick behemoth has always invigorated me. This colossal space shouts with the bravado of a carnival barker, "Experience the ancient one. Come join the fun!" Who am I to object when such epicurean delights leap out to present themselves?

I have some advice for visitors, though: Don't overlook the countless booths on the second floor—a massive shelter for tacky tourist trinkets. Stall after stall is filled to overflowing with Orthodox icons painted in China. Forget not the Babushka dolls carved in Vietnam, a fake crystal vase from who knows where and stacks of heavy-handed embroidery—prefect for draping Aunt Adrian's sofa.

Well, my notebook's reviewed and a fitting level of criticism heaped. I sense it's time to find the rail head. The InterCity to Belgrade leaves just before noon and I want to be on it. With a couple dozen stops, it's no express to the Serbian heartland, but that's okay. The ride will give me time to observe the locals, a writer's true pleasure in life. So, why do I insist on taking the train? First off, I love locomotives. And it will give me a chance to reflect on the crescendo of war threats now churning in that multiethnic Balkan backwater.

Notebook entry: By early '90s, Yugoslavia is plagued with problems... Foreign debt, inflation & unemployment cloud the air... Nationalist feelings & political snags fester, leading to crisis... Milosevic rejects ideas for a looser federation

But why must I again charge forward to report from such a political hotbed? We're entering the last decade of the 20th century; wake up people! Just look what's going on. Iraq has invaded Kuwait, East and West Germany struggle to reunite, Europe's commies are hanging it up and the World Wide Web has debuted—whatever that means. Bottom line: This should be a busy, busy decade. By extrapolation, it's the essence of a reporter's bliss, and more importantly, just what my editor ordered.

—⚍—

The cab driver's Lada wheezes and shakes its rusty shell toward a Gothic cathedral-like structure known as the Budapest-Keleti Rail Station. I pay him. He pops from the Marxist heap to gather my suitcase, shopping bags and attaché. I offer a second tip, but the cabbie refuses. Instead, he points toward a ticket kiosk and encourages me to step lively into my new adventure.

No one said I'd be riding the Orient Express, but I didn't plan on hiking half the Hungarian frontier just to board a train. Okay, so I'm dragging too damn much stuff, as usual. I soon realize the need to execute a few Manhattan-style sidewalk dodge-and-weave maneuvers, if I'm to proceed. It's an acquired urban skill that allows me to zigzag past hordes of peasant ladies who've begun swarming on to the platforms. I find it intriguing they're all laden with enormous bouquets of sweet-scented flowers. And not to my surprise, the cantankerous itty-biddies are pushing and shoving like miniature sumo wrestlers in a crazed attempt to board the train all at once.

I execute a mental slap on the forehead, realizing I've strolled smack dab into the middle of an All Saints, Souls, or Something Day mass exodus from the city. And now I'm surrounded by a colony of babushkas scurrying about like penguins waddling to the sea.

> *Notebook entry: Halottak Napja—Day of Remembrance... Instead of Halloween, Hungarians head to the cemeteries for All Soul's Day... Prayers believed to lighten the way for those living in purgatory... Death is nothing unusual here*

The poor women on the platforms are consumed by a single-minded purpose: Scuttle to their villages in time to put flowers on gravesites and light lanterns to lost loved ones before tomorrow's sun sets. Based on centuries of Balkan tradition, this is what the devout must do.

Mustering my own determination, I'm able to pass a multitude clad in multi-layered funeral garb. My knees are now aching in time with my fast-beating heart. I soon reach a railcar where seating appears available. I struggle up the steps and into the coach. A single, somewhat worn, dark green velveteen lounge seat, nestled with a petite, but chipped, wood-veneer desk, presents itself. It's a silent, but genuine, invitation to sit. I accept the offer and settle in for the journey.

My travel banquet is quickly put on display—a caviar tin is opened, Lipto cheese spread unwrapped and crusty artisan bread at the ready. It's time to "Prost!" this Mad Hatter sojourn with a shot of Hungary's finest. As I lift my glass of brandy, the train pitches forward and back, then begins its slow lumber out of the station.

—⁂—

Before long, my romantic repast is interrupted by a verbal exchange erupting at the far end of the coach. The commotion involves a boyish-looking conductor in an ill-fitting uniform confronting what appear to be three affluent tourists.

> *Notebook entry: Two trendy women & a male companion… Spent high end to gear down… Only East Coast fashion slaves have the style, acumen & cash to dress with such style… Ugly Americans at their finest*

"Ön a hibás a vonat," the baby-faced train official states.

"We don't speak Hungarian," the first sojourner replies.

"Ön a hibás a vonat," the conductor shouts.

"Parlez-vous Français?" the second female tourist asks.

Once again the youthful officiato hollers, "Ön a hibás a vonat!"

"Sprechen sie Deutsch?" the male traveler interjects.

"Ön a hibás…," is all the conductor will say, sounding shriller each time he repeats the phrase.

"Okay, last chance… Parli Italiano?" the first woman asks, as if resigned to the fact her question will only generate a repeat of the previous response.

And she's right. "Ön a…," the young man says yet again. This time it's more of a pleading attempt to solicit action from the three.

"Can you believe it?" the lad in the middle says with a huff. "Here we are, three seasoned world travelers who speak half a dozen languages, and we can't get this zit-faced bureaucrat to understand a damn word we're saying."

Then, as if on cue, a dapper gentleman rises from a nearby seat and steps into the fray. He tips his fedora and in perfect English quips, "Dorothy, you're not in Kansas anymore."

The ensemble's male member bites his lip in a desperate attempt to keep his laughter at bay. Then, the older chap begins to explain. "What your conductor's trying to tell you is that you're on the wrong train."

"What?" they all cry out.

Taking their tickets from the conductor for closer examination, the impromptu interpreter advises them, "You not only boarded the wrong train, you started out from the wrong station."

"What?" the three repeat their scream.

"You must return to Budapest, taxi to the Déli station and take the next train bound for Lake Balaton, if you wish to see Transdanubia. And you should do so now, as this train will be stopping soon."

The globe-trekking triumvirate begins dashing about, gathering belongings. They struggle, with bags held overhead, toward my end of the coach as part of a mad group shuffle to exit. All of a sudden, one of the side pockets on metro-man's suitcase bursts. As a result, his underwear tumbles on to a cluster of peasant ladies sitting nearby.

With what appears to be genuine concern for the traveler's lost belongings, a gnarled old woman stretches the waistband on a pair of the briefs and shouts, "Mister Hanes! Mister Hanes!"

The busted bag man collapses to his knees in a fit of uncontrollable laughter. He can't move, having been so completely struck down by the malapropos moment.

"Get up, you fool!" his companions shriek in unison. "Let's go."

"This is the last time you're put in charge of hangover detail," one of the women mutters as they cram the vestibule between cars.

The man's spirit is broken. He struggles to stand, then continues schlepping his belongings down the aisle. As the station nears, the train screeches to halt. The three disheveled wanderers disembark. Fumbling like klutzes, they begin waving and thanking everyone on board.

But, thanks for what, I wonder? I can't figure it out. Oh, forget it… No one else really knows, nor do they care.

The locomotive lurches and once more we're on our way.

Trying to repress a smirk, I glance toward the far end of the compartment. In a subtle farewell gesture, the gentleman who first interceded on the sojourners' behalf, pulls down the window, tips his hat and reminds the three, "Don't forget to follow the yellow brick road!"

—w—

PART I

CHAPTER 1:

RIDING THE RAILS LESS TAKEN

"I HAVE RETURNED!" globetrotter Heath Winslow blusters like a modern-day General MacArthur as he mounts the well-worn steps of a train resting in the seaside Croatian town of Ploče. The intrepid reporter's destination: Sarajevo—former Winter Olympic jewel and the current, still tattered capital of Bosnia and Herzegovina.

Oh, I could take a bus, I guess, but where's the romance in that?

Enlivened by the brisk, sun-drenched spring weather, Heath sheds his leather jacket. The middle-aged journalist lingers on the gangway, gazing at the cobalt Adriatic lapping the pristine pebbled beach.

How I regret leaving this whitewashed hamlet, along with my friends—the Kamenice oysters and bottles of Bogdanusa wine.

Heath then scribbles a reminder as part of his ongoing effort to capture such moments in prose.

Notebook entry: Forget not the in-love-with-life locals...
Beauty blossoms eternal along the Dalmatian Coast...
Irrepressible seafaring spirit in the air... Observations
meant for a sightseer's guide

Thoughts recorded, he slips the pad back in his pocket.

So, why go now? Oh, my restless nature needs a stretch, I guess.

Heath's off on yet another of his ambiguous, self-assigned writing adventures.

But I do have a goal in mind: Rediscover the Sarajevo I fear lost a decade ago… How? How the hell do I know?

Therefore, Heath will simply start by making yet another blind charge at the Balkan hinterlands. His latest literary trek follows a trip from Budapest to Belgrade in the fall of 1990. It was an excursion that coincided with the beginning of the end for the former Yugoslavia.

He then wrote with passion, "Its republics clamor for independence. The South Slav coalition crumbles under the ever-weakening support of several poorly brokered peace plans by a group of less than caring European neighbors."

Equally, Heath doesn't see his current jaunt as some pithy travel piece for any glossy tourist brochure.

No! This will be a journey of recollection and reconnection. I want to reunite with the very Bosniaks, Serbs and Croats I befriended during the war years. It's part of my quest to find out what they're all up to now.

With several old reporter notepads to jog his memory, Heath expects to stay busy, reflecting on what was, is and could be for the struggling Balkan expanse he's come to know and love.

Notebook entry: Insights are often based on slanted observations from the past… Be cautious about drawing conclusions from bizarre reflections… Always consider the circumstances surrounding the moment

As he recalls events, Heath's convinced his tribulations were based on a heap of blind charges made by the very people he met—each in mad pursuit of a personal Holy Grail.

Can someone tell me why those folks were so damn single-minded during that stampede?

"What? My chit-chat bothering you?" Heath asks, as if someone's standing nearby, ready to take up the argument. "I've long carried on lively conversations within myself—accompanied by a little devil and angel ranting around in my head. They're locked in a never-ending battle over what course I should chart."

Our self-talk bothers you, Mr. Winslow? Heath's devilish mind asks from deep inside. *Maybe there's a psychosis driving your love for internal banter. Did you ever think of that? We could look into that for you.*

Alright, I sense what you're doing... You devil spirit, you, the angelic one interjects. *You think our man should explore the darker side of his psyche. Is that it?*

"No!" Heath yells. "I've never linked such intercourse with any kind of mental flux. This ol' boy's just fine... Thank you two very much."

If you say so, Devilish grunts from deep within.

Heath's alter egos are convinced he's some kind of self-proclaimed intellect. He often latches on to the various elevator melodies playing in his mind. He can be found chatting himself up quite regularly, with no greater purpose than to vocalize his inner musings.

And they're not Freudian looks at the old' man's unconscious, the devil within insists. *They're more like in-house rap sessions where we get to join in.*

Yes, yes! That's it, the angel inside agrees. *I find them not only creative, but downright stimulating. So, put that in your pipe and smoke it, Mr. Winslow.*

"Aside from a few bats in my belfry," Heath mumbles, "what's my real game plan? And can I score when the pressure's on?"

Wow... Those are tough questions, Devilish notes. *But sir, you've been down this road before.*

Yes, yes he has and this is just more of that déjà vu all over again, Angelic thinks.

—⁓—

Heath turns to enter the carriage… Bam! A short, but strong-minded peasant lady has slammed open the passageway door. She's fixated on smashing her way to the next rail car. Being in her way, Heath's brushed aside while his overstuffed attaché suffers a direct hit. Its contents explode down the long aisle. Manila folders disgorge their contents in the process. Papers fly everywhere like celebratory doves bursting from a cage. His treasured spiral notebooks skate the corridor as if in a race for gold.

"Žao mi je! Žao mi je!" the hunched-over matron shrieks as she scurries to gather the strewn documents. Covered in crumpled layers of black lace that cascade from head to toe, the old woman continues screeching, "Žao mi je!"

"I know you're sorry. Yes, I know. I know," Heath whispers in an attempt to calm the aged woman. Her gnarled, arthritic hands scrape the floor in a desperate attempt to retrieve as many of the papers as possible, as quickly as possible. Realizing she doesn't understand English, Heath tries to engage the frightened figure, gently touching her shoulder and saying, "It's okay. It's okay."

The frail creature jerks to cower in the corner. It's as if she expects to be beaten for her transgressions by the almost larger than life figure hovering over her.

"Really, it's okay," Heath repeats in a gentle, reassuring tone while brandishing a smile and extending a hand.

The little lady hesitates, then grasps his fingertips. Heath lifts her from the floor. With a slight tremble, she passes him several crumpled papers. The octogenarian begins shuffling toward the door, the whole time mumbling, "Žao mi je… Žao mi je."

"Yes, I know. I do. I really do," Heath says as she lurches into the next car.

Seeing the first compartment is vacant, Heath tosses his near-empty satchel inside and gathers those items still littering the passageway. Once retrieved and stacked in haphazard fashion on the overstuffed and worn tweed bench, he lowers the window to hail a passing handcart pusher.

"Pivo! Pivo!" Heath hollers with thumb and index finger extended, flashing the European sign for two. "Oh please, please, my kingdom for a beer," he mumbles, awaiting the platform vendor's reply.

"Jedna minuta," the disheveled entrepreneur shouts back. He pulls two bottles of Karlovačka from his well-dented, rusty metal cart and slaps them in Heath's hand. Heath passes down several coins. He makes the universal shoulder-shrug, asking if the transaction is acceptable.

The street merchant glances at his palm. "Da, da," he states, brandishing a wide grin and exposing an urgent need for dental work. "Hvala… Hvala."

"No, thank you. Thank you," Heath chuckles and smiles, realizing full well he'd overpaid the peddler. Dazed by all that has passed, Heath crumples on to the faded couch. There's a clanking sound, then a slight jolt as the train slips out of the gray, socialist-era station. It's now rolling away from Marco Polo's home and heading toward Herzegovina's heartland.

—⟋∿⟍—

"Karte i putovnicu, molim vas!" a slender, virile man shouts into Heath's compartment while throwing open the sliding door with a deafening bang.

Startled by the youthful official's boisterous grand entry, Heath responds with an acerbic, "Excuse me! Must everyone slam things ajar in this country?"

"Arrogant British businessman on way to financial rape of poor Bosniak peoples… Welcome! Ticket and passport most please."

Heath pulls the documents from his coat pocket and slaps them in the tall trainman's outstretched hand. "And no, I'm not English. I'm an American journalist retracing steps taken during the '90s war. Thank you very much."

"Da… Američki welcome more, but journalist? Jury still out on that. As critic Dragan Šušić once say of us Slavs, 'We like truth so much that everybody got his own.'"

"Thank you, again. That's most insightful. And your English is quite good as well."

"Hvala. I work my way through *Sesame Street*, John Wayne movie and BBC *News Night*. With NATO soldier here now, I have many times to practice. Why you visit Jerusalem of Europe this trip, please?"

Pointing to the mound of disheveled documents, Heath states he's reviewing notes about people he met traveling the Balkans, reporting for the *International Herald Tribune*. "I'm trying to write a feature story about your country a decade after the conflict started."

"Da, I see." The juvenile conductor winks, lifting his cap and brushing back his wavy, dirty-blond hair. His ocean blue, deep-set eyes intensify as he begins to smirk. "Like American GI say, 'Your shit don't stink' Da?"

Being a natural communicator, Heath doesn't suffer fools gladly. "I think that's about enough… I didn't start the damn war, nor did I contribute to its anguish. I reported what I saw, as fair and balanced as possible. Besides, what the hell were you doing in those days?"

"So sorry, foxy newsman. Not want to make you go angry. I was not enough old to fight as soldier, but family, well, we all got war assignment. We are to be the killed civilian. It did not pay so good, but most of us had leading part in this drama."

Heath breathes deep and extends his hand to the stressed out youth. Relaxing his confrontational tone, he murmurs, "I'm sorry, too. My name's Heath. I want to start our conversation anew. Maybe this time we can reach a more positive ending."

"Heath like candy bar? No, just kidding. My name Sasha and I proud for to meet you."

"So, Sasha, a shot of slivovitz to christen our new friendship? I'm convinced Maraska is the best plum brandy on the Dalmatian Coast."

"Hvala, but no thanks you. Much work to do. A pivo in Sarajevo Old Town soon for sure I buy." And with that Sasha returns Heath's punched ticket and passport. He then steps out, sliding the glass door to a whisper close while taking exaggerated tip-toe steps down the corridor toward the next car.

—ɷ—

As the train ambles across the Neretva delta, Heath finishes the second beer. He can now relax while soaking in the fairytale beauty as peaks of the Velez Mountains rise to shape the eastern skyline. Ever the passionate traveler, Heath grins with childlike excitement. He's once again gazing on a rock-strewn, but lush emerald countryside—a landscape dotted with ruined Roman arenas, Venetian bell towers and Hapsburg villas.

The train's melodic whistle echoes through the valley. The railcar's restful rocking soon lulls the intrepid explorer to sleep. Memories begin swirling in Heath's head. As they rush by, he snatches subtle visions of his convoluted past. One remembrance after another kick off a series of fantasy dance steps deep in the brain. The gathered reveries produce a complex and conflicting ballet of the mind.

Ah, dream time. My cup of tortuous recollections now runneth over.

Notebook entry: Trace present-day posturing to distant memories... Thoughts are both pleasant & painful... Trudge forward until options are drained... Arguments

*often end before points can be made… Roads to
realization still under construction*

Having again displayed a grand sense of pomposity and self-importance, Heath's internal mockery fades to a quiet repose while the aging locomotive chugs through the mountain passes. The jostling, along with the motion of Heath's bobbing head, validates the rambling confusion of the moment.

The angelic and devilish ones are now engaged as mischievous DJs in the ballroom of Heath's brain. They spin, with sinister glee, a medley of country music classics. The tunes accompany their virtual waltz across the dance floor of Heath's mind while uncanny lyrics echo over and over…

Happy trails to you, until we meet again.

—⁓—

TRAVERSING TUNNELS AND SWITCHBACKS

THE 396 EXPRESS from Ploče snakes into Bosnia's Mostar rail yard… Then, boom! Cars lurch forward and slam back. Brakes grind out a deafening screech to halt. A semi-conscious Heath Winslow, not unlike a pudgy rag doll, flops across the compartment, ending up sprawled on the opposing bench seat. The mound of documents leapt clear of his awkward advance and now flutters to the floor. Manila and white rectangles carpet the cabin in a patchwork litter of paper.

"What the hell?" a dazed Heath yells. The train stopped well short of the station. There's no commotion. A deflating hiss, courtesy of the air brakes, is the only sound in the moment. Heath struggles to sit up and take inventory of what just transpired.

Conductor Sasha strides down the corridor. He slides open the entry to Heath's cubicle. "Big boom boom thundering storm in mountains. Lightnings hit pole. Cut off electrics to train. Motor stop. Brakes go bang, but you hear that… Da?"

"Yes. I heard it, felt it and pretty much flew with it."

"Engineer think maybe two hour for fix. So, I make announcement, then come get you for lunch with Uncle Thoma. Meantime, you clean up mess. This no way to do homework." Before Heath can comment, the compartment door glides shut and Sasha scurries on his way.

An announcement in Bosnian crackles through the train's public address system.

"Sound like Hollywood star, yes?" Sasha asks about his broadcast upon return.

"It was truly an Oscar-winning performance. So, do you mind telling me what you said?"

"Da… Train broke. Some time to fix. Go see my city and listen for whistle. Much more romantic in Bosnian, no?"

"Yes. And with our options limited, let's go meet and eat with this uncle of yours."

—⁓—

Heath hadn't planned on a stroll. Yet, here he is, stranded at an ancient crossroad of civilizations. He's marooned in a city where minarets share the skyline with church steeples, while the majestic Neretva River meanders through its core.

"So, you were born here, Sasha?"

"Da! Home of the Mostari—the bridge keepers—men who guard Old Bridge in old times."

Without notice, loudspeakers on minarets across the city sputter to life. Calls to prayer warble through the town and river gorge. In turn, Mostar's Muslims begin flocking to mosques. Sasha excuses himself to pray. "I be back soon. Meet you at bridge. Go down that way."

Heath nods and saunters toward Old Town. Gazing around, he can't help notice the burned out husks of buildings, pavement starbursts and bullet holes everywhere… proof positive this village was bombed to bits during the war. He soon reaches Stari Most, the 16th century Old Bridge and former icon of Yugoslav unity. It's but another casualty of the early '90s carnage.

Notebook entry: UNESCO & half-dozen donor nations on a 5-year plan to rebuild the city using ancient methods

& materials… Will keep craftsmen busy for years…
Religions imported by emperors, missionaries, bishops
& sultans… All have stars, crosses & crescents to bear…
Welcome to Europe's cultural fault line

"Bridge almost done!" Sasha shouts as he runs up the cobblestoned street. "Before war, young men jump off. That twenty-five meter down, like Acapulco cliff diver. Before leap, they make ruckus with tourist. They tease and tease… ask for money, more money, more money. When get enough, take big plunge… Crazy, no?"

"Crazy, yes. Did you ever do that?"

"No… Like GI say, 'I may be dumb, but I not stupid.' So, time to eat… Walk this way," Heath's Mostar guide insists. "See that place? Was park before war. Lovers come here. Childrens play. Everyone have nice times. But in war, we cannot go to cemetery, or sniper leave you there. We come here to bury peoples… old park, new cemetery.

"Enough bad news. Many good things now happen in my town. Winemaker come back. Farmers press olive again. Smart dogs sniff truffle in forest. Maybe Uncle Thoma have some for you."

—⚍—

As Heath and Sasha finish their amble, they turn a corner. A bright cloth banner waves above a corner restaurant. Sporting the blue and gold of Bosnia's flag, it's overlaid with swirling white script proclaiming the home of Café Sasha.

"You own this place? I'm impressed.

"No, no… This belong Uncle Thoma. He name it for wife, Sasha. Sasha a man and woman name both in Bosnia. Okay, sometime I tell young lady café mine, but this our secret…Da?"

"Nema problema," Heath whispers and winks as they enter the premises.

"Sasha! Sasha!" a voice bellows from the back of the café. "Dobra dan. Dobra dan… Come give your uncle a big wet kiss."

Sasha and a robust, middle-aged man share a bear hug embrace, then plant loving, moist greetings on each other's cheeks. "Uncle Thoma meet my new friend, Heath… He American reporter back to write big story about days before."

"Jebi ga! A journalist, you say? But that's okay; we've served communists here, too… No, no, Heath. I'm just kidding." Thoma chuckles as he thrusts his meaty paws forward, locking on Heath's right hand and forearm. He shakes them with intensity. "You call me Thoma. Sasha will tell you I'm a bit direct, as my diplomacy is seldom called into service."

"No problem," Heath states as he retracts his arm from the steel-like grasp. "And let me compliment you, Thoma, on your English."

"Thank you. I worked for years with my cousin in Dubrovnik. We managed a tourist hotel for the Brits. Between their haughty attitude and meager tips, I was able to rein in much of the Queen's English. I try to teach this one the importance of verbs, but he uses them less than vowels in a Slav surname."

Notebook entry: Thoma & his wife met vacationing on the Adriatic… Croatian-Catholic & Bosnian-Muslim marriage followed… Balkan interfaith unions common before the upheavals

The Sasha-Thoma reunion banter becomes animated, punctuated by hand waving, more hugs and plenty of shoulder slapping. Several times during the exchange, Thoma and Heath lock eyes.

Notebook entry: Bosnians are very sociable & hospitable… Curiosity makes them straightforward… Culturally appropriate to ask personal question… Eye contact important—implies honesty

& good intentions... Power of the collective spirit is omnipresent

"Okay," Sasha interjects. "Time for lunch. I soon have much train work to do."

"Burek is our specialty today, Heath. I think you'll like this. It's a light pastry pie with meat inside. I also have fresh lamb cevapi with baba's homemade cheese on the side. Musaka, of course, and tufahije—apple cake—for dessert."

"That all sounds delizioso. Can I accompany such delicacies with a fine local wine?"

"Zilavka Mostar is a renowned Herzegovian dry white. It's crystal clear and very clean. Might I pour you a glass?"

"You read my mind, Thoma. Maybe you should bring the bottle… Eh, Sasha?"

"Kefir for me. It common yogurt drink with Muslim. I have train to drive, you know. But make sure, Uncle Thoma, you bring dish of ajvar, too… Hvala."

"Ajvar is a condiment made of eggplant and peppers. Think of it as Bosnian ketchup with a kick. So, I'm off to the kitchen to work with the other Sasha."

Moments pass. A teenage waitress in traditional Bosnian garb approaches. She presents refreshments, including two small blue bottles of mineral water, with a demeanor well beyond her years.

"Hvala lijepo," Sasha says, thanking her for the delivery.

"Nema na čemu," she whispers as she bows and steps back from the table.

Heath and Sasha raise their glasses, lock eyes and toast their good fortune.

"I feel you confused about some of this. Also hard for NATO soldier to understand my homeland. But that okay. During republic time, we just as confused. Old joke go, Yugoslavia have eight different peoples in six republics. They have five language, three religion…

Orthodox, Catholic and Muslim. They also have two alphabet… Roman and Cyrillic. But have only one Yugoslav… Marshal Tito."

Sasha pauses to wipe his mouth. "Tito die and Yugoslavia quick to become big mess. I see breakup like cooking crazy Balkan goulash. Mix group of Serb, Croat and Bosniak with Yugo armed force. What you get? Bad politic stew. Now serve with too much spices to everyone across country in broken ethnic bowls… Christian against Muslim against Orthodox and vice versa. Then town against town, neighbor against neighbor."

Fearing he may have spoken too loud, Sasha looks about the restaurant before continuing. "Soon this bad stew boiling over with church after church, mosque after mosque destroyed by all kind of violent peoples. Pressure build to insane climax. No one turn down heat. Stew now boiling over. Many peoples burned. Stove and kitchen catch fire. House destroyed."

"Jebi ga!" Thoma shouts, bringing food to the table. "Only old people still speak of djubrad, lopovi i kriminalci. Sorry, Heath; that's talk of politicians, thieves and criminals. You should be chatting up rock bands, hot women and that Internet thing.

"Heath, you must remember time here is divided into before and after the war." Thoma leans forward to whisper, "It has often occurred to me I've never met anyone, from either community here, who saw the war as anything but a mistake.

"Bottom line: Everyone you talk to will have a different version of events. A very wise Bosniak once told me, 'Listen to all three sides—Muslim, Serb and Croat—then decide for yourself what you think.'"

"Da, uncle, what then you think so special being from Bosnia?"

"My restaurant, plus Sasha's great kebabs, of course." Thoma counters as he pats his protruding belly.

"You also be visited by Francois Mitterrand, Susan Sontag and Bill Clinton, but still make no difference," Sasha adds.

"Jebi ga!" Thoma screams in laughter, throwing his hands in the air. "You get to be bombed by a psychiatrist too, if you're so lucky."

Notebook entry: Radovan Karadžić—educated as a psychiatrist… Co-founded Serbian Democratic Party…. First President of Republika Srpska ('92-96)… Accused of war crimes against Bosnian Muslims & Croats during siege of Sarajevo

"Okay, okay. Enough, enough," Sasha insists. "We eat food before it go cold."

"Very good. You're right Sasha, enough is enough. Heath, let it be said we both think the Bosnian War was our Vietnam. But now is time to move on. And on that happy note, bon appétit."

"Wow… After that, I can't wait for dessert and an aperitif."

As Heath and Sasha finish lunch, a shrill sound is heard whistling in the distance.

"Our timing most excellent. We make way to station now. Uncle Thoma… Check please."

The kitchen door bursts open. In a fake, condescending tone, Thoma scolds, "Young man, you know your money's no good here. Yes, a couple Yankee dollars in the tip jar would be a good thing. Now go. Be good, strong men. Give my love to all the families. And don't wait so long to see us again."

"Thank you so much, Thoma," Heath states, extending his hand in gratitude.

"Ah, thank you, Mr. Pulitzer, but you'll be back. I know. You liked Sasha's food too much." Thoma grabs Heath, smothers him with a hug and pecks on both cheeks. He slaps Sasha on the shoulder for good measure and ushers them both to the street. Heath and Sasha start their saunter to the station.

"So, what does 'jebi ga' mean?"

"Some things best left not said," Sasha whispers as he lightly jabs Heath in the side with his elbow.

—w—

The lunch comrades, Heath and Sasha, reach the rail station platform.

"Your wagon right there. I check with engineer and make announcement."

Heath grabs the coach's handrail and ascends the steps, satiated and confident his rail journey can now continue.

"Vlak polazi u petnaest minuta!" Sasha's voice bellows from the loudspeakers. "Train leaving fifteen minute… Be on it!"

Heath chuckles at the crude bilingual effort, then slides open the door to his compartment. He's greeted by an elderly gentleman who's just lowering the day's edition of the *Herald Tribune*. The dapper fellow peers over his wire-rimmed spectacles. There's a meeting of the eyes.

"I hope you don't mind a little company? The other compartments were quite full and it looks like you could use some help with your filing system."

"No, that's okay… Welcome."

"Please excuse me. I should introduce myself," the man says as he extends his hand in greeting. "Dr. Bojan Marić."

"Heath Winslow… It's a pleasure to meet you and please excuse the paperwork mess. I'm still recovering from a surprise run-in with a rather determined babushka lady."

"That's a fight men will seldom win," Dr. Marić jokes.

"Wait," Heath says as an inquisitive web of wrinkles scuttle across his forehead. "Haven't we met? You look so familiar. Yes… I remember. All Saints weekend, 1990 on the IC from Budapest to Belgrade. Three young Americans… complete with flying underwear. You interceded on their behalf and translated the error of their ways."

"Exactemont! What a great memory you have, sir, and what a small world within which we live. I did not realize you were witness to that tourist debacle."

"Yes, I was there, but only as an observer on the other end of the coach. So, Herr Doktor, do you travel today on business or pleasure?"

"Well, it's a pleasure to meet you, Mr. Winslow, but please call me Bojan. Business is the essence of my excursion. I'm the new, if not somewhat old in years, Minister of Education for Bosnia and Herzegovina. I had a morning call here in Mostar. I will soon check in at the Sarajevo ministry. And then, I continue to a conference of old cronies in Belgrade this evening."

"That's quite the schedule, Bojan, regardless of someone's age. I'm glad you've joined me as part of your excursion, but only if you call me Heath."

"And what is the purpose of your travels, Heath?"

"I'm on a self-guided tour of the Balkans. My goal: To gain a greater understanding of where this region is headed in the new millennium. I also want to visit some of the old haunts… try reconnecting with some of the people I met along the way."

"Your trip sounds like quite a challenge as well, monsieur."

Bojan pauses to glance at Heath who's now in an almost trancelike gaze out the window. "Pardon my interruption, Heath. I think you should take a seat before you fall. Our train will soon depart."

"Sorry… I guess I was daydreaming. I'm afraid my mental locomotive may have already left the station."

"No need to clarify. I travel in that parallel universe on a regular basis. Might I suggest we bundle your documents and store them, to ensure they don't escape again."

As the two men stash Heath's journalistic mess, the train begins its crawl out of Mostar in route to Sarajevo.

Notebook entry: Tracks glimmer bright silver in the afternoon sun… Tiny twin ribbons of steel skirt the riverbank like slivers on the gorge floor… The train coils and climbs through a wooded tableau dressed in nature's finery

"Dobra dan, Dr. Marić… Hello again, Mr. Winslow," Sasha states as he bows through an exaggerated formal entry. "Please to enjoy upcoming Six Flags over Bosnia. You ride down mountain, over rivers and through the wood. Tourist come from world over to switch back to forth and whisper Agatha Christy story while in tunnels so dark. And no surcharge for biggest amusement park ride in all Europe… You most welcome. Ciao!" Yet again, Sasha makes a mad dash to exit.

"He's quite the character, that young man," Heath notes.

"Yes, but his spirit is a good sign to me. It's been a long, long time since we've seen young people smile from the heart in this country… So, Heath, have you traveled this stretch of the line before?"

"No, Bojan, I've not had the pleasure. And as a train buff, I'm more than just a little excited, especially now, with my own tour guide."

"I doubt I can provide any great narrative, but that's okay. This excursion is far more a feast for the eyes. Just lean back and soak it all in. Be sure to watch for Mount Radusa. It leaps out like magic… an enchanted border between forest and field. As Sasha says, 'Enjoy the voyage through our Magic Kingdom.' My personal joy is knowing that we can once again share it with the world."

> *Notebook entry: Mountain trains often chug past Konjac… Panoramic views vie for attention… spring-fed streams rush through rocky limestone crags… Glacial lakes pool in faraway valleys… Harrowing descents come free of charge*

"Thanks for the scenic homily, Bojan, but please tell me a little bit about yourself."

"Well, I was born in Jablanica. Our train stops there soon. My father was the lead engineer for construction of the huge power plant there. He soon fell in love, married et voilà! Here I am.

"My father knew well the value of a good education, so off to Belgrade University I went. After finishing my degree, I earned a master's in journalism in London. Tito's technocrats touted me as the next Association of Universities chairman. So, I was sent to Vanderbilt to write my doctoral thesis. And now, Heath, it's your turn."

"Born and raised in America's heartland. Studied journalism at the University of Texas in the mid-sixties. Between the drugs, sex, rock and roll… and endless anti-war protests, I was given a sheepskin and became a reporter."

Heath passes Bojan a dog-eared black and white glossy photo taken decades ago.

"I guess my anarchist writings for *The Daily Texan* paid off. The next thing I knew I was sipping gin and tonics on the balcony of the Intercontinental in Saigon. I waited every afternoon with these guys for the Army's press brief, or 'Damn 'Nam Follies,' as we called them. I'd file my Associated Press 'What the general meant to say was… ' fluff piece and then head back to the bar."

Bojan returns the photo. Heath glides it back into its protective sleeve.

"Well, after a couple of those reports ran in the *New York Times*, I was offered a job with the *Tribune* in Frankfurt. Later, I stepped out as a freelancer to cover the civil war in Rhodesia, Idi Amin's exploits, IRA fun times, the carnage in Ethiopia and a crumbling Lebanon. Oh, I can't forget the Red Army Faction… and last, but certainly not least, the great Balkan debacle."

"That's quite a series of adventures, Mr. Winslow."

"Yes, Dr. Marić, but age and arthritis caught up with me. As my ability to dodge bullets diminished, my focus on writing culinary features for globe-trekking carnivores increased… as did the money. So, I left frontline reporting. Now, I work out of my apartment in Manhattan, selling travel dribble to the highest bidder."

"Fascinating… Ah, I see the Tsar's Mosque piercing the horizon. Soon we'll be in the city. Heath, where will you stay in Sarajevo?"

"I was thinking the Holiday Inn… It holds lots of memories."

"The only thing good about that corporate rip-off is the bar. No. I will introduce you to my nephew, Danvor. I insist you stay at his guesthouse. The tram is but one block away. It will be perfect for your research, writing and relaxation. You'll see… Da?"

"I've already learned not to say no in the Balkans."

Bojan steps out to use the phone at the end of the carriage. He calls his niece and makes the arrangements. "So, it's set? Hvala puno… We'll be there soon."

—⁂—

As the train lumbers into town, Heath marvels at the juxtaposition of Ottoman and Austro-Hungarian architecture at its heart. His wonderment is soon blocked by one of the city's grand socialist-era eyesores, the main train station. This cold, gray concrete monstrosity does nothing to evoke the romance of travel, but Heath cares not. He's already sensing the latest of his adventures is well underway.

As they exit the train, Bojan points for Heath to place things on the platform. Bojan waves to summon a street porter. He instructs the man on taking the luggage to a Stari Grad address.

"Being baggage-free makes for a more leisurely walk into the heart of my city," Bojan says as they step forward.

The two soon reach the Kovaci Quarter. Danvor greets them on the street in front of his home. He ushers both down an alleyway to the guesthouse entry. It's outlined by an elaborate terracotta-tiled dormer. Beyond the small courtyard, an arched wooden door bids *Welcome!*

Danvor opens it, exposing a sun-drenched room with plastered white walls and a dark, wood-beamed ceiling. He walks across the red tile floor to the sliding glass door. It glides open, revealing a patio complete with a grape arbor canopy. It's laden with crimson-colored flowers. A plant-covered wall trellis heightens the olfactory experience.

Almost speechless, Heath remarks how sweet the Sarajevo roses smell.

Danvor is quick to reprimand him. "In this town, roses have nothing to do with horticulture. They only bloom on the footpaths, in holes carved by exploding shells that have, since the war's end, been filled with red rubber."

"My apologies… I didn't mean to insult anything or anyone."

"No problem, Heath," Bojan reassures him. "Like the pock-marked walls and charred spines of buildings that scar this glorious city, the rubber roses are a testament for many. For me, they're nothing but a morbid reminder of a stupid war and its legacy."

"I'm sorry, too," Danvor adds. "I don't mean to sound angry. It just wasn't that long ago." He turns to continue the apartment tour which includes a compact, but well-stocked kitchen; a bedroom complete with delivered suitcase; as well as a light-filled bathroom with a massive blue and white tiled ceramic shower.

"This will work for you?" Danvor asks with genuine concern for Heath's welfare.

"Perfecto!" exclaims Heath, as they shake hands to seal the deal.

Danvor escorts everyone out the door, locks it and then hands Heath the key. He gestures up and down the street, noting where the bakery, pharmacy and coffee shop are located. He stresses to Heath the historic Baščaršija Bazaar is but a few blocks away.

"Well, I'd like to celebrate my fortune with a glass of Montenegro red. Would either of you care to join me?"

Danvor says thanks, but explains he has house repairs to do and must be finished by nightfall. Bojan asks for a rain check. He reminds Heath of his pending stop at the Education Ministry and continuance to Belgrade.

Heath decides he'll take a tram to the Holiday Inn, hoping to reconnect with Eoghan, the bartender at what was once his favorite watering hole. Danvor and Bojan give Heath business cards and insist he call them whenever with any concern whatsoever. As quickly as the parties had united, they charge off in separate directions.

—⚏—

Heath steps into the corner pharmacy to buy a tram ticket. A clanking metal behemoth soon screeches to stop in front of the store. He boards the yellow trolley and slumps into a narrow plastic seat near the conductor. As usual, Heath's mind begins drifting. Meandering thoughts are soon stumbling through his semi-consciousness.

What's this resistance you have to examining the demons from your past, Mr. Winslow? A devilish voice asks from deep within Heath's mind.

Why spout inquisitions about those with whom Heath wishes to reconnect? An angelic counterpoint demands.

What? Is he afraid too much time has passed for anything to come clear?

Or, are you just trying very hard to mess with his mind?

"Enough already!" yells Heath at his quarrelling subconscious thoughts. He's again shouted himself out of a dizzy daydream and back to reality. "Can't you two just shut up for once?"

Having missed the chance to stymie his outburst, Heath looks about the trolley. He blushes after realizing everyone heard his flare-up. There's but one option: He pulls the signal cord. The tram soon stops. Heath lowers his head and shuffles to dismount.

"A beer… My kingdom for a beer," Heath mumbles as he saunters down the cobblestone street. He's drawn once again to that bright green hotel sign, a sanctuary of sanity for reporters who once covered the siege of Sarajevo.

You call this your port in a storm? The angelic one asks.

Is this all there is? The devilish one laments.

Take us back to a time when a peasant could be made drunk on a single glass of water and the lilt of a gypsy violin.

Did those days ever even exist?

"Oh, to hell with the both of you," Heath shouts aloud as he intensifies his gait toward the liquor lounge. "Just let me find a beer!"

—ɯ—

C H A P T E R   3 :

AN UNEASY CALM
BEFORE THE STORM

THE BALKAN SUN streams through the branches of a tree-lined boulevard. It warms Heath's shoulders as he ambles past a museum and the Ali Pasha mosque. He stops to consider the eternal flame memorial. "What a paradox!" the returning reporter scoffs. "An Orthodox cathedral and Catholic church now bracket the city's tribute to Muslims slaughtered in the siege."

> *Notebook entry: City blockade longest cordon of a capital in modern warfare… Republican Ruska & Yugoslav People's Army besieged Sarajevo with daily attacks… Bombardments rained down from April '92 thru Feb. '96*

Heath turns a corner, beginning his stroll down a street nicknamed Sniper Alley. It was tagged so in deference to those who dared use the bloody pathway during the war. Before him stands the mustard yellow and burnt-orange exterior of a once-modern inn built solely for the '84 Olympic Games.

It may have once been the latest in fashion and luxury, but I fear it now lives on little more than its former glory, Heath reflects.

> *Notebook entry: Holiday Inn-Sarajevo became a bloody symbol of ethnic conflict… Tattered walls photographed & printed in newspapers worldwide… Videos of*

the pockmarked façade aired globally… Hangout of choice for the press corps… Remained standing amid destruction—poignant irony of the war

Heath enters the hotel. Scanning the lobby, his eyes lock on a set of double doors with a small neon sign flickering *Lounge* above them.

Ah, could this be the passageway to my former domicile?

Being early afternoon, the historic watering hole is devoid of customers. A svelte woman wearing a navy-blue cocktail dress stops wiping the bar to glance in Heath's direction. Flourishing a smile, she purrs, "How may I help you?"

"I'm looking for an old bartender buddy named Eoghan."

"That crazy Irishman now runs a pub in Old Town. It's called Ballygoan. A lot of expats and NATO soldiers hang out there. Can I offer you a drink before you go?"

"Hvala, but no thanks."

"The bar is on the Ferhadija walkway. You can't miss the huge Guinness sign out front."

A cursory "Thank you" and Heath marches off. He weaves through side streets toward Stari Grad. In the process, he skirts a mix of charming houses, small mosques, graveyards and well-tended gardens patrolled by dozens of well-fed cats. Stepping into the pedestrian zone, he sees *Ballygoan* emblazoned in stout green Celtic letters on a massive burgundy billboard trimmed in gold.

"Subtle as Eoghan is large," Heath sniggers. "Oh, go ahead. Leap off the building, you big, beautiful sign. Grab my thirst-driven attention. I dare you!"

Heath squints through the pub window's afternoon reflection to see Eoghan dusting liquor bottles. His back is to the door. Heath enters in a stealth-like fashion and demands, "What the hell does a guy have to do for a beer around here?"

Without a flinch or turn in Heath's direction, Eoghan, a man with the physique of a massive oak, counters, "A bit o' civility might be in order, unless you're an half-assed American journalist, then there's little hope, I'm afraid."

The bright-eyed Irishman, with wavy silver hair and a double chin, swivels to face Heath. Eoghan, now wielding a smile as broad as his stature, throws down his dust rag and wipes his meaty paws on a frayed white apron.

"Mr. Winslow, ya ol' fool! How be ya?" Eoghan grabs Heath's hand, shakes it, then tussles his hair—a macho Irish sign of affection.

"A little slower on the draw, but no complaints. Besides, you'd neither listen, nor would you give a damn. Noting your waistline, I'd say you're doing quite well yourself, Mr. Barkeep."

"Can't complain; not that it would do any good… Your usual, sir?"

"I thought you'd never ask."

Eoghan pulls a pint while tossing a coaster in Heath's direction. The cardboard mat, inscribed with the pub's name in gold over a map of Ireland, lands in front of him and is followed by the placement of a perfectly drawn Bass ale.

"Sláinte!"

"To your health as well, my gleaming Irish friend."

"Jammy beggars you're lookin' good, Mr. Winslow. Dropped a few stone, did ya? And lost your limp, it looks as well."

"Well, Eoghan, I got a new knee, so I can move again. No Irish jigs, but regular fast-walking has dented the midsection. Eating a little better seems a benefit as well, but don't think that's a license to take my beer mug away."

"And what brings you to my neck of the woods? I'm quite sure your bar bill is paid. Don't be tellin' me you're a contractor, eh?"

"No, no. Nothing that shameful. I stopped writing for the *Tribune* a while back. Now I make good money freelancing out of my Manhattan flat. I write for travel mags. Oh, and I hooked up with the Center for Community Journalism. We work with media folk worldwide on stuff like safety, good governance, human rights—that kind of crap."

"And they invited ya in?"

"Yeah, can you believe it? Anyway, they're all about a more engaged kind of journalism focused on social change and growth."

"And they invited ya in? Next, you'll be tellin' me we're goin' to Mass on Sunday."

"Eoghan, you're still sharp as a beach ball, aren't you?"

"Okay, okay, sir, but what brings ya to Sarajevo? The truth now."

"It's a mix of things and they're all across Europe. I'm following some food and travel leads, going to a couple biggy reporter meetings and hoping to track down some of the folks I met covering the war."

"And why bring up that bollocks, eh?"

"Call me *The Inquisitor*. I don't know. If I can find any of the usual suspects, I'd like to hear what's going on in their heads, find out who has and hasn't made it. But, it's anyone's guess what luck I'll have."

Eoghan does a silent, "A moment, please," while pointing a finger in the air. He trudges toward the store room. After a moment of rustling, he returns with a box in tow. It's marked WINSLOW on the side.

"I applaud your enthusiasm ol' pal, but you're still a hard man to understand," Eoghan states as he plops the cardboard container on the bar. "And before I forget, these be your notes from the last time you skedaddled. Your brain may be cunning, my friend, but I don't see any continuity in your peculiar life."

"First off, thanks for saving this stuff for me, but you haven't noticed the most important fact: There's a gaping hole in my mug. For that matter, you've paid little attention to how long it's been there."

Eoghan pulls a pen from his pocket and makes a small "x" on Heath's coaster. "Trick I learned in Bavaria. When your deckle starts lookin' like the *Wall Street Journal*, I'll be tossin' your ars in the street."

"Well, then, let's start publishing."

Eoghan plops a freshly-drawn ale in front of Heath. "Okay, enliven me mind about these fascinatin' folks from your past. Let's see how many I still remember. We're the only bar flies here, so hit me with your best shot, Mr. Hemmingway."

"My other notebooks and news clips are back at the guesthouse, but there are a few folks imprinted on my brain—that young go-getter Andro Babich, for one."

Eoghan scratches his head and rolls his eyes. "Andro stopped by on occasion after you left. He's in Kosovo with the peacekeepers now. You remember his uncle, eh? An update on Andro shouldn't be hard to come by. Tell me, how far back do you boys go?"

"I met Andro in New York when he was working the docks. I still remember the first story he told me about Herzegovina, as well as the anger burning in his gut, what with the war blowing up his football dreams."

—∞—

Heath paints his yarn not unlike an orange glow enveloping the Bosnian countryside. He pictures the spring day's first rays glistening off the river as it zigzags across the valley floor. Golden shafts of light pierce piney alleyways in the neighboring woodlands. During the night, snow has dusted the mountainous expanse. The scenic wonderment is now apparent to the many forest creatures who pause in awe.

The gurgling sounds of the Neretva build as the river cascades down the mountain ravine. It rushes round jagged rocks and over icicle-draped waterfalls. The cacophony in the foothills is joined by church bells chiming through the basin. Their ringing echoes fade inside the canyon walls, followed by loudspeakers on minarets crackling to life. It's Saturday, April 11, 1992 and morning has come again to Konjic, in Bosnia and Herzegovina.

Andro Babich, rising star and contender for the Yugoslav National Under-19 Team, kicks and scores during a recent scrimmage against

FK Igman Konjic, the cutline to a sports action photo in *Scorer Football* reads.

"I coulda been a contender!" Andro explodes, aping Marlon Brando's classic *On the Waterfront* line. "But no, the Europeans say Croatia and Slovenia are free and Bosnia is not. There goes my club contract… Stinking politics."

The athletic teen slings the glossy journal across the kitchen table. It bounces off a chair back and tumbles into a trash can set next to the refrigerator. Andro hisses, "How à propos and good riddance." His chiseled good looks and wavy black hair accentuate Andro's deep-set brown eyes, now glaring across the room with disdain.

As reporters have noted, Andro's a gifted sportsman. Every day he practices dribbling, passing and shooting until exhaustion consumes him. At this juncture in time, the national football team is enjoying a modicum of success against a tough, international lineup. Yugo players kicked their way into the 1990's World Cup finals. Red Star-Belgrade is crowned Europe's champion. Andro's ego is riding this victorious crest like a wave of personal glory. But the Federation's break-up has chipped away at any chance of premier league prominence… for Andro, as well as the Belgrade team.

Clubs are leaving the union in droves. FIFA now threatens suspension, Andro laments. *Where's Yugoslavia… where's my team going? What am I to do?*

The last missed goal in this cruel grudge match occurs when Croat and Slovene clubs petition to separate. Balkan football and Andro's sport future now lie in shambles.

"Good afternoon," Andro's broad-shouldered father declares. The slender six-foot farmer in denim coveralls stomps snow off his boots while stepping through the kitchen door. "Might you be interested in helping milk the cows and take care of a few chores this morning? That's if you're not too busy solving the Balkans problem."

"I'm sorry, Father," the young man says with a sigh. "I just get sick when I think of the storm clouds hanging over us. Europe ignores our cry for help. Croats and Serbs thinking they own us. Then there's Alen's blown knee."

"Your brother's future should be the least of your worries. He was born to coach football. Clubs are already fighting over him… By the way, who elected you to parliament? You're barely old enough to vote. Already you want to solve a problem that's been festering half a millennium.

"Focus on your education, Andro… maybe in England, Canada or America. Your photo skills are a gift to be nurtured. With our family connections, we can make that happen. But first, let's get the damned cows milked."

Andro finishes lacing his boots and bolts for the door. The strapping adolescent moves with a degree of confidence and spirit reserved expressly for energized youth.

"Sweep the snow off the walk so your grandmother doesn't slip and fall," Andro's father yells from outside.

Not long after Andro's exit, a squat woman scurries into the kitchen, draping a heavy-knit scarf over her thick silver hair. Somewhat stooped by her advancing years, the lady in black stretches on tiptoes to lift a Loden cape from the hallway rack.

Quick-thinking and ever observant, the methodical Sofija scans the room for anything out of order. She grabs her purse, slips on gloves and charges the door in a rush to get to the church on time. With the pathway swept and roadway cleared, mission success seems assured, as it has almost always been for her through decades in memoriam.

—⚏—

Eoghan smacks his hands, interrupting Heath's latest tale. "Whoa! Not all the laddies in Scotland wear kilts me boy. Who's this dame you be throwin' at me?"

"Sorry, Eoghan. Remember Baba Sofija? She's Andro's grandmother… the matriarch of the Babich clan. Andro's mom died when he was born. It's a tragedy he's laid at his feet ever since. Anyway, Sofija became the de facto head of household after that."

"Okay. I remember now. My fog's a clearin', Mr. H. Do tell me more."

—◊—

Heath describes an enlivened parish priest who spots Sofija scurrying down the country lane. Sporting a thick beard and broad smile, the padre waves in her general direction.

"Dobra don, Baba Sofija," the pastor says, preparing to bless the senior churchgoer as she nears the chapel archway.

"Good morning, Father. Please save your blessing for those more in need. I sense a calm before the storm. I fear we all have much praying to do."

Since Tito's death, Baba Sofija has been obsessed with politics. She's constantly watching TV, listening to talk radio and reading whatever she can about the régime.

It's nothing but another mishmash, Baba reflects, *like goose-stepping Nazis and Ustaša beside the Partisans. But today, everybody's faking harmony and tolerance, convincing no one.* As the Babich elder often points out, the country's power is now divided along ancient ethnic lines.

A Bosniak President, a Serb leading Parliament and a Croat prime minister… What a glorious parade of skeptics that's become. And all this tension. What's to come of it? Slovenia and Croatia declare independence so Europe can salute them? What's that but a masquerade?

Like a spoiled political child believing its raison d'être was stolen, Bosnian politicos demanded a national referendum as well.

The result was what I expected… Serbs storming off in a huff as hotheads on all sides stand scowling at the ready, eager for a fight. They're all such juvenile brutes!

—⁓—

Andro sweeps the silage in front of several ruminating beasts one last time. Morning chores complete, his father switches off the lights as they head for the barn door. He clasps his son's arm. "You're a great worker when you put your mind to it, Andro, but where's all this anger and frustration coming from?"

"I don't know, father. I have this hunger for travel. You know that. I guess I just want to run free."

"I hear you, but I'm still worried. You've been successful at so many things—football… photography… music… but I don't sense a passion, something you'll follow through in life."

"I'm sorry if I've disappointed you."

"No, no, that's not it, not at all. We're very proud of you, Andro. You just seem bent on going to the extreme in all things lately. You make sudden decisions, or change your mind so quickly. I'm just saying you may regret such hasty moves later on."

"Well then, maybe it's time I leave the farm," Andro snips. "I was hoping a contract with Igman-Konjic might be in the offing, but the diplomats have crushed that."

"You and your brother with your football fantasies and premier-league dreams… You need a skill you can market long after your legs give out. Yes, the political mess is grim, but it could be a blessing in disguise. And if you want to leave, at least go to college and earn a degree. Stop kicking that damn ball and look to the future."

Andro's and his father's eyes lock.

"Listen, son, we've had this talk before and we always end up in a shouting match. So, let's drop it here. Better yet, how about talking with your grandmother? You've turned to her for advice so many times before. You two communicate in a special way. I love you, Andro, and I want you to make good decisions, but I really think Baba Sofija can help you find some answers."

"I love you too, Papa. And no, I don't want to fight. For what it's worth, I'll talk with Baba soon… I promise."

Andro and his father enter the farmhouse to find brother Alen hobbling around the kitchen, his leg bound in a splint. Set on the table is a tray laden with breakfast wares. The injured footballer reaches for a woven basket heaped with rolls and crusted bread. With morning Mass recited, the Babich matriarch finishes her amble home and steps into the kitchen.

"Great timing, Baba Sofija. Breakfast is served," Alen proclaims as the extended family's two youngest—thirteen-year-old Chapeka and Suzana, who just turned eight—scamper into the room.

"Dobro jutro. God bless us, everyone," Sofija calls out with sincere homage to Dickens' *A Christmas Carol.*

—m—

As Baba Sofija chops the last carrot for a hearty chicken soup, Andro swings a chair from under the kitchen table, straddles it and faces her. His eyes focus on Sofija's hands as they orchestrate the latest culinary symphony. Andro's fascinated by this hearty woman in her early seventies whose stiff, somewhat unkempt hair mingles with wrinkled olive-colored skin to validate her maturity.

Baba radiates such kindness. It's easy to see how people find comfort in her gentle ways.

More deeply, Sofija is simply showing restraint while acting dutifully. This is a matron with a preference for planning rather than spontaneity. She's determined to follow a strict schedule and pay attention to detail for all the family's sake.

Grandmamma may be short in stature, but she's long on character. I love how her bright green eyes, broad smile and welcoming ways combine to give off such a glow.

"Did we clean behind our ears?" Sofija scoffs. Much to Baba's dismay, Andro has taken to wearing a gaudy gold stud with fake diamond in his left earlobe.

"Earring jokes are no longer funny."

"So, what's our topic of conversation today, beside fashion?" Sofija asks over her shoulder, anticipating Andro's latest query.

"I'm so frustrated, Baba. Life's been good here and all, but what's out there? And how exciting might it be?"

"Yes, the grass is always greener, but be careful what you wish for. You may get what you think you want."

"Baba Sofija, please… I need more than old tried-and-true sayings today."

"Obviously… You've never hesitated giving an opinion before, even tactless ones. You dream of a life beyond the boredom that fills this valley. We understand that. You're curious and you appreciate the arts. You're sensitive to beauty. Those are wonderful traits, Andro, but there's little chance to expand your horizons in this quaint town. So, what's one to do?"

Andro senses his grandmother is about to weave a life lesson for him. It only amplifies the angst that's captured him as of late. Andro's desperate. He sees himself as incomplete. He's eager to embark on some kind of quest for fulfillment.

"Okay, so I don't know my potential, or my calling in life. But Baba, for heaven's sake, help me. What am I to do?"

"You're no longer a child, young man. Your sheltered upbringing is over. You need to wake up to the demands on your life. There's a blank portrait in front of you that needs to be filled. No one can put paint on that canvas but you."

Sofija injects a homespun parable for emphasis. "It's not unlike your father planting a new crop in the spring. He knows what seeds to use so he can harvest what he wants. The Bible teaches us, 'As you sow, so shall you reap.' I too keep this in mind. It's true no matter what season in life you're traveling through.

"Since we all want to stay fruitful as we grow older, we should look to God, the one who never ages or fails. He teaches us everything that will help us mature. The deeper we take root in our bond with the Almighty, the greater access we have to his boundless means."

After Sofija's allegory, Andro rises from his chair. "Hvala, Baba, I think," Andro whispers in Sofija's ear as he kisses her cheek, then saunters toward the kitchen door. He slips on a jacket and scoops his camera from the counter. "I'm off to shoot in the hills. And this time, I'll try looking at the world with a fresh set of eyes, focusing on what you've said, Grandmamma."

Sofija smiles as she whispers from the Book of Matthew, "You're not alone my son. I'll be with you always… You're not alone."

—〰—

With Heath's recollection complete, Eoghan calls out, smacking his hand on the bar, "I like that ol' broad!"

"Enough to draw me another beer?"

"X marks the spot," Eoghan jokes as he puts another tick on Heath's coaster and heads for the tap. "Look how Andro's turned out. Back then, he was a good kid. He was your typical teenager without a clue where he was goin' or what he wanted to do. As for granny, if anyone can keep folk on the straight and narrow, my bet's on her."

"You see what I mean, Eoghan? It was more than just a war for me. It's so much the people. I want to get it all straight in my head, or I'll never move on."

"Don't be so hard on yourself, Heath. I was fed a pretty big shite sandwich durin' those times as well, but look at me now. Things happen for a reason. And when the time comes to be revealed, well, it just happens, me boy. So, you met some real McNastys durin' those troubled times, eh? Have you forgotten 'em?"

"No, I've not. Trust me, comrade, but enough for today. Crush my deckle and give me the bill so I can blow your fancy gin mill."

"Your money's no good today, sir, but rest assured me cipherin' will improve—in anticipation of your regular return."

"And I'd expect nothing less, my lad."

"Dia dhuit, Heath Winslow!"

"God be with you too, my buddy, my pal."

C H A P T E R   4 :
DEVELOPING A DIABOLICAL PLAN

HEATH TIP-TOES THROUGH a maze of papers, folders and news clips piled on every square inch of sofa, chair and coffee table surface available in his Sarajevo flat. Even with all these creative building blocks stacked before the intrepid journalist, no constructive image presents itself.

"This drudgery will be done," he grumbles. "How else do I recall my '90s life story? I'm determined to finish this task once and for all, but why must my 'Balkans gone by' saga be such a fait accompli?"

As his cataloging continues, Yugoslav folk music gushes from a boom box left by a former music-loving tenant. The tunes are courtesy of cassettes Heath bought at the corner drug store. He revels in their sounds. *Caress me with slow tempos and rich harmonies. Your elixirs flow close to my soul. I feel so melancholy, so much in the moment.*

Notebook entry: Sevdalinka—traditional Balkan folk genre... Popular across region... Elaborate songs, charged with emotion, sung with passion... Composers unknown... Unique among Southeast European music

The patio door swooshes open. A furious rush of air thrusts up the heavy lace curtain, not unlike a giant white arm sweeping across the living room. As if on cue, Danvor the landlord enters just in time to watch dozens of paper piles take synchronized flight.

"What the hell?" Heath pleads.

"Žao mi je! Žao mi je!"

"I seem to be getting more than my fair share of 'I'm sorry' lately." Heath shakes his head in disbelief at how much destruction a single puff of wind has wrought.

"Really, Heath. I so very, very sorry."

"It's okay, Danvor. I know you didn't do it on purpose, but you couldn't have been more effective, even if you'd tried."

"Pardon, sir?"

"Oh, never mind. What's done is done. It's a sign. It's beer time in Milwaukee. Join me in a sojourn to the Ballygoan?"

"You know a good pub, sir. Da. I be honored, but only if I buy. My way of saying…"

"Yes, I know. You're so sorry and so am I."

—⚊—

"Welcome, me boys," Eoghan, the Ballygoan's owner and bartender extraordinaire, proclaims. "Beers all around?"

"Da!" and "Yes!" Danvor and Heath yell back in unison.

Brews set and coasters marked, Eoghan makes a sweeping hand gesture. "No soldiers. The castle's ours. Now, let's reminisce about another of your damsels in distress, Mr. Winslow."

"Sorry, Danvor, but this crazy Irishman insists on rehashing war stories from the '90s… when I was a reporter here."

"As long as beer is cold, I be fine."

"Okay, then, I'm glad we've got our priorities straight. So, my stout drafter of stout, I think you made reference to 'baddies' during my last visit. Well, let's talk about a woman so evil her photo's in the dictionary, next to the term 'she-devil.' Her insane escapades started in a tranquil valley not far from here in the winter of '91, if I remember correctly."

—⁂—

Heath describes the sunrise spilling over the Dinaric Alps as yet another majestic spring morning is born. Smoke-like wafts of fog rise off the Neretva River. Street lights dot Konjic's twisted roadways. Their globes glow in the mist, setting the stage for a new day's awakening. Welcome to postcard-beautiful Herzegovina.

Dragana Kowalchuk, a Serbian Guard and rising rebel star, finishes pouring over maps of the nearby city and neighboring towns. In defiance and disgust, the lady scorpion crumples page one of the *International Herald Tribune*, dated March 2, 1992. Its headline screams, *Turnout in BiH Signals Independence.* The self-proclaimed freedom fighter grabs her mug and storms out of the rustic hunting lodge.

"It's been more than two months since that referendum!" Kowalchuk shouts. "May Day has come and gone. When will federal troops start shelling this zone? We're organized. We've trained. We're ready to do our part. Just give me a sign!"

The woman's an angry enigma. Her personality is as alluring as she is wicked. One moment Dragana is talkative and confidant; the next, she can be cold and rude. She relishes being harsh with underlings and uncaring toward her peers. Kowalchuk might seem original, even droll at times, but her drive is the result of a hell-bent life—one long, arrested development.

Yes, a disappointing childhood it was. I was the oldest of ten. A nurturing home was not enjoyed by any of us. I can assure you of that.

There was constant fighting and so much dysfunction in the Kowalchuk household. Dragana's father was always yelling, with an endless, threatening tone. She lived in never-ending fear of him. Her stressed-out mother was seldom on an even keel, nor were her punishments. All of that, and so much more, just repeated itself for years on end.

Dragana left home at an early age, bouncing from kin to kin. Then, she took up with a street gang as a means of fending for herself, but her parents tracked her down. They forced Dragana into a convent, hoping the rules of the nunnery would improve her behavior. But that was not to be. She soon broke away from the sisterhood to become a member of the Guard.

I'm an Arkan's Tiger now. Okay, so most of these guys are Red Star football crazies, but under my leadership, they're now a fanatical fighting force.

—ɯɯ—

"I know of this woman!" Danvor shouts, interrupting Heath's story. "You know here too? You interview this wicked person?"

"No, we never met, but I'm convinced we travelled the war years in parallel. My writings and her actions were always colliding. Now, do you mind if I continue?"

"No, not at all. My beer still cold, but I do hear war stories of this nasty lady. Good to know she drive other peoples crazy too."

—ɯɯ—

Heath continues by describing Dragana's command post. It's perched atop the Borasnica slopes where the defacto ruler of this rugged region can soak in unobstructed views. She has committed to memory supply routes that switchback through the harsh mountainous terrain… all part of her ongoing need for control.

The hell gal takes a long, slow sip of coffee in an effort to quell the frustration over the Yugoslav army's snail-paced inaction. Taking a deep breath, she reflects on historic times when the Orthodox Church ruled this land as the spiritual guardian of all Balkan people.

You can trace our struggles to that 14th century putsch by Emperor Dusan. Like him, I'll restore a Greater Serbia. Pec will again be the heart of Balkan Orthodoxy... Mark my word.

Pec—that idyllic little town in northwestern Kosovo—was the center of it all. Church leaders of the day, along with their noble executioners, were obsessed with expansion. Their flocks were told to charge as far west as the patriarch's power could reach, spreading Canon Law to the hinterlands.

Saint Sava's message was simple and his preaching clear: The national and religious elite rule. Deviation was not to be tolerated! Present-day radicals, like Kowalchuk, use such religious text to justify razing churches and mosques, seizing land and uprooting people at will.

With such thoughts fresh in her mind, Dragana steps down from the porch and strolls to a nearby fire pit. Soon she's sharing her twisted tale with a motley group of hooligans. They gather around the blaze as Dragana continues to preach. It's as if she has some kind of magnetic power that pulls people close, appealing to the emotions and sentiments of her public far more than any trail of logic could ever do. Dragana, the political puppeteer, can sway an audience in any direction. This will be but one of her many performances intent on emboldening these separatists for the selfish struggle ahead.

"Remember Milošević at Gazimestan in '89," Dragana stresses. "As proud Serbs celebrated the Battle of Kosovo, he said, 'Every nation has one love that warms its heart.' Therefore, we must fight to regain our state, our nation, our integrity."

Although the devil-woman is driven to support the president and others, she has no intention of bloodying her own hands.

I can never be part of any engagement supporting any battle. Yes, I have clever ideas, but I function best in an advisory role.

Her accommodating push is a synonym for maintaining a distance from most anything and everyone. In many ways, she leads a double

life; one is acted out for the eyes of loyal followers and another script-
ed for personal indulgence.

Silhouetted by the dawn's early light, Dragana casts the shadow of
a tall, fit, yet willowy woman. Years of mental anguish and physical
abuse are apparent in her hard-edged features and pointed gestures.
Most people find it difficult to look at her face on. Dragana's beady,
almost black, eyes seem capable of piercing one's very core.

At the same time, this feminine warlord dresses impeccably,
whether it's military-like outfits or business attire. Every garment is
heavily starched and faultlessly tailored, but this attention to detail
does little to complement Dragana's appearance. Rather, it empha-
sizes the tragic woman's rigid, unforgiving stripe. It's as if the best
and worst of humankind have made her soul their chosen battlefield.

Out of earshot, fellow rebel leaders describe Dragana as insensitive
and uncharitable. It's a given her emotional state is far from stable.
She's moody and full of self-pity. She's the bottom line definition of
arrogance—a truly criminal, calculating creature.

"Sip that coffee slowly, ma'am," a rebel leaders is overheard saying.
"It may well be the only warmth headed your way for a very, very
long time to come."

—⁂—

Eoghan pounds his fist on the bar. "Laddy! As I've long said, that's
one bog Irish bitch. God help the poor bastard that brushes her bad
side."

"Amen," Heath and Danvor affirm.

"That kind of scary reflection calls for stronger sustenance, Eoghan notes. "Who's with me?"

"I think it's time for me to go upstairs."

"What? You have apartment here too, Mr. Heath?"

"No, Danvor, it's our code. You see, during the war, I stayed up-stairs at the Holiday Inn. Eoghan was head bartender there. The old bar had a railing above it where the fine liquors were kept. I'd tell big guy, 'It's time to go upstairs.' That was, and still is, Eoghan's cue to grab the good stuff."

"And if Mr. Pulitzer was too shite-faced to appreciate the better booze, I'd just pour him a heavy shot of rot-gut gin. Besides, tonic and lime camouflage a multitude of sins."

"Then a gin and tonic from the well it is. So, Rocky and Bullwin-kle, should I continue this fractured fairytale?"

"Da" and "Yeah," Danvor and Eoghan enthusiastically slur in agreement.

Heath begins describing a valley below Dragana's headquarters where Mara Cesarec is sounding off about the role of Muslim women in today's society.

"This is 1992, not 1692!" she shouts.

Her conservative mother tries reasoning the differences between the sexes are due to their divergent conditions. "It's all detailed in the *Qur'an*, young lady."

"Stop, stop, stop! Who the hell was Mara, again? And why are we debatin' the *Qur'an*? This be a non-practicin' Catholic lad you're preachin' to, Mr. Winslow."

"Sorry, Eoghan. Sometimes my memory gets the best of me and I just ramble on. You remember Mara's tragic tale. She was Andro's childhood sweetheart. She lived next door. And yes, she was quite the budding feminist. Mara's was always promoting women's rights, social justice and all the rest of that women's lib stuff.

"But there was another, finer side of this lady we all can appreciate. Trust me when I tell you Mara was as gorgeous as she was puzzling. She was stunning and intriguing, in a mystical kind of way. Her shimmering black hair begged to be touched. Her tresses were the ultimate compliment to her wide-eyed beauty and dainty chin."

Prior to Mara and her mother's morning exchange, the teenage beauty's day started with her scribbling, *Don't fence me in!* atop a new diary page. Hunched over a petite bedroom desk, she giggled and stroked her hair while remembering the latest furtive liaison with Andro in the Babich hilltop cabin. Mara's still surprised how simple it was to fall in love with someone harboring a call of the wild. She finds that untamed nature the center of Andro's masculine charm. Mara takes endless pleasure in stroking his chiseled physique, as well as sensing how he responds to her gentle caresses and soothing words of encouragement.

But Andro's as hard to pin down as he is charming, Mara scribbles. *He's not what anyone would call boring. The mystery makes him charming. He's truly the Prince Andro of my dreams.*

Mara's come to realize, if she's to share in Andro's life adventure, she must be strong enough to let him run free. In return for such abandon, Mara seeks only Andro's adoration and intercourse—in both the bedroom and of his mind.

"Okay, Mr. Romance Writer, we get the picture," Eoghan moans. "She's hot, they're playin' with puppy love and the sex is better than good. Now, tell us more."

"Sure, but don't be taken in by Mara's stunning surface. Her inner strength is a real contrast to her fragile-looking shell. Her character is that of a chameleon. One moment she's warm and outgoing; the next, she's distant and aloof. Mara's one forceful creature. She's also stubborn and even a bit bossy. Just ask her brother. He'll tell you."

—⁂—

Heath lets the tale unfold… Behind her back, Mara's brother, Aadil, often points out Mara's lack of concern for other people's problems. "She's not interested in others, period."

With himself as the example, Aadil tells his schoolmates that Mara insults people all the time. "Praise be to Allah. Our madrasa teacher says it's a sin for Mara to call me a pig or a dog. She should be punished. Just like me, she has to repent. And Allah knows best. So there!"

Although Mara accepts the world around her, she's determined to find order in the midst of its chaos. Wise beyond her 17 years, she's intent on driving the blocked progress of women in her village—to better define her life and the lives of those around her. As a result, the heated debates with her mother are likely to continue in frequency, duration and intensity.

"Let's table this talk for another time," Mara's mother suggests. "I'm worried about your father and brother. They saw the election results on TV and rushed off to the mosque mumbling about the future. What do you think it means?"

Mara senses her mother's concern and tries comforting her. She places both hands on her shoulders. "Don't forget the old Turkish

Sufi saying, 'You can bandage a cut for yourself, but you can't take out your own appendix.'"

"And what, Mara, is that supposed to mean?"

"Even as we learn and grow through our own work, for profound guidance, we need someone to lead the way. The men are at the mosque to seek direction from the imam. It's a matter of mathematics. As an ancient one said, 'Whoever travels without a guide needs two hundred years for a two-day journey.' After they get our leader's wise counsel, they'll come home."

"I sense you listen too closely at the mosque's door."

Mara begins to weep. "I ask that you listen only to me now, mama, not the holy ones, as I fear what I am about to say may break your heart."

"Good God, child, what's with all this drama?"

"I'm pregnant!" Mara yells as the words blurt from her mouth. "And I know it's true."

"Aslam Alukm, my daughter… Fall on your knees and beg Mohamed's forgiveness. Remember, as written in the Holy *Qur'an*, 'God does not place a burden upon a soul beyond what it can bear.' You must go to a private place and ask Allah to pardon you."

"It's not that simple. It's Andro's baby. What do you think of that? So, do I get an abortion, or what?"

"No! Reflect for a moment on what you say. Bear in mind what Allah teaches. On the Day of Judgment, each aborted infant and every child that was killed will come before its parents, whether married or not, and ask, 'For what reason did you murder me?' It's clear; is it not? No baby should ever be taken to destroy proof of fornication or mischief.

"At the same time, my child, having a baby out of wedlock is a brutal oppression. It's almost unimaginable. First, women end up having to raise the toddler. Any enlightened imam will tell you this form of cruelty can't be ignored. Men must shoulder the blame too. They must be made liable for what they produce."

"Mama, I too have studied the *Qur'an*. I know of Allah's divine guidance and the imam's teachings. That's not what I'm asking. What do we do about this seed inside me? Mama, please help me… Please."

"What's the solution, you ask? Are you not blessed with the least bit of sincerity and understanding? If so, there's no need to search far afield. Who better to guide us than the creator of men and women than Allah himself? It should be obvious where you've gone wrong. Allah can steer you back on the right path.

"Now, to your room, child. We'll speak of this again when a sense of calm comes back to this house and my mind is no longer on fire."

Mara bursts into tears of anger. Frustrated and confused, she rushes to her bedroom, crying into her hands and begging, "Why me, Allah? Why me?"

—⁂—

Meanwhile, on a distant mountain top, Dragana wraps up her impromptu lecture. She grabs a jug of *Bulls Blood* wine and heads back to the porch. "Bring me those books off the table," she yells to a lieutenant inside. "I need to review our plan of attack one more time."

Dragana has long been intrigued with strategies used by Confederate generals planning the South's defense during the American Civil War. She reads President Jeff Davis' tactics with keen interest.

"Remain on the defensive until the opportunity presents itself to launch an offensive," Kowalchuk mutters, parroting the Southern leader's stratagem. "Just as then, I'll promote to the world we're only acting in self-defense."

Through her studies, Dragana notices a criticism historians repeatedly unleash: Southern armies often took to the offensive too quickly, wasting meager resources, as well as lives, for little or no gain.

Guerrilla actions conserve resources and tend to draw out a conflict, Dragana surmises. The modern-day Jennie Reb has studied every

Confederate plan she could get her hands on and committed most to memory.

I read and re-read them with immense pleasure. I'm eager for the day I can put such tactics into action against those who oppose our dream of nation building.

Drained by the mental exercise, Dragana sips the robust red from a heavy, lead-crystal glass. Thoughts tumble back to her youth where so much of her current rage was incubated. Her present day pontifications near the steps of this forest fortress are but a culmination of the pain from her sordid past.

In light of all this and more, opponents of this modern-day Clytemnestra can be forgiven as they paraphrase Shakespeare, declaring, "Heaven hath no greater wrath than Dragana scorned."

—∿—

While putting dishes away, Sofija glances out the window, catching sight of Mara trudging up the pathway. Baba swings open the kitchen door and calls, "Come, child. Come in from the cold."

"Thank you, Baba Sofija, and a good day to you."

"Dobra don, Mara," the Babich clan leader replies. "Have you seen my son and grandsons? The phone rings. The next thing Alen grumbles something about an urgent football meeting. They grab their coats. And like a puff of smoke sucked up the chimney, all three are gone."

Sofija's anxiety has been building for days. She fears a prediction in a recent newspaper editorial: Bosnian Serbs, with support from the Yugoslav government, will launch a terrorist campaign against Bosniaks and Croats. The essay goes on to foretell Croats doing the same against Serbs and Bosniaks.

Such a three-way war, Sofija fears, could rage for years. Families choosing sides as the chaos grows. If you have a Serb mother and a Cro-

at father, you must pick one side or the other and your brother might choose a third.

She wonders what's next. *Will families train guns on each other? Will cities be turned to ruin? Has a world at war come to haunt us again?*

The sad truth of the moment is people on all sides of the argument are learning to live in a state of constant terror and endless fear. It's a dreaded scenario Baba Sofija can't get out of her mind.

"Every boy in this town, regardless his age, is obsessing over the possible break-up of the Yugoslav football league," Mara explains. "'My God… The premier footballers won't be able to play!' they scream. Every fan is waiting on pins and needles to see what FIFA does to their club. It's bigger, far bigger, than any kind of politics. And that, I'm sure, is the crisis at hand."

"I hope you're right."

"So, what is our remarkable Babich homemaker crafting today?"

"Just some paperwork. You know, Mara, taking care of bills and some banking; that kind of stuff. That's why I want the boys to come home, so we can talk vacation plans."

"You take great pride in serving as den mother, don't you? I see this love and devotion every day. And you can be sure it's not lost on anyone under this roof, especially Andro. He sees you as a very special grandmother. He calls you his 'mama with lots of frosting.'"

"That's sweet, Mara. You know it's not always been easy running this household—leaving Croatia, moving here after the Nazis, learning to manage this farm. Those were scary times. Then, the rug is pulled from under me. I felt so empty, so alone, when my husband died. I doubted I could carry on."

Baba Sofija glances heavenward. "When God took Alen and Andro's mother, I feared the roof might collapse. And then we took in the girls. After the car crash, they had no other place to go. And that's when God called to me. He said I had to step up. 'Move forward,' he said. God gave me the strength and skills I needed to survive. And with the Almighty's grace, we did it.

"Now we have you, too, Mara. You're such a beautiful part of our bigger family. Okay, we may be different in religion and background, but you know you're loved by us all."

"Of course I do. You're like my second mother. And your Andro is such a kind man." Tears well up in Mara's eyes as she reaches out to hug Baba Sofija. "And that's why I came today."

Just as the two embrace, an explosion smashes the tranquil moment. Sofija and Mara squeeze together in fearful response to the thunderous blast. Before they can question its origin, another detonates, then another. The eruptions span the valley, rattling windows, setting off car alarms and shattering the huddled women's nerves. The outbursts are followed in rapid succession by the syncopated rat-a-tat-tat of machine gun bursts and the clapping sound of small arms fire.

"What the hell?" Mara yells in terror and confusion.

"I fear the devil is at our doorstep," Sofija whispers. "You must run home, my child. Your parents will be worried. God knows what wickedness is about to unfold."

"But I'm so afraid!"

"As are we all, my dear, but it's most important we gather close those we love. We must pray to God for guidance—each in her own words and in her own way. Go now, Mara, please, and hurry."

The two frightened women lock eyes in deep understanding, clasp forearms and kiss both cheeks. This hushed engagement is a far more poignant farewell than any frightened words could propel.

As Baba Sofija feared, the quiet before the storm has been broken. She stretches to clasp her Bible on the kitchen counter. Collapsing to her knees, she trembles while making a Sign of the Cross. Tears stream down Baba's face, following the crevices of her weathered cheeks.

Sofija whispers from the Book of Matthew, "All who draw the sword will die by the sword. All who draw the sword will die by the sword. God have mercy on our souls."

—⁂—

"I knew it!" Eoghan shouts, throwing his hands in the air. "The damned war. You had to usher that in, eh? Póg mo thóin, Heath Winslow!"

"What that mean?" Danvor demands.

"Kiss me ass, if my accent detector's working."

"Very funny, Heath. Okay, I'm sorry, but like you said it's the people and that's what I hoped we might harken back to. Andro's a good kid. Grandma's bitchin'. Dragana's the bitch she's always been. And Mara, well, I wouldn't mind takin' her to the dance. So, to hell with the war, man."

"Have I to meet Mara and Baba?"

"Eoghan will catch you up, Danvor, but I think story time's over for today. It looks like we're coming up on happy hour anyway. The last thing I need is sitting in a bar with a bunch of drunken soldiers crying in their beer, recalling battles they never fought."

In a flash of sobriety and insight, Danvor interjects, "As a wise Serb poet once say, 'If needed, we invent new enemies. Our old ones are of no more use to us.'"

"That's not only deep, it's brilliantly scary, you simple wise man. And so, barkeep, what do the coasters say?"

"Da, and if you need handyman, I can work my way sober."

"Get your tails out a here, the both of ya. We'll settle up later. You take the high road. And you take the low."

"And I'll be in bed afore ya!" Heath laughs, grabbing Danvor by the arm and guiding him out of the pub as a squad of soldiers saunter in.

—⁂—

C H A P T E R   5 :

FROM PLOW SHEARS TO SWORDS

It's the Balkan spring of '92—a time when farmers lay down plow shears to gather up swords. Villagers are beginning to arm themselves. Barricades rise like weeds sprouting along the roadside as Serb, Croat and Bosniak defenders stand on point. Water pumps are smashed. Electricity and telephone lines are cut. TV stations flicker off the air. Residents on all sides of the triangulated divide are soon left in unknowing darkness.

Radio announcers broadcast updates. They warn of conflicts in the capital. "Gunmen attacked a wedding party in Sarajevo today. An Orthodox priest and a man carrying a Yugoslav flag were killed in the melee."

As an raid sirens blare, the sound of sniper fire zings down once tranquil village streets. Car alarms wail. Dogs bark as if wolves are approaching. Ambulances rush along deserted avenues, crisscrossing cities in a blind effort to aid the wounded.

"In but a few weeks," a newsman laments, "our beautiful Bosnia and harmonious Herzegovina have descended from tension into a state of terror."

—⁓—

Andro bursts into the family farmhouse. "Baba Sofija! Andro!" The two scream in near unison. "Are you alright? Are you okay?"

"Da, we're okay," Andro reassures his grandmother, lifting and caressing her. "Papa's hooking up the wagon. Alen's coming up the trail. Let's gather the girls. We're going to the cabin until things settle down."

"God grant me the serenity to accept the things I cannot change," the Babich matriarch begs. Then, as if struck by a jolt of clarity, Sofija rips down a jacket to wrap her shoulders. "I must see the priest at once, for all our sake."

"Baba Sofija, stop… Please! There's no time for church advice. Papa thinks civil war has come. We must find shelter in the woods."

"Don't doubt my actions, boy. We need a link to our home. Father Malinko may be our only conduit. Now, call the girls and throw some clothes in a bag. Don't forget socks and underwear. By the time you're done, I'll be back." With the discussion ended on her terms, Baba Sofija bolts out the door.

—⁓—

Mara dashes through an alleyway, desperately darting for home. She turns the corner by the family courtyard, as starbursts of dirt erupt from the street. She's dusted by an acrid-smelling gray cloud. Her face is peppered with cobblestone chards. Screaming in fear, the agile teen leaps a retaining wall and lunges for the portico.

A shaft of light from the open door illuminates Mara's mother re-coiled against the wall. She's weeping with hands outstretched, while whisper-chanting words of the Prophet, "God has no mercy on one who has no mercy for others… God has no mercy on one who has no mercy for others."

Mara falls to her knees at her mother's feet. "Come, mama. Let's get you in bed so you can rest. I'll wait with you for papa and Aadil's return."

"God has no mercy on one who has no mercy for others…"

"Yes, I know mama. All will be right with the world. Allah be praised," Mara whispers as she guides her mother to the bedroom. Cupping her mother's head and lowering it on to the pillow, Mara sighs, calling on all her strength to face what may lie ahead.

—⁂—

The mountain top's morning clam is shattered as tank commanders and artillery crews lob fire at mosques, churches and other targets considered suspect across the valley. The ear-splitting booms become muffled thuds as the percussion sounds reach the ridge line. The plink, plink, plink release of rocket-propelled grenades is followed by brilliant flash-bangs from their exploding rounds. These killing noises are attended by loud, sharp blasts as Soviet-made bazookas are unleashed.

Fragmentation grenades are next on the firing line. They shower ruination far beyond the fire cracker sounds their launchers make. All the time, infantrymen replicate the roar of massed kettle drums as thumb-size bullets blaze from their .50 caliber machine guns. The shells rip through anything in their path. Then, the barrage ends, as quickly as it started. The silence is deafening. The warriors have heard little of the death screams that accompanied so many of their bombs bursting in air.

The rebels' leader stands at parade rest on the cabin porch edge, her back to those assembled. Dragana's feet are shoulder-width apart, hands at the small of the back, fingers extended and joined, thumbs interlocked. For dramatic effect, she snaps to attention, executes a crisp about face, then clanks her heels to grab further attention.

"Those are federal troops firing!" Dragana yells as she points toward the valley. "Those are the orchestrated sounds of heroic people across the Balkans saying 'Enough is enough!' Today the patriots of Greater Serbia are taking up arms in self-defense. We're demanding the world recognize what we've known for centuries. Like our ancestors on the Plains of Kosovo, today we rally for our special truths."

The paramilitary crowd, sporting bomber jackets, leather caps and hunting rifles slung over their shoulders, erupts in a frenzy of cheers and wild applause.

As the ovation subsides, Dragana takes a step forward for emphasis. "You've been assigned to great patriots. Just as Serbs fought against the Turks in Kosovo more than 600 years ago, we come together to fight for our survival today. Listen to the leaders among you. You are the follow-on force needed to put our house back in order."

Dragana pauses for emphasis. Her dark, hollow eyes squint. "As the saying goes, if you love someone, set them free. If it's meant to be, they will come back to you. And if they don't return, hunt them down and kill the bastards."

The crowd of hooligans bursts into uproarious laughter and chants of approval. "For Kosovo! For Kosovo! For Kosovo!"

Pushing to heighten the fever pitch, Dragana shouts one of her treasured Machiavellian quotes. "'If an injury has to be done a man, it should be so severe his vengeance need not be feared.' Now, go and be part of our new history."

The rag-tag collection of rebels bursts into jubilation once again. As the commotion settles, insurgents break into small bands, encircling their group leaders for orders, not unlike footballers shoulder to shoulder in a pre-match huddle. Units peel off, dissolving into the dense forest. A massive trudge down the mountainside begins. Stomping boots trample footpaths toward the targeted towns now smoldering in the valleys below.

—m—

The sound of a tractor's sputter is heard outside the Babich farmhouse. Andro's father charges in. "Are we ready yet? There's not much time. Let's move!"

Little Suzana, casting a doe-eyed stare at her uncle, whines, "But why must we go to that clunky old cabin? There's no TV."

"Yaga Baba is hungry," her older sister teases. "You could be her lunch."

Children of all ages fear Yaga Baba. She's a witchlike creature of Balkan folklore. The hideous hag flies on a giant pestle. She kidnaps, grinds up and eats small children she finds along the way. With ghostlike strokes, the wicked old woman is known to sweep away her tracks with a silver broom. She lives in a thatched hut that stands on dancing chicken legs. The front door keyhole is a hungry mouth filled with razor-like teeth. The fence around her odd abode is made of human bones with skulls atop corner posts.

Desperate peasant people often seek Yaga's wisdom. Yaga Baba will dispense guidance to lost souls for a price that's not always gold. Seeking her aid can be a perilous undertaking for the weak at heart and soft of mind.

"Chapeka, don't scare your little sister like that. Besides, Yaga is grand mama's friend, so I'm sure we'll all be safe. Now, both of you help cousin Alen pack the food stuffs."

Chapeka chuckles, patting her uncle's arm. "That's a good one, but I don't know how funny Baba Sofija would find it."

"Find what?" the clan leader asks as she bursts into the kitchen.

"Nothing, mama. Are you about ready?"

Ignoring the question, Sofija bustles past her son to the coat room's far corner and begins digging. "I know that paint… Ah, here it is." Baba rises with a tin can in one hand and a small brush in the other. She pulls open the front door and starts smearing its outer face.

"What the hell are you doing, Baba?" Alen yells. "Have you lost your mind?"

"Desperate times call for desperate actions, beyond washing your mouth with soap, young man. Father Malinko said we should borrow a lesson from Passover, when Moses told the Israelites to mark their doors with blood. It kept the Angels of Death from taking their youngest sons."

Andro comes into the room carrying a suitcase and blankets. "But why the Russian cross, Baba Sofija?"

"Football hooligans and other fools on that rebel team are too dumb to tell the difference between a Serb and Croat cross. This three-beam version is unmistakable. One Orthodox will never desecrate another. Let's just hope the damn thing works."

Andro's father shakes his head in wonderment while ushering the girls out the door. He hoists them on to the flatbed. "Come on, everyone. Andro, help Baba Sofija into the wagon, then lock the doors. Alen, pull the main switch on the fuse box and bring that last crate of food. It's time to go. Now!"

—⁂—

Dragana's thugs continue charging forward with their ruthless campaign, ransacking unorthodox houses of worship, as well as any Muslim or Croat shops in their way. Barns and out-buildings are torched, setting the countryside ablaze while marking their paths of destruction.

Two rebels, using a grenade launcher, blast open the doors of a mosque on the outskirts of Konjic. It's the same masjid where Mara's father and brother are gathered with so many other men. Shards of metal and wood splinters rain on carpets lining the prayer hall, striking many sitting close by.

As the assembled recoil in shock and fear, the imam stands and extends his arms toward the interlopers. "Do not become angry and you will be relieved."

A popping sound echoes through the mosque as a flash streaks from one of the gunmen's rifles. In response, the imam lurches back, spins and falls to the floor. Everyone freezes. Two stout mosque workers, taking slow, silent steps, approach the trespassers from behind, with clubs in hand. They swing in unison, striking both intruders square on the head. The barbarians fall to the floor like sacks of grain tumbling from a peasant's cart.

Pandemonium erupts. Dozens of men and boys break into screams, scattering in every direction. Mara's father grabs Aadil. They rush through a side door, then bolt down the street and up an ally toward home. Not until safe inside does he sense the warm ooze between his fingers. A large splinter has lodged in the soft underside of the boy's arm. The puncture site is bleeding profusely.

"Allahu Akbar, Allahu Akbar," Aadil's father utters in shock as he tries to comfort his son.

"Allah will forgive the ones who do us wrong," Aadil whispers in a dazed effort to calm his father.

Mara runs down the hall from the bedroom. "Papa… Aadil… Praise God! Are you okay? What's happened?"

"Rebels attacked the mosque. Many, like Aadil, were injured, but the holy men took revenge. Allah be praised… That's when we fled. What happened to your face, my child?"

"Pebbles blew up from the street. I made mama rest while I cleaned up. It's fine now, really."

"So, help me stop this bleeding. I must get your brother to a doctor right away."

Mara gathers several kitchen towels while her father helps Aadil sit. The boy winzes in pain as father and daughter attempt to wrap his wound.

"Mara, you stay with mother while I take Aadil to the clinic. And don't let anyone through this door. No one! Do you hear me? Do you understand?"

"Yes, sir, but come back to us… Please."

—⁓—

Alen stands watch outside the Babich cabin, banging his boots together while pacing back and forth in a feeble attempt to keep warm. There's a rustle in the distance. A twig snaps. "Halt! Who goes there?"

"Alen Babich… Is that you?" a voice yells out from the forest's underbrush. "It's your cousin, Baldo Ivaniševic. Stop with the Nazi bullshit. And, if you're holding a gun, point the god-damn thing at the ground, will you? Jesus! And for Christ's sake do it now."

"Baldo? It must be you. There's no finer trash mouth in all of Herzegovina. Step out and show yourself."

Baldo emerges from the thicket and saunters toward Alen. The two strongmen slam chests together, share a bear hug and exchange kisses on both cheeks. "Great to see you too, you ass!"

"Hey, it's crazy times. How could I know it was you? We're all Slavs. We all look alike. Besides, what are you doing here?"

"My dad and a bunch of bitchin' neighbors are camped down the hill. They want to talk with your father about stopping the asshole rebel goons."

"And you, Baldo? You're a reservist. Why, with all this going on, didn't they call you up?"

"Like you, Alen, I have a friggin' football waiver. I just don't have your beautiful bum knee for insurance. Hell, they can sound the bugle all they want. There's been too much gunfire and crap already. I can't hear a damn thing they're saying any more." Both men laugh as the irony of it all slowly sinks in.

Just then, Alen's father steps out of the cabin. "Baldo, long time no see. Short time no hear. What brings you to our neck of the woods?"

Baldo explains. Alen's father agrees to meet with the others. "Why not? Who knows what nightmares we may dream tonight? Alen, I want you to join us. Go tell Baba Sofija where we're going… and have Andro stand watch."

—⁙—

Andro's time on point passes in slow motion. Bored by it all, he daydreams while spinning a tiny crucifix dangling around his neck. Perplexed, the young man sighs and shakes his head.

I don't get it. What's going on here? And why? Why? Why? There's got to be an answer. How do we end this insanity? It's tearing everything apart.

"And what's papa thinking? Andro asks aloud. "There has to be a better way than eye for an eye. How can fighting be the answer?

It's so strange what I'm thinking and how I feel right now. I want to act, but I'm lost on what to do. There's just so much fear in my gut.

"But I can't walk away," Andro announces to the woods. "Something must be done. If not, it'll come back to haunt me. It'll haunt all of us. Then things will be even harder to fix. From here on out, I'm going to commit. I must try to steer a course."

Baba Sofija was right. My calling has got to be about more than selfish me. It's now the ultimate game of good versus evil.

Andro continues pondering and mumbling his jumbled thoughts, gazing westward in time to see the mountains drink in what's left of the afternoon sky. Lingering sunlit beams seem to strike a fairylike prism hung somewhere in the firmament. Rich, warm colors, with smooth, blended edges, pour down from the heavens. Radiant streaks shoot skyward from a molten gold band caressing that place where earth meets sky. The sunset lets go shadows that creep across the foothills. They canvass the countryside in a curtain of darkness. Nightfall is soon to make its entrance.

"How can anyone not believe there's an answer out there after seeing something like that?" Andro whispers in amazement. Shrugging his shoulders, he resumes his guarded stroll, skirting the cabin clearing and waiting for who knows what from who knows where, or when.

—m—

CHAPTER 6:

STUMBLING THROUGH THE HERE AND NOW

AN ATHLETIC, WIDE-EYED rebel in paramilitary garb leaps the stone steps of Dragana's hunting lodge headquarters. He stops in front of the leader's massive wooden desk, thrusting a note in her direction. Gasping to catch his breath, he whispers, "First reports from our patrols, ma'am."

She-devil grabs the hand-scribbled memo.

> *Combined forces hold key points in nearby towns.*
> *Outlying sweeps complete. Stiff resistance in Konjic.*
> *Bosnian forces control strategic assets, armaments.*
> *Cannot penetrate city center.*

"This is unacceptable!" the villainous creature screams as she crumples and throws the report to the floor. "Who doesn't realize how important those military stores are? We gave those people more than 500 weapons and this is what we get?"

Dragana pauses in the midst of her rage… Gazing at the strikingly handsome chap standing square before her, she thrusts back her chair and swoops around the desk. She's now standing toe to toe with the youthful fighter. Fearing a verbal assault is eminent, he steps back, only to have his retreat blocked by the cabin's rough-hewn wall.

"No need to recoil," Dragana purrs at the frightened soldier-boy. She wedges her right leg between his, resting her thigh against his groin. "In the midst of all this activity, I'd forgotten my need to choose a new aide. Might you be interested?"

Flattered, but befuddled by Dragana's rapid advance, the man mumbles, "Yes, ma'am, but I don't know if I'm qualified to…"

"I'm sure you're more than qualified," Dragana says as a smirk slides across her face. Her fingernails rake the gent's skin-tight T-shirt outlining his barreled chest and rippled abs.

"Let me assure you I'm more than confident I have whatever else you might need." As she speaks, Dragana's mind races with the thought of dragging this man-child into her bedroom, tearing off his clothes and exploring every inch of his Adonis-like body.

In response to her emboldened offer, the lieutenant smiles, revealing stark white teeth bracketed by deep-set dimples and glistening green eyes. Dragana finds them alluring. She feels beckoned.

What a nice boy, but he's not a boy; he's a young man. So what if I'm a little older? The temptress yearns to have her way with this man-toy. And what Dragana wants, she usually gets.

"Do I need paint a picture of what could be?" Dragana asks as she slides her fingers inside his blue jeans and yanks forward his brass belt buckle. "Or, should I order you to comply?"

"Your… your wish is my command."

"Then come to me at 20-hundred hours. Use the back steps. My bedroom opens onto the porch. Now leave me. Storm out as if I gave you a reprimand. And about tonight, don't be late."

As the giddy young recruit charges down the chiseled front porch steps, he's met by a well-respected patrol leader heading in. "I hope you have your flak jacket on, sir," the young stud states with bravado. "The volcano's erupting as we speak."

—⁜—

"Comrade Jovanović, ciao. I've read the field report. You can kick that worthless wad of intel in the fire for all I care. Tell me: What's going on out there?"

"Stiffer resistance than we'd expected, ma'am. Two of our militia-men blew up a mosque and killed an imam. No one needed kick that hornets' nest. But I'm confident, with continued morning bombard-ments and afternoon mop-ups, we'll secure the region straight away."

"I'm holding you to that, Jovanović. I want our enemies to feed only on fear for survival. Do I make myself clear?"

"Yes, ma'am!"

"I know we're all committed to the mission, but we must do even more. Tell the others I'll be holding formation at eighteen-hundred today. No exceptions! Now, go clean yourself up and get some rest."

"Yes, ma'am. Is there anything else I can get you at this time?"

"No… Just go."

—ɯ—

Two shadows, long gray streaks in the moonlight, slide across the clearing. "Andro… It's your father and brother. Don't be alarmed. Is everything okay?"

"I hear you papa and everyone's fine."

Soon, the Babich clan is huddled near the fireplace with Chapeka and Suzana perched on Baba Sofija's and Andro's laps. Alen leans against the mantle next to his father. An uneasy tension radiates from the hearth as eyes dart back and forth in desperate, silent searches for counsel and comfort.

"Alen and I just met with our Croat brothers. It's clear we have neither the arms nor experience to confront the rebels now. We don't know much about their leader either, but rumor has it federal troops will keep on shelling Konjic until the town surrenders."

"Papa and I are leaving with the others to build our strength in Croatia."

"But Alen!"

"Mama, please let me explain. If we stay, we'll be captured and imprisoned. When they find out, and they will, that Alen and I are soldiers, it could be worse. Just as key, a brave man must stay to protect the women. And Andro, that's you."

"But father!"

"No, Andro, just listen, please. Alen and I discussed this at length. It's the best way. Alen's a trained radio man. The resistance needs his talent. My command skills may be rusty, but I'm obliged to heed the call. Baba Sofija and the girls need you. We have no other choice. Now, you two young ladies scoot off to bed. It's late and the adults have more of this boring talk, talk, talk to do."

—◊—

Baba Sofija tucks the girls in, kisses both on the forehead, then slips out of the bedroom.

"I'm scared," Suzana whimpers.

Chapeka pulls the blanket over their heads and hugs her sister. "I know. I think everyone's scared."

"Maybe it's time we go find Yaga Baba and see what a witch has to say."

"Sure, Suzana, but let's wait until morning. It's cold and I can't see in the dark. Just go to sleep. We'll be fine. Papa knows best and Yaga Baba will always be there."

—◊—

Three thugs—one tall and skinny, another short and fat, plus a third burley in-between—saunter up the lane near the Babich farmhouse. If not for their paramilitary dress and gun-toting swagger, they could be cast as three lost Stooges.

Noticing the paint slathered on the Babich door, burley man makes a Sign of the Cross. "Let it pass. These Russians are comrades. We move on." The other two in the tragicomic threesome shrug shoulders and continue shuffling down the lane.

As Mara strokes her mother's hair, there's a knock at the front door. She shrinks back in fear. Her mother awakens in a fog.

"Go see who… What is that my dear?"

"Never mind, mama. Papa said…"

"It's fine. Just go find it out… I'm okay. It's good."

Mara steps away from the bed and tip-toes down the hallway. The knocking becomes louder and more frequent. She lifts the curtain to peek outside. With a loud clunk, the door's kicked open and three thugs burst in. They halt to survey the main room. It's decorated as a resounding tribute to Islam. Traditional Ottoman motifs adorn the furniture, lamps and pillow tapestries that fill the sitting room.

The first intruder, sporting a face pocked by acne, exclaims, "No doubt Ali Baba's spent a thousand and one nights here."

"Is there anyone else, wench?" the second man, short and fat as the first is tall and skinny, demands.

Mara stands paralyzed in fear, unable to utter a sound.

"Check the back," the older, burley hooligan with a scraggily beard orders.

"No, please," Mara pleads, but pocked-face shoves her aside. She trips on the settee and falls to the floor. The gangster stomps down the hall, pistol at the ready. He enters the bedroom. There's a moment of silence, then two distinct shots ring out.

"Oh, great God!" Mara screams.

"The crazy bitch tried to shoot me!" the ruffian yells as he jumps back from the bedroom, "but I made sure she won't try that again."

"Let's get the hell out of here," the frightened, rotund one pleads.

The bearded brut steps forward to straddle Mara. "I think some-one should pay for being so inhospitable. Don't you, Javar?"

"Couldn't agree more, boss."

"I'll have no part of this!" fat man yells.

"Fine, Pavle. Just shut up. While we take a moment to please our-selves, you scope the house for money, jewels… whatever."

Mara retreats into a fetal pose while starring at the sadistic goons cowering over her. As they grab her wrists and ankles, she resigns herself to the impending abuse. Mara will come to see her rape as a sick tool, a sinful club hammered at her and so many other village women. Even these filthy muggers know theirs is a crude weapon, far easier to wield than any bomb or bullet.

The hooligan hogs plunge on top of her. As the attack commenc-es, Mara vows to survive her moral endurance test. She stares, with empty, wide eyes, at the far wall, festooned with Islamic verse. Mara wishes her ears were plugged so as not to hear the reverberating vio-lation. Her mind swirls with conflicting thoughts, fueled by anger and pain. There's nothing she can do about it now but swear revenge.

As quickly as the assault began, it's over. The room falls silent. In her delirium, Mara wonders if she'd gone deaf. Nothing's said. No one looks upon the other. The ruffians button their trousers. Everyone realizes they've been tainted by a vile deed beyond words or further action.

Pudgy Pavle stumbles back into the living room with a blood spat-tered pillow case filled with booty. "For Christ's sake, let's get the hell out of here."

"Dobar dan," the bearded brut snarls as he kicks Mara's shoulder and spits on her torn dress. "The pleasure was ours."

—⌘—

"It's time. Gather the fighters below the porch," Dragana barks to a nearby trooper. "I'm more than just a little angry and I can assure you everyone's going to hear of it."

Well out of earshot, two paramilitary bosses huddle to discuss the day's events, berating Dragana in the process. "I have observations for Kowalchuk, but we all know listening is the last thing she's capable of," Commander Djukić laments.

"There's no caring heart in that ice chest," Chief Kraljević adds.

"It's as if she puts up road blocks on purpose. They're built for her personal pleasure. Sure, we let her decide most everything, but why can't she see these are real people we're dealing with?"

"Who knows? Kowalchuk won't stand tall for anyone. She's never shown any interest in what others do… unless, of course, it serves her own end."

Another principal walks up and whispers, "Stop the bitch session, guys. The real one's about to take the stage."

The lady circus master steps out of the lodge and into an implicit ring of fire. The radicals lunge forward, displaying a false eagerness to hear the carnival barker roar.

"We can all agree today didn't go as well as planned." Dragana pauses as she makes searing eye contact across the entire front row. "I was sent here to run this show. My job is to guide and direct our way forward. And we will prevail!

"You know I demand perfection from all I oversee. And I can assure you I will fire any slow mover without a second thought. You also know I can't stand slackers or whiners. So, as the old general often bellowed, 'Either lead, follow, or get the hell out of the way.'

"We have a strong vision, but we only have time for action. All of you know where we're going and what we must achieve. I'm determined to reach that goal, but I can't get there without you. I'm just as concerned about results as you are. And we will get them. Is that clear?"

A unified shout rises from the horde, "Yes, ma'am!"

"Good… Then we meet again, right here, at zero-six-hundred. I'll have updated plans by then. I'll review and map out new strategies at that time… Dismissed."

"I rest my case," Kraljević mutters to his comrades. "Lions six, Christians zero and we still don't know who's going in the coliseum tomorrow."

It's just before eight the same evening. The wooden steps to Dragana's back porch creek from the weight of a fervent young man bounding on every other riser. Dragana swings open the wood-framed glass door to her bedroom and gestures for him to enter.

"Lieutenant Dub…"

"Shush," Dragana whispers, pressing her fingers against the soldier's lips. "No names. No talking; just kiss me," she says, stroking the man's smooth, dimpled cheeks, then slithering her digits through his thick, wavy hair. Dragana breaks the embrace, gliding backward to rest on her bed. As her legs cross, the silk negligee falls off her shoulder and slides opens. The lieutenant's eyes drop, transfixed on Dragana's thighs.

"Sit," she says, patting the Irish-linen sheets.

The two lock lips again. He-man plunges his tongue deep inside her mouth while his fingers slide through Dragana's hair and over her shoulders. They're in a mad rush to find and trace the small of her back, then cup her smooth buttock. Both whimper and groan in unison, tumbling back on the bed to commence their pleasure romp. For what seems like an eternity, the two writhe in a sea of carnal bliss, eventually collapsing in a tangle of arms and legs. The sex stud soon slips into a dazed slumber. As his deep breathes subside, gentle snoring begins.

"Sleep well my prince and happy birthday to me," Dragana murmurs. *This may not be the time to cut the cake, but can't I be forgiven for opening my present early?*

—◆—

Chapeka awakes in a haze. She rubs her eyes, then gazes about the room. Realizing Suzana, along with her bright orange jacket and blue boots, is gone, Chapeka scampers to the sitting room. She finds Baba Sofija asleep, slouched in the leather recliner.

"Baba Sofija… Baba Sofija," Chapeka squeals as she tugs on the old woman's arm. "Suzana's gone. I think she went to find Yaga Baba."

"What?" Sofija mumbles, half asleep. "There's no Yaga Baba, my child."

"We know that, but Suzana doesn't."

Realizing the severity of the moment, Sofija leaps to her feet. "Get your things. We must find her. Andro's at the camp and he'll be back soon."

Sofija and Chapeka notice the back door is ajar. As they push it open, tiny boot prints are revealed in the snow. They track in a dotted line toward the woods.

"Let's go. I'm sure she couldn't have gone far."

As they reach the crest of a knoll near the forest's edge, two scruffy men approach. The taller, younger one is clutching a squirming Suzana under his arm. "Might this be what you're looking for? She was circling under a deer stand hollering for Yaga Baba, if you can believe that."

"She's all upset," Baba Sofija replies with a timid ruse. "She lost her puppy and has been looking for it everywhere."

The country bumpkin fighter plops Suzana down. She dashes to Baba Sofija's side, then caresses her leg. Sofija gathers both children closer. "I'd tie a leash on her and keep it taunt, if I were you. Things are a little dicey right now, if you know what I mean?"

"Da, da… Hvala. We'll be going now. And we'll heed your advice. Thank you. Thank you, again."

"Our patrol is camped just beyond the ridge. Don't be alarmed by the cannon fire. It should end by noon. Then we'll sweep for resistance. Tell your men folk to come join us. Your Serbian Guard is here to make it right."

Sofija bows to the tough guys, then turns away. She begins a resolute march back to the cabin with the girls in tow. When they arrive, Andro has returned and is frantically stomping around, looking for them.

"Baba Sofija, Chapeka, Suzana! Where have you been? Are you alright?"

Sofija explains what transpired as she ushers the girls into the cabin. "Andro, I don't like it. Those hooligans frighten me in so many ways. In his dumb excitement, one told me who they are, where they're camped and when they'll be coming. It's not safe for you, my loving grandson. You must escape while you still can."

"Baba Sofija, I can't leave you alone. What would papa say?"

"Now it's what I say! I'm taking the girls back to the farm. Then we'll head to Sarajevo. I'm sure we'll be safe there. You follow the hiking trail to Mostar. Stay off the main roads. Go to the restaurant so Uncle Thoma can shelter you. Then head for the coast. Cousin Andelko should help you go south. Uncle Abeiron and Aunt Jadranka will take good care of you in Greece."

"But Baba…"

Sofija thrusts her open hand forward, making a stop-like motion, while digging deep into her carpet bag. She pulls out her old passport and a wad of money. "Here, take these. The papers should get you to Dubrovnik. And you'll need cash. Here are some dollars and Deutschmarks."

Anticipating refusal, Sofija is insistent. "Please, Andro, don't argue with me. We don't have time. This will work. I know it. God has given me a sign. But remember one thing: Father Malinko is our bond. Send your messages to him. The Church will never fail us."

As Andro casts a confused daze, Sofija pulls off her black woolen scarf. After tossing some rolls, cheese and smoked ham slices on it, she ties up the crocheted rag and thrusts it at Andro. "Take this and go. Know we love you. God will be with you."

Andro and Sofija hug in silence. Tears well in both their eyes. They kiss cheeks in a hushed goodbye. As he steps back, Chapeka and Suzana start crying and rush to his side.

Andro drops to a knee, caressing them both. In a whisper, he heartens the girls, "Be strong for Baba Sofija and watch over her for me."

Andro stands, turns and steps away. Sofija closes the door with a gentle push. Making a Sign of the Cross, she falls to her knees and begins weeping as Suzana and Chapeka huddle to her side.

—⬥—

C H A P T E R   7 :

CASTING FAMILY TO THE WIND

"Hey," Dragana murmurs to her bedside buddy. "Wake up."

"For God's sake, woman, what time is it?" her soldier stud mumbles as he rolls over, throwing his powerful leg across and anchoring Dragana to the bed.

"It's zero-five-hundred. Time for you to go," Dragana declares as she pushes him back and wiggles free.

"Are you shitting me? It's another hour until sunrise, unless you want to chop some morning wood? I'll gladly be your bushman."

"Stop it… I've got formation in an hour and I'm not doing it from my boudoir. Now get dressed and get out."

"What's with the ice bucket? I felt we had a pretty hot thing going here."

"A one-night stand and you're thinking unrequited love? Grow up kid. Not everyone wants to play that game."

The words "You caustic bitch!" tumble out of the young man's mouth. Before realizing what he's said, and to whom, Dragana lays the full force of her back hand into a searing face slap.

"To the porch now, lieutenant!"

The soldier-boy leaps out of bed, pulling on his socks and pants. He then slides into his boots while struggling to don T-shirt and bomber jacket. By this time, Dragana's wrapped herself in a heavy fleece robe and slid on slippers. She stands cross-armed and impatient at the side of the room, ready to swing the back door wide.

As her night fling stomps on to the porch, he jeers, "You're as cold in bed as you are at roll call."

Dragana spins toward him in a maddening rage, impaling the angry man's throat with a knife-hand strike. Dazed by the Karate blow, he stumbles, then slips on a patch of ice. Before Dragana can grab him, the rebel recruit tumbles over the porch railing into the ravine below.

My God! What have I done? Now what? Get control, woman. This is no time to panic. You're in command. It was an accident. Take action now.

Dragon Lady steps inside, scrunching her eyes in a frantic push to invent a cover-up. In a flash of brilliance, she rips open the nightstand, pulls out her Luger and fires at the wooden beam above the porch door.

Seconds later a guard bursts into the room. "I heard a shot. Are you alright, ma'am?"

"Yes, I think so," Dragana states with a fake swoon. "There was an intruder on the porch. I saw him silhouetted in the moonlight. I fired my pistol to scare him. I'm afraid he slipped and fell over the railing while trying to run. Have someone check it out. See if he's alive. If he is, kill him. First, bring me some coffee. I have to get ready for morning briefs. I need to warm up; you know."

—⚏—

A row of wood siding blushes red in the distance. "Come on, come on. We're almost there," Sofija urges the girls as they slip through the pasture gate. "Watch your step. We have enough messes to clean."

As they round the barn's stone corner, an elderly man pops out of the shadows. Surprised, the three freeze in place. The wiry old codger tries standing erect, as if assuming an attention stance. "Mrs. Babich… So sorry. I didn't mean to scare anyone. Back from the cabin for good?"

"I don't know, Mr. Hadžić. We've spent the morning dodging thugs roaming those hills. Now, you spring from our barn. I'm confused."

"As you might be, Mrs. B. The rebels' first wave did surge through here. They left when our Bosnian troops showed up."

"But our farm, our home… They've been spared. How can that be? I painted a big cross on our door in hopes of keeping the crazies at bay."

"And it worked. Then, when the tide changed, your neighbor, Ms. Cesarec, painted over it with a star and crescent—sacred symbols of the Muslim world. That the Bosniaks respected. So, I'd say everyone's God has been on your side."

Sofija throws her arms skyward, "Praise God and Allah, but why are you hear, Abdulah?"

"You're cows were bellowing for hay and their udders were ready to burst. So, I fed and milked them. I hope that's okay?"

"Da. Da. Bless you, sir, and hvala. Please, take all the milk you need. Offer it to the neighbors, too. Now, I must check on our home and thank Mara."

"Please tread gently, Sofija. Mara's head is in a strange place. We just buried her mother. She was killed by those roving brutes. Mara's still waiting for her father and brother to return. The young lady scuttles around all day, like a frightened lamb, in your back yard."

Sofija makes a Sign of the Cross and shakes her head in disappointment. *That poor child. Lord, give me the strength to do the work you have called me to do.*

—∾—

Sofija steps out the Babich house back door. She finds Mara curled and huddled against the wood pile. "Come to me, child. Together with God, we'll move ahead as one."

"Allah be praised," Mara cries and rushes into Sofija's arms. She begins howling and shaking in despair. Falling to her knees, Mara buries her face in Baba's apron.

"Let it out, child. As the Prophet Gibran once wrote, 'Your joy is your sorrow unmasked.' How else can it be?"

"I must get away from here, Baba Sofija. I must. I must get away."

"We all need to move on and we will, Mara. We will. I'm taking you and the girls east. Yes, my daughter-in-law is somewhat of an odd gypsy lady, but that Roma has a loving heart. We'll be safe there. We can start to heal. I'm sure of it."

Sofija begins rocking Mara and telling her about the cabin happenings. Mara's heart is torn anew by the news of Andro now trekking to the coast, but she accepts the need for his safety.

Lyrics to an old ballad swirl in Mara's head. It's a phrase out of time and place. It was first meant to strengthen her English skills. She gazes deep into Sofija's eyes and whispers, "Let us be content and the times lament. You see and I see the world is turned upside down."

"And if God is for us," Sofija affirms, "Who can be against us?"

As they prep to leave the farm, Baba Sofija tells the girls about the Romani. "Yes, Gypsy is another name, but think of them as a special people without a motherland. Unlike your Aunt Florica, thousands live in ghettos around the countryside. They're poor and many must beg for work."

"Does Auntie Flo have a crystal ball? Does she? Does she?" Suzana pleads.

"No, silly," Chapeka snaps. "And I bet she can't read tarot cards either."

"Let's not be so quick to judge," Sofija scolds. "Some people are born with special gifts. What makes Roma rare is how they get along with nature. Many bond with outdoor spirits. Do you know what that means?"

Silence is accompanied by wide-eyed stares from the girls.

"Well, their skills are pure and grow in harmony with Mother Nature. What could be better than communing with the cosmos? Okay girls, that's enough for now. Just remember: People believe different things in different ways. They deserve our respect. And in our case, plenty of thanks for taking us in."

—⁑—

With the aid of two glaring florescent lamps, a bespectacled Dragana pours over maps, staff notes and reference books heaped on her desk—documents so numerous several have slid to the floor, lying in neglect. She can now be found rethinking actions and reexamining conclusions at almost any hour. It's all part of Dragana's endless quest for validation.

"Comrade Jovanović is here, ma'am," one of the lieutenants announces.

"Good. Send him in."

Jovanović enters the room as Kowalchuk shoves back her chair, thrusts upright and marches next to the commander. Extending a finger, she points toward a lounge chair near the fireplace.

"Sit… Wine?" Jovanović smiles and waves off the offer. "Okay, let's talk. We've been at this for some time now. What's your latest assessment?"

"I think we've reached a stalemate," he says with hesitation. "Regardless how much we shell the area, we can't gain a foothold in town."

"Then we've got to find a way!"

"Permission to speak freely, ma'am?"

"Go ahead."

"Several of our troop leaders are concerned about your incessant review of the facts. They fear it undermines resolve. It confuses them. They can't predict what might come next, what actions will be taken. They feel the more you scrutinize, the more you drain assets from the campaign."

"Is that so? And when did they become field marshals? It's my responsibility to weigh the pros and cons, to examine how time and money are spent, how we prosecute this crusade. That's called leadership. My job is to assume control of all actions for which I'm responsible. Due to the incompetence of those around me, I will continue leading to the exclusion of others. Do I make myself clear?"

"Yes, ma'am!" Jovanović snaps, followed by a slide forward to the chair's edge, as if he's sitting at attention. "Then, there's the matter of the U.N. protection force."

Dragana's forehead blushes. Blue-hued veins swell in her neck. She holds nothing but contempt for the United Nations troops. "I'm cognizant the Smurfs are headed to town. I'm also confident NATO leaders and CIA operatives will come to appreciate our cause. Yes, I'm proud of my aptness in dealing with these issues. Understood?"

"Ah, yes, ma'am, of course."

"I realize command can be given, taken or surrendered. So, if you're determined to set another path, bring your proposals to me, but do it quickly. And stop trying to put bowling balls in marble bags. Just find a way to get the job done. Now, get the hell out of here!"

"It appears Kowalchuk has plenty to tamp in her campaign pipe," Jovanović mumbles as he walks well out of Dragana's range, "but is she prepared to smoke it? It might behoove her to mind the dissident who said, 'Serbia is not a twilight zone. Here you can see nothing at all.'"

—∽—

Sofija makes clear everyone's tasks as they prepare to leave. "Girls, we must bag our stuff like we're camping. Get your backpacks and lay out your needs. That means sleeping bag, flash light, bottled water, sun screen, soap, wash cloth, towel, a pocket knife and a change of clothes. Don't forget extra socks and clean underwear."

Suzana tugs on Baba Sofija's ski pants. "Should I bring my camera? We might see Yaga Baba on the trail."

Chapeka lets go a chuckle that sounds more like a scoff.

"I think a camera's a great idea, witch or no witch."

Mara slouches through the door, her talkative free spirit not to be found. "I can't do it, Sofija. I can't go back in that house. I just can't."

"That's my fault, Mara. I didn't think. You sit with the girls and I'll gather your things. Give me a minute to share our plans with Father Malinko as well."

Sofija scurries down the lane toward the church. Chapeka and Suzana start making a lighthearted game of their packing ritual, hoping to shed a few rays of sunshine on Mara's darkened world.

Sofija returns with Mara's stuffed back pack. She inspects the girls' efforts and ushers everyone out the door. "We'll take the old hiking trail along the ridge to Lukomir. Did you know it's the only traditional village left in Herzegovina? It has many old stone houses with roof tiles made of cherry wood."

"Are we going to Uncle Franjo's, or are we on a *National Geographic* tour?" Chapeka quips.

"Excuse me young lady, but I find talking often helps people move through troubled times. And now that I think of it, you should write a detailed report about our adventure. Suzana can be your nature photographer."

The hike out of Konjic is a wonderment for the eyes. Towering limestone peaks stretch skyward before the mountain trekkers. A maze of grassy alpine valleys and dense woodlands lay at their feet. They're entering an almost forgotten, pristine wilderness.

"Mara, you seem so far away. Are you okay?" Sofija asks.

Mara nods in the affirmative and in silence.

"I've never seen so many wild strawberries… and sweet too," Suzana notes. "Can we pick some Baba Sofija? Can we? Please?"

"Sure. Let the harvest begin. Then, on to Lukomir. I know someone who has a cabin there. It's a good place to rest for the night. And if we hit bad weather, there are caves where we can hold up."

"I don't know," Suzana cautions. "Yaga Baba could be hiding in them."

With the strawberries gathered, the troupe steps off again. Soon, they come upon a lofty wooden suspension bridge. Suzana starts to cry, petrified at the thought of crossing. Without a word, Mara passes her rucksack to Chapeka and gives the frightened little girl, eyes squeezed shut, a piggy-back ride to the other side. Eyes open once again, Suzana begins clicking photo after photo. Images framed by panoramic views and anchored in churning ribbons of whitewater far below.

—⟋⟍—

Andro scans a hiking map found in the cabin. He picks a route to Mostar through the mountains by way of Lake Barocko, then moves out to conquer the course. Andro's confident, if he keeps a steady pace, the ramble is doable in a day. Several hours later and near exhaustion, the youthful trekker reaches a bluff overlooking the village.

Exhilarated by the site, Andro runs down the slope and into Uncle Thoma's bistro.

The restaurant is empty. Thoma is startled by an unexpected guest bursting through the door. "Andro? Is that you? There's no need to rush. We're still open."

Dashing to his uncle, the two fall into a huge embrace. "Uncle Thoma must always be the clown. Have you not heard the shelling and seen the vigilantes?"

"Yes, Andro, but we must be strong, or they win before our first shots are fired. Okay, we have to be smart as well. Your Aunt Sasha is busy upstairs packing. We're off to the coast. I'm sure your cousin won't mind if you tag along. In fact, we insist."

"Sounds like a plan, but I'm starving. Is there anything left to eat?"

"You ask this in my canteen? Do I look like we're starving? Now go. Raid the refrigerator while I finish up here. Then we drive west, young man."

Andro yells from the kitchen. "I'm worried, Uncle Thoma. Papa and Alen have gone to fight with the Croats. Baba Sofija and the girls are hiking to Uncle Franjo's. And who knows about my girlfriend, Mara?"

"Crazy times, Andro. This conflict may be impossible to resolve. One side fights for peace while the other struggles against war. But our family's strength is in its numbers. Trust me; we'll preserve."

Stepping into the kitchen, Thoma keeps on, "Just remember that wise old saying 'The fearful are often more dangerous than the man who seeks to do you harm.' I'm convinced that's where we stand now. But with your help, Andro, we'll be even stronger. Eat up. Build your vigor. We're going to need it. God help us everyone."

—◊—

After a restful night snuggled around the cottage hearth, Sofija and her entourage hike toward Ilidža. Several hours pass and as many rest stops. The foursome reaches the foothills of Mount Igman. They gaze down in relief on the lush green oasis known as Vrelo Bosne. This pristine Sarajevo suburb is both their destination and hopeful sanctuary.

"Look at all the beautiful flowers!" Suzana exclaims.

"Bosanski Ljiljan," Mara explains. "The golden lily is an historic symbol of Bosnia… What? I'll have you know I'm very interested in flowers."

Sofija moves close, smiles and pats Mara's cheeks. "And I'm over-joyed you're talking to us again. God and Allah be praised… Welcome back, my dear."

"Suzana! All you do is shoot, shoot, shoot," her sister grumbles. "Aren't you out of film yet? You never know when Yaga Baba might show up. What will you do then?"

"Stop, Chapeka. Uncle Petar said Baba Sofija was Yaga's friend. So, I'm not afraid anymore."

Everyone shares a laugh as they stroll down the hill and into what's often described as one of the prettiest places on earth. Sofija so hopes this relative-rich safe haven will prove the refuge they all need. As if buying some type of spiritual insurance, she pulls a Bible from her satchel and whispers from the Book of Isaiah, "They shall obtain joy and gladness. Sorrow and sighing shall flee away."

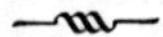

Dragana, wine glass in hand, leans against the cabin's mantel. She stares into the embers, soaking in the momentary warmth and tranquility. A creak escapes from a rough-hewn floor board behind her. The rebel leader turns to see Father Kraljić, a local Orthodox priest, entering the room.

"You asked to see me, Sister Kowalchuk?"

"Yes, Father. I'm in need of a clerical advice, but please, call me Dragana."

"How may I help, Dragana?"

"I've been studying, in great detail, historic strategies I believe can move our cause forward. I've uncovered tactics I'm sure will seize the moment. I'm now mapping out actions to support them."

"That certainly sounds like a logical approach to a complex challenge."

"So I thought, but many people now question my work—each and every day. Isn't it my job as a leader to flush out our strengths and weaknesses, to identify threats and prospects?"

"Again, I'd say yes, but as I'm sure you know, conditions are always changing and we may need to adjust accordingly."

"Of course, Father. That's why I review my plans, but I won't sacrifice my beliefs simply for the sake of change. What's so alarming and confusing about that?"

"Nothing, Dragana, but we can never forget the difference between responsibility and self-centeredness. On one hand, a person is liable for the results produced in their life. God holds us accountable for those outcomes—both good and bad. Conversely, a person shouldn't be so focused on self he forgets to serve others. That person could be seen as vain and lose influence."

"I hear what you're saying. And I'll admit I'm driven. I'm driven to reestablish the moral focus of our homeland. I want to reaffirm the values of a Greater Serbia in the here and now. This is what I seek without compromise. And I do it not for me, but for all our people."

"No one's questioning your drive, Dragana, but I've heard some are concerned about your approach. They see it as endless searching. For example, are you shutting your mind to the big picture, becoming blind to the greater good? If so, how can you know when an idea might be wrong? Are you blocking inputs at odds with your beliefs?

Will such an approach cause you harm? And how might it impact those close to you?"

"Father Kraljić stop, please. You've put forward nothing but a litany of questions. I need answers."

"Those can only come from God and you, Dragana. They come from deep inside you. Come with me. We'll pray together and seek His guidance. Forget not the wisdom found in Proverbs 20-18: 'Plans succeed through good counsel; don't go to war without wise advice.'"

—w—

Andro's busy in his uncle's kitchen, devouring a Dagwood-style sandwich while trying to make sense of his life's moment. Thoma pulls out the wooden bench, plops down and stares. "Are you okay with everything that's going on, Andro? Mama spoke so quickly when she called. I couldn't catch it all. Did what she and your father say make sense?"

"Yes, I think so, but I take much of it on faith. Baba said God gave her a sign. We've never questioned that before. What I don't understand is why we're in such a crazy place? If I could figure that out, maybe I could make sense of it all."

"Don't think so hard, Andro. Trust me; it will only depress you more. This country's fight is all about bigotry, propped up by a bunch of hotheads. Just remember: We were all South Slavs once. Hell, we still are. That's what Yugoslavia means… And religion's been recruited to feed the latest hate. All this pontificating only fuels the bigger lunacy that is war."

"You're quite insightful when you're not telling bad jokes, Uncle Thoma."

"Well, thank you, Mr. Footballer. And between us men, let's not get hung up on your grandmother's preaching either. For example, I have my own special prayer for times like this: Oh God, if you exist, help us. If you don't, tell us not to expect anything… That, and a couple grains of salt over the left shoulder, will get us through dinner most any day."

"Common sense is a good thing, Uncle T, but simply wanting to live within my own circle of friends, well, that can't be such a pie-in-the-sky idea. Can it? It's the question our old priest would ask all the time: 'Can life become richer, and people stronger, when we look beyond labels?' Why can't we value one another for who we really are?"

"With that said, Andro, I want you to listen to me. You need to be careful. Strong feelings can be serious barriers in the real world, especially if you try putting such words into action."

"But Uncle Thoma, I'm just saying what I feel."

"I'm afraid the elitism you preach may be the very source of your unhappiness. Take the quarrels you and your father have. They happen when both of you get stuck on a singular point of view, or some silly opinion."

"I'm sorry, but now I am confused. Did I come here to be lectured by you as my father in absentia?"

"I tell you these things because we love you, Andro. You're going through a hell of a hard time right now and I'm not just talking about the war, or our family. You're becoming a man. That's one rough road to travel, but you need not go it alone."

"Okay uncle, so what's your advice? Say something that will lift the dampness from my spirit."

"Be open and flexible, Andro. It's as simple as that. Your blind faith in beforehand views can hurt you. Be careful. You often refuse to question attitudes. That's a weakness. Try this approach: Look at your fixed ideas as prejudice."

"Now you think I'm prejudice?"

"No, no, no, young man. I'm not saying that at all. What I mean is you should look at things in another way. It's called introspection and it might help clear your mind. In the end, you'll see. Fixed attitudes are far from an unmixed virtue. Bottom line: Don't let your bullhead-edness check your progress… ever."

"Uncle Thoma, you have such passion and perception. Where's my tape recorder when I need it?"

"Shut up, kid. That's what too many beers and too many years as a bartender will do to your brain. Now, help me box some food. It's time we head for that Pearl on the Adriatic, before it's too late."

C H A P T E R   8 :

PUTTING PLANS TO WORK

OUTSIDE A DECREPIT bus station, half-hidden on the northwest coast of Greece, an exasperated driver shouts, "Ne, ne, ne… Da… Jawoh… Yes, yes, yes… This express to Athens!"

Passengers strain to hear while huddled under a dilapidated canopy. It's the only protrusion large enough to offer escape from the blazing sun. With the announcement made, a gaggle of tourists charge the bus, clamoring to get aboard.

For Andro, this is leg three of a bizarre sojourn. It's one more wild ride arranged by crazy cousin Andelko. Andro endured a six-hour sea crossing from Dubrovnik to Italy's heel on day one. Any thought of food on that sail was soon left overboard. The next afternoon, he boarded an overnight ferry from Bari to Patras. It was a far less tumultuous Adriatic cruise. At the same time, the crossing took more than 16 hours of undulating boredom to reach Greece's shore.

At least the food was good and plentiful, Andro remembers. *Although, being introduced to Mr. Grappa might not have been the best courtesy afforded me.*

Remnants of the traditional Italian firewater still throb on Andro's forehead as he staggers onboard the tour bus. He must now endure three more hours of winding, pothole-covered mountain highway in order to reach Uncle Abeiron's abode. And today's scorching heat should only enhance the smell of rotting fish and sunbaked cargo containers waiting near Athens to greet the Bosnian wanderer.

—m—

Baba Sofija and her entourage stroll a tree-lined Sarajevo boulevard elegantly dressed by historic Hapsburg homes. As they pass a park entrance, Suzana spots a horse-drawn carriage. Its costumed driver tips his hat and winks.

"Baba Sofija, can…"

"Another time, Suzana, but yes, we'll go for a ride soon."

The cackle of ducks and swans mixes with gurgling sounds from a nearby stream and splashing waterfall. As nature's inviting clatter fades, the foursome turns a corner. Sofija's son and daughter-in-law are standing outside their bungalow, eager for mother's arrival.

"Dobra dan, mama! Dobra dan. What a joy to see you," Franjo shouts. Tall and handsome like his brother Petar and nephew Andro, there's little doubt he's a member of the Babich clan.

"And I, you. God bless us, everyone."

The afternoon passes with pleasure as Sofija, Franjo and Florica step on each other's conversations in repeated eager attempts to reconnect. Chapeka and Suzana race around the patio table, chasing their cousins Abraham and Nahida in an impromptu game of cat and mouse.

"Children!" Baba Sofija shouts. "Stop before you break something, or somebody trips and falls."

"They're just bored. They're trying to burn off some steam," Florica notes. "Mara, would you escort them to the park? I'm sure our gabbing is of little interest to you."

"There's a photo kiosk on the way," Sofija adds. "Here's some money. Have Suzana's film developed and get everyone some ice cream. Hvala, Mara."

Mara shepherds the gaggle of children down the street. Those remaining resume their banter, oblivious to the political storm clouds gathering overhead.

—◊—

As Heath pours his morning coffee, he glances at the table where a plastic milk crate is now filled with dozens of manila folders. The globe-trotting reporter beams with pride, knowing his anal-retentive need for journalistic order has been fulfilled.

This apparatus should ensure my documents won't fly helter-skelter any more. There will be no more papers masquerading as floor covering in my house.

Heath's fingers flip through the files. He pulls a folder labeled *Radio & TV*. Sliding the patio door open, he steps toward the small wrought-iron courtyard table. The doorbell rings, interrupting his transition. Heath sets the folder and places a large ceramic mug on top. It's his feeble attempt to secure the contents. He then heads to the door.

"Mr. Heath Winslow?" the deliveryman inquires.

"Yes, can I help you?

"A parcel from America. Sign here please."

"What's today's date?"

"12 March 1999, sir. It's Liza Minnelli's birthday."

"Well, that's a special moment on the world's stage, isn't it?" Heath scoffs as he takes the package. The two exchange pleasantries and the courier leaves.

Heath saunters back to the patio, unaware he'll soon set a Rube Goldberg moment in motion. His carless disregard while ripping open the shipment results in the wobbly mug being struck. It tips over. Coffee spills across the manila file. The remainder drips through the table grates on to Heath's bare feet. The burning sensation causes him to jerk. During the recoil, Heath's new knee hits the table's edge. Papers inside the folder are set free. A breeze ensures each scrap is given flight to a far corner of the patio and numerous spots in between.

After a brief pause in amazement, Heath shakes the remaining drips off the errant folder, then starts gathering the news clips now littering the patio.

Well, I believe this is yet another sign. A walk to the coffee shop appears in order.

After a two-block amble, Heath enters Café Fez. He orders two bosanska kafas and a wedge of baklava to go. "Might as well get a sugar rush, as long as I'm drinking high test," he chuckles with the clerk.

Back at his own café table, Heath reopens the still damp folder. He starts skimming the ruffled stories devoted to the early '90s scandal involving Yugoslav radio and television. Back then, the communication arm of the government became a propaganda puppet under Milošević. And its director, Adrijan Ackov, was having his strings pulled on a regular basis.

Notebook entry: Jugoslavenska RadioTelevizija—
national broadcasting system... 8 production sites...
Belgrade denies TV & radio stations air rights... High
fees force others to close... Milošević soon controls the
airwaves

What a bizarre encounter... my first meeting with that strange little man. Ackov was always promoting himself as some modern-day press officer. He never realized the ruling elite had made him a propaganda artist. He was their defacto Mr. Yellow Journalism at his finest.

Ackov and his crews produced little real news. Instead, they used sensationalized reporting to sell the party line.

Oh, their clips were impressive, in an odd and sad kind of way. I actually found it quite amazing to watch such a massive half-truth machine in action.

—⁓—

Heath approaches the Yugoslav Ministry of Transport & Communications, admiring its brushed steel and smoked glass façade. He enters the building and is directed to a conference room where a sign declares: *Media Brief—1200 1 April 1992—Legitimate Press Only.*

"Nothing more need be said," Heath chuckles.

Through the room divider's gray tinted Plexiglas, Heath can see Communications Director Ackov huffing and puffing on a cigarette while scurrying around his disheveled office. He's making last-minute preparations for the briefing. The topic of today's meeting: *Restructuring Yugoslav Communication Services.* His anxiety spiked moments earlier when advised several senior bureaucrats will also be attending today's brief.

This added stress is not a good thing. Poor Adrijan's not in the greatest of shape. He's almost fifty, short and stout with a pronounced beer gut. His thick, wavy coif is defined by a well-receding hairline. And Adrijan insists on wearing his basic black-framed glasses with Coke bottle lenses slid half down his nose.

Tubby man's teeth are stained from years of drinking strong coffee and lighting too many cigarettes. He's known to fidget and sweats profusely in pressure situations, not unlike the one for which he's trying to prepare. Adrijan makes a sad, but strong, fashion statement in his ill-fitting and outdated wool suit. It looks like a hand-me-down, courtesy of a sympathetic mid-level Soviet bureaucrat.

Looking back, Adrijan's spoiled, decadent upbringing contributed to the emergence of a cold and inconsiderate brat of a young man.

So, how did my parents respond to my rebellious attitude? Adrijan asks himself. *Defiantly: They whisked me away to boarding school so they could keep on sipping champagne from crystal flute glasses.*

Realizing their unimaginative son would be too much of a distraction while they waltzed through elitist Serbian circles, Mama Majka and Papa Otac set Adrijan up with his own apartment.

Then they cut my purse strings and bid me ado… Damn right I was mad and alone. From that moment on, I set out to prove Ma and Pa Ackov wrong… so very, very wrong.

In a near stroke of genius, Adrijan somehow helped raise great sums of money for Belgrade's children's book center.

That's where I was bitten by the editorial bug. I wanted to drink deep from that journalistic well. And he wanted to do it through exerting little effort in the process.

Back to the briefing at hand… Heath listens as Adrijan's double-speak drones on and on across the half-empty meeting room. He's only paying him the courtesy of attending because Heath has a meeting with Adrijan right after this session.

—⁊⁊—

"Mr. Winslow, I presume?" Adrijan asks, stepping out of his office about 30 minutes after the briefing.

"Please, call me Heath."

"Come in. My apologies for the delay… And yes, call me Adrijan."

Bureaucratic impediments aside, their initial meeting gets underway. Heath and Adrijan consider themselves members of the Fourth Estate. In their own egotistical, flamboyant ways, they both represent a unique societal force. But in this current propaganda war, Adrijan is everything Heath is not. He's constantly searching for ways to compete with Heath and all the man stands for.

"It's obvious," Heath notes, "we're both dedicated professionals, predisposed to seeking out the truth while attempting to tell fair and balanced stories."

"Agreed, sir, but one must be wary of any obsessive manner that might contribute to contentious, even dangerous, situations. Such actions require great tact and cunning as a means of disengagement."

Fancy words and arrogant attitude aside, Heath is quick to realize Adrijan's impulse is to resist any stereotypical editorial role.

This bastard's only intent is finding ways to package government crap so the public will swallow it, Heath soon realizes. *And he wouldn't mind snaring me in his spider's web of misinformation along the way.*

"Enough with the philosophical garbage, Ackov. You're no more than a contemporary half-assed impersonation of that finger-shaking, goose-stepping, Goebbels prick. You called me here just to make me wait so you could chew my ass, then whine about what some of your cronies call scathing… That being my editorials on your government's misinformation campaigns."

"Insinuations aside, I find your attitude and conduct reprehensible. I'm tempted to have your credentials pulled and ask you to leave our country."

"Bullshit, Ackov! You haven't the balls to do any such thing. Nor are the neo-Nazis you work for willing to endure the wrath of the *New York Times* or *International Herald Tribune*."

"Then you force me to respond in kind. Our producers will address your accusations across the airwaves. Our listeners and viewers will then know the truth."

"Go ahead, Adrijan. Your propagandists wouldn't know the truth if it bit them on the butt. As for me, I'll continue researching and reporting what I see and hear. We'll let the readers be the judge."

"Considering your intransigence, I would say our business is over, Mr. Winslow."

"And may the best man win, Mr. Ackov!"

—⚹—

Mara wanders the playground as four hyper-energetic kids scurry from jungle gym to swing set to teeter-totter and back again in a sequence of unending wild dashes. The park-like steeple chase is accompanied by an ensemble of squeals and laughs. Oh, the simple bliss of children at play. What a joyous contrast this is to the horrendous final moments in Mara's home just days before.

"Who wants ice cream?"

"We do. Me. Yes, please," the four rambunctious ones yell in tumbled unison.

"Okay then, follow me. And if Suzana's pictures are ready, we'll pick them up too."

With a mix of chocolate, vanilla and strawberry cones smearing their smiling faces, and photo sets in hand, the playful gang returns to the park.

"All frozen dessert lovers must sit on the grass until their icy treats are gone." Mara perches on a wooden bench within view of the munching munchkins and begins scanning the photos.

"Is this seat taken?" an attractive middle-aged woman with reddish-blond hair inquires. The mystery lady is also enjoying a cone on this warm, breezy Bosnian afternoon.

"Please, make yourself comfortable," Mara responds.

"You've got your hands full."

"Just supervising a little park outing."

"Pictures from a recent vacation?"

"Photos the little one took as we trekked here through the mountains."

"How stunning. May I see?"

Mara glances at the pics, then passes them on. Throughout the photo review, the two women smile, chuckle and share simple observations.

"I'm sorry. I should have introduced myself. My name's Jasna. And you are?"

"Mara... Mara Cesarec from Konjic."

The two shake hands and nod. Jasna then pulls a set of reading glasses from her purse and squints at one of the photos. "How unusual. They look like gun emplacements. Do you see?"

"Yes, I suppose that's what they could be. There are little bug marks like that on a lot of these. See? They're on the hillsides everywhere. How strange is that?"

"Maybe you need to take these to the authorities, or I could take them for you?"

"Excuse me?"

Jasna sits upright and slides forward to the edge of the bench. "Really, I wouldn't mind. I know the commander at the local garrison. I'm sure he'd be interested. And you'd be doing an important public service."

Mara looks away, stands, takes a couple steps forward, then turns to face Jasna. "You think I should? Maybe I should ask Baba Sofija first."

"I'm concerned there might not be time. These bug specks could be rebels who want to bring us harm. Someone needs to see these photos, figure out what to do."

"Okay, but how will I know what... ?"

"We'll meet here tomorrow at the same time," the woman in business dress suggests. "I'll update you on what I've done, as well as what the commander had to say. But for now, let's make this our little secret."

"I guess that will work."

As the children start walking toward Mara, Jasna gathers several photos, leaving the duplicates. She scoots off the bench and strides out of the park, slinging a tweed jacket over her shoulder.

"Who was that, Mara?" Chapeka asks.

"Just a lady who likes pretty pictures. She was sharing her special eye for detail. That's all."

———m———

As Heath storms out of the Communications Ministry, Dragana, in a dapper, dark green suit, stomps past in a determined rush to enter.

"So, that's what Cruella de Ville looks like in broad daylight," Heath sniggers, not knowing who he'd just encountered.

"Ms. Kowalchuk is here to see you, sir," Adrijan's secretary announces.

He adjusts his tie, then buttons his coat. "Send her in and bring us an aperitif."

"Mr. Ackov, good to meet you," Dragana states, thrusting her hand forward. "I have little time. So, please, let's dispense with the formalities and get down to business. I've spoken with numerous officials and we concur: There are several journalists and other staffers at your network who must be laid off, then fired, since they can't support the party's information program. We all know how urgently that's needed."

"Yes, yes, ma'am." Adrijan resigns himself to the fact he will now become the voice behind Dragana's Bosnian broadcasts. Let it be said each holds the other in reticent contempt. These are two fanatics bound together by twisted personal and professional drives. Yet, both must support the regime while trying to influence the public's points of view.

"I'm here to help in any way I can. My lieutenants are available for interview. Your crews can visit my camps. Whatever you need, just let me know."

In response to this zealot's desires, Ackov states he'll direct his production staffs to shoot spots focusing on Serbian Orthodoxy and jingoism. He'll demand the clips air on all radio and TV outlets several times daily.

There's a pause in the conniving conversation. Adrijan's assistant enters with a silver tray supporting two crystal shot glasses filled with plum-pressed brandy. Both take up the offer.

"I sense we have a good understanding. I look forward to hearing and seeing such ideas on the airwaves. Please don't disappoint me… Ziveli!"

"Let's live long indeed," Adrijan agrees as they toast their twisted communication plan. Dragana and Adrijan have conceived a course of action so filled with anger and vengeance it can't help but eventually explode in their faces. It could well be the ruination of all their grand plans. Expect video at eleven.

—⁂—

Andro exits the bus, exhausted and confused. He trudges across the parking lot, swings open a taxi door and tosses in his backpack. He's soon slouching on the seat.

"Taverna Poseidon, parrakallo."

"Excuse please, but what you say?"

"The Poseidon restaurant in Piraeus."

The driver starts to chuckle, then gets out of the car.

"What did I say? Did I upset you? Where are you going?" Andro pleads as the cab driver opens the door, grabs Andro's arm and begins pulling him from the vehicle.

"Stop, please… I just want a ride to my uncle's seafood place."

The smiling, robust man takes Andro by the shoulders and turns him 180 degrees, facing the harbor. The mystery of the moment is revealed. A huge blue and white sign with stylized Greek lettering screams *Taverna Poseidon*. It stands sentinel over a two-story white-washed brick and clapboard edifice, complete with sidewalk café and canopied balcony reaching toward the sea.

"I see. Efkaristo," Andro mumbles as he offers his waterfront guide a generous tip for his service.

"No, no. Thank you. My laughter payment enough. Welcome to Greece. Now go eat good food and tell Abeiron to serve you fine retsina. Avrio… That mean goodbye."

As Andro steps into the café, he's greeted with unbridled exuberance by Uncle Abeiron, Aunt Jadranka, the restaurant staff and most every patron. "Εμπρός! Ευπρόσδεκτος!" many yell as they slap Andro's back, hug him and holler more joyful salutations.

"Everyone say, 'Hello and welcome!'" the boisterous Abeiron shouts as he side-squeezes Andro in a one-armed bear hug. "I know Greek tough language, so we try speak English for you, okay?"

"Hello, thank you and yes, English works for me."

Andro's restaurateur uncle is full of health and vigor. Standing nearby is his aunt—Abeiron's voluptuous wife. Jadranka's statuesque figure could serve as a model for any classic sculptor. She's a stunning compliment to this loving environment into which Andro's been so warmly welcomed.

"We have room for you upstairs," his uncle notes. "You start work in kitchen, but first we drink, eat some fish and smash plate. This all what good Greek peoples do."

—⚏—

Well, memories of Ackov don't age well, do they? Heath reflects while relaxing on the patio. He's still stacking newspaper clips and placing them back in the media folder.

Why do you still let Adrijan's arrogance get under your skin? the devilish one asks from deep inside Heath's mind.

A journalist is more than twice as likely to be a left-winger on any-one's political spectrum, the angelic one points out from the same mental locale. *So, why would Adrijan march to such a different drummer?*

Heath begins verbalizing his heretofore internalized conversations.

"Adrijan shouldn't be considered a member of the Fourth Estate in the first place. Damn socialist technocrat!" Devilish exclaims.

"I see that, but it doesn't clear up much for me," Angelic replies.

Heath strolls the porch perimeter, continuing to vocalize his mind babble while admiring the flowers and soaking in the flagstones' radiant heat.

"But just regurgitating the party line," Angelic notes. "What reporter would do that?"

And still obsessing over Ackov's role as a propaganda practitioner, Devilish demands, "Where's the pride that comes from being a goddamned independent?"

"Am I naïve to consider journalists as social reformers?"

"No! And if so, what the hell are we doing here?"

"Is chatter I hear on patio a cry for help or cold beer?" Danvor the landlord calls from the alleyway.

"No help necessarily, sir, but I like your beer interpretation," Heath replies.

"I have ticket for FK Sarajevo verses Željezničar. Game this afternoon, if you interested? Number two play number three in Premier match. Maybe we stop by Ballygoan for refreshment on the way. Eoghan always good for little entertainment."

"Well then, let the games begin!"

—⁓—

PART II

C H A P T E R   9 :

INNERMOST DESIRES

WHEN ANDRO'S GREEK uncle offered him a job, the Bosnian youth had no idea it would translate into near-slave labor at the end of a mop handle. With the dubious title of chef's assistant, the new Jack of all Trades is liable for a spotless, shimmering kitchen that includes continually swabbing a red-tiled floor, repeatedly washing a massive auto-mixer, scrubbing a "jaws of life" chipping machine, as well as endlessly cleaning a cache of knives and cutlery.

Don't forget prepping food faster than it can be ordered, Andro laments. All day I wash, trim, peel, repeat... Wash, trim, peel, repeat... Repeat, repeat, repeat! And make sure the chef has everything he's ever wanted, let alone needs.

Andro executes these tasks while also observing a multitude of hygiene and safety rules. *Far beyond what anyone else in this bizarre food prep arena ever follows!*

The restaurant aide has been schlepping in a heavy rubber apron, complimented by sweaty plastic gloves, for more than a month now. He takes a mid-morning break on the patio, gazing into the harbor and daydreaming about exotic ports of call as ship after ship slips over the horizon in slow, silent procession.

His doe-eyed, petite, yet buxom, cousin Alcina glides up and slaps the back of Andro's head. "Congratulations, pot scrubber!"

"What?" he says, spinning to face her. "What was that for?"

"Don't be so naïve, Andro. You don't think papa's going to keep you chained to the kitchen sink forever, do you?"

"I'm beginning to wonder, but I still don't understand what your 'best wishes' slap was all about."

"It's time to change course. It's time to leave your culinary career and head to Athena's harbor. I'm taking you to work with me. Papa's arranged for you to become the newest employee of the Hellenic Container Corporation."

"Great… I finally figure out the kitchen and now I must worry about being squashed like a bug by crane operators!"

"Stop complaining! Dock workers make good money. Besides, the job takes brawn, not brains. Trust me when I tell you there's no diploma required. There are only a few skills needed. Even a farm boy like you has them. They're called good health and references. Papa's already paid the union bribe… And yes, you'll be expected to pay it back.

"Andro, your kitchen work was just a test. Papa wasn't going to recommend you for a longshoreman's job if he didn't think you could handle it. It's obvious you're trustworthy, good with math and have real people skills. Sure, you'll load and unload plenty of containers, but you'll do a lot of security work too, checking cargo and pushing papers. That's where I can help."

"And I already know how to swab the deck. So, when do we cast off?"

"Go take a quick shower. Be sure to knock off some of those fish scales. Put on a clean shirt and we'll head to the wharf."

—⁓—

Baba Sofija storms across the slate patio of her son's suburban Sarajevo home to snap off the radio. "How can they air such garbage and call it news? Does that announcer eat with the same mouth?"

"Mama, watch your blood pressure," her son chuckles as he steps into the back yard.

"It's not funny, Franjo. In fact, it's absurd what's being said nowadays. It's the same propaganda pitch those Ustaše puppets spewed as Hitler's war dummies. It's not only wrong; it's frightening. Someone must put a stop to it!"

"Yes… and I wonder who that could be?"

"Okay, I've been pondering this for some time. I'll be the first to admit I've latched on to this thing and I refuse to let go until it's settled."

"I understand, mama. I do. It's clear you want to do something to keep your beliefs from being worn down, but such acts may not let sleeping dogs lie. You could be stirring up all kinds of negative things. Are you prepared for that?"

"God and common decency are on my side. How can I fail? I will ask the priest to raise the issue after Mass. If there's a following, we'll plan our next step. A march on that rotten propaganda palace sounds in order."

"Mama, please call the station manager first. Make an appointment. Talk to him about your fears."

"My loving, naïve son… What good would that do? I'm too old to have some condescending bureaucrat pat me on the head and tell me everything's fine. We need action now, before this gets out of hand. We need newspaper and TV support. The only way we'll get that is by holding some kind of demonstration. Don't worry son. I'll be careful. Besides, these are educated people, right? What could go wrong?"

—〜—

Another day passes. Mara strolls beyond the Vrelo Bosne entrance, still pensive about her pending encounter. She nods, acknowledging the carriage driver in his forest green suit, complimented by a derby with pheasant feathers flittering in the breeze. She takes a seat on a nearby bench.

Jasna appears as if out of nowhere, then bends over the seatback to say, "Good afternoon, Mara. How about we stroll around the park?"

Mara leaps from the bench, leans in close and locks arms with her rendezvous partner. "What did you find out? What did the commander say? What was in those pictures?"

"Eager, are we? Well, you did the right thing, my dear. Those spots appear to be rebel gun placements, lots of them. Please accept our gratitude for sharing such important information. Now, what do you think? Are you prepared to do more?"

"What? You want me to be a spy or something?"

"How about keen observer? It describes so much better our intent. Look, Mara, you're a smart young woman. You seem ambitious. Wouldn't you be proud doing work that will help your fellow citizens? Besides, there's money to be made. As a matter of fact, the commander wants you to have this as a token of our appreciation."

Jasna hands Mara a small black clutch bag encrusted with ruby-like rhinestones. She opens it and several crisp Bosnian 100-dinar notes are revealed. "But I…"

"Yes, Mara, you can. This is simply a business transaction. You know—the cost of developing film and prints."

"Yes, Jasna, but didn't you say you wanted more?"

"Okay, we know what happened to your mother. And we're afraid we know what they did to you. We also know who's leading those murderous goons. This Kowalchuk creature has long been fascinated by conscious dreaming. She's studied ancient shamans and seeks out Roma who are gifted fortunetellers. She considers Gypsies prized for their psychic skills. To her, they have a special gift… attracting good luck, or destroying life with a curse."

"But I'm no Roma."

"No, but Sofija's daughter-in-law, Florica, is. I'm sure she's willing to share her spiritual knowledge with you. That would get you close to Kowalchuk, gathering information about her activities along the way."

"I don't know. This is all coming at me so fast."

"It's okay. I understand. Just know I've worked with Franjo and Florica before. They're aware we're talking, but no one's pushing you, Mara. This has to be your decision. Yes, you may want revenge, but don't let rage cloud your judgment. Rather, look at this as a means to an end, helping limit a horrible threat hanging over all of us."

"Okay, I'll do it, but let's make one thing clear: If I want out, that's it. I'm out. No questions asked."

Jasna makes a quick scan about the park. "Agreed. And as your case officer, I'll be with you all the way. Florica will start your training soon and Franjo will supply the window dressing, as well as let you know about meetings. You're doing the right thing, Mara. Your family, your imam, your country, we all thank you."

—⁓—

Days pass. "Don't tell me to calm down!" Adrijan screams into the phone. "That crazy old broad has organized hundreds, if not thousands. They're marching on the Sarajevo office as we speak. Belgrade Radio is promoting this garbage. Dozens of college kids are banging drums. Some umbrella group of dykes called SOS Telephone has fired up the Women in Black and Mothers of Sarajevo Soldiers. And the damn preachers in town—Orthodox, Catholic, Muslim and Jew—all linking arms to sing *Kumbaya* for Christ's sake."

"Settle down, Ackov!" Dragana yells back. "Making a mountain out of a mole hill will only play into their hands. Let the protesters march. Call a few into your office. Listen to them bitch. Act like you care. Don't call the police unless there's damage to the building. This will blow over and in a couple days everyone will forget. You'll see.

"I'll make sure Grandma Protestor is taken care of. If we cut off the snake's head, the serpent will soon wither and die. You got it? Now sit down! Have a drink and leave the heavy lifting to me," Dragana bellows, slamming the phone into the cradle without pausing for a response.

—⚭—

Later that day: "Franjo, Florica, Mara… Come into the living room now!" Baba Sofija shouts in jubilation as she turns on the television and cranks the volume to better hear the newscast.

"What is it? What's going on?" they ask. Franjo lowers the TV sound to hear Sofija's report.

"The rally was fantastic. So many more people than anyone expected. Students, the clergy, feminists and mothers… oh, so many mothers. And the press was there, too, doing interviews, shooting lots and lots of pictures. There was TV coverage too, just like this," Sofija states, gesturing to toward the screen. "It was epic.

"And we met with Mr. Ackov, the TV director. We told him broadcasting propaganda wouldn't be tolerated. A Woman in Black complained about the military. She shouted against pushing army ideas, using war-like words. And this Orthodox man jumped in saying the news was spreading hate and destruction, not information and understanding. He said the clergy is without words to express its anger. It was electric. We spent a long time trying to reach an agreement, but we'll get together again and finish that work… I'm sure of it."

Franjo paces back and forth as Florica and Mara clutch together for support. "That all sounds good, mama, but don't count your chickens before they hatch. Who knows how the misinformation brigade will cover this event?"

"Franjo's right," Florica interjects. "For such a movement to grow, it must be bold, with a message that's easy to understand… one that everyone can support. Otherwise, the nationalists will tear you to shreds. They'll find ways to pit one group against another. They'll fuel the fire until all of you are consumed.

"We've seen how our country can be destroyed. Things are miserable now. Before, we lived a rather good life. Okay, it wasn't to high standards, but somehow we had pretty much everything we needed. It was quite easy to get a flat, go on holiday, buy food and clothes. We could go to restaurants, travel and have free medical care. But now? All our money just goes for food and not much of that."

"Like you, Sofija, my grandmother lived under Hungarian rule," Mara adds. "Like you, she came to despise the in-fighting. She believed the rulers stoked it just to feed the hatred. She lived near the Italian border then. Those were the early fascist years. She spoke out against it, too, as I'm sure you did.

"When the war began, Gram was living in Zagreb. They were forced to leave because they were Muslim. They settled in Belgrade. During the war, there was no prejudice from above. First, they were bombed by the Germans, then the Americans.

"Grandmamma told us how excited everyone was when Yugoslavia was born. Until her death, she called herself Yugoslav. It was her political choice. I was raised with those ideas. Now we must build on those values, ones we will need for a new Bosnia."

"Bravo, Mara… You should be the movement's spokeswoman. You have such insight, such clarity, such simplicity. Thank you, all of you, for helping me see what is right before my eyes. And with these thoughts, I'm off to see Father Drazeta. The rally leaders are meeting at the community center tonight. We need to review our ideas, to see if they're still valid. We need a no-nonsense approach. At the same time, we can't let the hurdles in our path trip our resolve."

"But mother…"

"Enough, son… My mind's made up. Help me with my shawl. I have miles to go before I sleep." Her shoulders wrapped, Baba Sofija marches with determination to and out the front door.

"Robert Frost aside," Franjo confides, "that woman's on a mission we cannot stop. What troubles me is seeing all of them so focused on effects. I fear they'll just talk and talk about outcomes, rather than figuring out the cause. That is, until it slaps them square in the face."

"It's as if they're in some communal state of denial," Florica adds. "They refuse to admit traditional views may no longer hold true. They won't let go of the past. And your mother proves how much stubbornness is on display. They're eager to resist, but they have no goals, or even a clear course of action. I fear for their safety."

"I think you expect too much too soon, Florica. Give it time," Franjo stresses. "Their movement needs to gel. They need to become one. From that, a plan and a purpose should come to light. But yes, I share your concern."

"We all must do our best to protect Sofija from outside forces, as well as herself," Mara points out. "In the meantime, we'd better start on my Roma training, or do the Gypsy lady and her husband have other tricks up their sleeves?"

—⁂—

Andro jogs around the corner of the dock-side office building to find his luscious cousin leaving work for the day. "Alcina… I've come to walk you home."

"Good God, man, please keep your distance. You look like Mafia thugs kicked the devil out of you and you paid them handsomely for the pleasure."

"Very funny, pretty lady. So, I'm a little sweaty and a bit dirty. I spent all day dodging container cranes. They swoop down like space aliens trying to devour the earth. I worked hard today and the boss liked it. He told me so. It felt good. And I have you to thank for it." Andro leans in and gives his elfin cousin a peck on the cheek.

"Settle down, Mr. Stevedore. And please stand down wind. Okay, I'm glad you're glad and had a good workout, but you're just a few days into the job."

"Yes, I know, Alcina, but I think it's the end of the beginning. It's the answer to my prayers. Now I can grow, help the family and so much more."

"Andro, stop and listen to yourself. It's a stinking laborer's job on the waterfront. Anyone with lots of muscle and a little brain can do it."

"Okay, okay. When we get to the taverna, I will clean up. You grab a bottle of wine, add an antipasto or three and meet me on the patio. Then, I will explain."

Half an hour passes. Andro struts out of the restaurant wearing a pair of tight-fitting, well-worn blue jeans and a raw silk shirt with the sleeves rolled up.

"You clean up pretty well, sailor," Alcina proclaims. "Hot date tonight?"

"No, this is just how I like to dress. As second-class kitchen help, I didn't have much chance to do so."

"Okay, pretty boy, so share your platitudes and enlighten me on Andro's Zen moment."

"It's not that monumental, Ms. Smarty Pants. I had a fine day. It's a beautiful night. I'm feeling great. And I want to share that with someone who helped make it possible."

"Really, Andro? I told you what papa said and walked you to work. That's it. I was glad to do it, but you earned it."

"Thank you anyway, Alcina. It means a lot to me. Being ripped from my family, slipping out of Bosnia, sailing to Greece, then working in your father's kitchen. Well, it felt like the lowest point in my life. But now, I sense I'm in some sort of transition. I'm like a Zenith rising from the ashes."

"And in Greece, no less."

"Please, don't laugh. I now sense I can move on—from the old world to a new self."

"I think you need to slow down, Andro. Take a moment to smell the roses. We all know you're good at using your wits. And you can find your way out of most any predicament. At the same time, you're an impulsive man. Who's to say Andro the Swashbuckler won't take off on a new adventure just when things are being put in order here? Are you ready to handle more than one challenge at a time? Who's to say you won't be waylaid by another quest? How do you know where your path will lead?"

"Thanks for the encouragement. You sound as much a downer as our Uncle Thoma. Well, just think about it. You both live over a tavern."

"Settle down, big guy. Believe it or not, I'm one of your major fans. I want to move on and see the world too, just like you. I'm telling you what I sense, because I like you. I want to be your friend, not just your cousin… Are you still interested in photography?"

"Yes, but what has that got to do with anything?"

"I just remember when you were a kid you found few things more enjoyable than taking pictures of wonderful moments you shared with friends. You even won some photo contests. I'll have you know there are many parts of Greece just as stunning as Herzegovina. Let's drive around town this weekend and see what your lens can find."

"Alcina, that sounds great. I'll get more film. We can take a picnic and just explore. And you're right. Maybe I do need to slow down a little, but I still think it's time for Jonah to exist the belly of this whale."

"Pardon?"

"Nothing, really. Let's say I'm more than just a little excited about what may lie ahead. And I'm ready to set sail."

—∽—

A lone bell in the cathedral's tower strikes the eight o'clock hour. Baba Sofija, along with student union reps, women's group leaders, clergy and news media, mull around the reception hall. They're buzzing with energized small talk. The doors swing open and troopers from the Sarajevo Police Service storm the room.

"Everyone remain calm and we'll have no problems," one of the Bosnian-Serb paramilitary men, dressed in black denim, sporting a ball cap embroidered with the SPS crest, declares in a monotone.

"What's the meaning of this?" Sofija demands. "We have the right to peaceful assembly. Tito's dead. Communism's over."

"Not when we receive word of a conspiracy against the public," the officer states as a chilling response. "You people view the government as a tool to achieve some kind of gain at the expense of other citizens. Such tyranny cannot be tolerated."

"What?" Sofija screams. "You don't even make sense!"

A voice is heard echoing from the hallway. "Let me enlighten the woman." The armed intruders step aside as a tall, slender Draconian figure steps into the room. Dragana Kowalchuk, dressed in starched and pressed fatigues, scans the faces of those assembled, making sure to stare into the eyes of each and every one. "News media out… Now!"

After the press departs, the doors are shut and Dragana continues. "All of you are aware of the civil and criminal penalties for those who perform acts against people of other races, religions or lifestyles."

"That's what we're here to discuss."

"Silence! There's no question one should suffer the same consequences, regardless if one commits an offense against a Serb, Croat or Bosniak. It should make little difference, legally, if the perpetrator and victim happen to share a certain ethnicity, or end up being totally distinct. Efforts like yours to twist and manipulate the law only further divide our society, while trying to set up special privileges for members of certain groups."

Dragana takes a deep breath, puffing up like a peacock. She steps to the front of the auditorium and makes an about face. "Should a criminal who harms me be treated any differently than a criminal who harms you in the same manner? Isn't the goal equality for all under the law? Is justice blind, or does she favor certain ethnic or social groups, one over another? Does it matter when you are robbed whether the perpetrator wants your money or commits that act out of sheer hate?"

Kowalchuk pauses to again stare at those assembled. "What are you doing here? You're seeking protection at the expense of everyone else. Therefore, in order to maintain equality under the law and keep the penalty for crimes consistent, we must do away with such obstructionist movements."

"If anyone's twisting words and intentions, it's you!" Sofija hollers. The others in the room shout in the affirmative, vocalizing their strong, unified support.

"Enough, already!" Dragana shrieks. "Take them to the station and book them for obstruction of justice. We'll interrogate them later."

Glancing toward the uniforms on her right and left, Dragana yells, "What are you waiting for? Did I not make myself clear? Arrest these people. We must get things in order… It starts here and it starts now."

C H A P T E R   1 0 :

MEETING A MERCHANT MARINER

THE YEAR IS 1999. The Ides of March cast shadows across Eastern Europe as Poland, Hungary and the Czech Republic step into NATO's fold. During the makeover, Heath, the ever intrepid reporter, becomes ever more frustrated, wrestling with the writing disorder his milk crate filing system was meant to address.

What the hell is behind this paper chaos? Heath demands as another mental point-counterpoint sessions kick in.

And how'd we get into such a fix? Inner voices, Devilish and Angelic, ask in unison.

So far, Heath's analytical efforts have produced little more than a dining table jumble of manila folders, a score of scattered newspaper clips and dozens of barely legible sticky notes glued helter-skelter.

I might as well dump this damn box on the floor for as much help as it's given me.

Is there a reason for this messy madness? Devilish asks. *What's the purpose of your exercise, Mr. Winslow?*

Don't you get it? Angelic notes. *Heath wants to better understand what his Balkan brethren have been through the last few years. He wants to explore their ecstasy and their angst.*

Hell, it would be nice to understand what we've been through as well.

Heath, still surprised his quaint apartment came furnished with a full set of encyclopedias, reaches for Volume 18.

"So, what does Funk & Wagnall's have to say?" Heath mumbles.

Order: A condition of methodical or prescribed arrangement among component parts.

"I couldn't have said it better," he adds.

Then, why aren't clues leaping out to tease us? The angelic and devilish ones demand.

"Oh, the joy of writing… especially with you two helping out," Heath sighs. "And people wonder why journalists drink… Andro, Dragana, Baba Sofija, Mara and Adrijan where are you? Somebody talk to me, please."

By this point, both sides of Heath's brain have come to agree on one thing: His band of Balkan belligerents is driving everyone quite mad. For example, endless untamed stabs at life's markers are beginning to leave tell-tail scars, especially on Dragana and Andro. They're both charging madly through points in time, poised like vultures ready to pounce on any opportunity that dare present itself.

Can't you break this down into some logical order? Devilish wonders.

Maybe he can… maybe not, Angelic adds. *Look at it this way: Dragana's focused on success while Andro is off chasing humming birds in hopes of catching a rainbow of joyous delight.*

"Okay now, you'll both have to admit that's a bit condescending," Heath states.

Admitted, but let the feathers fall where they may. The devilish one thinks.

"What?" Heath asks. "You're saying I shouldn't care? I want to know why these folks are so intent on tearing each other apart. It has to be more than just their struggles to win."

How quickly we forgot, Devilish points out. *It's all about finding the Holy Grail… And what a joke that is. Everyone's running in different directions while no one moves forward.*

If you could impact how they think or act, maybe then you could change their attitudes, Angelic suggests.

So, you're saying Churchill had it right? Devilish asks Angelic. *I'll never forget that line of his… Attitude is a little thing that makes a big difference.*

"Okay, stop it," Heath demands. "Both of you… Just stop it. That's more than enough messing with my mind for one day."

Wait! I think I hear a beer calling, Heath's devilish side announces. *Yes, yes… I'm sure I do.*

Quick… Grab a coat, Mr. Winslow. The angelic one orders. *It's time for refreshments… Let us trudge to the nearest watering hole.*

—⁓—

"Well, if it isn't the John Cameron Swayze of Sarajevo… Fancy a pint do ya?" Eoghan asks with a wink and a smile.

"Yes. Anything to drown the marbles rattling 'round in my head."

"Well, Lucy's psychiatrist stand may be closed, but the bullshit at Ballygoan never stops flowin'. How might this maître d' of malarkey be of service, good sir?"

"I'm driving myself nuts trying to make sense of the notes I've gathered over the years, especially those you held for me. I can't seem to find that proverbial light at the end of the tunnel."

"Deep breaths, me boy, deep breaths. Set yourself down and let these lovely hops caress your mind and soul. From the little I know about the batty Balkan blokes tormentin' your life, I'd say you're not seein' the forest for the trees. Take a step back. Give it all a simpler look. They're only human and concerned with their own deepest wishes.

"And be a little respectful. These are the very feelings that form a man's tone. You're pluckin' at the messy fibers of the soul and ya wonder why it don't sound all neat, clean and pretty?"

"Okay, are all bartenders certified shrinks?"

"No, just those of us with a 'BS' degree."

"Well, Eoghan, for sure you've spread plenty of bull butter in your lifetime—enough to earn an honorary doctorate, I'd say."

"Thank you, kind sir, but just look at the folks you've introduced me to. Andro's consumed with findin' a way to heal his homeland. The bitch Dragana seems barmy with desire to restore a Greater Serbia. Baba Sofija wants everyone turnin' to God for answers. Mara will only be satisfied when she gets revenge. That self-centered ass, Adrijan, wants but to bask in the limelight while doin' as little as he can. And then there's my buddy, Heath. You, me wide-eyed freelancer, are forever driven to find one more story, regardless the cost. That about nail it?"

"Pretty much."

"This man's prescription: Open up me boy. Be willin' to have another look at what's goin' on 'round ya. Be a little more broadminded and receptive. Then, it'll come to ya. I'm sure of it.

"And a little resistance is a good thing too, I say. You can be pickin' up so much speed you'll cross the finish before the others even line up. That's where a bit of frankness comes in. It thwarts the upshot from all those folks pushin' you forward. It may even let you slow down long enough to enjoy a cool brew or two with an ol' friend."

"Doctor Eoghan, you're not going to put this on my tab are you?"

"That's why I love ya, Heath Winslow. You couldn't afford me… So, I've done me part. Now, how about you? Another character from your collection of *Fractured Fairy Tales*, if ya don't mind, sir."

"Let's see, I don't think I've told you much about Jason Banks. Picture a barrel-chested 6-foot, 4-inch, 260-pound black man stomping into your bar. Like you, he's got broad cheekbones and a wide smile that telegraphs his agreeable nature. Jason gives off confidence in all he does. He makes everyone just feel at ease.

"The guy's worked almost forty years as a merchant marine, so he's one fit hombre. But his rough exterior hides a far gentler man inside. Like you and I, his salt and pepper hair is his only age giveaway. Oh, I'd say he's now sixty or so."

"Sounds like your African cousin would be an interestin' bloke to meet, but what's he got to do with all the other folks you've rambled on about?"

"Correction: He's African-American. Yes, Jason's a Yankee, but I'm sure he considers himself more a citizen of the world. I don't think there's a port on this globe to which he hasn't sailed.

"He and Andro met on the docks in Piraeus not long after the lad got to Greece. The two hit it off right away. As Andro's self-appointed mentor, Jason started working hard at building Andro's trust. He helped the kid open up and explore his soul. Yeah, it sounds hooky, but that's the sort of mensch Jason is."

"Well, someone had to look after you," Eoghan notes, patting himself on the back. "So, Jason as Andro's seafarin' guru makes sense, but how did ya meet him, Mr. Landlubber?"

"It was after an awards ceremony aboard the Intrepid on Manhattan's west side. Man, that was years ago, but I remember it like it was yesterday.

—∞—

Notebook entry: USS Intrepid—(CVS-11) now a national historic landmark... Commissioned & sailed in WW II... Pulled 3 tours off Vietnam... Did submarine surveillance during the Cold War... Aircraft carrier museum opened in '82...

Heath stands silent, burning a cigarette on the fantail of the Intrepid Sea-Air-Space Museum's hanger deck. Sunset is at hand. An orange glow ripples across the Hudson as the Jersey skyline is made a silhouette. The lights of New York City twinkle at his back. With more than 41,000 tons of steel beneath his feet, Heath's mesmerized by the moment. This is his inaugural protocol event on Pier 86.

All this hoopla means the Museum Foundation is hosting yet another gala fundraiser. Mr. Happy-Go-Lucky Boris Yeltsin, President of the Russian Federation, is receiving the 1992 Intrepid Freedom Award as part of the festivities. Heath's here for a far more important reason: an interview for a *New York Times* feature. The chap in question was just awarded the Merchant Marine Distinguished Service Medal.

> *Notebook entry: U.S. Merchant Mariners are nationalized in times of war... Become nation's 4th defense arm... Merchant ships deliver military supplies worldwide... Essential to American sea power*

A hatch creaks open and a giant of a man in full dress uniform steps on to the deck. "Mr. Winslow, I presume? I'm Jason Banks. They said you wanted to interview me?"

"Yes, Mr. Banks, I do… And please, call me Heath."

Jason pulls a cigar from his breast pocket. "Then you call me Jason." Holding up the stogy, he asks, "Do ya mind, Heath?"

"Not at all. I'm one who smokes too damn many cigarettes. The arthritis in my hands is pretty bad, though. Do you object to my using a recorder? I want to make sure I get it right."

"Makes sense to me," Jason mumbles as he puffs to fire up his cigar. "So, what ya wanna know?"

"Well, I understand you were born on December 7th, 1941—that illustrious day in infamy."

"Yup. My pappy was a share cropper on a small plot of land outside Hattiesburg, Mississippi. The war broke out and we moved to Harlem so he could land a better-payin' factory job. I graduated from Rice High just off Lenox in '59. That summer, with my folk's help, I applied to the Merchant Marines out on Kings Point. We even got a classy nomination letter from Mayor Lindsay. He was our Congressman back then.

"I liked the academy. There were 275 in my plebe class—cadets from every state in the Union and every side of life. Every race, creed and background you can imagine studies there. As a young black man applyin' for college… Well, let's just say things was a bit different back then. After I graduated…"

"With honors, I understand."

"I took the exam and received my maritime license from the Coast Guard."

"So, Jason, you want to talk about 'Nam and being federalized?"

"Nope… Sorry, Heath, but you've got a copy of the citation. You heard the bull crap introduction. What I did back then wasn't for any shiny medal. It's what any sailor in harm's way would do. This award ceremony just helps them get over the guilt of forgettin' to honor mariners all these years. And hell, the World War II vets are dyin' off so fast they won't have to do any of it much longer.

"Sorry 'bout that. I just get riled up at times. Everyone's a goddamn hero nowadays. Bull shit! The heroes are the ones who didn't come home. Okay, how about this: Let's blow this tin can and I'll show you my real New York. Then we can talk all you want."

"Lead the way, sailor. All hands off the deck." Heath and Jason flick their smokes overboard and head for the nearest lift.

———⟋⟍⟍———

Reaching the end of the pier, they both scan the West Side Highway for a taxi.

"Damn… No cruise ships in town. I guess we hike to Tenth for a ride. You gots ta wave large, white boy, if we's gonna catch a cab."

"Whoa, Nellie…"

Both big men stop in their tracks, turn toward each other and snarl, not unlike a couple junk yard dogs at first meet. The pregnant pause seems to stretch forever.

"I may not have a Jewish grandmother whining off a balcony in Rego Park, but your Bojangles' step an' fetch it crap ain't gonna fly with me Mr. Banks. I don't play dat, homey."

The awkward moment continues.

"I think it was Bogart who said, 'This could be the start of a beautiful friendship,'" Jason whispers. The silence persists until both gents spit loud and long lines of laughter, slap double high-fives and bear hug on the street corner.

A few steps in front of them, one of New York's bravest is strolling their way with a bag full of pastries for the firehouse crew. "Hey, dudes… Why don't ya just get a room?" the fireman suggests as a smirk slides across his face.

"Piss off, mate," Jason snaps back with his best attempt at an Aussie accent.

"Australian for none of my bloody business… Point taken."

In unison, Heath and Jason throw forth two thumbs up, laugh and lock arms over each other's shoulders. They continue heading east on 45th in search of that elusive public conveyance. Jason soon waves down a taxi and swings open the door. Mimicking a pompous chauffer, he makes a sweeping arm gesture for Heath to slide inside.

"Well, thank you, Jeeves."

"The C-Note, corner of Avenue C and Ninth," Jason directs. The cabbie nods and begins weaving his way toward Lower Manhattan.

"Excuse me, Abhi. Can we knock off the Panjabi music and extinguish the smudge pot for the remainder of the trip, please? Thank you."

"Now who's bein' racist?"

"His name is Abhi. It's right here on the operator's card. My asthma can't take that incense shit. And yes, I'll be the first to admit I hate snake-charmer music. If that's racist, Uncle Tom, then so be it."

"Just forget it… This jazz club we're goin' to is a first rate neighborhood bar. It comes complete with a daily dose of tunes startin' 'bout three bells. And take note: The program changes most regular like, embracin' all manner of fine music."

Notebook entry: Since '40s bebop inception, New York jazz scene has been hot… Improv moved out of New Orleans… Syncopated rhythms connected with people of Gotham… Greatest evolution occurs in the Big Apple… Now the world's jazz capital

Ebony and Ivory enter the club with Jason leading the way. They head to the bar where a double shot of Maker's Mark awaits, along with a small box of wooden matches and a large cut glass ashtray meant to hold Jason's favored Cuban cigar.

"Been here a couple times before, have we?"

"Jazz, where ad-libbin' plays the lead, is more than just music. It's an attitude. Sit down, my man, and feel up the blues."

Sweet jazz pianist Gil Coggins, one of Jason's longtime artistic pals, nods and smiles from behind the keyboard. "Gil played with Miles Davis and Sonny Rollins for years. He jams here pretty regular like."

Creative key strokes fill the room with a sexy, harmonious vibe. Jason's foot begins to tap as he listens to the riffs, signaling the onset of a most excellent evening of entertainment. Mellow time passes. Occasionally, the not so ancient mariner nods his head or points his cigar, greeting friends around the saloon.

Heath slides his cassette player on to the bar and flicks the record button. "I read somewhere you've been with the Ocean Futures Society for more than two decades. So, what's that all about?"

"It's like this: The Society's on a mission to explore the high seas. Along the way, if we inspire some kids or educate some ol' folk to protect it, well, that's a good thing, right? Like fine music, we look for that connection between man and nature. We celebrate the sea—how vital it is to our planet, to our survival."

"Heady stuff, Mr. Banks."

"Mighty crucial, Mr. Winslow."

"And how do you advance that goal?"

"Just as jazz accents Mr. Coggins' music-speak, I see myself as one mellow voice of the deep."

"I'll be damned, Mr. Blues Man, that's one rich story," Eoghan utters in a slow whisper. "I got a couple Billy Holiday tunes on the juke-box. What say we compliment 'em with a bourbon of our own?"

"Works for me," Heath replies. "Like jazz, we too have the ability to absorb and transform many a troubled times, with drinks included."

"No 'Twenty-three Skidoo' for you, Mr. Syncopation."

"Shush, my man. Let the lady sing the blues."

CHAPTER 11:
ACTORS PLAYING AT BIT PARTS

It's a lazy Saturday afternoon. Andro and Alcina breeze into the Taverna Poseidon after their cityscape outing to find Abeiron busy dusting liquor bottles.

"Hey, Sexy Juan," Alcina teases her father. "Can a couple parched tourists get a retsina or two from a seaside stud like you?"

"I'll give you 45 minutes to stop such talk," Abeiron barks, then turns to face his playful daughter. "So, how was your Athena excursion?"

"Quite nice, uncle. Alcina knows the theater director, so we got the VIP tour. Kastella itself was amazing. What money in that town. And the views of the gulf, Mount Hymettus and the ancient city. They were all magnificent."

"This came for you, Andro. Brother Iesos dropped it off."

Andro's face pales. The young man appears stunned as he picks up the envelope, along with his wine. He turns slowly, walks out of the bar and descends the patio steps on to the beach. Andro parks himself on a hammock strung in the shade of two gnarled olive trees.

Alcina starts to follow, but Abeiron clutches her arm. "Maybe it's best you give your cousin some time alone with his mail, my dear."

Andro opens the packet bearing the crest of St. Nicholas Church with his name scribbled below. Tears well up as he slides out the onion skin paper and begins reading.

Friday, June 15th, 1992

Dearest Andro,

We received the postcard noting your arrival in Greece, Abeiron & Jadranka's warm welcome and the restaurant work. So good to hear you're safe and well cared for.

I wish I had such good news from Bosnia. As you've seen on TV, Sarajevo is under siege and being shelled daily. Fortunately, we live close to the airport and haven't been touched. U.N. soldiers are coming to help secure the place. My job is fine, as is our house and all within. Chapeka, Suzana, Abraham and Nahida play together like loving brothers and sisters. Your friend Mara is with us too. What a fine young lady.

Got an update from Father Malinko in Konjic saying Petar & Alen are both safe and sound. They're with a Croat self-defense unit outside Makarska helping set up the community of Herzeg-Bosnia— whatever that is.

Baba Sofija's been detained by the police on some trumped-up sedition charge. Florica and I are working with legal aid and the bishop to secure her release. I'm quite sure it will come soon. I will try calling with any updates.

We're always eager to hear news about your adventures. Use the church as your conduit. I hear the mail is being searched. Parish to priest updates work for many.

God's speed to you, Andro…
from Franjo & the extended Babich clan

Andro refolds the letter and places it back in the manila envelope. With one swallow, he gulps the tart white wine, then tosses the tin cup aside. Alcina can no longer bear watching from afar. She runs to the beach, kneels before Andro and cups her hands around his. "What can I do? How can I help? Talk to me."

"The mess back home. It all hurts so much. I can't keep pretending to be what I want to be." Andro wipes a tear from his cheek as his face twists in anguish. "It's time I step up and help my family. It's time I stop walking away from the mess in my head."

"Changing direction is never easy, Andro. There's a cost for going down that road and plenty of roadblocks along the way. It'll take a lot of work to overcome them, but that path's not impossible to follow, not if you're gritty enough to make it happen… And I know you are."

"When did you become so wise and insightful? And a bit Pollyanna, I might add."

"Like you, cousin, I have a few too many books in my library. As for my outlook, I bend more toward Scarlet O'Hara, 'As God is my witness, I'll never be hungry again.'" Alcina makes an overly dramatic swoon, with hand pressed wide against her forehead.

"Come on," she begs as a grin brightens her china doll face. "Grab that goblet and let's head back to the bar. If we're going to solve world problems, we can at least do it with a little nectar of the gods."

"Efxaristo, Alcina."

"And thank you, Andro, for letting me in."

⁓⁓

It's been almost two weeks since Sofija was taken to the Remand Prison on trumped-up charges. She's escorted to a small, stark meeting room where Dragana paces from near to far wall, puffing on a cigarette. "I trust your accommodations are acceptable?"

"As if you care. And what are you doing here, anyway?"

"Although you may not notice from your cell, Sofija, I'm hoping you will see the light after our conversation today."

"Why don't you save your breath, Dragana?"

"Listen, Sofija, you're an enlightened woman. Take a moment to reflect with me on our country's history. It's need for stability. The time is now. We must stop playing martyrs and restore our sense of national pride. And we must do it together.

"Have you forgotten the horrors of World War II? Remember the days of Chetnik on Partisan. That was worse than anything the fascists did. Such in-fighting has followed our people throughout history. And what have our leaders done about it? Nothing but cower and compromise, hurting all of us. You know it. I know it. This sad state has lasted for centuries. It's time to say, 'Enough is enough!' Unity, cooperation and honesty, that's what we need to move forward."

"Yes, Dragana, it's all about your Greater Serbia. Isn't it? But what about Bosnia and Herzegovina?"

"You miss my point, Sofija. Unity will bring prosperity to everyone, regardless their background. We need one and the same relations among all Slavic people. Tolerance, cooperation and fairness should be the hallmarks of our region. You and I must be a part of this new direction. It's where our world is headed."

"You're right: Enough, Dragana, enough… Compliments to whoever put those words in your mouth. He has a real gift for twisting reality. Your methods may be crude, Ms. K, but they've been effective. Your artillery barrages kill. Property is taken straight away. People are forced to move. And that's just the short list. We're all South Slavs, Dragana. That's what the word Yugoslavia means. We're not that bunch of radical Bosniaks, Croats and Serbs, like you, who want to pull it all asunder."

"Enough from you as well… Guards, take this arrogant old woman away."

Sofija makes the Sign of the Cross as she's led from the room. She then begins a whispering recitation of the Holy Rosary.

"Why can't they get it?" is Dragana's bombastic yell. "The problems of prejudice and hostility are by-products of a nation lacking focus. Clearly, diversity must be eliminated. The discord that springs from it must be silenced. What's not to understand?"

—⁂—

"Might there be somethin' behind that bar that will wet the lips of an ol' sea dog?" Jason inquires as he saunters into Abeiron's taverna.

"Good lord! His ship's come in. To what pleasure do we owe this honor, Mr. Banks?"

"Uncle Sam's birthday, my good man—July 4th, 1992—the 216th year of American independence."

"Hell, I've got a couple bottles of wine older than that."

"Then pull their corks and pour the devil's brew... Please excuse my loud mouth," the sailor says in the direction of Andro and Alcina. "A few too many weeks at sea and the volume tends to go way up."

"Jason, you remember my daughter, Alcina. With her is my nephew Andro Babich from Bosnia."

"Your once charmin', but slightly ugly ducklin' has blossomed into a beautiful swan. Excuse me for not complimentin' the gent beside you, Ms. Alcina, but we've only just met. And I prefer drinkin' to stickin' a foot in my mouth straight off the boat."

"Jason is chief mate to some freighter pilots who plow these waters," Abeiron informs Andro. "Who knows, he might find you shipboard work someday."

"Easy, my good man, I've still got my sea legs, but you never know. So, Andro, what brings you to this Mediterranean seventh heaven?"

"Troubles in the Balkans, I'm afraid. But don't let me bore you. Please, tell us about your adventures sailing the high seas."

"Great... You've started it now," Alcina jokes. "Bring on the Makers Mark, papa, and ready yourself, Andro, for a dark and stormy night. Jason, tell us about the Cherokee stunt. You know, crewing that barge full of Jeeps down the Nile for some TV commercial."

As Jason sets the Luxor scene, the retcina begins flowing. Abeiron's toothsome wife, Jadranka, approaches carrying a serving tray laden with bowls of hummus and tahini, surrounded by toasted pita points. More retcina's poured. Alcina clicks on her reel-to-reel music mix. The bar is soon filled with a subtle blend of laid-back New Age melodies. The sounds drift into the dining room, then float off the patio to welcome nearby beach strollers.

Two large ceramic platters covered with antipasto and soft pita rounds appear. More retcina flows. Later, a cheese tray arrives. It's followed by generous slices of baklava, accompanied by a Greek version of café frappe. The evening's reunion is filled with food, wine, laughter, storytelling, song, the occasional expletive and lots more laughter. It's topped off with shots of ouzo. These are toasts from which Andro abstains. Ah, life is good and then comes sleep.

Sofija sits on the edge of a prison cot, reciting the Holy Rosary. She prays for courage while meditating on the third sorrowful mystery. Moon beams stream through a small hole on the far wall, creating a bluish oval pool near the center of the cracked and stained concrete floor.

The slow, repetitive "clack, clack, clack" of a guard's heel clips becomes louder as the sentry approaches. The boot strikes stop in front of Sofija's cramped quarters. A note is launched through the door slot, fluttering to rest in the middle of the floor, highlighted by the lunar follow spot. The heel clacking begins again, fading into the distance as the guard departs and silence returns.

Sofija kisses her rosary, placing it on the tattered wool blanket. She kneels on the floor and picks up the yellow memo. Slowly, she unfolds it. The brief note reads…

Mama Sofija,

Working hard to earn your release. Father Draze-ta believes if you fake a mental breakdown, we can have you transferred to Konjic sanatorium. Symptoms of Stockholm syndrome include view-ing your guards with kindness, feeling positive toward them, expressing adulation for Kowalchuk and stating your desire to submit.

We know this is much to ask, but we're quite sure it will work, with no one the wiser. Prison library may have more info. Call up your best acting skills. You can do this.

We love you, miss you,
Franjo, Florica, Mara & the Children

Baba Sofija clutches the note to her bosom and smiles. A tear of joy and relief trickles down her cheek as she whispers, "Let the show begin."

—ɷ—

Earlier, Dragana stopped in front of a full-length mirror at the end of the prison hallway to self-inspect and adjust her storm trooper-like outfit. Satisfied with her appearance, she marches out of the complex to an awaiting staff car. She's whisked back to the mountain fortress where she spends yet another evening alone, studying maps, memos and manuscripts. Without realizing it, Dragana is again reconsidering all her actions, reorganizing each strategy and revisiting every supposition. It's all part of her never-ending attempt to bear out their soundness… And Nero fiddled as Rome burned.

Like her response to the protests, she now resists movement by any group she hasn't already sanctioned. This twisted special interest pleader will keep on using stereotypes to assert her prejudices while Sofija, Adrijan and so many others are made to bear the brunt of Dragana's sadistic reasoning.

—⟋⟍—

A few days after the American independence night soiree, Jason runs into Andro waiting on a bench outside Alcina's dockside office.

"Andro, great to see you. Got a minute?"

"Sure, Jason. I'm waiting on my cousin. Have a seat. What's on your mind?"

"I've been watchin' you from afar and talkin' with the longshore-men about your work."

"Is there something wrong, Jason? Please don't tell me I'm being fired. I can do better. I just need to know what, when and where."

"Calm down, man. It's nothin' like that. In fact, it's quite the op-posite. In your short time here, you've impressed even the crusty ol' stevedores. Hell, I have a hard time doin' that. As chief mate of the Vale Quito, I'm prepared to offer you a shipboard job. I have a sea-man's apprentice position comin' open in about a month, when I get back from my next cruise. Are you interested?"

"Absolutely, but, Jason, am I qualified?"

"That's pretty much my call. There's nothin' glamorous about bein' a low-level seaman. Most mariners consider them no more than sea-goin' caretakers who tie up ships. Duties include sweepin', moppin', dustin' and cleanin' the head. We don't chip or paint the ship's hull any more. That's contracted out, but you'll be expected to serve as a lookout, checkin' for things that might block the ship's path."

"Be a janitor and sentry. I can handle that."

"While I'm at sea, I expect you to take some certification courses—CPR, basic fire fightin', knot tyin', semaphore and Morris Code."

"I already know the flags and code. I was certified when I was in Junior Achievement. Papa and my brother were in the Yugoslav army and they tested me often."

"That's great. Alcina can help you sign up for other courses. Trust me, they're not hard classes and they don't last long. A few nights a week this month and you'll be done. Okay, they're not needed, but they make puttin' you on the ship's visa that much easier. Besides, who knows when they might come in handy?"

"Thank you, Jason. I don't know what to say."

"Don't say anythin' now, Andro. This is a big decision and I want you to think it over. And talk it over with Alcina before you decide."

"Talk what over?" Alcina asks stepping out of the Maritime Building and into Jason's conversation. "And decide what?"

"That it's time for a glass of wine and some crusty bread. Will you join us, Jason?"

"I can't. I've gotta watch the cargo loadin' and make sure the maintenance is done. The captain wants to set sail late tomorrow. So, Andro, I'll see you in about a month. Alcina, give your father and mother my best and take good care of this boy."

"Efxaristo, Jason. Adio."

"Yes, thank you, Jason," Andro adds. "Fair winds and smooth sailing."

C H A P T E R   1 2 :

FROM GYPSIES TO UNCONSCIOUS DREAMS

DRAGANA LEAPS FROM the porch and springs into her somewhat impractical, yet classic, MGB-GT lift-back. The lovingly restored '76 red roadster with its sexy wire wheels and black leather upholstery begs to be driven. "I'm off to Belgrade for a meeting. Don't expect me back until late."

The lady racer has long reveled in the rush that comes from sitting on the floor of a coupé with her legs outstretched and the wind blowing through her hair. Once settled into the cozy cocoon of a cockpit, she zooms off and down the mountain path, glancing at the odometer and rear view mirror as the miles and smiles zip by.

Kowalchuk ponders what lies at the end of her rocky road trip. This she-devil has long considered vision quests as pathways to inner health. It's her route to ultimate truths. She's studied ancient spiritualists and believes in gaining insight through conscious dreaming. Dragana's shamanic reveries have transformed over time. For the most part, she no longer uses drugs or denial to induce her dream state.

Relaxation and reflection now spur me to go deeper. Those in the know remain skeptical. *This is neither the beginning nor the end of my self-guided healing process.*

It's but a step in Dragana's overall excursion and goes far beyond her current fantasy Grand Prix down an alpine trail. *This is my true out of body travel.*

If so, Ms. Kowalchuk might consider synching her psychic seatbelt, as she may be in for a very bumpy ride.

—⚬—

Dragana pulls around back of a small, whitewashed datja outside the Serb capitol. As she drives up, a gnarled babushka lady is seen pulling back a laced curtain on the glazed veranda of the clapboard country cottage. The elderly charwoman shuffles to the door.

"Is my room ready?" Dragana demands as she steps inside. "My time today is limited."

"Yes, ma'am. All has been prepared."

"Then leave me, but let me know when that Gypsy girl arrives."

"Yes, ma'am and sweet dreams. May your fantasies find a most positive purpose."

Dragana steps into the candle-lit and incense-filled sitting room, closing the door behind her. The dark velour curtains are drawn tight. She slips off her riding boots and stretches out on a purple velvet chaise. Dragana soon slides into a trance-like state, eager for her imagination to become a springboard that will catapult her to an inner world whose majesty is beyond belief… Sweet dreams indeed.

—⚬—

"Roma Mara, I think you're ready," Florica announces with pride. "There's always more to learn, but if you stick to palm reading, you'll do fine."

"But how do I gain Dragana's confidence?"

"Remember what we discussed. Tell her your gift is personal, not some newspaper horoscope filled with clichés. Tell Dragana you're the way to finding both the future and a healthy life-force. She's all into that spiritual stuff and will eat it up. I'm sure. You'll be pointing out her strengths, so that she can capitalize on them; and her weaknesses, so she can improve those. Besides, who doesn't want to know hidden facts about their lives?"

"But it's not about Dragana. It's about Sofija, right?"

"Of course, Mara," Franjo throws in as he steps on to the patio. "But we help Sofija, and our people, by first befriending the rebel leader. Then we share what we've learned with those who can make a difference. So, let's review your cover story."

"Again?"

"Yes, again. You must convince that conniving woman beyond a doubt you're a true Roma with very special gifts. Okay, what's your name?

"Mirela. It means to admire."

"And your ancestors?"

"I can trace my family history back to Prester John. He was an ancient priest who ruled our vast empire in North Africa—home to the lost tribes of Israel."

"So, you speak Arabic?"

"Copts speak Arabic because we're from Ethiopia."

"So, why do you call yourself Ashkali?"

"My grandparents are Balkan Egyptians who live in Kosovo. They're proud members of the Coptic Orthodox Church of Alexandria. They support the Serbs. I couldn't take the abuse the Albanians were piling on, so I moved in with a clan here in Sarajevo. We're building a new Roma settlement in Gorica right now."

"Excellent, Mara… You've learned your homework well."

"I have a good instructor."

"So, the meeting with Dragana is set for this afternoon at her country home," Franjo explains. "Take the local. There's a train stop no more than a kilometer from the cottage. Just remember to keep it short and sweet. And don't forget to bring up Baba Sofija."

"What if she won't let me go?"

"You're a Roma," Florica declares. "Threaten to throw a curse on her. Say that a menace in her dream sessions is looming. Something tells me that will get her attention."

The Roma training and Gypsy prep complete, Franjo and Florica join hands, bow their heads and begin reciting, "Hail Mary full of…"

Mara steps back, swipes the palms of her hands before her face, lifts them toward the heavens and begins to recount, "Allahu Akbar, Allahu Akbar…"

Katya senses something moving outside the datja. She looks up from her embroidery to glance out the parlor window. An elaborately dressed young woman can be seen strolling up the garden path. The old hag scurries to the door, swings it open and with two gnarled fingers pressed against her lips, whispers, "Shush, the lady sleeps. You must be the palm reader, yes?"

"I am what I am," is Mara's cagey comeback.

"Fine, then. Come in, but make yourself quiet." The elderly woman takes and folds Mara's shawl while making a pushing gesture for her to walk straight ahead, out on to the veranda. Katya stares in silent amazement at what stands before her.

Florica went all out gathering costume pieces to replicate a Gypsy from Tirgu Mures. A dark green pleated silk skirt flows over a pair of cream-colored bloomers. It's complimented by a provocative, bright red blouse with tatted lace trim, low-cut collar and puffed sleeves. The chemise is layered with a form-fitting blue velvet vest trimmed in gold embroidery. The draw strings are pulled snug to cinch the waist and bolster the bosom.

The costume spectacle continues as Mara stands poised with a multi-colored scarf tied as a sash. It drapes over her hip and is secured by a belt made of sunburst medallions. Speaking of ornamentation, this Roma waif is covered in jewelry from head to foot. An anklet made of tiny bells is strung on thin silver ribbon. The ornament sets off a pair of pointed velvet slippers embroidered with multi-colored beads in an elaborate geometric pattern.

With the dress modeled, Katya begins admiring the mystery lady's face. Mara's hair is wrapped in a blue paisley bandanna with jewel-encrusted gold fringe. It holds back a mound of thick, black hair that cascades off her shoulders. Ridiculously long false lashes ride eyelids powdered with turquoise shadow and traced with black liner. Glossy, dark plum lipstick is paired with even darker rouge.

"Well, you certainly dress the part."

"Clothes make the woman, do they not, Madame Kowalchuk?"

"Oh, no, no, no. I'm but Katya, the housemaid. Ms. K is in the next room. She's lost somewhere in a dream session. That is why we must speak softly."

"Such techniques can be most beneficial. Has she been practicing long?"

"She visits twice monthly, for over a year now. Dragana is always 'practicing'. She's trying to connect with her higher self or soul, if, indeed, she even has one."

"Katya, you put little faith in spiritualism?"

"I put my faith in God… The Lord needs not send anyone else."

"Are you asking me to leave?"

"No. That is not my place. Dragana travels in her dreams to strange places. I believe God has a better path, but if this brings her peace, then so be it."

"There are many reasons to do hypnotherapy. The most important is to seek guidance. In that special dream state, Madame Kowalchuk can act as her own protector. Her higher self can mend many of her childhood wounds."

"I neither understand nor welcome such goings on, but these are the visions of a strange woman. I give her a wide berth when it comes to such things."

A southing classical guitar melody from a scratchy Segovia recording is heard resonating from the sitting room. "Ah, it sounds as if the dream gathering has ended," Katya notes. "Let us retreat to the parlor and I will inform her you are here."

As Mara stands waiting in this strange home of strangers, she feels transported to a Victorian wonderland. The room is chucked full of ornate maple furniture. A serpentine-backed Queen Anne's chair is paired with a dark green velvet divan, over-stuffed and buttoned deep. An elaborate sideboard stands nearby, fitted with a gigantic gold-speckled mirror. Its shelves are stuffed with dried floral arrangements that reek of lilac. Textured Persian-styled wallpaper dances below the chair rail as a multi-colored stencil streaks around the room, brushing the crown molding.

"Madame Kowalchuk, your Roma guest has arrived."

"Thank you, Katya. I'll be right out. Please fetch something for us to drink," Dragana replies, then muses, *She's prompt. I like that. This will be good. I can feel it.*

Dragana enters the decorative time capsule without pause for admiration. "You must be Mirela."

"Princess of the Ashkali."

Dragana offers the Gypsy princess a seat as Katya returns with a tea set and savory griddle cakes. They engage in trivial conversation as an ice breaker, as well as a means of measuring each other's reaction to the moment.

"Chitchat aside, Mirela, what insights do you bring me? I hear you are blessed by the mystics. This intrigues me."

"I'm gifted in the art of palmistry and I accept that certain parts of the body have independent spirits. Everyone should see their hands as a special chart of life. Your left hand chronicles your past, while the right maps your potential. For this reading, I will look at your lines, mounts and hand divisions to tell the past, present and future."

"That all sounds fascinating. Shall we get started?"

"Shukran jaziilan," Mara whispers as she rubs Dragana's left hand, sensing its rough texture and rigidity. She turns it to examine the nails and color of the skin. Pressing the base of Dragana's index finger she murmurs "The Mount of Jupiter shows you're a natural leader with strong ambitions." Taking the second finger, Princess Mirela sighs, "and the Mount of Saturn denotes a serious woman full of wisdom, but with a sadness deep in her heart."

"My childhood, to say the least, was no bed of roses."

Mara takes up the ring finger. "I now explore the Mount of Apollo. I see brilliance, happiness and success in your future."

"Excellent! Please continue."

"The base of your fourth finger is the Mount of Mercury. It says Ms. Kowalchuk is a shrewd, but level-headed woman. And finally, your thumb, the Mount of Venus. Although you may not be looking for love, you're a woman filled with passion."

"Thank you. So true, but you're too kind."

"This is what I sense," Mara says as she trails her right index finger over the rest of Dragana's hand. "Where I see courage and bravery, I also see aggression. Might I suggest you find ways to temper your antagonism?"

"Fine! Here. What about my right hand?"

After taking a moment for examination, Mara says, "You have no need for romance, but you appear to have a very strong sex drive."

"Okay, that's enough of that. What else do you see?"

"Your head line is short. That means you think simply and directly. Right now you are pondering the fate of an elderly woman in a confine close by. You cannot step around, prevent or escape from dealing with this problem."

"And why should I? I'll examine the predicament and take action to address it."

"But controlling others by instilling guilt and fear may not be the most effective answer, Madam Kowalchuk."

"Enough! What gives you the right to question me? This session is over. Katya, pay this story telling tramp and show her the door."

"I'm sorry if I upset you ma'am, but again, I only speak of what I perceive. As a chirologist, I read palms for spiritual and beneficial reasons, for people's comfort and interest. If we seek the truth, then the truth must be told."

"Apology accepted and mine extended. I will think on what you've said, especially about that old woman. I may need to call on you again. Is that possible?"

"Princess Mirela is always at your service," Mara says as she stands and makes a broad, sweeping gesture with her arm. She then swirls on toe point across the room to the cabin door. "Your wish is but my command." The marauding Roma grabs her black knit stole. As she steps out the door, Mara remarks over her shoulder, "Ilaa al-liqaa… I'll see you soon." And poof, she's gone.

When Mara reaches the lane's end, she turns toward the cottage and thrusts both arms skyward to recite an ancient Gypsy curse, "May you wander the face of the earth forever, never sleeping twice in the same bed, never drinking water twice from the same well and never crossing the same river twice in a year."

Katya's hunched over silhouette is seen dropping the lace curtain, then scampering away from the window and Princess Mirela's spell.

"My work here is done," Mara says with a haughty flair. The Roma renegade then swirls about and begins her stroll to catch the next tram back to town.

—⁂—

Heath stumbles out of the hotel elevator, dragging himself across the lobby floor.

"Excuse me, Mr. Winslow," the desk clerk interjects. "There's a Telex for you." He places the folded note on the counter and slides forward a pressed wood clipboard with pen attached by beaded chain. "Please sign here, sir."

Heath scribbles his name on the receipt stamped 5 July 1992. He grabs the memo and continues his trudge to the lounge.

"It appears a little hair of the dog might be in order, Heath, me boy."

"Turn down the volume, Eoghan, you damn loud-mouthed bartender. And may the United States of America never celebrate another Independence Day with such gusto."

"Not only were you in fine spirits last night, I think you put a significant dent in your country's trade deficit… So, what's with the message?"

"Pull me a beer and we'll read it together."

3 July 1992 0932 EST, New York, NY

Mr. Winslow—Be advised your Aunt Adrienne van Peel has died. You are designated executor of her estate. Initial reading of her will is set for 18 July at 1000 EST in the Manhattan law office of Larry Grossman, LLC. Funds to cover cost of your flight home will be wired to Holiday Inn-Sarajevo. Please notify me of your availability ASAP.

Phone (212) 668-7000

"For Christ's sake," Heath moans. "What's next?"

"Sad to see you're so choked up, ol' boy. Damn. Pay me to fly home? I don't know, but that all rings of good money to me."

"I thought you were Irish, not Scotch."

"I'm just sayin', if they're gonna go to all that trouble to get your tired ars Stateside, there must be some kinda pot at the end of auntie's rainbow."

"Oh, I don't know how well off the ol' broad was, but she does have a two-bedroom condo in Hell's Kitchen and a little house on the Hudson. I'm pretty much the only relative left. Maybe it's time for a trip to Gotham City. After all, I can't beat the price."

"Speakin' of price, might we settle last night's bar tab before you hit the road?"

"I think you'd better pull another pint if we're going to do that much math."

—∾—

Dragana fiddles to adjust the collar of her suit coat before entering the reception area at Remand Prison. It's been two months to the day since Sofija was incarcerated and only Dragana's second visit.

"I'm Ms. Kowalchuk. I understand the prison psychiatrist wants to see me."

A slender, distinguished looking man with salt and pepper hair, wearing a white cotton lab coat, strolls across the room and extends his hand. "I'm Dr. Nikolic. Pleased to meet you, ma'am." The middle-aged shrink drops his grasp and brushes past Dragana to thrust open one of the side doors. "Please, come in. Have a seat."

"Thank you, doctor. I don't mean to sound abrupt, but I'm a busy woman. Why did you call me in?"

"One of our detainees, and now, sadly, a new patient of mine, needs long-term psychiatric care beyond my capabilities here. Her name's Sofija Babich."

"What is that crazy old bitty up to now?"

"Precisely my point, Ms. Kowalchuk. I'm convinced Mrs. Babich suffers from a phenomenon known as Stockholm syndrome. Her erratic and irrational behavior is having a negative impact on the staff, as well as other inmates. The situation continues to intensify. It is my professional opinion that comprehensive treatment is in order and needs to be initiated soon."

"What's this silly Scandinavian snivel you're talking about? Give me some examples."

"Sofija's exhibiting all the classic symptoms. She has strong, positive feelings toward her controllers, in a very maternal kind of way, I might add. Then there's her negative stance toward her family and friends. They visit and try offering support, but are rebuffed. I think she's come to buttress many of your beliefs as well. And of keen interest to me, she no longer shows any real concern about being incarcerated."

"Those aren't symptoms; that's just bad acting and you've been sucked up in her drama."

"This is not some provincial guard unit. And I'm not your puppet on a string. You filed the arrest papers on Mrs. Babich. She will appear before the magistrate next week. And as her doctor, I will testify as to her mental state. Do I make myself clear?"

"Perfectly, but be assured you've not heard the last from me." The Dragon Lady leans forward, spreading her hands on his desk like a vulture's claws ready to grasp its pray. Then, as if to make a final threat, Dragana stares deep into the doctor's eyes and slowly declares, "No one ever takes for certain what rightfully belongs to me."

C H A P T E R   1 3 :

SETTIN' SAIL AND DOIN' WHAT'S RIGHT

"Mr. Winslow, please, please take a seat. I know you're upset, but the sooner we go over executor tasks and New York probate law, the sooner we can settle this."

"Mr. Grossman, I'm not a law student. You're the big attorney for all this, right? According to the will, Aunt Adrianne put complete faith in you. We've been screwing with this for more than a week. Why in the hell did she appoint me administrator, if you're here?" You don't find that a bit strange?

"As Ms. Van Peel's long time personal counsel, I could not ethically allow her to designate me as executor of her will."

Notebook entry: New York probate—inventory assets, appraise property, settle debts & file taxes... Myriad of financial considerations... Minimize taxes on estate transfers to beneficiaries

"Wow, Ariel, that's incredibly un-lawyer-like, but that's what you're going to do, right? As I said before, I don't feel comfortable working with a bunch of parasite accountants, bureaucrats and realtors, or any other vermin who think they can infest my aunt's wishes. So, just get it done... Alright?"

"Yes, sir. Since you've retained me to help with the process, I will conduct a full accounting of what the deceased owns and what she owes."

"I gave you all the insurance policies and bank records I could find. Hell, Auntie A was more anal and kept more stuff than me. Bottom line, Grossman: You research, file, fiddle and putz to your heart's content, then just bill me when the mess is over, okay?"

"Very well, Mr. Winslow. When complete, assuming there are no probate actions, I'll make disbursement according to Ms. Van Peel's desires."

"Good… You can reach me through the *Times* news desk. Please, make this your top priority. And Ariel, money's not an object. I need to get back to Europe as quickly as possible. Are we clear?"

"Absolutely, sir. I should be able to wrap this up by the end of the month. Don't worry about a thing. I'll be in touch. Thank you for your support and confidence."

"Right. Just remember: I didn't ask for this job and I don't expect anything out of it. Now, I think it's time for a drink, if you'll excuse me."

—⁂—

The Vale Quito—Panamanian Registry
Captain's Log Aug. 5, 1992

1. *Ore cargo secured*

2. *21 crew accounted for (Deck-9, Engineer-6, Steward-6)*

3. *Andro Babich—registered as seaman's apprentice to Chief Mate Jason Banks*

4. *CM Banks to mentor SA Babich*

5. *Bulk carrier setting sail for Bayonne, NJ—1600L*

6. *Ship scheduled for corrosion survey upon arrival*

"Welcome aboard, sailor," Captain Jansen shouts to Andro as he trudges up the gangway with a gray canvas bag slung over his shoulder. "Drop your gear here, then report to Banks. He'll direct you to your quarters. Go starboard, near the bow."

"Yes, sir! And thank you, sir," Andro shouts back as he plods forward, dragging a sports satchel with one hand and balancing the bag with the other. He reaches the quarterdeck and slings his belongings against the rail.

Andro steps forward to find Heath examining the anchor winch and chain. "Seaman Babich reporting as ordered, sir."

"Jolly good, young man. Let's get you settled." Jason guides Andro to his sleeping area. "You'll berth here with three other mates. They've all sailed before and can show you the ropes, to include the forecastle store where you'll warehouse your gear. Everyone has their own locker. You're expected to share the chest and writing table. Head and shower are down the passageway. I know this is all a bit overwhelmin', but you'll get the hang of it straight away."

"This is going to be quite the adventure, Jason."

"This can be a great journey for you, Andro… on many levels. Accept the coachin', mentorin' and other things that come your way. Allow that you don't know everythin' and that others have value to share. Be open-minded and curious. And don't be too proud to admit the error of your ways. Process things, but temper your opinion. Trust me; yours often come across as tactless. Bottom line: Grab it and go for it. Experience livin' in the moment. You may not have this chance again for quite some time."

"Banks!" Captain Jansen yells. "We're ready to cast off. Are you?"

"All's square, sir. I'll join you on the bridge straight away."

—⚐—

Now well out to sea, the evening meal's finished and the mess is scrubbed. Andro strolls on to the quarterdeck. He sees Jason leaning on the rail. Andro walks and stares into the darkness.

"So, Jason, why did you put to sea?"

"Good question and I guess I'm still answerin' it. Pretty simple: I want to see as much of this beautiful planet as I can before I die. And I enjoy that feelin' of solitude in the middle of the ocean, thousands of miles from everything. It's a great place to just relax and unwind. All in all, it makes for a pretty laid back cruise."

"But even so, this life isn't for everyone. Is it? Months at sea, separated from loved ones, the solitude. It's driven sailors to leave, right?"

"True, Andro, but for me, the rewards far outweigh the price. What could be better than goin' to far flung places, steppin' ashore and havin' the time of your life? Plus, I'm gettin' paid for it. Sure, it can be hard work and sometimes lonely, but it's only as good or bad as you make it.

"Come with me. I want to show you somethin' that'll help you understand." Jason leads Andro up a series of ship ladders to the weather deck where he unfastens and unfolds a pair of aluminum chairs. "Take a seat, lean back and gaze at the sky."

With no ambient light from anywhere, the two are enveloped in almost total darkness. A cool ocean breeze and the sound of the ship's generators mix with the splashes of water being cut. The background noises only enhance the night's tranquility.

"My God! It's as if I could reach out and touch them."

"And there's no admission charge for a night full of such magic. All you need is a curious mind. Just think about it. Stars have amazed people for ages. Astronomers have studied 'em for centuries. Poets and musicians write words and songs about 'em. Painters try catchin' their charm with a brush.

"But the heavens are more than romance, Andro. This is where you can ask the big questions, even if you don't always get an answer. This is where you can open your mind and be curious—all the way to the end of the galaxy. This place is intoxicatin'. And it's all ours. So, drink up, boy; drink up. You have my permission to night dream here whenever you like."

—⁂—

A rickety Redbird subway train screeches to a halt. Metal and glass double doors, covered with scratchity, struggle, then jiggle open. Heath steps out and on to a mobbed 42nd Street platform. It was a brief, but quiet, one-stop ride on the No. 7 Flushing Local from Grand Central. The deafening sound of jackhammers, concrete debris being tossed into giant metal bins and the whirl of chalk-colored dust pretty much says the calm has passed. The Times Square underground rat maze is a hot and acrid hodge-podge of metal stanchion pathways, pillars wrapped in orange webbing, ceilings draped with plastic sheets and walls festooned with hand-scribbled directional signs, all propped up to compliment the massive reconstruction effort now underway. Yet, hardly a commuter is fazed. Welcome to New York!

A shiny new steel escalator glides Heath out of the commotion. Above his head, a vast neon and colored glass sign with train route symbols flashes for all to see. This is the MTA's silent omage to the Crossroads of the World. Heath heads north. His destination: Midtown West where Aunt Adrianne's condo sits vacant. His trek is interrupted by commotion in front of the Armed Forces Recruiting Station.

Notebook entry: AFRS—nicknamed The Booth... Has stood sentry on Times Square traffic isle since '46... 520-sq. ft. station is a unique office for Army, Marine Corps, Navy & Air Force recruiters

On this day, a rather disheveled, greasy-haired character in soiled fatigues has chained himself to the concrete atoll's flag pole and is ranting about Vietnam vets needing shelter and medical care.

A Marine, who's had enough of the protestor's delusional rage, marches across the street to a small glass and brushed steel building. Its diminutive size is overwhelmed by a series of gigantic letters in blue neon on the roof—a couple letters not lit—trying to proclaim *N w York Pol ce Dept*. One of the city's finest puts down his donut and lumbers across the street with the recruiter to question the whacked out activist.

With no prospective arm to twist, Sgt. First Class Cashton Steel steps out of the booth to observe the interrogation. Sergeant Steel has been blessed with what the Army would describe as recruiting poster good looks. Truth be told, the square-jawed, six-foot strapping Soldier maintains a rigid exercise routine that ensures he's never an ounce over 190 pounds or two percent body fat. Cashton exhibit's a degree of conceit through his tailored uniform that only draws further attention to his physique.

"Excuse me sergeant," Heath asks. "I'm a reporter. What's going on here?"

"Nothing for the record, sir."

"Good, because I sure as hell don't want to spend happy hour filing some bullshit vagrant's story," Heath jokes, trying to break the ice.

"I thought the Marines were staging another damn recruiting stunt to draw a crowd, until the gunny went over to call on the cops."

"So, this kind of thing happens a lot?"

"You could say that. Not long ago this guy walked in with a loaded gun. He sat down and wouldn't leave. He goes on and on about being one of the *Born Gangstarz* and how he has to lay low for a while, outside the hood. So, one of my recruiter buddies walks over to the police station. The cops get all stoked and surround the booth. They take a while, but nail our visitor. And we're back to normal."

"Only in New York."

"Welcome to Times Square!"

"Good story, sergeant, and thanks, but could you point me toward a decent watering hole? I'm a Second Avenue Irish pub kinda guy and not familiar with the West Side."

"Sure, a block up and over is Barrymore's at 45th and Eighth. It's a laid back saloon, but not a theater fern bar. A lot of stage hands and union guys hang out there. Since we don't have a head in this dump, they let us use their bathroom; that which it is. Anyway, it's a good place, decent food and great bar crew. In fact, I'm as good as done here. Let me secure my desk. I'll walk you over and introduce you. Susie-Q or Elizabeth-Ann should be bartending now."

"Barrymore's it is. Quick time Sergeant Steel, before the curtain falls and the can-can girls get away."

Notebook entry: Theatre District — Midtown Manhattan where most shows staged… Filled with restaurants, hotels & other "entertainment" venues… Includes Times Square & Great White Way—name long ago given this section of Broadway

—⁂—

It's a brisk September morning in Belgrade. A clunky black desk phone rings. "Remand Prison. Dr. Nikolic's office."

"Dragana Kowalchuk for the doctor."

"Hello, ma'am. I was hoping to hear from you. How may I be of service?"

"Let's cut the crap, Dr. Nik. I've considered your diagnosis, reference the Babich case, and I concur. She should be provided whatever treatment you deem appropriate."

"How benevolent of you. I'll fax over a release statement and related court documents for your signature. Upon receipt, the patient will be transferred to the Kovacev Institute for long-term care."

"I'll have a courier deliver the papers this afternoon. Advise me when the transfer's complete." Dragana slams the receiver and plunges back into the mound of self-generated red tape heaped on her desk. "Problem solved. Now, where was I?"

—m—

"Susie-Q! How's my Madame Butterfly?" Cashton asks as he ushers Heath into Barrymore's.

"Chop! Chop!" Susie snaps in response. "Take seats here, now, before they gone. And who this with you?"

"Susie, meet Heath, a reporter for the *Times*. We met at the booth. And I offered to show him a good bar nearby."

"So, you come to write big story about crazy Thai lady, or you just got to pee?" the petite barmaid with high cheek bones and brown doe-like eyes leans forward to ask.

"No tail, no toilet. I'm fine, but I wouldn't refuse a beer, if you'd be so kind."

"What kind?"

"Cold."

"Good answer. And you, Soldier Boy?"

"Rocky Mountain Light please, ma'am."

"That no beer," Susie exclaims while pulling a pint of Bass for Heath and adjusting the large silk orchid in her hair. "That why you pee all the time."

"I can already tell the level of intellectual banter in this establishment is going to fit perfectly with my afternoon demeanor."

Heath and Cashton prepare to toast the moment. Susie brushes her hips, adjusting her ankle-length, form-fitting cocktail dress, then grabs her bourbon from the back bar. The three revelers clink glasses in unison. The good times roll and several beers flow. Numerous people enter and leave. Many acknowledge Cashton's presence and a few even stop to chat.

"Well, thanks, GI, but I've got to head out. There's an estate I need to settle. This has been great. And you too, Ms. Susie. Please, what's the damage for the both of us?"

"What? Bathroom damage again? Oh, at the bar, you say? Fourteen dollar."

"Cashton," Heath whispers. "It's got to be more than that. We both had at least three beers a piece and sent a couple shots down the bar."

"Three or thirty, doesn't matter, Heath. Susie-Q likes you, so you get the special rate. Now, you leave a twenty on the bar as we walk away and she'll love you for life. Welcome to Barrymore's!"

—⚎—

Meanwhile, a Greek cargo ship is being secured to a wharf on the New Jersey banks of the Arthur Kill. Dock workers scurry to unload its freight.

"Cleaned up and ready to go, I see. Got your duffle bag and a change of clothes? How about your passport?" Jason drills Andro.

"Ey, ey, captain! And you? Got a copy of the ship's visa?"

"Roger that. We'll take a taxi to the rail head, then catch the PATH at Hoboken. Before you know it, we'll be toastin' Midtown Manhattan."

—⚎—

"How's my spicy little Thai princess?" Jason shouts as he and Andro enter Barrymore's. The place is packed with the usual pre-theater crowd, but two bar stools just came open.

"Sit, sit my chocolate Goliath. You park boat just to come see me? And who this?"

"Docked in Bayonne this morning. I hope to flirt with you for at least a week. And this is my new shipmate. Andro, say hello to Empress Susie, Queen of Siam."

"It is an honor and a pleasure your highness," Andro says with a wink and a smile as he reaches for Susie's hand and kisses it.

"You teach boy good, Big Guy. He soon talk more bullshit than you."

"Not possible!" three or four patrons shout out in unison far down the bar.

"Thank you. Thank you very much," Jason barks back. "I feel humbled to be so warmly welcomed home."

"Here your Makers Mark, Jason. What you have, Andro?"

"A beer will be fine."

"You just miss Cashton. He stop by with reporter. Have a couple beer and run off—some recruiter thing at Arthur Ashe Tennis place. But he leave these. Can you use?"

"Wow… Yankees verses Mets tonight. These are MVP tickets on the third base line. Interested, Andro?"

"Of course… I'm more of a footballer, but I know the basics. The Italians are crazy in love with baseball and basketball. We watch it on TV. I even have a Yankees T-shirt. Tonight I can get a cap. Thank you, Ms. Susie. Thank you."

"No thank me. Thank Cashton. You tell him, Jason."

"Sergeant Cashton Steel's a recruiter who works out of the Times Square booth. He stops by here regular like to throw back a beer or two."

"And to pee," Susie interjects.

"Anyway, those guys get a lot of comp tickets to games, Broadway shows and other stuff. When Cashton can't use his, he'll drop 'em off here."

"Damn… My head's spinning and I haven't finished my first beer. This morning I said hello to Lady Liberty. We ate lunch at a fine Polish place in Jersey, then tunneled to Broadway. I fall in love with Susie-Q and now we go to see the Yankees play. No one will believe me back home."

"Keep spreading the news, my man," Susie shouts and laughs as several gleeful drinkers along the bar chime in to yell, "Cheers!"

A silken baritone voice resonates through the public address system. "Ladies and gentlemen, welcome to Yankee Stadium. Now speaking, your announcer, Bob Sheppard. Please rise, remove your hats and direct your attention toward home plate…" The national anthem concludes and the crowd of thousands roars, "Play ball! Play ball!"

"Wow, you get this crazy before every game?" Andro asks.

"Yup, they do," an eager, and somewhat inebriated, Yankees fan pipes in.

"And the announcer's voice. He speaks with such class and style."

"Reggie Jackson nicknamed Sheppard 'The voice of God,'" Jason notes. "He's been the announcer here for more than forty years. Hey, man, your cap looks good. You likin' the Hebrew National?"

Andro tries to mumble a response while chomping on his gourmet hotdog. He's resigned to nodding his head *Yes!*

"So, with food and drink in hand, get ready for about three hours of nonstop spittin, ass-scratchin' and crotch-grabbin," Jason wisecracks, "as the Bombers try to blast the Mets back to Queens."

The game moves forward. "Three up, three down for the Mets as we go into the bottom of the fifth," Sheppard announces. "Yankees lead, 5-3. A reminder: Disorderly conduct isn't tolerated. Respect your fellow fan and refrain from any unruly behavior."

A couple more innings pass. "The Mets go three up, three down, again," Sheppard announces. "Your attention please, ladies and gentlemen. Rise and join me in a seventh inning stretch."

"Now what?" Andro asks.

"Like the man said, stand up and stretch," Jason replies. "And if you like, sing *Take Me Out to the Ball Game* loud and off key, like everyone else does. It's tradition."

The game moves to the bottom of the ninth. Yankee third baseman Mike Gallego drills a ground ball off the front of home plate. It takes a huge hop over the shortstop's head and dribbles into left field.

"Damn!" Jason exclaims. "All these years watchin' the majors and this is the first time I've seen a Baltimore chop."

"Damn strait, dude. He shoulda used a nine iron," another fan notes.

"Brilliant!" Ando yells. "Let me buy you a beer, Jason, to mark this special occasion."

"Thanks, man, but we're past the seventh. No more suds for sale, unless ya wanna belly up at Stan's after the game? It's just a block away."

Andro looks back with curiosity at Jason. "Whoever Stan is. I'm sure he's part of the whole Yankee thing, right?"

"It's a die-hard Bombers' bar. Besides, I could do with some food. So, we'll catch a couple extra innings there."

—⁓—

Later, at the sports pub, Andro waits in the corner as Jason, using his massive frame, edges his way to the bar and grabs a couple beers.

"Here, have a cold one. That was tougher than talkin' sense to a Boston fan."

"Thanks. So, what do you think, Jason? Baseball's a lot more than just a game, right?"

"What? Like baseball's a metaphor for war, or somethin'? That's pretty naïve; don't you think? I get your worried about the fightin' back home, but I don't have much time for such talk. What front line grunt wouldn't love to suck down a few beers while watchin' a silly pissin' contest between a couple jocks on a ball diamond?

"Baseball's nothin' but a game, Andro. In war, the stakes are a bit higher. Okay, a good game can show us hope, I guess. There's always another series, another season. Maybe baseball is about immortality, or a chance to win. Hell, I don't know. Ask the thousands who died in 'Nam for their definition. How final were those losses?"

"I'm sorry, Jason. I never meant to strike a nerve."

"It's not your fault, man. I just keep too much of that shit bottled up inside. Maybe you're right. Maybe we should look at sports in a positive way. Look beyond the failures. Try to become better. And maybe we get it right next time. Take the simple crap from baseball, I guess. Apply it to the crazy world we live in. Maybe then we can go home safe—to the places we left long ago."

"On that note, I think our burgers are ready... And I'll grab us a couple more beers."

—⁓—

C H A P T E R   1 4 :

GOTHAM CITY'S GRANDEUR

IT'S MID-SEPTEMBER. MOTHER Nature has her son, Autumn, painting a brilliant canvas across the Bosnian hillsides. Bright yellow and vibrant red leaves are transforming the landscape, courtesy of his magical brush. The makeover marches forward as trees parade their vivid hues through every valley, with branches held high.

As nature's wonderment passes in review, Franjo stumbles to put down the receiver in the hallway of his suburban Sarajevo home. He grabs the phone stand, hoping to steady himself. His eyes swell with tears, then a smile slides across his face. "Florica! Mara! Come quickly, quickly. I have great news."

"What is it?" the two women ask in excited unison as they rush into the room.

"That was Father Drazeta. His cousin, Dr. Nikolic, the prison psychiatrist, called to say we're in luck. Kowalchuk has relented. The charges are being dropped and Sofija is being moved back home."

"Praise God! Allah be praised!" Florica and Mara exclaim in harmony.

"Things are pretty rough outside Konjic right now. So, the doctor will have Sofija stay at the sanatorium for a while. It's safer there and easier for us to visit. I'll call Abeiron so he can let Andro know. Father Drazeta can get word to Petar and Alen through their priest relay."

"Thank you, Mara. Bless you for what you've done," Franjo states as he reaches to take her hands, then squeezes them in gratitude.

"It wasn't much. I read Dragana's palms and listened to her rants."

"But it pushed her to reconsider," Florica stresses. "I'm sure of it. Do you plan to see her again?"

"It sounds like she's interested and will be in touch. I'm off to the park now. Jasna wants an update. Finally, a sense of justice and fair play is rolling our way. I'd almost forgotten how to feel pleasure in something for its own sake anymore."

—⁓—

It's late September, almost 7,200 kilometers to the west of Sarajevo. "Ah, this is morning in Harlem," Andro proclaims as he stares out the apartment window, watching the sun glisten off the Hudson. "How sweet it is."

"Sweeter yet when we grab a coffee and schmear a bagel," Jason adds.

"Please thank Ms. Andi for letting me stay the night. It sure beats the ship."

"You can do that tonight. Hamilton Heights is my crash pad when I'm in town and you're my guest. Besides, Aunt Andi's always walkin' 'round with her arms open wide. She would have made us breakfast, 'cept she had to rush off to work."

With steaming java in hand, Jason and Andro stroll into St. Nicholas Park, an uptown commons serving locals as an oasis of greenery and tranquility. It was long ago forged by nature into a mass of rugged rocks and inviting trees.

"This whole area feels like it oozed money once upon a time," Andro observes.

"In the late '20s, north Manhattan drew in a lot of wealthy Blacks. It was nicknamed Sugar Hill 'cause life here was so sweet. A lot of famous folk lived 'round here over the years, like DuBois, Thurgood Marshall, Duke Ellington and Billy Strayhorn."

"He wrote *Take the A Train*, right?"

"Damn, you got your music down, boy."

"Thanks, Jason. I wish I could figure out life as well as I feel music. I'm going nuts. It seems like my mind is lunging in a dozen directions all at once, as if I'm in some kind of panic to find answers to everything."

"See? There you go again, tryin' too hard. I, I, I… It's all about 'the me' in you, ain't it? You gotta chill, man. Remember those nights aboard ship… starrin' at the stars? Didn't they bring you some kind a peace or clarity?"

"Yes, but I still have so many questions. I'm trying to figure out how things are. What's going on at home? How's my father, Baba Sofija and the others? Should I be there to help?"

"That's what we need to talk about, Andro. I called your uncle just after we docked to tell him we're safe and you're fine. He'd talked with your Uncle Franjo and said things are much worse in Bosnia. The good news is Sofija's been moved to a hospital near your home. She's doing well. On the other hand, it's a civil war now with everyone fightin' everyone. Each side's tryin' to draft all the men they can, by order, or with a gun. If you go back, you're sure to be pulled in. Abeiron says goin' back now would be like committin' suicide."

"And you were going to tell me this when?"

"When the time was right. That's why we're sittin' here, talkin' now. Dig?"

"Okay, so what should I do? How can I be of help from here?"

"Abeiron and I talked options before settin' sail. He and I agreed: If things got worse, you should seek asylum here. You qualify—facin' persecution, if you go home. But we've gotta be quick, Andro, before those damn INS agents nose their way into our business. I don't know how clean your papers are, but Immigration has the right to deport folk at any time, for almost any reason."

"But doesn't someone have to sponsor me?"

"That would be me. Eventually, you get a work visa. With it you can stay for at least a year. The whole time you could send money back home. God knows they're gonna need it. Are you willin' to try?"

"It sounds like I don't have a choice. Either get a green card, or go back and fight."

"I doubt it's that black and white, but there's only one way to find out. Immigration stuff is a jumbled up mess of rules and regulations. We're gonna need an attorney to help us sift the chaff from the grain. For years, my cousin Chet's been workin' at a firm nearby that takes on nothin' but asylum cases.

"Okay, in the end it's still up to a judge, but I'm sure Chet can help us build a good case. So, let's go see him and get things started. And don't worry, my man. In due time, that lady out there in the harbor will lift her lamp beside your golden door."

A couple hours later, Andro and Jason take a pause outside the Harlem law office where Chet the Paralegal works. "My head's whirling again. What is with this mountain of paperwork Mr. Lynch gave me?"

"Nobody said this would be easy, Andro. So, you fill out the forms, then Chet reviews and files 'em. The sooner the better. In about thirty days, the INS will call you in for an interview. And like Chet said, it can take four to five months before any decision is made. If your application's approved, and we're damn sure it will be, you get to stay. If it's denied, we ask for a review. Denied again, we appeal, but it'll be approved. Trust me. I can feel it in my bones. Once you get asylum, you can file for residency. Then you get that sacred green card from the Immigration boys and live happy ever after."

"That all sounds great, Jason, but how do I ever thank you and Chet?

"What goes 'round, comes 'round, my man. As for Chester Lynch, it's a cash carrousel, but let's not put the cart before the horse. I know you want to see your uncle's relatives. They live in Astoria, right? Well, small world, Sergeant Steel rents a flat in Queens. Let's head downtown so you two can meet."

"Can we ride Mr. Strayhorn's A Train?"

"Straight to Times Square, my man, but we gotta hurry and get on board. 'Now it's comin'. Listen to those rails a-hummin.'" Jason croons the song's jazzy refrain. "Let's take the A Train indeed… And let the good times roll."

—⚊—

As Jason and Andro approach the recruiting station, Cashton throws open the booth's door and leaps outside. "You crazy black bastard!"

"Super Sergeant Steel… You be lookin' spit and polished as ever."

The two men lunge into a bear hug, loudly slapping each other on the back.

"God, it's great to see you, man."

"You too, my nautical friend."

"This is my new cohort in crime, Andro Babich. Andro, meet the Army's real life recruiting poster, Sgt. First Class Cashton Steel, Esquire."

"An honor and a pleasure, sir. And thank you for the Yankee tickets."

"The name's Cashton. And you don't sir a sergeant. We work for a living. The *Post* says you guys saw a hell of a ball game. Here, let's stand on the island and talk. It's too noisy and crowded in that tin box."

"I need to check back in with the ship real soon. I told Andro you might be able to help him find relatives in Astoria."

"The family name is Papadopoulos. They live in a house at 32nd Street and Ditmars Boulevard," Andro adds.

"That's crazy! I rent the upstairs apartment. Mr. and Mrs. P have three of the most beautiful daughters in all of New York, or Greece, I would imagine. They said they had a cousin coming to visit. That must be you."

"Yes, that is I and they are them. Can you take me there?"

"Sure, but I have a couple appointments this afternoon… Wait here just a second." Cashton rushes inside the booth and shuffles through the contents of his old wooden desk. "Ah ha, I knew I had one left."

He marches back outside. "Take this pass and walk up the street here. See those two red double-decker buses? Get on the one that says *Downtown Loop*. It'll take you all over Lower Manhattan. That should take at least two hours. By then I'll be finished, you'll have a feel for the city and we can head to Queens."

"That sounds great, but I don't want to put you out, sergeant."

"Hey, I gotta go home, right? And it's Cashton. You good with that?"

"That should work out for everyone," Jason throws in. "How about we circle the wagons at the Edison. Say two bells? We can flirt the night away with Ms. Karen and I might just pick up the tab."

"Gotham's last great piano bar, plus free cocktails," Cashton surmises. "How could anyone say no?"

The three huddle and stack hands as Cashton yells "Hoo-ah!" It's that proud Army battle cry meaning anything and everything, except no. With the holler made, the triumvirate splits to conquer separate agendas, later to reunite at the Rum House.

—m—

A couple hours pass. Andro steps through the door of the recruiting station.

"Hey, you're back. How was the tour?"

"Excellent. Thanks a million. There's just so much to see. I could ride all day, or all week, for that matter."

Andro notices what looks like a hand-woven teardrop mobile, about a foot in length, hanging behind Cashton's desk. He steps closer to inspect the handiwork. Slender leather strips wrap around the quills of multi-colored feathers, fastening them to a bent wood frame that's crisscrossed by knobby, hand-spun yarn.

"That's an Ojibwa dream catcher. My Minnesota grandmother made it. The webbing's supposed to look like a snowshoe. Indian women make them as charms to protect kids from nightmares. At night, the bad dreams get caught in the web. They melt away in the morning sun, but the good dreams flow to the center, then float down the feathers and bless those nearby."

"It's beautiful and appears to be working."

"Thanks, dude. I'm glad you get it. In these steel canyons, any spiritual help's appreciated. Well, I'm pretty much done here. Let's head for the ol' BMT Astoria Line. We'll take the N to the end at Ditmars." Andro looks dumbfounded at Cashton and cautiously follows as they descend into the Metro's labyrinth.

"So, let me get this straight, Andro. The shit hits the fan in your homeland. Family and friends are scattered to the four winds. You run off to Greece where you meet a giant black man. Then you hitch a ride with him on a freighter to New Jersey?"

"Pretty much, that's it in a nutshell."

"Damn, dude. I've got snake-eatin' Special Forces buddies who haven't seen that much action… You ever thought about joining the Army?"

"Cashton, please slow down. I still have my sea legs. And now I'm zooming underground to God knows where with an Indian dream catcher some people call a super hero. That's a lot to process."

"Ah, come on, man, I'm a recruiter. I'm supposed to scare people. Besides, you'd be amazed how many times it works. Seriously, Andro, take my card. If you do want to talk about signin' up, you know how to reach me. And that's all I'll say about it tonight. I promise."

"Good, I'll hold you to that. Wow, I should have called the Papado-poulos to let them know I was coming to visit."

"Don't worry, pardner, I already did. And your cousins say a little apokries is being planned."

"Cashton, there's no such thing to Greeks as a small feast. Well, I hope you're hungry and thirsty, for I fear we will not be able to leave, nor meet Jason in the city."

"Got you again. Jason called me and we've moved our midtown madness to Saturday. We both know that somewhere between the feta and the ouzo, neither you nor I could find a subway platform. So, just accept the fact you're crashin' at my pad tonight.

"And yes, I have garlic hanging above the door to ward off the evil eye. Your gal pal cousins have draped onions over the banister so we can call on their special healing powers. I'm betting we'll need 'em in the morning. See, I did my homework. Indians appreciate mys-tic powers just like the Greeks. I just haven't mixed a lot of it with moussaka before, but, what the hell, right? Let this special Olympics begin!"

—⚍—

It's early Saturday evening in Sugar Hill. The neighborhood oak, maple and elm trees are dressed in their autumn finery. "And where is this bar we're visiting?" Andro asks.

"In the Hotel Edison," Jason states. "It's home to the melodic sounds of Ms. Karen Brown, the crown jewel of that vintage piano bar. Beyond the fine music, you'll love the crowd. It's more Europeans than most London pubs I've been in."

"I can't wait, but I'm famished."

"Man, when you're not tryin' to solve world problems, your stomach's rumblin' for more. No sweat, Andro, I've got ya covered. We're headed to Maria's Mont Blanc on 48th. She serves up the finest Swiss food you can imagine, along with some great Austrian wines. It's truly an Alpine delight. Plus, Maria loves me."

"Of course she does. Who in New York doesn't? Or, who in this town don't you know, Jason?"

"Chill, bro. With age comes opportunity and a lot of free cocktails. It's that 'goes around, comes around' thing. Give from your heart, my man, and it'll come back ten-fold. It's not rocket science and trust me it's not hard to do."

—⁓—

Jason and Andro push back from their gourmet meal. A waiter swoops in with two cappuccinos and a bowl of brown sugar crystals. "Enjoy," he whispers as he slips away.

As the two prepare to leave, Andro takes Maria's hand and says, "La nourriture était excellente!"

"And your French is most excellent as well. Merci beaucoup. So, Jason, you're off to the Rum House, I suppose?"

"Yes, for a musical nightcap after yet another great visit to Clinton's culinary castle."

"I couldn't have said it better. Be safe and come again soon. Au revoir, my sweet black prince."

As they leave the café and mount the basement steps, Jason pauses to fire up a cigar. Andro pleads, "Is there no bad food in this city? And please tell me we're going to walk this off a bit."

"We have a nice stroll to the next waterin' hole. And as for dinin' out, this is New York, my man. You're eatin' from 'round the world and everyone wants you to sit at their table. Why shouldn't it be a delight?"

—∿—

Strolling through the Edison's sleek art deco lobby, they near the Rum House door. Jason raises his arm to block Andro from moving forward. "Emily Post says we wait until the song's over and applause subsides. We are in the Theater District after all."

At the right moment, Jason swings open the brushed steel and smoked glass door. The two step through. He peers around a massive wood-paneled pillar and spies a couple vacant stools. In front of them arcs the piano bar, behind which Ms. Karen Brown, with the voice renowned, is holding court.

"We're heaven blessed. Grab these two before we're overcome with guilt and feel the need to give 'em up to someone far less deservin.'"

"Damn, you're in a campy mood tonight," Andro observes. "Waiting for Bette Midler, are we?"

"Young man," Karen winks and whispers from her piano bench, "Her hairdresser already called and Bette should be here about midnight. As for you, Mr. Banks, might I send a little ragtime your way?"

"That would set my foot a tappin', Ms. Brown. And this is Andro. He's fresh off the boat from Bosnia, via Greece."

"Hello, Andro, and welcome to America. Although, I must say I do question the company you keep."

"Any port in a storm, ma'am, any port in a storm."

"Cashton left message he'll need a rain check. A soldier got sick and he has to cover at West Point. Jason, look who's just come in."

An elegant woman in her late twenties has stepped through the wooden vestibule wrapping the 47th Street entrance. She stops and scans the lounge, not only as a means of seeing who is present, but to afford those already gathered the opportunity to validate her arrival.

As if lit by a follow spot, a recessed overhead highlights the vixen's silken black hair while serving to accentuate her wide-set green eyes, super-model cheekbones and flawless ivory skin.

"Who's the diva at the door," Andro asks.

Jason almost spits his drink across the bar, then coughs to keep from choking on what's left in his mouth. "It's uncanny, man, how good you are at nailing it tonight."

"Okay boys, before you even start, no potty talk over my piano. The stunning, somewhat high maintenance woman upon whom you gaze is Anita Antonucci. She's a longtime acquaintance of mine. Mind your manners and I might introduce you."

"And if she doesn't, I will," Jason boasts while slapping Andro on the back.

Tonight, Anita has dressed her tall and slender frame in an almost costume-like collection that includes a green pleated skirt and lacy gray silk blouse. It's complimented by an exotic fringed shawl, simple pillbox hat and just the right sprinkling of over-sized costume jewelry. Looking toward Karen, Anita throws a single wave with her extended left arm. Having made eye contact with Jason, she appears to almost float as she strolls across the room in her retro-fashion ensemble.

After laying a light peck on each cheek, Anita scrunches Jason's shoulders and giggles, "How's my star-kissed hunk of the high seas?"

"Better now, for sure. So, cast as a Pan Am stewardess tonight, are we?"

"You just stop," Anita chides while swatting Jason on the arm with a glove. "Can't a girl play grown up now and then? And how long before you introduce me to the hunk, I mean, friend of yours?"

"Anita Antonucci… Andro Babich. Andro… Anita."

"My… my pleasure," Andro half-stutters, blushing with excitement and interest. "Excuse me. Please, please have a seat."

"Well, thank you, Andro. You obviously didn't go to charm school with Mr. Banks."

"Anita," Karen cuts in. "Would you like to sing tonight?"

"A voluptuous woman and a vocalist too? Jason's friends never cease to amaze me."

As Anita strolls around the end of the bar, Andro leans toward Jason and asks, "What's her story?"

"Pretty interestin' one. Anita's a gifted singer, as you'll soon hear. She was bitten as a kid by the actin' bug and she's been chasin' a show biz career ever since. Her family made her learn a real skill to fall back on, should the Broadway lights not shine so bright. She went to business school and landed in the city, workin' for some boutique firm on Wall Street. Now she juggles her vocation with her avocation, but she's always lookin' to land a role on the *Great White Way*."

With Karen's skilled accompaniment, Anita finishes her impromptu medley. It includes a Patsy Cline lament, Cole Porter number and rafter rattling rendition of *Georgia on My Mind*. As the applause subsides, Anita sachets back to the bar stool next to Jason.

"That was quite amazing, Ms. Antonucci."

"Well, thank you, Andro. And what did you think, Mr. Banks?"

"Ah, Karen and Anita: that's a musical match made in heaven."

"Okay, that will cost you a piccolo, my fine sir."

The banter continues, the drinks flow and several others step up to sing with Karen.

Anita glances at her watch and squeaks, "Oops!" as she scoops up her belongings. "I've got to catch the 12:10 to Hoboken. I have a vocal audition in Philly tomorrow, early afternoon. Sorry, Karen. We'll hit the duets next time. Love you, Jason," she whispers while kissing his forehead. "Here's my card, Andro. Call me, or die," Anita jokes as she gives him a quick peck on the lips and rushes out the door.

"Wasn't it Alice in Wonderland who said, 'Would you tell me, please, which way I ought to go from here?'" Andro asks.

"Yes," Karen chirps in. "And the Cheshire cat responded, 'That depends a good deal on where you want to get to.'"

"Touché, Mr. Babich," Jason adds. "I'd say the ladies have tricked us yet again. Sounds like it's 'bout time we catch that A Train back to Harlem. You, or I should say we, have a ton of paperwork to do… Happy trails Ms. Brown, until we meet again."

—ɷ—

CHAPTER 15:
TAROT MIXED WITH INCENSE

It's July 25, 1992. Dawn is breaking over central Bosnia. Dragana, the ultimate *Scorpio Rising,* bursts out of her mountain lodge, lunges to the porch rail and lets go a primordial scream so convincing it's assured to frighten most any man or beast. "My plans aren't working! Why can't we exact the ultimate sting? Why can't I bring this campaign to its rightful end?"

This woman has been heard screeching a lot lately. The priest thinks it may be her unique way of unleashing pent up energy. The devil woman's convinced it's part of a mystical process to rebalance her personal power. Either way, Dragana's shout outs are heard by others as bizarre calls to action, flashpoints for turning desires into deeds. The lucid dreamer stomps back into the lodge. Dragana consults her diary, reviewing notes about her latest vision and trances, hoping to spot what's lead her to this juncture.

Is this all some kind of false awakening? she wonders. *Or, am I recounting a previous dream while still floating deep inside a more recent one?*

Such a quandary is more than enough to make anyone stand on a mountain top and scream. "Let her bizarre Wagnerian opera play on," one of the lieutenants is overheard chuckling in the distance as he shakes his head in disbelief.

—✹—

An hour or so later, Dragana plops in an overstuffed leather chair, staring into the lodge's massive fireplace. She hears boots clomping across the porch.

"It's Comrade Jovanović. You called?"

"Sit. We need to talk. And I insist you speak candidly, or leave now. Bottom line: What's your read on our situation?"

"The stalemate continues."

"What a brilliant account of the obvious! Can you at least try putting your finger on a possible cause?"

"There are those among us with fixed ideas that serve as prejudice. Such bias prevents us from looking at information that's different from previous conclusions."

"And through your euphemistic bullshit, Jovanović, you're now placing the blame at my feet?"

"No, ma'am, there are plenty of feet to go around. When differing feedback is no longer a part of good analysis, the ability to lead can be impacted. The result: actions, or inactions, that work to our detriment and possibly harm those around us. We must be willing to adjust our plans, or we're destine to repeat our mistakes."

"Rather than pontificating like some half-assed Soviet strategist, why don't you give me just one example?"

"Okay, Madame Kowalchuk, let's talk *Operation Anaconda*. I've also studied military history. Your plan is no more than Winfield Scott's *Great Snake Campaign* used in the American Civil War. Not unlike that grandiose design, you insist we blockade Adriatic ports, then advance down the Neretva—our Mississippi—to cut Bosnia in half. You've argued your plan is like the coils of a snake suffocating its victim. I, and several others, believe your approach is too passive. We need bold action. No more second looks in hope we stumble upon something that might work."

"You have no concept of the big picture, or the pressures being put on me and our Serbian brothers. Agreed, we must move massively, but subtly, if we hope to cross the political minefield put down in front of us."

"That's why a decisive victory is needed, if we're to achieve success," Jovanović argues. "A triumph will send a message, to the Smurfs, Clinton and all the other meddlers, that we have this matter in hand. The bourgeois Europeans have never given a damn about us. Why in hell do you worry about them now?"

"Get out… Get out now! And on your way, why don't you consider running for office, you pompous, blubbering twit. Just leave the war planning to me."

—m—

Later that morning, Mara is found strolling alongside the duck pond in Vrelo Bosne. Without notice, Jasna bursts on to the park pathway, causing Mara to flinch and the waterfowl to scatter.

"Do you always have to make some dramatic James Bond entry? You startled me."

"Sorry, that was more of a trip than a surprise. I'm a bit of a klutz. My shoe caught on a water sprinkler. Anyway, how was your meeting with Kowalchuk?"

"Interesting, to say the least. She seems wise beyond her years, but is at a loss when it comes to her own happiness. Dragana has this magnetic power. She appeals to your emotions straight away. Yet, she's a sad and angry woman, filled with contradictions."

"Good intel, if I was a clinical psychologist, but what were you able to glean about the rebel's plans?"

"It was a simple palm-reading session in her country cottage. Dragana wasn't going to talk about military campaigns, but I did manage to snatch this," Mara states as she places a small, leather-covered pad in Jasna's awaiting hand.

Jasna flips through its contents. "Excellent… It looks like battle-field notes and timelines. We'll have this analyzed right away. Thank you. Thank you much. It should prove most helpful. So, do you plan on meeting Kowalchuk anytime soon? At her mountain headquarters, I hope."

"I expect she'll call again, but I won't go into her lion's den, Jasna. Besides, she's too clever for that. There must be clergy with all those soldiers. Father Drazeta helped with Sofija's release. Maybe he can connect you with a priest at their campsite."

"And now you're telling me how to do my job? Okay, okay. I'm sorry. I understand your reluctance, but do continue meeting with her. And I wouldn't try lifting anything next time. It's too risky. Be careful, Mara. I'll be in touch."

—⁓—

Father Kraljić nods as he climbs the porch steps, extending a greeting, "Sister Dragana, I heard earlier what sounded like a call for help. Might I offer some comfort?"

"Thank you, chaplain, but I was just vocalizing my frustration at the moment."

"Try not to dwell on the negative, ma'am. Don't be so critical of yourself. It can get in the way of life's greater achievements."

"Thank you, father. I'll take that under advisement. But tell me, what do you think is the best approach to moving our campaign forward?"

"I'm but a simple priest, not a tactician. Yet, I champion a crusade focused on winning people's hearts and minds. And what I deal with are problems of perception. Never forget that true power is the ability to achieve purpose. And the most powerful are those who do so through persuasion, not coercion.

"Sure, that's over-simplified, but stubborn problems must be solved using bold strokes. In the end, it's all a matter of legitimacy. If the masses don't see authority as genuine, they'll withdraw support, then power evaporates. People are willing to obey, if they consider the control valid. We'll never win hearts and minds if we're not willing to empathize with our brothers and sisters. Jesus said it best: 'First, remove the beam in your own eye, before you try to remove a speck from the eye of another.'"

"Interesting perspective. That's pretty much what Jovanović said, but with far less eloquence. Thank you, Father Kraljić. You've given me insight into a part of our operation that may need more emphasis."

Dragana steps back into the lodge, picks up the phone and calls Katya. "Yes, this weekend. Call that Gypsy girl right away. I want her at the datja Saturday afternoon. Tell her I want to focus on the past as a prelude to my future."

—⁂—

About a week later, an ocean and a continent away… "You're shittin' me, Ariel!" Heath yells into the phone. "The condo, lake house and money to boot? Are you sure that's right? Did you know she was sittin' on that kind of dough? Who else is in on this? What do I owe in taxes? When can we settle?"

"One question at a time, please, Mr. Winslow," the lawyer Grossman begs. "I recommend you come to my office so we can review your inheritance in detail. Ms. Van Peel's estate has cleared probate and we can settle, but I have documents we must review and several more you'll need to sign."

"I'll see you right after lunch, if that's okay? And thanks, Ariel. You've made my day."

—⁂—

A lazy swirl of smoke rises from the chimney of Dragana's datja. Fog hovers everywhere. "Enter please," Katya says to Mara, who's again dressed to the hilt in her Transylvanian garb. "Ms. K will soon finish her dream session, then I will announce you. A cup of tea, perhaps?"

"Yes, please and thank you," the false Roma replies. "I'm proposing a Tarot reading today. May I clear the coffee table and prepare myself?"

Katya nods yes, then shuffles toward the kitchen. Hearing music from the study, she realizes another daydream has ended. Katya hollers, "Your Roma has arrived."

Moments later, Dragana slides open a pair of hand-carved pocket doors and steps into the parlor. "Mirela, good to see you again."

"And you, ma'am. Princess Ashkali at your service."

"Ah, a card reading. I'm impressed. You've developed so many psychic skills in such a brief lifetime."

"I think the analogy of singing is apropos. Everyone can sing, yes? It's just that some people resonate a lot better than others, especially with practice. So, shall we begin?"

Mara lights the devotionals at the far ends of the table, then the incense, placing it in an ornate, egg-shaped brass burner. Her bejeweled hands capture the rising smoke with a circular gesture. "Please hold these cards, close your eyes and clear your mind. I will be laying out a blank slate for our session today. What question do you want addressed?"

"Can you look at my past in order to predict my future?"

Dragana opens her eyes as Mara spreads the cards in a pattern resembling a Celtic cross. "I call upon the powers of the Major Arcana, and the suits of the Minor Arcana, to come forward. Bring your wands, cups and pentacles. Ta'ala… Oh, come to me."

Mara turns the first card. "You're at a crossing, Dragana. You have important decisions to make. The High Priestess card holds the mystery of your unconscious. She represents your inner voice. She's trying to send you a message. Be patient and open to hidden whispers."

Mara turns the next card. "Something in your recent past is still being felt, but will soon pass. To admit you are afraid will give you the strength to conquer your fear. When you give up your desire for control, everything will begin to work as it should. You are running as fast as you can only to stay where you are. This Hanged Man says stop struggling so that you can move forward.

"The Six of Cups," Mara murmurs. "Now that you have looked back, the way will be clear to look forward. There is nothing wrong with gazing into the past for inspiration when things aren't going well.

"The Ace of Pentacles. This is your spiritual foundation. It's the fertile soil in which your ideas can be planted, grow and mature. The success of your harvest is almost assured. If you want to succeed, start now. It's not the time to dream and fantasize when there is work to be done. Keep your feet planted in the earth and let common sense guide you to success.

"And finally," Mara sighs as she turns the last card. "The Eight of Swords shows what happens when you abuse the power of the rapier. The knife will turn against you. Don't let your mental clarity be replaced by blindness. Free yourself from the bonds of fear and doubt." Mara again circles her hands over the incense, then mixes all the Tarot cards in one rapid swirling motion.

"Is that it? What else do you see?"

"That is all the Tarot can share with us in the moment."

"Okay, okay. It makes sense. What Jovanović said may have stung a little, but Father Kraljić said much the same. And now you've reinforced it. Tough, but good. I'll take it. Thank you, Princess Ashkali.

"Katya, call Ackov at the TV station. Have him set up dinner for tonight. Tell him we have hearts and minds to win. My past is my present. And I will now begin to shape my future. Yes, Mirela, I do think I've seen the light."

With a melodic tone, Mara locks eyes with Dragana and whispers a phrase from the Hindu mystic Kahlil Gibran, "May your joy be your sorrow unmasked." She then gathers her paraphernalia and rises. Making a broad, sweeping gesture with her arm, Mara swirls on point across the room and exits. Another rouse is complete.

It's late September, a little more than a month has passed since Andro's Big Apple arrival. The INS has granted him asylum while his application's reviewed. Through the efforts of his gregarious cousins, Andro's now working the docks with New York Waterways in Long Island City. And Cashton has offered his sofa-bed as a temporary port in the storm of Andro's transition. The phone rings in Cashton's apartment. Andro answers.

"Hey man, it's Jason. I just got a call from Chet about your INS interview. He knows the agent pretty well. You did great and it sounds like things should move quickly."

"That's fantastic news, Jason. Thank you."

"Yeah, but I've got to set sail in a couple days. It's a round-robin to Amsterdam. I should be back in about three weeks. Everythin' okay with you and Cashton? You've got Chet's number, right? Eatin' well? Got enough money?"

"Yes, mom," Andro scoffs. "Thanks for your concern, but all is fine. The next step is up to the INS, I guess, but you will be back soon. Let's meet at Barrymore's about six to get caught up before you cast off?"

"Book it Danno."

That evening, back in Belgrade, Dragana steps through the ornate cherry wood and frosted glass doors of the historic Manjez restaurant. The maître d' greets and directs her to a tree-lit terrace facing the park. She spots Adrijan laid back at a side table, swirling a glass of welschriesling in his pudgy little hand.

"Comrade Kowalchuk, welcome," the network manager says as he stands to greet Dragana. He makes a broad sweep with his arm toward the sculpture garden. "I hope this is acceptable."

"As long as you're picking up the tab, Ackov. Old Town, a four-star hotel and special seating. What the hell are you thinking? I'm here for work, not a three-hour Balkan feast meant to impress some fat cat diplomat."

"My apologies if you find a decent respite for an evening meal somehow offensive."

"Just drop it, Ackov. Time's short. So, let's get to the point. I've had a revelation of late and I want you to launch a new media campaign for broadcasting our nationalist goals. Take a fresh look at all our outlets. See them as your communication arsenal in our latest charge. They will be the key weapons in my crusade to reaffirm our identity.

"Those broadcasts reach almost four million people. You must enlighten listeners. Your staff must develop stories that define us as legendary. No one should ever forget the tragedies we suffered at the hands of the Ustashe. We were the victims and martyrs of history. I want messages about attacks by Bosniaks and Croats on Serbs. Air them over and over. They must appeal to the unconscious in all of us. They should trigger fear and terror, if necessary.

"And Adrijan, don't forget who you work for. The media directors decide who'll be promoted, demoted, dismissed or condemned. A new media law is being drafted. It'll create a special court to try violators. It'll have the power to fine and seize property, if needed. Do you understand?

"There's no need to respond, Ackov. Just sit there and take notes. Here's your approach: Keep it simple. Rely on folklore, tradition and history. Don't hesitate airing unverified stories as fact, if needed. Do what you have to do, but build that national consensus. Are we clear on what I expect?"

"Yes… yes, ma'am," Adrijan responds in a cowering fashion.

"Good, then I'm out of here." Dragana grabs his glass, downing the wine in a single gulp. "Bon appétit, you little rat bastard."

It's Wednesday afternoon of the same week in New York City. Cashton strolls back to the bar from the men's room as Andro, Jason and Heath jostle in Barrymore's doorway.

"Hey, Andro… Cashton, buddy… Heath! Great to see ya'll again. You too, Jason, Cashton, Andro… Hey guys! How's everybody?"

"Shut up with the salutations for Pete's sake," Elizabeth-Ann demands from behind the bar. "Sit your fat asses down and listen up: Maker's Mark, Bass ale, make that two, and a near-bear, right? Good… Happy hour starts now."

"Good to see you too, ma'am," the four state in unison as they mount stools along the short end of the bar.

"So, lots of news, I understand," Cashton states. "Who wants to start?"

"Well, I'm buying the first couple rounds," Heath boasts. "Aunt Adrianne's lawyer called and I'm set to inherit a butt load of money from the dearly departed dame."

"Congratulations," Andro says. "And Jason, you're setting sail for Europe soon?"

"Yup… Should cast off Saturday for a quick trip."

"Sláinte!" Cashton shouts a toast as the others lift glasses to join in.

"Cheers!" most everyone down the bar shouts back, not unlike a spirited and supportive echo leading to the loo. The conversation continues as the foursome attempt to make up for lost time and gain clarity on current events.

"I've got an idea," Heath proposes, "now that I'm the owner of a condo on Tenth, just a couple blocks from here… Cashton, would you consider being my tenant? That way, when I'm off on assignment, I could stop flushing rent money for that dump on Second Avenue. And you could walk to work. Consider the maintenance fee your rent."

"If we follow on that," Andro adds, "I could take over Cashton's upstairs apartment in Astoria. I'd be close to my relatives and work."

"Hey, don't be lookin' at me to move, or nothin'," Jason pipes in. "I've got my sweet deal with Aunt Andi in Harlem and I'm gonna keep it."

"Yeah, it makes sense to me," Cashton concludes. "How about we seal the deal with a shot of tequila?"

"Might as well; can't dance," Heath quips. "Damn knees."

Anticipating a call for special refreshments, Elizabeth-Ann has already lined up five shot glasses, just waiting for someone to call their poison.

"Sláinte!" Cashton shouts again as Elizabeth-Ann joins the guys in their latest toast.

"Cheers!" Another spirited echo ripples down the bar.

The reunion and celebration continues with Heath, Cashton and Andro working out details and timelines for apartment shuffles and key swaps.

"As much as I'd love to stay, there's a big Army recruiting gig on Jones Beach tomorrow. I've gotta drive our special humvee out there. I swear that thing's like the world's biggest boom-box on wheels."

"I'll head back to Queens with you, Cashton. I need to update family on what I'm doing."

Andro and Cashton grab their coats, then share farewell wishes with Heath, Jason and Elizabeth-Ann. When they attempt to put drink money on the bar, Heath brushes them aside, reminding both he's now a gentrified resident of Hell's Kitchen. They all laugh. Andro and Cashton head for the door.

"Ciao, everybody," they call over their shoulders.

"Cheers," is the bar echo heard once more.

—⁓—

Cashton unlocks the Astoria house stairwell door. He picks up a small plate of sugar cookies resting on the banister's newel post and begins the trudge upstairs. "Damn, I'm going to miss this," he says to Andro. "Mrs. P puts treats out every day. I usually take them to work. If the recruits don't eat them, the cops will. But whatever you do, don't forget to take the plate upstairs. And be sure to put it back empty in the morning."

"Noted. Cashton, can you make a couple, three copies for me at work? I won't have to write so many letters then."

"You can go with me in the morning to Fort Hamilton. We'll stop by headquarters and use the Xerox."

"Can we walk on Doubleday Field? He was the general who defended Fort Sumter, you know."

"Andro will have Civil War battles for $300, please, Alex! You're quite the trivia expert, dude. You should be on *Jeopardy*."

"And what good has it done me? I still can't see the forest for the trees."

"Don't worry, Andro; it'll come to you. Don't forget: I'm with you man, but I've gotta grab some Zs. Write a good letter home, take a chill pill and get some rest. Tomorrow's another day."

"Divna noch, Cashton… Have a beautiful night."

Sept. 20, 1992

Dear Everyone,

I have made copies of this note so they go to papa, Baba Sofija, Uncle Franco and Aunt Jadranka all at once. Jason has updated me. I'm so glad all is well—considering. I'm now living upstairs from the Papadopoulos family. How great is that?

Jason has been a saint. He has helped me make many friends. I have a good job on the docks. It is only a short walk from the house. I will start sending money home soon. I want to and will do more. My asylum request was approved. The government interview went well. I may get a decision about becoming a permanent resident in 4-6 months.

I read the papers, listen to the news about Bosnia and I'm so concerned. I sense a crazy few are driven by their blind faith in country, religion and history. They just accept all those things without any kind of proof. I now believe such stubborn-ness only adds to the problems we face. Is this what has caused the divides among our people and forced everyone to fight?

Enough of all that. Know I am well and I hope this finds you the same. I wish you the best of health and that your spirits stay strong. I love you and miss you and pray for you—and for peace— every day.

Andro

—⟋⟋⟋—

PART III

CHAPTER 16:
AN OFF, OFF BROADWAY PLAY

Sixteen tires extend like giant rubber claws. They scre ch as TWA Flight 121 touches down after an uneventful eight-hour flight from JFK. Heath is busy stuffing notepads into his attaché as the chief purser announces, "Welcome to Frankfurt where the local time is 6:42 a.m., Sunday, September 20, 1993… Meine damen und herren: Willkommen in Deutschland. Die lokale zeit ist…"

The valiant reporter clears Customs and steps into Europe's heartland. He's greeted by a spit and polished American airman holding a placard with WINSLOW printed in large block letters.

"I'm Heath Winslow with the New York Times."

"Sergeant Sonny Webb, sir," the airman replies as he grabs Heath's luggage. "Welcome to Germany. I'll be driving you to base operations where you'll receive your preflight briefing. These are your travel orders. Please review them prior to takeoff."

Notebook entry: Operation Provide Promise—21-nation U.N. coalition flying Sarajevo resupply missions… U.S. Air Force part of food & medical lifeline… Daily American, French & German cargo planes launch from Rheine-Main Air Base

The sergeant drives to the base checkpoint. It's dressed by an archway emboldened with massive blue and white letters proclaiming it the *Gateway to Europe*.

"Welcome to the home of the 435th Operations Group and the Blue Tail Fliers," the gate guard snaps with pride.

At the counter in base ops, Heath is met by a burley airman in a zipper-covered, drab-green flight suit. A hand thrusts forward. "Tech Sergeant Skip Green, Mr. Winslow. Glad to meet you and proud to serve. I'm the loadmaster today. Excuse my bein' a little pushy, but our flight's been moved up due to bad weather in the AOR. I have you on the manifest and your bags are being secured. Please step into the VIP lounge where the PAO will brief you. The AC will then escort you to the plane… Excuse me, sir, but you look confused."

"I'm a little rusty on military-speak. What does AOR and the other acronyms mean?"

"My apologies, sir. AOR stands for area of responsibility, VIP means you're our very important person, PAO is the public affairs officer and the AC is our aircraft commander. Clear?"

Before Heath can acknowledge, another airman whisks him into an adjoining room where the unit's PAO waits with a three-ring binder choked full of fact sheets, news clips, photos and maps detailing the relief operation.

"I'll take it from here," a tall, slender pilot with stoic demeanor says. "Apologies, Mr. Winslow, but we're in a bit of a rush. I'm Lieutenant Colonel Barry Perugini, your aircraft commander. Sergeant Green will give you a safety brief once we're on board. Be forewarned we fly a VFR approach into Sarajevo, regardless the weather. Welcome aboard. Let's hit the tarmac. We're wheels up in thirty."

"Clarification please: VFR, wheels up, thirty?"

"Sorry. VFR means we use visual flight rules and 'wheels up in thirty' means I hope to be airborne in 30 minutes."

"Thanks. Now, what about a report in the *Herald Tribune* that says airdropping supplies into Bosnia may result in attacks on U.S. aircraft? Or, that Muslim forces might stage some kind of incident in hopes the Serbs are blamed?"

"Good questions, Winslow," the colonel replies, "but I leave politics to the politicians. These flights are about butter, not guns. Besides, none of the warring factions are dumb enough to fire on an American aircraft. That's an invitation to get your ass kicked.

"I was briefed you can travel with us only if you report on the airlift. I'm holding you to that, but your focus should be on Sergeant Green. This is his 50th relief mission. His first was July 4th. How ironic is that? He has a wealth of war stories to tell, I'm sure."

"Roger, commander," Heath responds. Understanding only about half of what any of the aircrew have shared with him, Heath falls into a quick route step with the flight boss. Soon they're marching up the aircraft's tail ramp. Heath is ushered past a dozen massive palates of cargo lashed to the floor with a maze of orange nylon tie-downs. He straps himself into a web seat hinged against the aircraft's metal honeycombed wall.

Hours pass, then flaps extend while landing gear drops and locks in place. The Hercules begins rolling without warning. It's now spiraling downward like a slow turning bit in a giant power drill. By the time Heath figures out what's happening, the wheels touch down with a reassuring thud and the aircraft rolls to an abrupt stop on the runway.

"What the hell was that?" Heath yells.

"Welcome to Sarajevo!" Sergeant Green exclaims. "That corkscrew got us down the good Lord's staircase and away from any assholes with shoulder-fired missiles."

"It sounds like something out of a flying circus."

"And you're in the Big Top's center ring," Green shouts back as he lowers the tail ramp. "Okay, stand up, step down the ramp and halt.

Safety first. Someone will take you inside. I've got candy to deliver. We'll talk later."

—⚬—

Heath steps inside the gray, Stalinesque terminal and is greeted by a slim man in his late 30s sporting a light gray suit with open collar. "Welcome to Sarajevo, Mr. Winslow. I am Franjo Babich, cargo operations manager."

"You're shittin' me!" Heath shouts. "Oh, excuse my language, but you're Andro's uncle, right? He said you worked here, but I had no idea. And please, call me Heath."

"It is a small world, Heath. And yes, Andro is my nephew. Now, you must be tired. Let me get you to the Holiday Inn where all the journalists are staying."

"Thanks, Franjo. I sure could use a drink, but are the roads safe?"

"There is only one way to find out… Seriously, there are corridors guarded by U.N. soldiers. We will be fine. And I would like a beer as well. We have much to talk about."

—⚬—

"What the hell does a guy have to do to get a beer around here?" Heath yells as he steps into the hotel lounge.

"Keep your head down and your powder dry," Eoghan replies, "or so the soldier boys tell me. Oh, and put a hand on your glass to keep the plaster dust at bay."

"How the hell are you, you bullheaded Irish buffoon?"

"You're the one who's come back to a city under siege. And I'm the clown? You likeable idiot… By all the saints, how'd you even get here?"

Heath shares the tale of his latest travel adventure and introduces Franjo. He then recounts how Cashton opened the door to Barrymore's, charts Andro's byzantine journey to America, as well as the path to inheriting Aunt Adrianne's pot of gold.

"Okay, the bountiful ol' broad leaves you a cart-load of booty. So why come back to this hell hole?"

"It's where the action is, Eoghan. History's being made here. I want to witness and report on it. It's in my blood."

"You think you are going to behold a solution to this insanity?" Franjo asks.

"That's the question that drives me. It would drive any journalist. Even if these Balkan problems are solved, I'll bet money the political bullshit will just droll on and on."

"Well, don't bet the farm," Eoghan insists. "You've still got a few ticks on the deckle, me boy. Besides, your Hunter S. Thompson shenanigans seem to put you in your own stories as often as you try writin' about 'em."

"Thank you for that insight on gonzo-journalism, my beloved bar brainiack." Heath notes as more beers are drawn and the stories grow.

"Okay, you men test my English too much. Eoghan, my bill please, as I must head home. And Heath, we will get together soon, so I can hear more about Andro."

"Absolutely... I'll be here for a while, leaning on this very end of the bar. Besides, there are many things I want to ask about your family. And there's much Andro wants me to share with you. I know where to reach you, Franjo. So, we're set."

"Good to meet you, kind sir," Eoghan adds, "and put away your money. This inaugural visit's on me." The three shake hands and Franjo darts out the door.

"Don't you find that a little strange? I mean, we meet, the beer's flowin', I have all this info about his nephew and poof, he's gone."

"This is only bartender rumor, but I hear tell the whole Babich clan is caught up in this bloody war. First off, they can't be Muslim, or he wouldn't be tippin' beers with us. Franjo's brother Petar and Andro's brother Alen ran off with the Croat militia. Franjo's mom was arrested a while back for leadin' protests at the TV station. His wife's a CIA informant. And word on the street is they've taken in a Bosniak girl who's pretendin' to be a Gypsy. It's her way of gatherin' dirt on the Serb rebels, I guess."

"Well, if even part of that's true, it makes sense Franjo would want a little time to get his house in order, regardless how much I may know about his long-lost kin."

"So, Mr. Winslow, let's be droppin' that crap. Tell me more about what sweet ol' Auntie A left ya."

"First, I need to go upstairs. And no, I don't mean you pouring me a gin and tonic, Mr. Trickster. I have to clean up. I'll be back, if for nothing else than to fight off the jet lag."

"You're a top drawer player, Heath, me boy. The blessin' of God and Mary be upon ya. And rest assured I'll hold down the fort until your safe return."

—⚬—

Weeks fly by as the Balkan conflict escalates. Heath stays busy filing report after report with the *Tribune*. He investigates rumors of tunnel supply routes and black market warehouses around Sarajevo. Winslow documents precarious treks by U.N. convoys coming from the Adriatic. With Loadmaster Green's help, he routinely hops on C-130 shuttles between Bosnia and Germany, while working to build trust with Franjo and his extended family.

Notebook entry: Balkan warring factions constantly change aims & allegiances... Ethnic cleansing is in place—sterile reference to attempts at wiping out the opposition... War of nationalism at levels not seen since the Nazis... Religions are recruited to fuel animosity

—∞—

Times Square basks in the summer's sun while Sgt. First Class Steel barks orders at his fellow recruiters. "The battalion XO just called. The CG's stoppin' in our AOR in route to the hotel. This place is messed up as a football bat. We've got a narrow window to GI this dump. Now, let's not screw the pooch on this one. And make sure your chest candy's on straight. Hoo-ah!"

"Excuse me," Andro says to the petty officer just inside the recruiting booth door. "Is this a bad time for me to speak with Sergeant Steel? I didn't understand his remarks, but they sounded intense."

The Navy recruiter chuckles and says, "That's just Army-talk. Steel is trying to motivate us to tidy the place up a bit. For your info, XO means executive officer. That's the guy who just called. The Army commanding general, or CG, wants to visit the booth. Like a football bat implies our stuff's all scruffy. GI means to clean for a general inspection. And we don't want to screw the pooch, or mess up, on this one.

"Fascinating. And chest candy?"

"That's your ribbon rack. Make sure it's clean and on straight."

Cashton lunges into the discussion as the petty officer steps back. "Shoot man. What's up?"

"Double-checking meet up time and place for the Fleet Week gala," Andro explains.

"We rally at the Intrepid, Pier 86, Twelfth and 46th no later than 1900."

"Nineteen hundred? When did you American's learn how to tell time?"

"That's the Army way," Cashton snaps. "Sorry, Andro, a lot's goin' on and my fuse is burnin' a bit short. Just let Anita direct the show. She's done all this before. Gotta run, buddy. See you both tomorrow night."

—m—

Just before seven the next evening, the driver swings the limousine door open. As Andro and Anita step out, Cashton approaches from the pier's entrance. The super sergeant is resplendent in his dark blue mess dress uniform bedecked with a gold chain, cufflinks, braids, miniature jump wings and a crowded medal rack.

"Cashton, how do you plug in your Army Christmas tree?"

"Very funny, dude. I must say a chocolate tux is an interesting pick, but you pull it off quite well."

"Thank you, sir. It was Anita's choice."

"Ah, yes, Ms. Scarlett. How ravishing you look in red."

"Fiddle dee dee, Rhett. This ol' thing."

Fiddle indeed. Anita's southern belle gown of burgundy velvet is bedecked with rows of rhinestones to accent the low-cut bust line. An ostrich feather boa floats on her bare shoulders. Elbow-length silk gloves compliment the garnet velvet shoes adorned with gold-rimmed crystals and bows.

"Andro, shall we escort the princess to the ball?"

With Anita in the middle, Andro and Cashton each offer an arm. The threesome begins strolling the red carpet. Before reaching the main entrance elevator, four herald trumpeters snap to attention and sound an harmonious fanfare.

Befuddled, and at the same time curious, the three look behind them to see what dignitary has been announced. To their surprise, there's no one else on the carpet. By this time, several guests have gathered at the flight deck railing and are peering down to see who the special arrivals might be.

One of the event coordinators, adorned with headset, clipboard, penlight and walkie-talkie, scurries to the musicians' side. "What are you doing?" she hisses. "They're not VIPs. I didn't signal you. Why did you sound off?"

The elder of the four leans forward and with a deep, gravelly voice says, "Because they just looks hot."

Anita, Andro and Cashton, bent over in amusement, fight to hold back their laughter. Composure regained, they step into the lift and proceed to the museum's reception hall.

"Excuse me while I do my final troop check. They won't budge an inch without a direct order."

"Let's grab some champagne and attack the hors d'vours," Anita recommends.

Chimes sound and the assembled are ushered into the hanger deck ballroom. As people find their tables, an unseen announcer begins introducing distinguished guests. "Ladies and gentlemen, please rise for the posting of the Colors by the Joint Service Color Guard from Washington, D.C., and remain standing for the singing of our national anthem by the daughter of a great World War II hero, Ms. Anita Antonucci."

"That's my gal," Andro says with a smug whisper to those around the table.

The "stars are spangled" and the troops march off. Welcoming remarks are made and the invocation is offered. Anita approaches the table to take her seat next to Andro. Several of the assembled applaud and compliment her on the performance.

"Fiddle dee dee. It's always a joy to sing in honor of our brave men and women in uniform, wherever they may be standing in harm's way."

"Hoo-ah!" Cashton toasts.

The others at the table lift glasses and shout "Hoo-ah!" in response.

—◊—

The self-indulgent Fleet Week extravaganza begins drawing to a close. Sergeant Steel excuses himself as dessert is being served so he can attend to the flag detail. Anita gives Andro a quick peck on the cheek as she whispers her need to float among the tables, inviting several naval officers for post-gala cocktails at the Rum House. Her tuxedoed, window-dressing stud is now alone in a sea of pretentious humanity.

A discerning gentleman with a stylish white beard, sitting a couple chairs to Andro's right, reaches out and offers his business card. "Judge Bloom, U.S. Circuit Court. Have your lawyer give my aide a call tomorrow. I think we can do something to expedite your green card application."

"Thank you, sir… Thank you. Thank you very much."

"Don't mention it, son. Just keep that young lady of yours singing. Now, excuse us as my wife's tired and I must hold court in the morning."

—◊—

As Cashton thanks the drill team for their stellar performance, Anita scurries back stage, bursting into his work area with a question, "Are you coming to the Rum House?"

"Doubt it. I have to get these guys on a bus, glad hand a bunch of ROTC commanders and prep for tomorrow's ceremony at Yankee Stadium."

"Well, excuse me, sergeant… I just thought you might want to enjoy the moment, for a moment."

"Anita, these are the things I'm charged with doing. I must be sure they don't fail. Go play the struggling starlet with wild abandon. Sing like a bird and drink champagne from a ruby slipper. Have a damn good time, okay? But just let me do my job."

"Fine, Cashton! As you like it. At least Andro supports me," Anita finishes with a huff. She spins, sweeps aside the black velvet curtain leg and struts into the ballroom.

Cashton mumbles under his breath, "Hell hath no fury like a woman scorned, especially an Italian dynamo dressed like that pissed off diva."

—⁓—

"Then the judge hands me his card and says phone him," Andro recalls for Anita as the yellow cab bobs and weaves through midtown traffic, eventually screeching to a halt in front of the Hotel Edison.

"… and Cashton mocking me like that. What the hell was that all about?" Anita asks with a shrill.

"Did you hear what I just said?"

"Yes, yes, lovey. Now, you just pay the driver. I have to powder my nose. Order me a piccolo and let Karen know I'm on my way. Hurry… The fleet will dock soon."

As Andro steps into the Rum House, the lounge is already swarming with a dozen Navy officers in their white dress uniforms, hard-charging businessmen parading in penguin suits and several women in opulent evening gowns.

An arm reaches out and pulls Andro toward the piano. "Drop a bomb on this place and you'd wipe out half the Pentagon," Jason chuckles from his perch at the bar's end.

"What a great surprise. I thought you would be at the event."

"I can't abide those ass-kissin' soirees. Besides, I have to protect the crown jewels," Jason states as he gestures toward Ms. Brown at the keyboard.

"Welcome, Sir Andro. You look dapper tonight. Will Ms. Antonucci be joining us?"

"Yes, ma'am."

"Primpin' for the grand entry, I suspect."

"Stop now, Jason," Karen chides. "Some ladies just have more needs than others."

No sooner is the observation made than Anita pushes open the lounge door and strides into the bar with all the confidence of a grand dame at a spring cotillion. The crowd parts as she sashays around the room, alighting next to Karen. Anita picks up a microphone, and in her best Tallulah Bankhead voice, grovels, "If you want to help the American theater, don't be an actress, dahling; be an audience."

The crowd erupts in laughter. A gregarious tone is set for the evening. Drinks flow, songs are sung and the boisterous chatter rises in an almost deafening crescendo. As the hours pass, the crowd thins and the '50s-era cocktail lounge-lizard intimacy returns. The bartender announces last call. Karen thanks the devoted bar flies for their indulgences and encourages them to tip generously.

"Come, we head upstairs. I booked us a room," Andro tells Anita. "This could be a very special night for us."

"Thanks you," Anita slurs in a half-inebriated, exhausted stupor. "That's so sweet. Au revoir, mes amis," she mumbles as the two stumble out of the bar.

—◊◊◊—

Holding Anita by the waist in a stalwart attempt to keep her upright, Andro slips the card into the lock, antsy for it to blink green. He pushes the handle and the door swings into a quaint, but cramped, mini-suite. Andro maneuvers Anita close to the bed. As he takes her boa, gloves and purse, she timbers, face first, on to the bed like a freshly fallen magnolia. Andro unhooks her gown and begins pulling on the zipper.

"Oh, God," Anita growls as she lurches from the bed and storms toward the bathroom. The next thing heard is the melodious sound of forceful heaves, intermixed with repeated moans of "Oh, God... Oh, God."

"Are you okay, dear?"

"Just peachy, Andro. Pull the frickin' door shut, will you? Give a woman some peace," Anita groans as Andro complies.

The green tweed lounge chair extends an invitation to sit. Andro accepts, then grabs the remote control and begins surfing late-night TV channels for nothing of interest. After a brief eternity, Anita emerges from the porcelain palace. Her face is ashen, but for streaks of mascara down her cheeks. And her hair's a fallen mess, flattering the soiled dress now rolled to her waist.

Andro tries to fight back a snicker as Anita grumbles, "What's so goddamn funny? Help me get out of this stupid thing."

Anita staggers forward. Andro lends a helping hand. Gown and petticoat removed, Anita tumbles back on to the bed, banging her wrist against the headboard. "Oh, God... Why me, Lord? Why me?" Anita asks, passing into a sleepy daze which is soon followed by robust snoring.

"Well, isn't that special?" Andro asks, mocking the *Saturday Night Live* Church Lady. Realizing the remote control would be his only companion for the evening, he pulls a downed comforter and pillow from the hall closet, then kicks off his high gloss shoes while hanging up the tux. After adjusting the footstool, he snuggles into the chair for a memorable night of poor sleep... Sweet dreams, young prince.

—w—

Late the next morning, Andro rolls a food cart next to the night stand and begins pouring coffee. The aroma teases Anita's senses. She sits up and begins rubbing her eyes.

"Voila!" Andro exclaims as he pulls away the stainless steel plate cover.

"Oh, good God… Food? Get that shit away from me before I puke again… Coffee. The lady needs coffee; nothing but coffee. Understood?"

"I'm sorry. I thought you'd be pleased, especially with the blue velvet case."

Anita picks up the tiny box, opens it and lets it drop in frightful response. "God no, Andro. This is so wrong. What were you thinking? How can you spring this on me? An engagement ring? Even the thought of marriage… I'm so not ready. No, no, no. Please, no. Take it all away!"

"Okay, Ms. Prima Donna, I have had enough. Your Oscar-winning performance as a drunken diva notwithstanding, I am out of here. Just drop the key at the desk, please. I am sorry if I hurt you, but I really must go now," he shouts, slamming the room door behind him.

"Woman," a somewhat decrepit, hunched-over Columbian janitor quips as he watches Andro board the elevator. "No can live with them; no can live without."

—⁂—

After discussing the hotel debacle with his three shapely cousins, Andro's encouraged to seek counsel from a priest. So, he boards the R Train for Times Square, then strolls west to Saints Cyril & Methodius Roman Catholic Church. As he ascends the steps of the old Croatian house of worship, a young priest pulls open the massive wooden door.

The cleric gazes at the downtrodden lad and says, "I'm Father Cerkez. How can I help you, my son?"

"You are a priest? Sorry, I am just surprised. You seem so young."

"I started college when I was 16 and graduated in three years. Then I went to seminary. I became a deacon four years later. Six months after that, I took my vows."

"Most impressive… I apologize if I said anything that may have offended you."

"No offense taken. I guess my baby-face doesn't help sell the story much either. But this is my calling and I'm loving it."

"Father, please help me, for I know not what to do."

"That's okay, but let's drop the theatrics. There are plenty unemployed actors in this town rehearsing similar lines. Our task is to look for the root of your problem in hopes I can propose a solution."

Father Cerkez leads Andro down a stone-arched hallway to the rectory. He encourages Andro to sit in one of the well-worn lounge chairs while he pours them both a cup of tea. "Okay, what's bothering you?"

"I fear I come to you with a broken heart. I thought I had found all powerful, all encompassing, unconditional love."

"The only thing that strong is God's love, young man. What you found is temptation. Someone has enticed you with lust to stray from your spiritual journey. Or, she just got really mad and told you off."

"Pretty much the latter, but it still hurts."

"Of course it does. If it didn't, I'd be out of a job. So, you've got some critical choices to make, Andro. Like whether or not to pave the West Side Highway—pot holes verses a pleasant drive. You must choose between a good, hard path, or a bad, easy one."

"I guess that makes sense, Father, but don't we need to consider my choices?"

"Choices… Everybody wants choices. Nobody said this was going to be easy, but don't worry. I think we can get you there, if you learn how to concentrate, young man. But, if you continue letting your mind lunge helter-skelter all the time, you'll never find that focal point."

"That makes sense, I guess."

"Of course it does, but it's just the start. You've got to understand that securing a goal in life means knowing not only what you possess, but that which you've already achieved, as well as what you've lost."

"So, Father, what writings of the Apostles might help me focus better?"

"Good question. I'm pretty much hooked on the works of Kahlil Gibran at the moment. Here, take this book and read it. *The Prophet's* an example of what scholars call inspirational fiction. The author's the third best-selling poet of all time, behind Shakespeare and Lao-Zou. Pretty impressive, don't you think?"

"Excuse me. Are you a man of the cloth, or some weirdo pushing me to read the words of a mystic?"

"Relax, Andro, Gibran was born and raised a Maronite Catholic. His theology is a union of several different faiths—Christianity, Islam and Hinduism. Anyway, please read it and think on it. Then, come back so we can talk more. Okay?"

"Agreed. Thank you, Father. And I shall return."

"That's the spirit. And bless you, Andro… Now, don't forget: Focus on your goals. And like the folk thinker Frank Clark once said, 'If you can find a path with no obstacles, it probably doesn't lead anywhere.' Ciao my friend."

—∞—

CHAPTER 17:
KNEE-JERK REACTIONS

"Okay, Ackov," Dragana huffs as she storms Adrijan's Belgrade office. "You've got to do more. Better my image and that of the nationalist bloc… Now! Your programming is drawing in the dregs of society. They're people without the likes and dislikes of the masses. They're acting like the body of our movement and they disgust me."

"I told you as much when we started this campaign. Careful what you wish for, I said, you might just get it."

"You sniveling pudgy Pomeranian. Who cares what you think? This is about me and how we right this ship."

"As you often say, Ms. K, 'Enough is enough!' Standing alongside your emotional rollercoaster hasn't been easy. Besides, when you go negative about something, you just get in your own way. I don't think there's any question I'm here to serve the cause. Pile on all the intimidation you want. It won't change the facts."

"Well, what is this? Is Adrijan Ackov finally standing up for himself? Congratulations… I'm impressed. Okay, I'll admit I'm a bit intense at times, but my whole life's been driven by my faith in our country and its religion."

"And that's my point exactly. People now question such blind faith and orthodoxy. They're convinced it only adds to the bigotry. They think the media has created it, causing Slavs to take up arms against each other."

"We've been at this for over a year now. Maybe our broadcast tenor has grown a bit shrill. Europe's criticism has been harsh, but I don't think the U.N. will pull the plug, or jam our signals any time soon."

"The U.S. just hit the airwaves with a huge radio campaign. It's nothing more than racial stereotyping and propaganda. They're acting like cheerleaders for the opposition."

"That's why we must refocus our drive, Adrijan. We must take a military approach by clearly defining our goals. I see three: Arouse the public's interest. Second, and maybe with more subtlety, continue quashing those 'inconvenient ideas.' And third, avoid telling so many untruths. If we focus on those points, we can still achieve our purpose."

"I can buy into that, ma'am. I'll call a staff meeting for tomorrow morning—a strategy session for a new way ahead. Might you want to join us?"

"No. I think you've got it. And if not, I'm sure we can find someone who does." With that, Dragana sweeps out of Adrijan's office and down the gray marble hallway. She leaps into her MGB parked just outside the entrance and zooms toward her mountain retreat where the rebel crusade marches on.

—⟨⟨⟨—

It's the second Saturday in June. The *116th Street Festival* in Manhattan's El Barrio is winding down. Thousands upon thousands have reveled through a sun-drenched day filled with salsa music, Latino food and plenty of people watching. A sea of young Boricuas still strut about in shirts, flags and caps emblazoned with the island's colors. Men and women show off every part of their bodies, especially those stained with paint. Puerto Rican maps, dragons, flags, hearts, weapons and names are inked everywhere—constellations of tattoos with love on one hand, hate on the other.

Recruiter Cashton Steel is having a good day as well. He's spit and polish in his short sleeve white shirt with all its accoutrements and

Army blue trousers bloused above his shiny black boots. Now it's time to secure his mobile booth and head back to Bay Ridge.

His pimped out military ride is awash in Army green cammo paint and covered with black and gold *Be All You Can Be* decals. The rig has a jam music system which got a workout today, as well as the video screens and computer war game consoles. It's all meant to grab the eye of potential recruits cruising Spanish Harlem events like this.

At first, he was a little apprehensive about setting up shop here among so many cocky young people. Add to the mix scores of macho muscle dudes and throngs of screaming kids all wanting something. But many passersby told Cashton they were happy he'd joined the party. Most of them were genuinely interested in what he had to show and tell.

Now late in the day, one of New York's Finest pulls aside a metal barricade so Sergeant Steel can drive up Third Avenue, leaving the fiesta's mayhem. As he turns right on 118th Street toward the FDR, the sergeant senses a commotion. He hears a woman screaming in a nearby vacant lot. Steel rams the humvee up and over the curb. He starts blaring the horn and yelling in the general direction of the ruckus. Three punks in gang colors, tight jeans and high-top tennis shoes scatter as the one-man military assault approaches. Left behind is a disheveled young woman in a light green sun dress, quivering as she cowers against a crumbling tenement building.

Cashton leaps out of the vehicle and rushes to the victim's side. "My God, are you okay? Are you hurt? Can I help you?"

"I'm fine. Who the hell are you?" she demands.

"Sergeant Cashton Steel at your service, ma'am. I heard the hubbub and thought I could help. Those thugs ran off, but I'll feel better when I get you out of here."

"Thanks. I'm sorry. I didn't mean to yell. I was just scared and confused is all."

"Totally understandable, ma'am."

"And stop calling me ma'am. My name's Denasha, Sergeant Steel."

"Okay, Denasha, but only if you call me Cashton. Now, let's get you away from this mess. Do you need to go to a hospital? Do you want to call the police? Is there any place I can take you?"

"No, no and yes. I'm fine, really. My pride's messed up more than anything. I'll take a lift in that snazzy ride of yours, if you wouldn't mind driving me home."

"My pleasure entirely, if you're sure you're okay?"

Cashton helps Denasha into the humvee. They head toward her apartment on Second Avenue. He walks her to the entrance, then passes Denasha his business card. Cashton jots down her name and phone number, assuring Ms. Rivera he'll be checking back next week. She thanks him and scurries up the squeaky wooden staircase to her flat.

All the time Cashton is maneuvering his Army ride south, he can't get the vision of Denasha's striking beauty out of his head. Her china-doll face and thick, silken hair have been known to catch many a man's attention with ease.

Now that's a recruiting challenge I'm willing to meet head on, Steel thinks. *Be all you can be, indeed!*

—⁂—

About a month after Judge Bloom passed Andro his business card at the Fleet Week gala, the phone rings in Aunt Andi's Hamilton Heights apartment. "Hello?"

"Yo, Jason… Glad you're back. It's Chet in the hood, down at the law office. Great news, bro. Andro's gettin' a green card. The INS dude just called and…"

"Son of a frickin' sweet Jesus… Excuse me. That's just me goin' half-assed happy."

"I can dig it, man. I pretty much flipped, too. So, when your aunt's done washin' your mouth out, we need to roll up with the feds downtown. You know—lots of papers to sign and that sorta stuff. We straight?"

"Sure, man. I'm on it. Trackin' Andro down now. Thanks for the call, Chet. We owe ya big time."

"I don't know who the kid knows, but some heavy cut a boat-load of red tape. But who cares? It's a done deal and the Babich man's legit! Holler when ya can."

"As always, Chet."

—⁂—

Later that afternoon, Andro, Jason and Cashton are found greeting each other in the entry to their favorite Theater District bar, shaking hands and slapping backs, as Susie-Q yells, "Why you come to Barrymore? Nobody else want listen to you?"

"We come to celebrate with you, our princess. And hear your lovely voice," Jason assures the bartenderess.

"Where my reporter buddy, Heath?"

"Crazy ass took his money and ran," Cashton jokes. "Actually, he's back on assignment for the *Times* in Andro's home of Bosnia. He said, 'To be a witness to history,' or some crap like that."

"So, what we celebrate today, you blowhards?"

"It's Flag Day… and the Army's birthday," Cashton adds.

"Cheers… Cheers… Cheers," is the familiar echo that ripples down the bar.

"And I'm getting my green card."

"Andro, you faster than Jason hand on my butt. Congratulation… We study to be citizen together. Okay?"

"Thank you, Susie, but I don't know. I am afraid many years must pass before I can become an American."

"Not necessarily," Cashton interjects. "Green Card Soldiers can be naturalized after just a year in the Army."

"Sign me up, sergeant!" Susie squeals.

"I'd say she's past the age limit," Cashton whispers to Jason, "but I prefer drinking my beer to wearing it.

"Seriously, Andro, legal residents just like you, serving in the military, can apply for hurry up citizenship. As a matter of fact, there are tens of thousands with Uncle Sam right now. Most of them able to do just that."

"Easy now, Steel," Jason states. "That's a damn serious decision. It can mess with a man's head, as well as his heart. It's not a choice to be made lightly."

"I couldn't agree more. And I wasn't making light of it. I'm just saying Andro has options. Besides, it's not uncommon for refugees to take pride in our country, then want to show their patriotism by serving. I've seen it many times in my career. Lots of young people today, just like Andro, carry on a long tradition of immigrants to America."

"I hear you and I appreciate you pointing that out. But like Jason said, this is something big I must think about. I prefer not to do it with a drink in my hand."

"Okely dokely, then," Susie jokes. "Flanders say next drink on me. We toast good old U.S. of A… But now you talk about boobies, no bullets."

"I like the way this lady thinks," Jason chimes in.

The banter continues as the three men keep Susie-Q busy with drink orders and snide remarks. At the same time, Cashton enjoys a mild sense of accomplishment. He's confident the enlistment seed has been planted in Andro's mind. And the adroit Army recruiter will make every effort to cultivate its growth in the days and weeks to come.

—⁓—

Ten days have passed since Cashton's happenstance in Harlem. His excitement has grown as well, but not over the bustling circus of activities enveloping Gotham. He's more intrigued by the goings on of a certain Latino lady—his self-proclaimed damsel in distress. It's time he call upon Denasha once again.

"Hello, Cashton, and thanks for checking back. Seeing you in uniform that day got me thinking. I did a lot of soul searching after our encounter. Did you know my cousin, Anselmo, is a recruiter with the New York Army Guard? Well, we talked and he laid out many good reasons to become a citizen-soldier. So, I'm taking the test next week."

"Wow… That's fast, but sounds great," Cashton replies, voicing false enthusiasm while masking his emotional setback. "What jobs are you thinking about?"

"I want to be a computer technician. It seems like a hot, up and coming field. There's an opening right now with a Brooklyn unit."

"That's a smart choice. Your Army training will mean college credits and the Guard can pay for school. You could become a computer programmer. Every company in the city is looking for those folks."

"And I have you to thank for it."

"That's nice of you, Denasha, but I think your cousin deserves the credit. At the same time, if there's anything I can do, or you change your mind and want to go on active duty, just give me a call. I want to make sure you're being all you can be."

"That's clever; Cashton and I'll keep you posted." A doorbell rings in the background. "Perdone, that's my friend, Joaquin. Thanks again for everything. Ciao."

"Well, that search and secure mission is terminated," Cashton mumbles as he hangs up the phone. "Okay, time to set new grid coordinates, sergeant. Time to launch *Operation Babich* and commence fire."

—⁂—

As Andro enters the stairwell to his Astoria apartment, he picks up the plate of cookies waiting on the banister. He then notices a folder on the steps with a note attached.

> *Andro—Don't think I'm being pushy, but here's some info about becoming a Green Card Soldier. Read it. Give me a call with questions.*
>
> *—Cashton*

Andro spends the evening reviewing the pitch package, weighing the pros and cons while running it over and over in his mind. He's now latched on and refuses to let go until a decision is made. Andro realizes full well this will stir up a range of reactions from many people in his life… those both near and far. He rushes downstairs to bounce the idea off his caring cousins.

"Why the sudden interest in soldiering?" Alecia asks.

"I feel so incomplete. It's time I find some kind of fulfillment."

"What about those sessions with the parish priest?" Daphne poses.

"And the writings of Gibran?" Andro adds. "They've both come up short."

"So, just like that, you think the Army can fuel your potential, or fill you passion?" Melinda demands.

"I don't know, but I'm sensing it's my special call to duty. Maybe it's a sign of my true nature."

"That doesn't sound very enlightened," Alecia points out.

"You need to sleep on this before making such a huge decision," Daphne insists.

"So, sweet dreams, Mr. Recruit," Melinda says with sarcasm.

"Sweet dreams indeed," the other cousins spout as they turn to leave the hallway impromptu.

—∞—

Another week passes. Andro strolls into Harlem's historic Morningside Park with two large coffees in hand. Sunbeams bathe the cliff-like hillside in ribbons of gold, glistening off the cascading waterfall and warming the stone walkway. He spots Jason sitting on a bench, taking in the heights matchless view of the mighty Hudson.

"Ms. Andi said I'd find you here… Coffee?"

"And so you have… And so you have."

"What's with the blues, Jason?"

"It's such a small world, man. You can never escape your past. Never," Jason sighs as he sips from the cup and fires up a cigar.

"Tell me about it," Andro states in resigned agreement.

"Okay, but it stays with us. That beautiful Puerto Rican gal Cashton rescued the other week. Well, she's my daughter."

"What? You never mentioned…"

"Nor did I plan to, until Cashton ran into her."

"But what? How? When? Why?"

"Chill with the drill, man. Go back 22 years. It was one of those 'just off the boat' summer romances, see. Margarita's husband was killed a couple months earlier in a bodega shootout. She was lonely, I guess. Well, the next thing I know, she's pregnant with Denasha. I try doin' the honorable thing. I offer to marry, but her family won't hear of it. There's no love lost between light Latinos and Blacks, Andro. I'll never understand that prejudice, but you can bet it's still there.

"After bein' told, in no uncertain terms, I wasn't welcome east of Fifth Ave, I headed back out to sea. I tried to visit, but Denasha's brother and uncles threatened my life. I got the point and didn't try a second time. Yes, I sent money over the years, whenever I could, but I never saw Margarita again. And I've never met my daughter."

"Wow… So, are you going to try now? Cashton and I can help."

"Thanks, man, but I doubt it. There's a lot of water under that bridge. Margarita's remarried and I'm sure the relatives would welcome me with the same open arms. Besides, Denasha's a strong young woman now. Why upset all that? You've gotta give weight to the past when thinkin' about the future. Don't forget that. This is gonna take a while for me to sort out, Andro."

"And I'm here to help you, Jason, if I can. Just like you have helped me. I too have made a big decision, but I would like your opinion before taking the next step."

"What's up, man? You're not goin' back to Bosnia, are you?"

"No, not yet. The war is only getting worse as the violence spreads. I've been reading and re-reading a lot of stuff Cashton gave me about becoming a Soldier. And I'm pretty sure that's what I want to do."

"Pretty sure isn't good enough! Ya gotta be damn sure it's what you want. Be sure of what's right for you."

"I know; I know, Jason. I meet the fitness criteria. Cashton is convinced I'll do great on the exam. I have my green card now. I speak Serbo-Croatian, English, German and Italian. Besides, you'll vouch for my moral character, right?"

"That's a given, man, but the Army? Are you sure that's what you want? What'll you do?"

"It's a one-year ticket to citizenship. And yes, I want that more than anything. The Army is also my way to give back. Cashton thinks I'd make a great civil affairs soldier, helping in emergencies, doing reconstruction and relief work. Those are the things that get a country running again. Those are the things we'll need in Bosnia someday."

"I'm impressed, Andro. It sounds like you've really thought this over. So where's the trainin'? How long will it take? Where will you be assigned?"

"Slow down, Jason. You ask more questions than me. Basic is at Fort Bragg in North Carolina, I think. Then I go for thirteen weeks of special training. After all that is done, I will be stationed with a Reserve unit on Staten Island. How cool is that?"

"Sounds like a plan, my man, but you must tell your family and friends. No secrets allowed. This is the ol' man talkin'. We're playin' this one by the book. You hear me? I want everything to work out fair and square. I'm gonna let Cashton know that too."

"Then, let's charge ahead."

"Hoo-ah!" Andro and Jason yell in unison, breaking into laughter and slapping each other on the back as a reaffirmation of their plans and friendship.

———

A couple weeks later, Andro, Jason and Cashton are again found greeting each other in the entryway of their beloved Hell's Kitchen watering hole. It's a Yogi Berra "déjà vu all over again" moment. This time Elizabeth-Anne is putzing around behind the bar.

"No shenanigans allowed in Barrymore's. You know that. Now get your butts in here and order something before my welcoming attitude goes south. And no comments from the peanut gallery," she cautions those sitting further down the bar.

"Even your loving hospitality won't ruin our day, Ms. E," Jason remarks.

"So, what do Moe, Larry and Curly have to celebrate?"

"I can explain everything," Andro states.

"Then we'll call in an interpreter to go over it again," Cashton jokes with his own reference to The Three Stooges.

"Here's the list. One: I join the Army next week. Two: Jason sets sail for Rio in a few days. And three: Cashton is going back to being an airborne Ranger."

"Then who will be left for me to insult?"

"Don't worry, Elizabeth-Anne," Jason explains. "I'm sure Heath's gettin' tired of waxy east European toilet paper. He'll be back to entertain you soon."

"Awe, Cashton, please stay. Rangers go to war, you know."

"Hey, young lady, I can't be a recruiter forever. Besides, 'Rangers lead the way,' right? I run the odds, but that doesn't mean I can't change direction. That's how I steer clear of life's little dangers," Cashton adds as he knocks back a whiskey.

"And that's how come you're so damn fickle," Annie snaps back. "I knew it… You haven't made any effort to stay."

"Sometimes, no action's the best response, but that doesn't mean I'm sitting still. I'm following a course by not interfering. The Army's calling me. Refusing to move out of harm's way is how I stand up to the bad guys and stop them from hurting all of you. And that's that!"

"Yo, Cashton," Jason interjects. "I think you're goin' ugly early there. So, let's order another round and try changin' the subject, if ya don't mind."

"Here, here," are the grumbles heard down the bar.

"I'm sorry if I pissed anyone off," Cashton mumbles as he slams another shot. "It's just, well, we've always been really open with each other and I'm gonna miss that a lot. Being honest beats holding a hard-ass point of view. Don't you agree? We're all pretty broad-minded and tolerant of things. Am I right, or what?"

"That's enough Cashton," Jason states. "We get it, man. You take pride in your frankness. We understand. You wanna protect your memories. That's cool. Your chance for change is here, but your half-assed, drunken push to find a happy endin' doesn't settle much. Now does it? Don't worry so, man. None of our friendships are over, regardless how hot-headed we get. Don't be so set on bringin' it all to a finish. Enjoy the fact we're more spur-of-the-moment kinda guys."

"Wow," Andro observes. "Sounds like you and my priest have been sipping the same communion wine."

"Amen to that brother," Elizabeth-Anne interjects. "And it's time for the sermon to end. We've got enough hot air in this place already… Hell, I'll even buy the next round, if Cashton and Jason just shut up."

"Here, here," is the unified response as the rumble from down the bar gets louder.

—◊—

C H A P T E R   1 8 :

DRESS RIGHT, DRESS!

IT'S MAY, 1993 in troubled Yugoslavia. Beyond the blooms and migrating birds, Belgrade's spring signals yet another sad awakening: Its world has turned upside down as the civil war heaves on and on. The only temperatures rising are those of hotheads screaming half-truths. In resigned response, more and more Slavs plug their ears from the incessant bombardment—both on and off the airwaves.

Reacting to Dragana's push for a new media campaign, Adrijan schedules a press briefing at the TV network headquarters. As the boring presentation ends, a dozen or so journalists shuffle out of the building, leaving Heath alone in the conference room, scribbling in his notebook.

"Well, Mr. Winslow, what a pleasant surprise. And why might you be here?"

"It's a free country, right? Sorry, you don't have to answer that, Adrijan. But I do have another question: What the hell's different in this drivel from the last?"

"Since you insist on misinterpreting the focus of our information efforts, I must ask for clarity with regard to your accusations."

"Adrijan, you master of misinformation, it's all about biased reporting, plain and simple. You selectively present your facts, or should I say you lie by omission? And why? To fire up emotions instead of rational responses… Right? Then you push, push, push for attitude change that will further Milošević's agenda. It's like this role's second nature to you. You're waging political warfare. Can't you see it?"

"Heath, sometimes, I swear, you should have been a drama critic. Just give me one example of what you speak."

"One? Just one? Okay, tell me why your reporters sling around pejoratives like Ustashe hordes, Vatican fascists, Mujahedin madmen, jihad crazies and Albanian terrorists? They're making racist slurs part of the lexicon, or is that your intent?

"And how many more unverified stories, presented as fact, I might ask, are you going to tell? For example, saying Bosniaks were feeding Serb children to animals in the Sarajevo zoo for Christ's sake. What the hell was that? The more you fear someone different, the easier it is to justify killing them?

"There are a dozen more I could list with ease. I know it and you know it. Adrijan, it's got to stop. This bloody war will end soon. It has too. When the instigators are judged at The Hague, they'll be hanging lots of folks out to dry as they try to save their own scrawny necks. You've got to step away from this propaganda madness, if you want to survive.

"Okay, I've said my piece. Why don't you come to the Holiday Inn sometime where the real journalists stay? You'll get an earful, as well as your ass kicked for making all of us look so bad. I don't hate you, Adrijan… I don't, but I despise the garbage you produce and the impact it's having on people all around here."

"Enough, already… Heath Winslow, the flag bearer for the Fourth Estate, has spoken. Your comments are duly noted. You can now exit, stage left!"

Shaking his head in disappointment and disbelief, Heath leaves by the side door. He soon reconnects with the U.N. observer team—his transport back to Sarajevo. Then, it's straight to the hotel lounge where Eoghan will have a cold beer waiting, he hopes.

—⁘—

A few days after the guys' drunken soiree at Barrymore's, Anita rips open the door to the Armed Forces Recruiting Station in Times Square. She storms to the front of Sergeant Steel's desk. "Cashton, you conniving, back-stabbing ass! You put Andro in the Army without telling me? And I have to find out second-hand from Jason and Karen."

"Excuse me, ma'am. Unless you lower your voice and adjust your attitude, I will be forced to move this conversation…"

"Ma'am! You condescending S-O-B. Who the hell do you think you're talking to? I'm Anita Antonucci, sergeant."

"And I'm a noncommissioned officer in the United States Army. If you can refrain from your tirade long enough, I have but three things I'd like to share, ma'am.

"One: Conversations between recruit and recruiter are privileged. It would be unethical for me to share the contents of those meetings without that person's consent.

"Two: If Mr. Babich wishes to disclose information to you, that's his choice. Although I doubt, after your hotel implosion, you should expect further contact with him.

"And three: Until you apologize for insulting and embarrassing me in front of my fellow NCOs, I have nothing further to say," the recruiter barks as he picks up his brief case, service cap and aviator shades. "Excuse me, ma'am. I have an appointment to keep. You have a great Army day."

The charismatic diva wannabe is left speechless, standing in the middle of the room. She looks about, locking eyes with the nearby Navy petty officer.

"Pretty impressive," the seaman says. "That was a Tony award-winning performance, if I say so myself. And I've seen my share of Broadway shows."

"Oh, shut up!" Anita snorts as she stomps out the door. "Just keep playing with your silly grenades and guns."

—ෲ—

Friday, Oct. 1, 1993—A crisp morning breeze snaps through the home of the Airborne, just west of Fayetteville. The pomp and ceremony surrounding Andro's basic training graduation is on full display across Fort Bragg's historic parade field.

The executive officer on the reviewing stand drones on and on about those in attendance. "… and a special welcome to Mr. Jason Banks, recipient of the Distinguished Service Medal, the highest award that can be bestowed on a Merchant Mariner. It's the equivalent of the Army's Distinguished Service Cross."

As the crowd breaks into a rousing applause, Andro's shocked to attention by the realization Jason's in the VIP section. As soon as the graduates are released, Andro rushes to where Jason's chatting with fellow attendees. "Mr. Banks, you're here. How fantastic, but why didn't you tell me you were coming?"

"Well, Andro, I didn't know for sure I could make it. And you didn't want me callin' your drill instructor, embarrassin' you in front of your buddies, did ya? Besides, look how nuts they went anyway."

"You deserve it, sir!" the brigade commander thunders as he approaches. "We're honored you joined us. You're a role model to these young Spartan warriors."

"Thank you, colonel," Jason says, shaking the officer's hand. "I'm privileged to be here. Today's soldiers are the noblest strata of our society. We should all be proud."

"Hoo-ah! Couldn't have said it better. Enjoy and welcome again. Airborne!"

Andro chuckles as the commander steps down the reception line. "Let's head to the barracks. I'll change into civvies and sign out. I have a weekend pass and I'm dying for a beer."

Andro and Jason spend the next couple days checking out the Carolina countryside. "Life, liberty and the pursuit of a scratch handicap," Jason snickers. "That's how the chamber of commerce describes this place. Makes sense. Some of the finest lookin' golf courses I've ever seen."

Sunday night, before Andro's return to post, they stop at a local watering hole. Between beers, Jason asks, "So, what's next, Andro?"

"I head across post to the Kennedy Special Warfare Center… Airborne! I'm supposed to yell that any time I mention the school or Bragg. Anyway, I'll be assigned to the 3rd Battalion and study there for the next three months. Cashton set me up for language tests and to get certified on a whole bunch of other stuff, but I'm cool with that. It all means more pay in the long run."

"Well, it should keep you out of the gin mill; that's for sure. Then you come back to New York?"

"It depends. I think I'll try for jump school. It's a three-week course right here. Then I head back north."

—⁂—

After her basic training at Fort Leonard Wood in the Missouri heartland, Denasha ships off to Augusta. She spends the next five months at Fort Gordon—a filled in Georgia swamp on the sloping banks of the Savannah—learning cutting edge skills as an information technology specialist, i.e.: how to become a camouflaged computer geek.

She soon discovers how to explain, with diplomacy, what operator error really means. *Before I knew it, I was installing and fixing all kinds of computer software and networks. I can actually make systems work. How rad is that? And jammin' with customers. Well, that just comes natural to me.*

Denasha's soon arranging password protection and system security like a seasoned conductor leading an orchestra through a symphony of bits, bytes and bandwidth.

—⚏—

Weeks later inside the Central Harlem Armory in New York City… "Corporal Rivera reporting as ordered, ma'am," Denasha says after coming to attention and snapping a salute in front of the headquarters company commander.

"At ease, corporal," Major Stellwagon states, returning the salute, "and welcome to the 369th Sustainment Brigade, home of the Harlem Hellfighters. You're training record is impressive. You were a distinguished graduate and outstanding basic trainee. Congratulations."

"Thank you, ma'am. I approached both as opportunities to excel. And I received a lot of support along the way."

"Well, how about another such opportunity? Although you're being assigned to 187th Signal in Peekskill, I've asked that you be detailed here to help with our computer hardware and software upgrade. As a matter of fact, we've just been authorized a civilian technician slot as a full time computer specialist. Are you interested?"

"Interested? I'm overwhelmed. Thank you, ma'am. That means I could live at home and work in the armory full time. Wow, that's being more of a soldier than I ever imagined I could be."

"Don't be so modest. You've earned it, corporal. Besides, it would be nice to have another woman on staff. So, discuss it with your family. Then, let me know, but soon. I need to fill the job quickly. And don't worry, you're more than qualified."

"No need to think anything over, ma'am. I'm your go-to-Soldier for computing. My instructors said America's building an information superhighway. I want to help build the Army Guard's on-ramp right here, right now."

After shaking hands, meeting the secretary and several other staff members, Denasha steps on to the balcony of the massive art deco, brick and mortar armory. She cracks a smile as tears well up, realizing she'll soon be a full-fledged cross-town bus commuter.

I've never seen the intersection of Fifth Avenue and 143rd Street look so fine. And standing at the gateway to Sugar Hill is very sweet indeed.

—⁂—

It's Friday, March 4, 1994. Andro's returned to the city. "Welcome home, Soldier-boy!" Susie-Q screeches as he steps into Barrymore's. "Have seat. Jason come soon. I get you beer. Tell me war story, now."

"Thank you, Susie. Hello, everybody!" Andro yells down the bar.

"Welcome back, dude," the bar flies reply in unison.

"Okay, as you may know, I just finished airborne training. The jump school commander let me go on a special nighttime exercise with a parachute regiment. I sat next to this lieutenant. He was looking a bit pale, so I asked him, 'Are you scared, sir?'"

"No," he replied, "but I'm a little apprehensive."

"What's the difference?" I asked.

"That means I'm scared, but with a college education."

"Now, Andro," the bartenderess chides, "That happen?"

"No, but it makes a good story, yes?"

"I say you stick to jumping out of airplane and we tell joke. Okay?"

Just then Jason steps through the entryway. "Salutations, Specialist Babich… Susie, did Andro tell you he made quite a mark down south? He graduated with honors from all his Army schools. He's already close to having more rank than me when I was in."

"Doubt it," one of the regulars quips. "You're about as rank as they come, Jason."

"Very funny, Brian. I never cease to be amazed by the respect I'm given in this place. Anyway, how the hell ya doin', young man? And what's up?"

"Another celebration soon, I hope. My Reserve commander wants to keep me on active duty until I meet the one-year residency requirement. That's just three months from now. Then, I take the naturalization exam right here in the city."

"But I thought you'd been reassigned to a unit outside Syracuse?"

"Yes, the 403rd Civil Affairs Battalion in Mattydale, but I'm attached to the headquarters on Staten Island for as long as needed to become a citizen."

"Sounds like it's a done deal… And don't worry, we'll all help you prep for the test."

"And plan big party," Susie-Q interjects. "Congratulation. You beat me, but I still happy for you."

"Cheers!" several of the patrons shout out.

As Susie steps down the bar, Ando stares into Jason's eyes. "I was helping the recruiters at a high school career day last week when I met your daughter. She's a computer technician now, working full time at the Harlem armory. How crazy is that?"

"Andro, please, keep your voice down. The folks here don't know about Denasha. Susie gets wind of the story and it'll be like firin' up the Times Square news ticker."

"I hear you, Jason, but you must meet her. Denasha is so bright and beautiful. She's an incredible woman. I didn't say anything about you, but I don't know how long I can keep that up. We are going on one of those Circle Line cruises next week. The USO is putting it on. You should come along. I can feel it. It's time you face the music."

"Music? What kind music you want, Andro?" Susie asks, returning to their end of the bar. "Enough this show tune crap. Agree?"

"Agreed!" the cynical clientele shout back in harmony.

—⚊—

A few days later, the public address system in the 369th Regiment Armory crackles to life. "Corporal Rivera, you have a guest in the reception area. Corporal Rivera to the lounge, please."

As the young soldier enters the sitting room, she encounters a tall, broad-shouldered Black man admiring the World War I photographs hung around the room.

"Hello, Denasha," he says. "I'm Jason…"

"My God, you're my father… I just know it. I can feel it. Tell me I'm right."

"That's right. I'm Jason Banks, your biological father."

"But why are you here? Who put you up to this? My mother, right? Talk to me."

"We have a mutual friend: Andro Babich. He and I sailed together from Greece some time ago. I've become his mentor and citizenship sponsor. After meetin' you at school, Andro told me you work here and how he knew it was time we met."

"I don't know what to say," Denasha swoons. Somewhat dazed by the magnitude of the encounter, she slumps into one of the Naugahyde armchairs.

Jason sits opposite her, perched forward, hands resting on his knees. "I don't either, but I can start by sayin' I'm sorry."

"No, no, no. Don't even go there. Mama told me about you years ago, after my stepfather left. I'm no longer that naïve little waif from the Barrio. And I won't be the target of anyone who wants to take advantage of me either."

"Andro said you were a kind and gentle lady, but he didn't mention your grit. You're as feisty as you are strikin'. And how is your mother, by the way?"

"She's doing well. When Antonio ran off with that tramp a while back, mama was hurt of course, but she's rebounded quite well. Margarita thinks of you and speaks of you often. And before I forget, as she'll never say, thank you for sending money over the years. With Tony's drinking and carousing, it meant the difference between having and not having food on the table."

"If I only coulda done more. I wanted to marry your mother, but…"

"I know. I know. My macho brother and cousins went gangsta on you. And without Abuela Carmen's support, who knows what might have happened to mama and me. Grandmamma was our savior. But as you know, no Rivera was ever going to marry a Black man. So, I learned to go through life bending to the whims of those around me. I did what mama wanted, what my teachers, friends and relatives expected."

"But now you've got an impressive new career."

"And a great skill."

"I'm so glad you're not resentful, Denasha."

"I was, in my teens, but mama and grandmamma painted the big picture in a way I could finally see. I'm frank about my feelings, but with the Army's help, I've learned to take responsibility for my actions."

"It feels good we can zero in on our feelings. Don't it? And not be bogged down by all kinds of other stuff."

"We're adults; aren't we? I think we should expect that of each other. Sure, I still want to know the truth, but it beats being defensive all the time."

"And I want to hear you out, young lady. Ask what you want. I like you bein' honest. And I promise to do the same. We've got so much to talk about. Beyond this fine Harlem gig, what really catches your fancy, Denasha?"

"I've always been fascinated by music, especially when it's tied to a Latin beat. Music's the heart of Puerto Rican cultural and I've studied so many different styles of dance. I love salsa, meringue, plena and bomba, but I want to learn their roots. And the Boricua art scene… It's so important to me. It's so engaging. I'm sorry. Just listen to me go on and on."

"No, don't stop. This ol' man's likin' it. I think we're connectin'. Do you feel it? I've got a friend in the theater you should meet. Anita's network could serve you well in the music and dance world. Well, I know you've gotta get back to work. Do you think it's possible a father could hug his daughter after such a long time?"

"Oh, papa, papa, papa," Denasha swoons as she plunges into Jason's arms. They fall into a deep squeeze, twisting from side to side.

"I love you… And I you," the two whisper as tears of joy trickle down both their cheeks while reveling in their extended embrace.

—◌◌◌—

It's mid-Monday morning on Staten Island's historic Fort Wadsworth. As Andro starts reviewing a new set of training manuals, his supervisor shouts, "You're wanted in the conference room."

"Come in, Specialist Babich," Lieutenant Colonel Gahly, the command executive officer states. "Please take a seat in one of the chairs along the back wall."

Six time zones to the east it's mid-afternoon in Vicenza, Italy. The commander of the 3rd Battalion, 325th Airborne Combat Team is assembling his staff.

"Sergeant Steel. Am I correct?"

"Sir, yes, sir," Cashton snaps to as he enters the secure room.

"Welcome to the Blue Falcons. I'm Captain Gramer, the unit XO. Please take a seat along the side wall."

As Brigadier General Wolf van Rijn, commander of the 353rd, enters, the exec calls the Wadsworth conference room to attention.

"At ease, but remain standing," the general says. "Specialist Babich, please step forward… By the authority vested in me, and in recognition of your outstanding academic achievements, I hereby promote you to sergeant in the United States Army."

The general then proceeds to ceremoniously rip the Velcro-held specialist patch from Andro's battle dress uniform and slap a 3-chevron insignia in its place. As he congratulates the newly noncommissioned officer, van Rijan shakes Andro's hand, slipping him a commander's coin in the process. Andro fights back a grin and renders a proud salute. The staff breaks into applause and shouts, "Hoo-ah!"

Meanwhile, in the Southern European Task Force command post, Colonel Olyn Gunhus, the 3rd Battalion commander, enters. Captain Gramer calls the room to attention.

"At ease, but remain standing for a minute," the colonel says. "Sergeant First Class Steel step forward. With the authority the Army's given me, and in recognition of your great military service, I'm proud to promote you to the rank of master sergeant in the United States Army."

Again, a chevron's ripped from the sleeve and replaced. A coin's passed and salutes rendered. Applause fills the room, followed by the group shouting, "Blue Falcons!"

"Now that I have everyone's attention," the colonel states, "We have orders to move out. They read in part:

> *The President has directed the Secretary of Defense to establish a joint task force, headquartered in Entebbe, Uganda, to sustain Operation Support Hope. The U.S. military will provide immediate relief for the refugees of the Rwandan genocide, allowing a smooth transition to full humanitarian management…*

"… blah, blah, blah, unquote. Our mission in support of this operation is to secure the area for U.N. personnel and civilian contractors. Captain Gramer will now begin the deployment briefing."

Meanwhile, back on Staten Island, General van Rijn advises his staff of pretty much the same, indicating the 403rd from upstate will deploy in support of the task force.

"Their command staff is being notified as we speak. The unit will process through Fort Dix and be airlifted out of McGuire next door. As always, the focus of our work will be on establishing and maintaining communication with civilian aid agencies and other non-governmental organizations. Colonel Gahly, you may begin the activation briefing."

—∾—

C H A P T E R   1 9 :

OUT OF DARKEST EAST AFRICA

AN AUGUST SUN showers the City of Palladio as morning rises over northern Italy's Vicenza Air Base. In the headquarters building, the 3rd Battalion executive officer is busy reviewing an almost endless set of slides prior to the battle staff's arrival.

"Captain Gramer, you asked to see me, sir?" recently promoted Master Sgt. Cashton Steel inquires.

"Yes. SecArmy wants the press to have full access during our Africa operation. With that said, we have a veteran war correspondent flying on this mission and you'll be serving as his escort."

"But captain, I've been…"

"Excuse me, Sergeant Steel," the exec interjects. "I believe you know the gentleman. He asked for you specifically."

At that moment, Heath steps into the briefing room with the unit commander. "Well, Cashton, you zebra-striped, gung-ho grunt. How in the hell are you?"

"At ease," Colonel Gunhus tells the captain and sergeant. "And for Christ's sake Steel, loosen up. At least say hello, or shake Winslow's ink-stained hand. I've been briefed on your Manhattan bar escapades… Damn good work, sergeant."

Everyone in the room lets go a sigh of relief, then glad-hand through introductions.

"So, you're covering the airlift?" Cashton asks. "I thought you were still in Bosnia."

"Back and forth on those C-130s out of Frankfurt. The *Trib* editor sent me here as soon as the story broke. Clinton says he wants to 'stop the dying' by making sure aid gets where it's needed. I'd say that's a pretty noble story. And here's the small world angle: soldiers from Andro's Civil Affairs unit in New York may hook up with us."

"That's Sergeant Babich to you, sir," Andro jokes as he steps into the room.

"Damn… If we had Jason on board, we could ask Susie to set up a round," Cashton cracks. "This is great. It's like old home week. We get to kick some ass and do some good all at the same time, while Heath writes stories and takes pictures."

"And we all get paid for it," Heath points out.

"Everyone take a seat," Captain Gramer announces. "The brief is about to begin."

"Can't wait," the colonel grumbles. "Death by PowerPoint, again. Commence fire."

Notebook entry: July 22, 1994 President Clinton announces Operation Support Hope—military to provide African refugee relief… 800,000-plus slaughtered, 2 million Hutus in camps… Americans airlift supplies to former Belgian colonies

—⁓—

It's early evening a few days later at Forward Operating Base Alpha near Goma, East Africa. Colonel Gunhus and Heath are swapping war stories at a small folding table in the far corner of the mess tent.

"Excuse me, colonel," Captain Gramer says, stepping in. "Master Sgt. Steel is taking a detail on patron. Any last-minute instructions, sir?"

"Remind that hard-charger he's a squad leader now. He's not to be on point. Steel's determined to do anything he asks his men to do and do it better. He's mission ready and I'm sure he'll do fine, but make that point."

"Yes, sir."

"Now that's a story worth telling, Winslow. It may not be sexy, but risk management, that's the key to success in this brave new world of humanitarian aid and nation building—identify, assess and control. That's what we've got to do. Make decisions that balance costs with benefits. Accept no unnecessary risk."

"I think it was T.S. Eliot who once said, 'You have to risk going too far to discover just how far you can go.'"

"You risk your poets and I'll protect my Soldiers. Goodnight, Winslow. Keep your head down and your powder dry."

Notebook entry: Winning the peace—Replace rogue regimes with responsible authority... Governance & nation-building require fewer soldiers... Can later be handed off to others... Based on BS theory by Pentagon Puzzle Palace pundits

—⁂—

Silhouettes of seven Soldiers appear and dissolve in the dessert's dim moonlight. The team darts from point to point on the outskirts of camp. They sprint through faintly lit intersections, guardedly checking mounds of trash where explosives could hide. They speak in whispers or use hand signals passed down from Sergeant Steel. Noise is limited to the sounds of swishing water canteens, soft radio beeps or a soldier's occasional trip in the road's sudden dip. The crunch of combat boots on garbage-strewn streets and gravel pathways is the only other hint of their stealthy advance.

Out of nowhere, a roving pack of dogs announces the squad's presence. Steel signals for everyone to halt in place until the barking subsides. Soon, the patrol is moving again, with the canine contingent sniffing close behind. The team's mission: Talk with the locals. Build trust and get tips that might help counter daytime attacks, or stop the bad guys from planting roadside bombs.

"So, what the hell are you doing on patrol with us?" Cashton asks Andro as they crouch near a dusty alley.

"I'm your interpreter," Andro whispers back.

"You speak French too?"

"Not so well, but it's pretty much like Italian. Just tie your hands behind your back."

"Okay, Sergeant Smart Ass, stay close. Your intel's no…"

Before Steel can finish, the night is turned into day as an explosion—phosphorus white with intensity—lights up the street. Cashton and Andro are blown against a shuttered storefront. The fireball subsides, but its impact is yet to be realized. Andro collapses on top of Cashton. He senses he's alright, but soon realizes he may be hurt. His hands and face feel like they're on fire. Andro abandons thoughts of safety as he jumps up and drags his unconscious friend into a nearby passageway, hopeful shelter from further attack.

"Cashton, Cashton… Are you okay?" There's no reaction. Blood is now oozing from a gash on Cashton's face. Andro grabs his handkerchief to use as a compress. "Medic!" he yells into the night. A corpsman is soon by their side. He cups Andro's face in his hands and starts examining him.

"No, no, not me. Sergeant Steel. He is not responding."

The medic checks Cashton's vital signs, then starts CPR. Andro joins in the coordinated rescue effort. Steel reacts to the first aid, coughing and spitting, not unlike a guy stumbling out of a seedy whisky bar.

"Lay back, sarg," Andro orders. "You've been hit, but you're going to be fine. We have your back, man and we're heading to camp, pronto."

Two more battle buddies circle around to Steel's position. "Grab that blown off door and form up tight," Andro shouts. "We can use it as a litter. Like you always say, Cashton, 'Adapt and overcome.'"

In no time, their scout leader is hoisted into place. "Ready, lift," Andro commands. "Now, quick-step toward base camp… Go!"

Andro calls for another soldier to bring the radio. "Incoming wounded," he transmits. "I-E-D attack with shrapnel wounds. Will need a doctor A-S-A-P. Do you copy?"

—◊—

Once they here the patrol's been attacked, Colonel Gunhus and Heath sprint to the medical tent where Sergeants Steel and Babich are being treated. A nurse asks them to stand fast. "I'll advise the doctor you're here." Not long after, the medical chief emerges, approaching the two men.

"Doc, this is Mr. Winslow with the *Herald Tribune*. He's also a close friend of both your patients. How are they doing?"

"Well, commander, the younger Soldier has second-degree burns to his face and hands," Dr. Besich explains. "Sergeant Steel didn't fare as well. He was hit hard with a lot of debris. The damage to his right eye, ear and arm is significant. Once he's stabilized, we'll medevac him to Landstuhl for further evaluation."

The nurse escorts the colonel into the treatment area.

"This is an impressive setup Dr. B… Tell me about it," Heath says.

"The first one of these portables was fielded in '92, I think. We can be up and running in an hour. Or, we can break down and move in less than two… We even have an operating room."

"Amazing. You have state-of-the-art resources with a worldwide reach. I'd like to be part of Sergeant Steel's medevac, if that's possible? I want to tell the whole treatment story from here to Germany through the patient's eyes."

"If there's space available and the PAO says okay, I don't know why we can't make that happen."

"But Heath," the colonel interjects, stepping back in the room. "You just got here."

"This whole hospital in a box thing is intriguing. Besides, it's just a quick trip to Frankfurt. I'll catch the next flight back. You don't expect to win all the hearts and minds in the Horn of Africa without me, now do you?"

"Alright, Winslow, we'll start ginnin' up the paperwork."

Just then, Andro steps out of the treatment room, escorted by a corpsman.

"Damn, son," Heath chides Andro, "You've got to cut back on time around the pool."

"Very funny, but don't tell Baba Sofija. She would rub me down with mustard and camphor cream for a week… How is Sergeant Steel, doctor? Can I see him, please?"

"He's resting now, son. I gave him a sedative. Maybe in the morning, before we transport him."

"Come on, Andro," Heath says, taking the young soldier's arm. "Let's get you to a bunk so you can rest. Dr. Besich is plenty busy and I can fill in the blanks."

"I'm proud of you, Soldier," Colonel Gunhus says. "You did right by Sergeant Steel and your battle buddies. You're a natural leader—a person of character with presence and intellect. And yes, Winslow, you can quote me on that."

—〰—

Early the following morning, Heath sips coffee with the medical team's first sergeant. "Here's your travel orders. You understand this ain't no joy ride, Mr. Winslow?"

"Roger that, Sergeant Crocker. Do you know what bird we're flying and who's holding the stick?"

"Should be a Blackhawk belongin' to the Fightin' Knights of 5th Battalion out of Katterbach. Those dudes from Deutschland know their stuff. Once you land in Entebbe, the blue suiters take over and fly ya'll to Ramstein."

"Got it. Thanks. And what do we fly out of Africa?"

"What I hear, to make room for Steel, they've kicked some State Department big wig off a C-21. It's an Air Force Learjet. That oughta piss off the pin-strippers."

The Blackhawk crew chief sticks his head in the door. "Mr. Winslow, you ready? The patient's on board and the pilot wants to pull chocks."

"I'm right behind you, chief. Thanks, sarg."

"Hoo-ah!" the first shirt barks.

—◊◊◊—

October's bright blue sky welcomes a giant C-5 Galaxy as it makes a majestic final approach to Stewart Field just outside Newburgh. The 28 tires supporting its landing gear screech out the plane's arrival at the upstate New York Air National Guard base.

Andro and his team gather belongings as the aircraft's huge nose and aft doors swing open to disgorge vehicle after vehicle and pallet after pallet of Army stuff. The battalion's sergeant major is standing on the tarmac. He yells for everyone to fall in on him. Once assembled, they're called to attention.

"First and second squads stow your gear under that bus and board right away," the senior enlistee shouts as he points toward the hanger bay. "Three and four to the next. We'll debrief at the armory. Welcome home and dismissed. Now, move out. Hoo-ah!"

Andro slumps into a seat and gazes out the window at the orchestrated madness swarming over the flight line. His thoughts drift back to that squalid little town outside Kigali. The name of the Rwanda village criss-crossed with red dirt streets escapes him, but not the memory of good works done there.

—⟋⟍—

Flash back to Andro and two other Civil Affairs Soldiers looking like young American tourists in their universal uniforms of khaki pants, t-shirts and baseball caps. Instead of cameras and a sightseeing map, or even a Soldier's weapon, they're armed with shovels, pipe fittings and a tool box. They stop at a tea vendor's rickety wooden table, sip chai and eat some fried dough. It's a simple celebration for a job well done. They're but one of several teams the Army sprinkled across the region to paint clinics, refurbish schools, fix phone lines and more.

Andro's completed project means women and children will no longer need hike to the town's single spigot to fill buckets and jugs. Instead, small water lines have been laid down most every village street. The three chuckle remembering when the women in town grew impatient with the pace displayed by male workers. So, they banded together and finished digging the trenches themselves.

Back in the present, Andro shakes his head realizing the only trenches being dug across the former Yugoslavia are for the countless war dead piling up. *How long before I go home? How long before the madness ends and Bosnia can be beautiful again?*

—⟋⟍—

It's a frigid mid-January morning in the Borough of Queens, complete with blustering arctic winds, plummeting thermometers and snow swirling everywhere. Warm and sheltered in his Astoria flat, Andro hesitates opening an envelope addressed by the INS. Soon, tears are plopping on the computer-generated form letter as he reads its content over and over again.

> *...are hereby notified to appear for a Naturaliza-*
> *tion Oath Ceremony on Monday, Feb. 20, 1995 at*
> *Federal Hall, 26 Wall Street, Manhattan, New York*
> *no later than 1 p.m. You must bring the following*
> *documents with you...*

"Alecia! Daphne! Melinda!" Andro yells to his curvaceous cousins as he bounds down the hallway stairs. "I am about to be a real American, just like you."

The sisters throw the door open to Andro's announcement. They embrace and start jump-dancing through the kitchen to the living room where Papa Papadopoulos has already grabbed the ouzo and several glasses.

"Let's call Uncle Abeiron with the news," Melinda says as she punches an endless series of numbers into the phone. It's soon emitting a gurgling ring tone. "Alcina? It's Melinda in New York... Just a moment." She pushes the phone into Andro's hand.

"Hello, Alcina. It's your American cousin. Yes, they will make me a citizen next month, but how are you? How is Greece? Have you heard from my father, Uncle Fanjo or Baba Sofija?"

"Staying in touch is hard, Andro, but we try. And the priests are always helping. No letter from your dad or brother, but Father Malinko has heard they're well. Fanjo, Florica and the children are fine. Mara is okay, too. Baba Sofija's resting in Konjic, but the war goes on. Some say it will end soon. They say your President Clinton wants to bring peace to Bosnia. So, how are you? Will you run for mayor of New York soon?"

"I must get my Social Security card first. Okay, this must be expensive. So, I will hang up. Give my love to everyone and I promise to write soon… Ciao."

"Thank you, thank you, thank you," Andro says kissing the cheeks of the Papadopoulos clan. "I must call Jason, then pen a letter home. Put February 20th on your calendar. I so want you to be there. If only Baba Sofija could join us, too."

—❧—

A United Nations of people stream toward Federal Hall, navigating a labyrinth of cobblestone paths to converge on Wall Street. Many pause to gaze at the larger-than-life bronze statue of George Washington, then continue up the marble steps, past the massive Doric columns, to enter the site of America's first capitol.

Andro, with Jason by his side, steps into the Pantheon-like rotunda to hear the refrains of a wind ensemble floating through the hall. He's directed to the sign-in table while the group plays *Over the Hills and Far Away*. Andro's reluctant to release his green card, but the INS official assures him he'll be receiving a permanent certificate soon.

The chamber is packed with people of all ages, colors, shapes, sizes and dress. They're flipping through programs and shaking small American flags placed earlier on every folding chair. The gathering is trumpeted to attention by the echoing harmony of a patriotic fanfare. The musical flourish is followed by a distinctive, yet silken, baritone voice stating, "Ladies and gentlemen, please rise for the entry of our distinguished guests and remain standing for the posting of the Colors."

"That's Yankee's announcer Bob Sheppard, right?" Andro whispers to Jason who winks back a confirmation.

A parade of dignitaries, including General van Rijn and U.S. Circuit Court Judge Donald Bloom, step on stage and take their places.

"That's the judge I told you about from the gala," Andro whispers.

"He's the fox sent to guard the hen house," Jason jokes.

"And the general is my commander at Fort Wadsworth."

"At least we have one honest man standing watch."

The official party's entrance is followed by the click of boot heels on marble. The Veteran Corps of Artillery Color Guard, in Army parade dress uniforms, curia 1812, marches forward, shoulder to shoulder, hoisting flags of the city, New York State, the Army and the Nation. They're resplendent in dark blue, close-fitting jackets trimmed in gold braid with tight white trousers and Napoleonic headgear. Whispers of admiration and approval ripple through the crowd.

After welcoming remarks by several on the dais, Judge Bloom steps forward to swear in more than 500 new Americans from almost 80 countries around the globe. He asks the new voters to join him in the *Pledge of Allegiance* and singing of *The Star Spangled Banner* as lead by the reigning Miss USO.

As soon as the anthem's sung, the crowd bursts into cheers, waiving their flags with abandon while hugging and kissing everyone nearby. Andro and Jason slap double "high fives" and shout "Hooah!" in unison. From the balcony, the Boys Choir of Harlem bursts into a joyous rendition of *This is My Country*. As the jubilation subsides, General van Rijn steps to the podium.

"Congratulations, everyone… As commander of the 353rd Civil Affairs Command on Staten Island, it is my honor to call forward one of our new citizens for special recognition. Army Reserve Sergeant Andro Babich report to the stage."

"What the hell did you do now?" Jason jokes.

"I don't know, but this is not the place to disobey a direct order," Andro says as he steps forward.

"I am humbled," van Rijn says, "not only to be with all of you today at this, the very site of Washington's inauguration, but to recognize a great American who now defends our very right to assemble in such places. Captain…"

"Attention to orders," the captain states. Members of the dais rise, followed by the audience. The award citation is read and a Bronze Star is presented to Andro.

"Airborne!" the general yells after pinning the medal on Andro's uniform, saluting and shaking his hand. "You have to yell that if you knowingly jump out of perfectly good aircraft." The audience responds with a rousing applause and much more flag waving.

As the general steps back and Andro prepares to leave the stage, Mayor Giuliani gestures toward the podium, encouraging the newly-minted American to say a few words. Andro's dumbfounded. He looks across a chamber filled with jubilant attendees, musters his courage, then clears his throat.

"Thank you and I salute you, all of you. What can I say? We are now U.S. citizens. Whatever country you came from, your allegiance to that place is gone… And we are not hyphenated Americans. I am not Bosnian-American. You are not Vietnamese-American, Mexican-American or African-American. We are simply Americans. We are united and we are now one."

For a third time, there's a spontaneous roar, applause and waving of flags. It's a blissful conclusion to an historic day.

—⁓—

A boisterous and inebriated version of *For He's a Jolly Good Fellow* reverberates from Barrymore's small dining room as Andro and Jason enter the bar. "Congratulation, super sergeant!" Susie-Q squeals as she plants a big wet kiss square on Andro's lips. The bar crowd roars, laughs and applauds with gusto. "I would be downtown, but Jason no call me girlfriend, so I cannot go."

"You wouldn't have liked it. It was so stuffy there. This is much more special. Thank you Ms. Susie for doing so much. So many people and the signs… How cool."

"You go away. I just pour a few more beer, that all."

About then, Elizabeth-Ann yells from behind the bar, "Andro! Phone call."

Surprised, he takes the handset and shouts "Hello!" over the din of the crowd.

"Congratulations, stud."

"Cashton… Thank you. How fantastic that you called."

"Well, I'd rather be there with ya'll, but the therapist has me workin' out until I almost pass out."

"So, how's it going? And when can we come see you?"

"Slow, but sure. My mom's here now. She stays at the Fisher House for free, so that helps. You guys can visit any time."

"Jason is back in town for a while. And I want to see my new nation's capital. So, we'll be down soon."

"Hey, I hear the noise. Time you get back to your party. Say hello to everyone for me. And congrats again, Andro."

"Thanks, Cashton. I couldn't have gotten here without you. I mean that. Get better and we'll see you soon."

As Andro passes the phone back, Heath steps through the saloon door. "What does a guy have to do for a beer around here?"

"You're late, Mr. Winslow… Elizabeth-Ann, pull this gentleman a beer, please."

"I was finishing an interview with the mayor and your commander, if you must know. I won't put in print what I uncovered. This can still be a good news story for Sunday's magazine. First, a beer. Zivjeli!"

"And cheers to you, sir, but I didn't know you were at the ceremony."

"Nor should you have. Today's all about you, Andro. I'm just the reporter. I was in the press pool, getting to write good news for a change. Now, let's get back to your party. We'll talk more later."

"It's all still a blur," Andro reflects as he throws his arm around Heath's shoulder and escorts him toward the reception area. "But I feel like I'm getting to the heart of things. You and Father Cerkez were right: Without substance, there is no meaning."

"Whoa, Andro, don't dive into the deep end of that drunken swimming hole… not today. Seriously, you're a real self-starter, kid. Your heart's in the hunt to find out what to do. That's great and more power to you, but don't ever forget what the old Roman, Cicero, once said: 'The pursuit, even of the best things, ought to be calm and tranquil.' Well, looks like we need more beer," Heath notices as he steps back toward the bar. "And again, welcome to America. I lift my glass to toast your golden hour."

"Truly inspiring," Elizabeth-Ann says with a scoff, as she pulls a couple drafts. "What's Ms. Liberty charging for a political license nowadays?"

"No charge. It's not unlike a trip to the loo. Just make sure you finish all the necessary paperwork."

—⁂—

C H A P T E R   2 0 :

HOW THINGS CHANGE

"Adrijan!" Dragana yells over the phone from her clapboard datja outside Belgrade. "Did you read the article in today's *Tribune* by that Winslow hack? He's trying to turn that Babich brat into some kind of Bosnian Wunderkind—a modern-day Mark Anthony—for Pete's sake. But hey, the kid ran just when the fighting started, right? Anyway, I thought you had that bleeding-heart journalist under control? How much more of this Croat superman garbage am I going to see in print? You need to tell the rest of the story once and for all!"

"When did you buy the *International Herald Tribune*?" Adrian demands. "And when did you get a seat on the *New York Times* editorial board? Heath Winslow's not on our payroll. Neither you nor I have any control over what he writes, nor what they print."

"Then find a way to discredit him. This has got to stop."

"Maybe it's time you do a reality check, Dragana. Try getting beyond your blind views for once. Try to understand what's happening in the real world. You're more concerned with the way things appear than what is. Lately, you seem to be caught off-guard by any little thing that's not just what you think it should be."

"Thank you, Sigmund Freud. So, Adrian, you've finally grown a pair. Maybe we need to steer you in the right direction."

"Enough with the castration jokes and obtuse threats, Dragana. You're so damn proud of how you manipulate people. God forbid you'd ever get your own hands dirty. Who do you think you are? Answer me that simple question. Will you, please?"

"Are you done? You sniveling, pudgy prick… If I were you, I'd find a box and start clearing your office."

"Consider it done, Comrade Kowalchuk. Good luck finding another puppet whose strings you can pluck so easily."

"Settle down, Adrijan. You're not going anywhere. You know I have to blow off steam to stay in the game. I'll be in your office tomorrow. We'll talk strategy then. So, be ready." Dragana insists as she slams the receiver down. She then storms out of the house to stomp around in the snow.

—m—

Andro and Jason rush New York's Penn Station to catch Amtrak's 185 Northeast Regional bound for Washington. Both have large cups of coffee in hand, as well as bagels and cream cheese in their bags.

"The big board says Track 9," Andro notes.

"All aboard!" Jason mimics as they ride the escalator down to the platform, board the train and ready for a ride on the rails to the Nation's capital. "This sure beats five hours on a bus sittin' next to a 300-pound gorilla who hasn't bathed in a month."

"Yes, the train is nice, but seeing Cashton is what I'm looking forward to."

As passengers scurry to grab vacant seats, Jason makes an observation. "Well, you certainly seem at peace with yourself lately, young man, almost in a state of bliss."

"It's strange. I feel like I'm in heaven, beyond the strife, so to speak. Maybe it's time I take a little rest and reflect. Is it wrong, Jason, to revel for a moment in what one has accomplished?"

"Hell no, man. You've had your share of excitement—gettin' your green card, joinin' the Army, servin' in Africa and becomin' a citizen. I'd say you've earned a little R&R. But then what? What's next?"

"That's the question. I feel like I'm on an endless quest. It started before I met you. And now, it's as if I might actually reach my goal, but I'm at a loss to put it all in words. Do you think I've found my holy grail?"

"Too deep for me, Lancelot, but I'd say a good job with a chance to grow might be a bit more to the point. And with that said, I've got a friend in D.C. I want ya to meet."

"Great… Who is it? What's the business? What's it all about?"

"First things first, Andro. We hook up with Cashton. Maybe we take a stroll on the Mall. Then it's off to the Ol' Ebbitt for a cool one. That's where we can talk about the future."

The train makes an on-time arrival in Washington. Andro and Jason grab duffle bags from the overhead, step on to the platform, then stroll inside the colossal turn-of-the-century Beaux Arts masterpiece that is Union Station.

"Let's throw our stuff in one of those lockers. The Metro's right this way. We take the Red Line to Takoma and it's just a few blocks walk to Walter Reed."

"Lead on McDuff. You are the guide extraordinaire."

—◈—

With Jason's encouragement, Anita arranges a meeting with Denasha at the El Museo del Barrio. As she emerges from the subway, a stiff March breeze puffs down 104th Street to greet her. Taking firm strides against the wind, Anita soon reaches the museum's sparkling new glass façade. She quickly steps in, leaving the cold to play sentry outside.

"Anita? I recognize the tweed coat and gray scarf you mentioned."

"Denasha? It's great to meet you. Jason has told me so much. How about we find a hot cocoa and continue the conversation?"

"Right this way… Here's your pass. I volunteer here. So, today you're my guest."

"Thank you. Jason tells me you're fascinated by the Latino arts."

"Yes. I've studied many different styles. With the curator's help, I'm now researching Boricua dance, our Taino, Spanish and West African roots—all of it."

"That's fantastic, Denasha, but what are you doing with everything you've found?"

"Well, the arts are important to our island's culture. And they're one of the best ways to understand our mixed heritage. Besides, they're great entertainment."

"Now, I think we're getting somewhere. Have you thought of directing a show?"

"Si, Anita… I even have a title: *Musica Folklorico de Baile*, the music of Puerto Rico, of course."

"Jason says you're a gifted seamstress as well, with an eye for costume design. Not to brag, but I have quite a network of contacts in the city. As my friends have risen in their jobs, I've stayed in touch. I often call on them for support."

The women's excitement levels soar to the ceiling of the multi-story atrium. Anita pulls out a legal pad and pen while Denasha throws back the flap on a well-worn satchel stuffed with notes, sketches, sheet music and a mound of other creative tidbits. They continue their banter for hours as the chocolate changes to coffee, then tea.

Through talk, laughter and an excess of hand gestures, Anita and Denasha lay the foundation for a special union. It's clear neither wants to waste any more time living alone in a city of eight million. It's also clear that each, in her own way, needs a refuge… a sense of belonging somewhere.

"You're a Cancer, aren't you?" Anita asks.

"Si. And I sense you're a Leo, right?

"Correcto mundo. I knew it. You have that driving desire to feel safe all the time. And Leo's like me are just born to, well, to be fortunate. What a team we shall make. Okay, so most Cancers are a bundle of contradictions, but I can tell, Denasha, there's a softness deep inside you. It's that thing that makes you someone very special."

"Thanks, Anita, but do you think we can do this?"

"With lots of positive-thinking and even more sweat, I'm sure of it. Together, we'll be unstoppable."

"What a fantastic first meeting this has been," Denasha notes. "I can't wait to tell Jason. I hope we don't scare him too much with all of this."

"He may find our sisterhood a bit frightening, but I suspect he saw it coming all along."

———※———

Andro and Jason stroll westward from the Washington Metro to the Walter Reed medical center entrance. "My God, I had no idea this place was so huge," Andro gasps.

The two check in at the reception desk. They're told Cashton's recuperating on the seventh floor. The lift stops at three where several patients in light blue hospital gowns are waiting to board. Cashton and his mother are among them.

"Jason, Andro!" a wheelchair patient sporting an eye patch, his right arm in a cast, shouts. "Step out here."

"Cashton, that you in those jammies?" Jason asks. "What's the matter? You lost?"

"No, smart ass."

Cashton's mother quickly slaps his good arm and chides, "Watch your mouth."

"No problem, ma'am. We're more than use to it by now."

"Thanks, Andro… The cafeteria's on this floor. We just ate. Are you guys hungry? No? Okay. It's such a fine day, let's sit in the courtyard. Mama likes it better, too."

"No, no, son. I'm going to catch the shuttle back to the Fisher House. You boys must have a lot to talk about. So, go ahead."

"Is she alright?" Andro whispers with genuine concern.

"They take care of her every possible concern. And don't worry; she's learned to milk it for all it's worth."

"I heard that and plead guilty."

—⁕—

Andro, Cashton and Jason spend the afternoon reminiscing in the hospital quadrangle as the sun blankets their early spring day, further warming this long-overdue reunion.

"Well, I gotta say, you're in a hell of a lot better spirit than I'd ever expected."

"Please, Jason," Andro interjects. "The man has been through hell. Take it easy."

"No, it's okay. A near-death experience has quite an impact on you. Trust me. Sure, I had plenty of baggage in my rucksack when I got here—my fair share of flashbacks, nightmares and the like. The whole time, my brain was trying to sort it all out. Man, I was one irritable bastard to be around then."

"Wow, Cashton," Andro says, "That's a lot to work through. How did you do it so quickly?"

"It was a group effort. I had the hospital team, chaplain and especially my mom. What a rock she is. She went through the same hell when dad was killed in Vietnam. Yes, she's a proud Chickasaw, but she's a real '60s hippy at heart."

"Well," Jason notes, "I'd say she's quite the medicine woman, even for someone as bullheaded as you."

"Okay," Andro says. "So, what's next?"

"It's pretty obvious I'm not gonna be fightin' bad guys any time soon. So, mom and I had a long talk. She says I'm needed back home.

The council wants me to liaison with the Oklahoma Guard. To work on tribal relations, partnerships and stuff. Anyway, that's what their letter said."

"I'd say that dream catcher your grandmother made is still working. It must be a sign. You and your mother are blessed with good luck and harmony."

"On that cosmic note, I need to find the head," Jason quips.

"Inside, just to the right," Cashton states as he gestures toward a pea-green door on the far side of the quadrangle. As Jason strolls off, Cashton grabs Andro's arm. "I'm glad we have a moment. There's something I need to tell you."

"What is it, man?"

"You've been a great battle buddy, Andro. The night of the bombing, you had my back. Once the fur started flyin', you put your life on the line for me and…"

"Of course, but you would have done the same."

"Please, pardner, let me finish. You guys risked it all that night. You saved my life. Thank you, Ando, for being there. I don't know what else to say but thank you."

"There is nothing else to say. It's what comrades do. Now, let's find the strength to win this battle. We need to get you out of this medical foxhole and back home where you can fight the new fight."

"So, what you ladies gabbin' about now?" Jason asks upon his return.

"How they'll let most anyone become an American nowadays," Cashton jokes.

"It's your fault… You are the one who made me a Green Card Soldier in the first place."

Emerging from the McPherson Square Metro stop, Andro shouts, "Jason, look. It's the White House!"

"Yup, 1600 Pennsylvania Avenue, my man. We're headin' to a bar close by."

As Andro and Jason step through a neo-classical façade, they're engulfed by 140-year-old mahogany and velvet booths lit by flickering gas lamps. They step up to an ornate bar set in marble, brass and beveled glass.

"Welcome to The Old Ebbitt Grill," Joey the bartender beams while greeting the intrepid visitors. "What'll it be, gents?"

"Maker's Mark straight up," Jason replies. "A gin and tonic for him. And a dozen oysters, barman's choice. Thanks."

"Very good, sir."

"Jason, this place is incredible. It's just oozing with history."

"If these walls could talk. The Ebbitt was a hangout for Grant, Harding and Teddy Roosevelt, to name a few. It's still a place where folks come to be seen, but now it's politicos, journalists and theater trash."

"I can see Heath belly up to this bar. Too bad Cashton couldn't join us."

"I think we talked all the steam out of him. Bottom line: He's doin' great and he's got a plan of attack all laid out."

A silver tray, covered with an assortment of oysters on a bed of crushed ice and rock salt, arrives with a flourish. "Bon appétit," Joey states and the gluttony begins.

After the bivalve mollusks are devoured, a dapper man in his mid-50s, wearing a wool three-piece, approaches the end of the bar. "Any port in a storm, eh, sailor?"

"Mr. B, how ya doin', mate? Pint o' Bass Ale for the suit, if ya don't mind, Joey. Have a seat, my man. Andro, this is Mr. Douglas Breen, PR honcho with the U.S. Agency for International Development. They do the same things you do in the Army, only they get paid a lot more and dress real fancy like."

"It's a pleasure, Mr. Breen. Andro Babich at your service."

"Good to meet you, Andro. Call me Doug. Jason's been telling me great things about you. So, let me cut to the chase. President Clinton will soon have the Dayton Accord worked out. Then, USAID will step in. As part of the peace, we'll be doing a big push to revitalize the news media in the old Yugoslavia. You interested in jumping on board?"

"Thank you, Doug, but we've just met and I fear your beer may be getting warm."

"I like your grasp of the obvious, young man, but I'm serious as a heartbeat. Jason says you're from Bosnia. You speak half-a-dozen languages, just became a U.S. citizen and have an Army security clearance. You're a Civil Service recruiter's dream."

"Thank you again, Doug, but what do you see me doing?"

"I read the *Tribune* article about your African escapades. Congrats… In the Balkans, we'll launch a two-pronged drive, one focused on professional media standards, and the second on nurturing news start-ups. Sound like something you'd be interested in?"

"Absolutely, Doug, but…"

"No buts about it, Andro. Jason, have this young man hook up with our resource folks in the morning. I'll make sure they're ready for him. By the time we get his paperwork done, the war will be over and the peace treaty signed." Completing his narrative, Doug grabs the pint of Bass and chugs about half of it.

"Very good, then. Sorry, but I have to run. I'm off on another mission of shameless self-promotion. Jason, we'll catch up soon. Andro, great to meet you and welcome aboard." As quickly as Doug appeared, he's pushing his way through the revolving front door and stepping off toward the Treasury Building.

"My God, Jason, what just happened?"

"Well, sounds to me, Andro, like you had a pretty good job interview. So, you're buyin' the next round, right? Set 'em up Joey and don't forget yourself this time."

"Thank you, sir. And again, welcome to The Old Ebbitt."

—⁘—

Dragana's housemaid hobbles down the datja's snow-covered porch steps, waiving a tattered kitchen towel in Mara's direction, trying to signal the false Gypsy to stop. "No, no," the charwoman sighs as she staggers up to Mara, grabbing her arms for support. "The She-Devil, she's mad this morning. I fear a trap has been set. Please go back. I can't have bad things happen here. This is my house of peace."

"Katya, settle down, please. What makes you say these things?"

"She was screaming on the phone, 'Mirela this' and 'Mirela that.' Then she's yelling about a woman named Mara. She goes crazy, then hangs up. Dragana is in one of her dream sessions now. I'm to wake her when you arrive, but it's not right. I know it's not right. I can feel it. You must go. Please go, but bless me first, Princess of the Ashkali. It cannot hurt."

Mara places her hands on the old woman's scarf-covered head and murmurs, "May the blessing of light be on you. And may the light shine out of your eyes like a candle set in the window, bidding wanderers to come in from the storm."

"Thank you and bless you, too," Katya sighs, squeezing Mara bejeweled hands.

"Back to the house now, before we're discovered. And thank you, Katya, for everything. I have words in mind for Dragana as well. Mark this curse: In the hour of her greatest success, may she sow the seeds of her destruction." That said, Mara swirls a black silken cape above her head, spins and strides away.

—⁘—

It's a clear, crisp mid-December morning in Paris. A procession of black limousines streams through the monumental gate of le Palais de l'Élysée, delivering passengers to the fortress' majestic courtyard. Massive windowless walls stand as stoic sentries, guarding the gush of dignitaries entering the residence of le Président de la République Française.

Heath adjusts the lanyard on his press pass, then joins the gallery in the square. Noticing a fellow curmudgeon, he shouts, "Bon jour, Monsieur DePaul. Ça va?"

"Very well. Thank you for asking, Mr. Winslow," the somewhat pompous political reporter for *Le Monde* replies with an exaggerated British accent. "And how is the world treating you this final month of 1995?"

"Like you, freezing my ass off waiting for the Balkan belligerents to agree peace is at hand."

"Exactement… Come, avec moi. We will find a hot coffee and warm room where we can wait. This is France. Everyone hurries to be late."

Inside a palace reception chamber, Heath and his French counterpart cup large mugs of café au lait, both to warm their hands and to savor. "Good to see you again, André. So, are we really covering something historic today?"

"I fear only time will tell. Although your president may have hailed this agreement from the Rose Garden, I think the quick scribbles last month in Dayton tell much more about how fragile this peace may be."

"Point well taken, but ending years of terror and bloodletting… Well, that can't be a bad thing."

"Certainement. I agree. It was Europe's worst hour since World War II."

"I just know too many Slavs who are tired of dodging bullets, digging graves in snow drifts and screaming for help to a world that will not hear."

"Oui. And just underneath all of today's haughty self-congratulation is the knowledge there are still too many questions left unanswered."

"Okay, André, I guess it's time we take our cynical selves into the ceremony. We shoot the shots, write a review, drink a little cheap champagne and swallow our journalistic pride one more time."

"That's what I like about you, Heath… You have not lost your basic, distrustful nature."

"Where cynical means skeptical, of course."

"Ah, once again, monsieur, I get to see you hoisted on your own petard. Santé!

"And cheers to you, André—complete with your vision of fire crackers up my ass."

> Notebook entry: General Framework Agreement for
> Peace in Bosnia & Herzegovina—known as the Dayton
> Accords or Paris Protocol… Peace pact reached at
> Wright-Patterson AFB, Ohio… Formally ends 3½ year
> Balkan war

—⁐—

The engines on an Air Force C-141 Starlifter whistle in the distance as the cargo plane makes its final approach to the Međunarodnog aerodrome, Sarajevo's international airport.

A unique reception party, each member holding a small American flag, has assembled behind the chain-link fence near the control tower's base, eager for Andro's arrival. Uncle Franjo and Aunt Florica hoist son Halim and daughter Amra on their shoulders for a panoramic view. Cousins Chapeka and Suzana jump up and down with excitement. And childhood sweetheart Mara holds high a sign in Croat and English proclaiming *Dobrodo sli ku'ci… Welcome home.* As the newly-minted American deplanes, his family ensemble bursts into screams of joy, waiving their tiny pennants with abandon. Andro runs to the fence where a security guard unlocks the gate, letting him pass. The Babich clan falls into a heap of hugs, kisses and tears. "Welcome, Andro," Franjo says. "It's hard to believe you're home."

"I know. I know… And God bless us, everyone."

"I talked with your supervisor. You're coming with us tonight. I'll bring you to work in the morning. But now, we go home to eat, drink and catch up on all those stories you haven't told."

"Mara, it's so good to see you safe and sound," Andro whispers as he pulls her close.

"Come, get in the van. As Allah would say, let's mix people with good attitudes. Welcome home, Andro… Welcome home."

—⚏—

Adrijan steps into the reception area of the TV network's Belgrade headquarters. "Mr. Babich, I'm Adrijan Ackov, the network manager. Pleased to meet you."

"Yes, I am sure, Mr. Ackov. I wish I could say the same to the man who persecuted my grandmother in the press, broadcast bold-faced lies about savagery in Sarajevo and insulted the Holy Roman Church in the name of nationalism. Ah, but I digress.

"I am not here to discuss your propaganda campaigns, or other possible war crimes. That we leave for judges at The Hague. I am here to lay out the way ahead. How we will unite in promoting democracy to the people of this divisive land. Do I have your attention? Good.

"Initially, I will be spending time with your production staff, brainstorming ideas for a range of new programs, to counter the negatives spewed these last few years. Our intent: Create news that's consistent, objective and balanced.

"I am confident we can be successful, if we focus on points in the USAID proposal. Let me highlight some of them for you: Create outlets that are a real option to the state-run propaganda machine. Train journalists and raise standards, thus helping ensure the free flow of information. Help listeners relearn what news should be.

"Yes, I think that is pretty much it. Any questions? No? Good. I look forward to working with your staff on this dynamic experiment. Yes, Adrijan, it should be one hell of a creative ride. And with that, I will say good day."

Andro places the briefing papers in a folder and hands them to the dumbfounded bureaucrat, standing in a silent daze behind his stylish teakwood desk. Andro snaps closed his attaché, grabs his Loden coat and stares at Adrijan. "I believe it was Duško Radović, the young Serb dissident, who said, 'If you can't figure your way out of a situation, change the situation.' That might be something to contemplate, sir."

As Andro exits, Adrijan slumps in his leather high-back chair, pours a healthy shot of scotch, then places his hand on his chest, mumbling, "Did you hear that, Elizabeth? I'm comin' to join you, honey. It's the big one." Adrijan's quoting a common refrain by comedian and '60s TV star Red Foxx, but nobody's laughing this time.

"Sonja!" Adrijan yells to his secretary. "Get Dragana on the line. It's time she hears that Patton's on the march."

—⟋⟍—

CHAPTER 21:

DRAPED IN BLACK LACE

FRIDAY, JAN. 12, 1996 fades to sunset at the Harlem armory. The building's unusually quiet. Many of the Army Guard employees left early to get a jump on the holiday weekend. Denasha pushes back from her latest computer project to stroll along the second story catwalk. Stepping into the company commander's reception area, she asks, "You wanted to see me, ma'am?"

"Yes, Denasha," Major Stellwagon responds. "Let's step into my office." The tall, slender, self-assured commander closes the door behind them. She perches on the edge of an over-stuffed lounge chair and gestures for Denasha to sit opposite her.

"First off, you're not in any kind of trouble. In fact, it's pretty much the opposite. I'm impressed—as are many others in the brigade—with your performance. At the same time, I'm sensing there are a couple folks showing a strong jealous streak. I've heard rumors you're being harassed. Are they true?"

"I'm glad people like my work, ma'am, but I'd rather not say any more."

"Don't be shy. You're the new kid on the block. It's easy to become a target, but there's no reason you should be mistreated by selfish or greedy people who refuse to be part of our team. Trust me, Denasha, I want to lend a hand, be a confidence builder, but I can't help you, if you won't help yourself. You can't just wait until someone comes along to rescue you. Sharks don't give a damn about the gold fish swimming nearby."

"I appreciate your concern, major, but I'm sure any misunderstanding will pass."

"Trust me, Denasha, by doing what everyone else wants all the time, you'll never realize your full potential. I know. I've been there and I don't want to see you waste time wandering the same path. I want to be your mentor, if you're open to that. This is a great organization, but there are still plenty of glass ceilings you and I, as strong women, must break through. I don't want to take the journey alone, nor do I want to watch you struggle."

"Thank you, ma'am. I'm flattered by your offer, but that's a lot to process. So, if I could have some time to think on it… say, this weekend? I should be back with an answer first thing Tuesday."

"That's fair. That's all I can ask, but don't just go through the motions while dreaming something better might come along. If you do, you may have a long wait, not unlike me."

—⚏—

As thumb-sized snowflakes flutter to the ground thousands of miles to the east, Andro and Mara sit starring at the fireplace in Uncle Franjo's suburban Sarajevo home. "I'm going to see Baba Sofija in Konjic tomorrow. I want you to join me," Andro says.

"I can go to the sanatorium, but I can't go to my home. There are too many ghosts inside those walls."

"I understand, Mara, really, I do. That's why I'll ask grandmamma if you can take her home, stay with her and care for her until you're both strong again."

"That I can do, Andro. And I think it's a good plan. I can be there when our fathers and brothers come home."

"Besides, I don't feel good about that scare you went through in Belgrade. Getting you out of Sarajevo is the right move. Those hooligans don't know where my special Gypsy gal is from, do they?"

"I don't think so. My cover's been I'm living in a Roma village. I came there from Kosovo. We've tried to keep Franjo, Florica and the children safe with that story too."

"Good… Also, my cousin Alcina will be arriving soon from Greece. She's quite the environmentalist, fighting to save marine life in Athens and all that. Their ministry hired her to do some survey work here. She's to find out if the fishing's been hurt. If Alcina could stay with you and Baba, she wouldn't have to drive to Sarajevo all the time."

"Three strong women in one house? Andro, you'll be afraid to visit."

"It may be difficult, but I've been known to do similar dangerous things in the name of God and country."

"I've so missed Sofija," Mara sighs. "Some people say she can be fussy and narrow-minded, but not me. When Sofija shines, nothing matches her inner light. She has so many magical traits. She's like an orchid that needs care to blossom into her unique beauty."

"Well, if there's anyone who can cultivate those qualities, it's you. Like you, she's put a lot into making people feel happy. It'll be good knowing you're nearby during these tough times."

"The joy is all mine, Andro. With Sofija back in my life, I'll have someone who understands and cares about me. A friendship based on such faith can only reward both of us. So, when do we leave?"

—◊—

"Might one purchase a malt-based beverage for consumption in this establishment?" Heath asks as he steps into Barrymore's.

"Don't know, mister," Susie-Q states, "but I have cold beer for sale. Have a seat, stranger. Long time no see. You solve all Europe problems, now come home to work on me?"

"I heard tell you and Elizabeth-Ann are running out of schleps to pick on. So, I figured I'd do my part and step back into the fray."

"Don't worry, Heath," a silken voice quips from behind a pillar just down the bar. "Susie and Liz have a non-discriminatory clause in their bartending contract that ensures all customers are insulted equally."

"Well, Ms. Antonucci," Heath realizes as Anita peeks around the bar obstruction. "What a pleasant surprise. Might that stool next to you be vacant?"

"It only costs a cocktail. So, please, come sit down."

"I keep making Cosmopolitan. Ms. Anita have much gossip to tell you."

Heath and Anita spend the afternoon sipping adult beverages and catching up on the last several months of their lives and friends' lives.

"Andro join Uncle Sam to wear three-piece suit," Susie interjects. "Now back in Bosnia. Cashton go home from big Army hospital. Indian chief want him for powwow."

"Sorry, Anita," Heath whispers. "I heard about your falling out with Andro. I so hoped you could have joined us at his citizenship celebration."

"Well, some things just weren't meant to be, I guess. I'm no longer angry with Andro and I've since written to tell him so. But in the long run, we just weren't a good fit. I'm glad we discovered it early on. So, what's next for you, mister world traveler? Why are you back from Europe so soon?"

"The peace treaty's signed, U.N. troops are flooding into the Balkans and the big boys at the *Times* want to chart a new course. They think Bosnia's old news."

"But the landmines, the refugees, the hatred. Those things all need to be addressed. You've said so yourself."

"I know, Anita, but it's not my call. It's how the newspaper business works. Besides, these old joints tell me it might be good to pursue another path right here in Gotham," Heath says while rubbing his sore right knee.

"Hey! Turn up the TV," someone yells from down the bar. "Isn't that Jason in that crowd of cops?"

Susie grabs the remote and boosts the sound for all to hear.

"Reporting from just outside the 369th Regimental Armory, this is Sandra Barber, WABC live breaking news."

TV coverage switches to news anchor Ned Winkleman, commenting from the station's midtown studio. "To repeat, there appears to have been a drive-by shooting in the vicinity of Fifth Avenue and 142nd Street. Several people have been injured and taken to the Harlem Hospital Center on Lenox Avenue. Their conditions are unknown at this time. Tune in to *Channel 7 Nightly News* at five for the latest on this breaking story. We now return you to our regularly..."

"Anita, grab your coat," Heath orders. "We're heading uptown. There's no question that was Jason. He may need our help. Who knows?"

"And Denasha? Where the hell is she? Let's go right to the hospital... Now!"

"You call with update!" Susie-Q yells as Anita and Heath rush out the door to hail a taxi. "We pray hard for you."

—∞—

A couple hours earlier that same day... Jason approaches the armory, taking a seat on one of the low-slung concrete walls flanking the main steps. The day's crisp and the sky's clear. His daughter will soon join him for a laid-back holiday weekend with Aunt Andi and who knows how many of Banks' relatives.

Too good to be true, Jason smiles while thinking of what lie ahead. *Too good... and so sweet.*

"Papa! Papa!" Denasha shouts with glee as she steps through the building's giant red wooden doors. "The weekend's here. Ready to play?"

"Sounds good to me. The weather's great. Ya wanna walk?"

Denasha nods yes and grabs her father's hand as they step through the parking lot toward Fifth Avenue. Out of nowhere, three young men in gray sweats with hoods pulled tight bolt on to the scene. One slams into Jason as they try racing by. A second slips and falls while turning the corner. The third leaps behind a nearby car, yelling, "Yo, nicca. Park it here! Get down. Whip a comin.'"

Before Jason can finish yelling "What the hell you punks think you're…" a silver Escalade with tinted windows screeches to a halt in front of Jason, Denasha and dozens of unawares bounding down the armory's steps. The doors of the SUV fly open, followed by a series of flash bursts, as the van occupants unload a cache of pistols and semi-automatic rifles in the general direction of the three terrified teens. In a clumsy response, one of the gangster youths slings his arm over a car hood and unleashes round after round from his Luger in the attackers' general direction.

Jason's mesmerized by the sound of guns blasting, bullets whizzing and shells ricocheting off concrete and marble. Closer to the armory, people unaccustomed to even running begin leaping behind shrubbery and diving under cars to escape the onslaught.

It's already a given: Many people will be hurt this day. Some will die, but bullets don't care. Slugs don't carry names. They fly in all directions. Innocence is no shield from a vigilante's vendetta.

At that very moment, Major Stellwagon's in a second floor conference room, peering out the window overlooking the curb-side mayhem. She grabs a phone and punches for help. Following what seems like an eternity, there's an answer on but the second ring.

"9-1-1 operator. What's your emergency?"

"Major Stellwagon, 369th Armory at 142nd and Fifth. Shots fired on main entrance. People down. Send police, fire and ambulance…

I'm going on scene." The major mashes down the switch hook, then punches 1-1-1 to engage the building's public address system.

"Attention all personnel. Shots fired on main entrance. Do not exit the building. Repeat: Do not exit the building. Security assemble at 143rd Street entry. Medics gather first aid packs and stand by. This is not a drill. I repeat: This is not a drill."

With her adrenalin pumping, the major rushes down the stairs to continue the coordinated response. Outside, Jason has thrown himself atop his daughter in an attempt to shield her.

Denasha grasps Jason's hand and whispers, "I'm dizzy and sleepy, papa, so sleepy."

The gunfire stops as abruptly as it started. The street punks scurry down the block like rats in red high-top tennis shoes. The van thugs slam doors shut and squeal away. Jason looks back to his fallen angel. He sees a pool of blood soaking Denasha's padded jacket. He grabs his handkerchief, rips open her coat and presses against the wound.

"Hold on, baby. Papa's here. Hold on." Denasha's dainty hand goes limp, slides from Jason's and plops on the sidewalk. "No baby, no… Medic! Medic!"

"Mr. Banks," Major Stellwagon says as she kneels in front of him. "You must let go. You must let go so we can help."

As two Army corpsmen slide Denasha from Jason's protective hover, a policeman leans in and asks, "Sir, can you hear me? Sir, are you okay?"

In a trance-like state, Jason points down the avenue. In a cold monotone, he drones, "Silver SUV, New York plates… alpha, delta, victor, three, six, niner, one… New York A-D-V-3-6-9-1… ADV 36 91… Get the bastards. Go! Get the bastards… Now!"

"Got it, sir. I'm calling it in. Someone look after this man."

"I'm here, Mr. Banks," the major says as she leans in to comfort him. "I'm here."

"I'm so tired of castles in the air," Jason mumbles, heaving a sigh. "God let my revenge be sweet."

"Don't step down to their level, my friend. Pass it over, Jason. Rise above the fray. Do it for the good of the guiltless… Do it for Denasha."

—⁓—

Although the third Monday in January, 1996 marks the 10th anniversary of Martin Luther King, Jr. Day, it holds a far deeper, gut-wrenching significance for Jason Banks. Three days before, he lost a little girl who'd grown up to be his friend. She was struck down in a senseless hail of bullets only yards from where he now sits. Anger and remorse fight for Jason's attention as he tries listening to the preachy, politically correct narratives echoing through this massive assembly hall.

The three-tiered balconies of the 369th's medieval-inspired drill shed are filled with New Yorkers who've come to celebrate Dr. King's legacy and honor a young woman from Spanish Harlem. The stage is packed with dignitaries. Mayor Giuliani is joined by Congressman Rangel, the Manhattan borough president, the NYPD's 30th Precinct captain and the Reverend Al Sharpton, to name just a few.

The Harlem Boys' Choir offers its rendition of Dr. King's favorite hymn, *Take My Hand, Precious Lord*. They're followed by politicos and preachers waxing philosophical about the civil rights leader's achievements. At Major Stellwagon's insistence, Jason's been made a last-minute addition to the program. While Anita spent the weekend consoling Denasha's mother, Heath worked with Jason, to draft remarks for this moment.

"Good morning Mr. Mayor, distinguished guests and friends. I'm humbled to be here. As you well know, the 369th Infantry owns a special place in American history. It was the first Black regiment to fight in World War I… And that was under French command, because of America's segregation policies back then. That irony shouldn't be lost on any of us today.

"Please forgive me as I try to deal with a similar paradox. Last Friday, my daughter, Denasha Rivera, and two others were gunned down just outside this building. I come to you today proclaimin' their deaths, like Dr. King's, must not have been in vain. From Spanish Harlem to Sugar Hill, more than two dozen gangs are now grabbin' territory and pullin' triggers over nothin' more than a pair of fancy sneakers. The damage they cause is immeasurable, but it doesn't have to be permanent.

"A couple years ago, Congress called for a nationwide push to transform this federal holiday into a day of community service—a vehicle for solvin' social problems. Today, I'm askin' you to join me in a new crusade. I want you to become modern-day Harlem Hellfighters. Enough is enough! The violence has got to stop. We can't be afraid of our children anymore.

"We all have a part to play in gettin' these gang bangers off our streets and out of our lives. We can rationalize all day long, but if we do nothin', we're as much to blame as those thugs. And denial won't make the problem go away. The best solution to our gang problem is to stop them from formin' in the first place. How, you ask? I don't know, but together, I'm convinced we can find answers.

"As Dr. King once said, 'Everybody can be great because everybody can serve.' Join me, please. Let's inaugurate a King Day of Service right here in Harlem. Let's make it a day that honors his legacy of nonviolence and the three beautiful people we just lost. Let's transform this holiday from a *day off* to a *day on* that will strengthen this borough, empower our people and work to scale the hurdles of hatred.

"On behalf of my daughter, I thank you. I'm going to take a seat now at that table in the back of the hall. Stop by when the program's over. Pick up an info card, if you're so inclined. Fill it out and mail it back. Major Stellwagon and the great soldiers of the Fightin' 369th have offered to serve as a clearin' house for this campaign. They have and will continue to open this armory and their hearts to help all of us. And for that, we should be forever grateful."

There's a deafening silence as Jason leaves the stage. An applause begins. A clapping crescendo soon ripples through the crowd. Citizens begin standing as the ovation grows. Jason maintains his march to the rear of the room, streams of tears run down his cheeks as a smile creeps across his quivering mouth.

Denasha would be proud, Jason reflects. *Denasha would be proud.*

—⁂—

"Ackov, my buddy, you seem tense today," Dragana jests, stomping into Adrijan's Belgrade office, sliding off her long brown leather gloves and plopping into an over-stuffed lounge chair.

"Tense? Oh, that's rich. Go ahead. Revel in your cynical understatements."

"Relax, Adrijan, the peace accord's been signed and you've still got a job."

"Easy for you to say, Dragana. That golden boy Babich marched in here the other day like a Nazi storm trooper telling me how things are going to be under the new order. And hinting I should be concerned about war crime charges for Christ's sake."

"He's just flexing his muscles. Between the U.N., NATO and the Red Cross, a bureaucratic mess is forming that will be so huge nothing will get done for years. In Bosnia alone, the Serbs, Croats and Bosniaks will each have their own government function. Isn't that what started this crazy conflict in the first place?"

"Some people in that new Office of the High Representative are already calling my work racist propaganda, a tool of war in the hands of rebels. Why must I be held responsible?"

"If you think Atlanta's burning, Adrijan, then maybe it's time to get out of town. That's what I plan to do."

"What?" Adrijan asks in stunned amazement. "What did you say?"

"Face it, Ackov, it's over. We fought the good fight. Now they must wage the peace. I'll have no part of it. I'm headed to Kosovo. Those brave Orthodox partisans are being ambushed daily by gangs of Islamic terrorists. Someone must stop their violent jihad. And Belgrade wants me to help lead the charge. Besides, why should I stay here and end up a scapegoat for the other rats now abandoning ship?"

"That's great for you, but what about me?"

"What about you? For God's sake man, learn to fish or cut bait. And don't give me that dumbfounded look. It's time to put up or shut up, Adrijan. Only you can make that call. And with that, I'm out of here. I wish I could say it's been great working with you, but we both know the length of that lie."

Reveling in her latest snide remark, Dragana leaps up and swoops toward the door. Without looking back, or breaking stride, she's out of the building, down the steps and secure in her sports car, ready for another political road rally to the next battle.

"To hell with you, bitch, and good riddance," Adrijan mumbles, watching Dragana's exit. "As the Bosnians say, 'In matters of great importance, it's not the cream that rises to the top, but the foam.' May you choke on your own froth, you heathen devil-witch."

Anita ascends the pulpit of All Saints Church to speak about her new-found and just lost friend. The Saint Patrick's of Harlem is filled with mourners from across El Bario. In pious proclamation, beams of God's bright light stream through the clerestory's wheel windows, highlighting the patterned brickwork and terra cotta details of this historic house of worship. Bouquet upon bouquet of flowers cover the alter steps, smothering the lace-draped coffin while filling the sanctuary with the smell of spring.

"Gracias por esta oportunidad. Although I only knew Denasha briefly, we became friends the moment we met and I'll carry those joyous memories forever. But I am not here to eulogize Ms. Rivera. Rather, I want to share with you our creative dream and ask for your help in making it a reality—a living memorial to our loving friend.

"Denasha, like you, knew dance and music are the heartbeat of Puerto Rico's heritage. She and I were crafting a Latino review when tragedy struck. Now, I need your help finishing this project. It's to be a celebration of your Taino, Spanish and African roots. I'm asking all Nuyo Ricans to join me in this salute to Denasha and your proud history. My goal is to stage the premier during this year's 116th Street Festival, complete with a float in the Puerto Rican Day Parade, but I can't do it without you… No lo puedo hacer sin ti.

"I know the fascinating and alluring woman we praise today would be overjoyed by your backing. This is how Denasha's magic can still touch us. Please become a willing companion on this special journey. This can be a miraculous moment for us all. It can be a celebration of life and a tribute in death. Gracias y vaya con Dios."

Anita steps down, then stops near the alter to pick up the microphone resting on a music stand. A lone trumpeter's lament tumbles from the church balcony. The choral lead-in to a long-popular Puerto Rican love song, *Madrigal*, is proclaimed. The notes lilt off stone pillars and stained glass windows, enrapturing the assembled mass. The brass fanfare soon melds with gentle strumming from a folk guitar as the lady balladeer whispers, "This song's for you, Denasha. And Señor Feliciano, let me do you proud."

Soon, tears are gushing down Anita's cheeks as she thrusts her arm toward the sanctuary's dome, crooning the song's closing lines with the timbre of a classic contralto. "Porque llevo tu amor en mi pecho, como un madrigal!"

The vocal tribute complete, she stops to kneel in front of Denasha's mother. Gentle weeping can be heard throughout the Nave. Anita takes and caresses Margarita's hands. "Denasha would be proud," the mother says with a vibrato-like sigh that highlights her sorrow. "Si, I know she is proud… Gracias, Anita, gracias."

Anita slumps into a nearby pew as the children's choir begins singing the well-loved Latino hymn *Caminando Juntos—Walking Together*.

—※—

Back in Bosnia, the spring sun glistens on the cobbled streets of Konjic, melting the snow into ribbons of wet silver that slither down the roadway. Andro and Mara, appreciating the March morning's brisk beauty, decide to walk from the station to the institute. As they round a corner, the three-story Bauhaus-style structure presents itself. It's become a symbol of strength and security in this mad, mad world.

"We're here to see Sofija Babich," Mara tells the receptionist.

"She was reading next to the fireplace in the welcome hall. Go through those large double doors to your right."

As they step into the greeting room, a fragile senior with bristled silver hair can be seen running her finger across the page of a book while rocking a gnarled wooden chair.

"Baba Sofija, can it be you?" Andro murmurs in loving disbelief.

As Sofija turns to look in the voice's direction, her eyes lock on Andro. She bursts into a joyous scream. "Andro, my baby! Andro, Andro, Andro!"

He rushes forward. They fall into each other's arms, hugging intensely. After showering him with kisses, Sofija looks around Andro's broad shoulders to view the other visitor. "My God, Mara, it's you. It's you… Come to me, my darling." They too share a long and loving embrace.

"There's a coffee pot and cups right there, Andro. Please pour us some. We can all sit around the fire and just talk forever."

"You look fantastic," Mara notes as she perches on the sofa's edge next to Sofija. "And your spirit seems solid. Tell me I'm right. Tell us you're strong."

"Yes, child, I'm fine. At times I felt helpless, but I fought Dragana's weapons of influence and made certain my battle was won."

"What do you mean, Baba?" Andro asks. "What weapons? Did someone hurt you?"

"No, Andro, they were missiles of the mind, but Dragana had no idea who she was firing at. I was committed to what was right. I still am. Her tricks weren't going to take that away. When it comes to obeying someone, a higher authority is the only voice I've ever listened to. The good Lord pilots my ship. He always has and always will.

"And there were all these people helping me in so many wonderful ways. Then I'm moved to this special safe house. Yes, I've been lonely at times, but prayer, and your adventure letters, kept me strong. They pulled me through. But now, it's time to go home. Yes?"

"Yes, Baba. That's why we're here. That's why we're here," Andro whispers. He then shares his plan for Mara to stay with Sofija as everyone readjusts to village life. Unanimous in their eagerness to move forward, Mara returns to the reception desk, asking to speak with the director. He agrees to Sofija's discharge, with the stipulation she visit on a regular basis to inspire other residents.

"There will be no objection from us. How could there be?"

"Let's go home, Baba Sofija," Andro says as he wraps his strong arm around her frail frame. "Let's go home."

—⁓—

C H A P T E R   2 2 :

CURTAIN UP ON NEW BEGINNINGS

IT'S A DRIZZLY, gray March morning as Jason saunters up the marble steps skirting a house of worship in the heart of Hell's Kitchen.

"Welcome," says a boyish-looking priest, swinging open the rectory door. "You must be Jason. I'm Father Cerkez. Andro's told me so much about you. Please come in."

As Jason and the priest exchange pleasantries, the cleric pours coffee and puts forward a plate of sweets. "They're Balkan crescent cookies the church ladies make. They're dryer than dust, but I'm pretty much forced to offer them."

"Thanks, father, but…"

"Please, call me Peter."

"Okay, I'm no church goer and I don't put much faith in scripture, but Andro said you're a good listener. So, if I tell ya what's messin' with my head, you'll help sort it out, right?"

"We can try, brother. Let's face it, losing a child is like losing your innocence. When you lost Denasha, a future full of hopes and dreams vanished too."

"It's like this huge, empty space inside is rippin' me up. It's so real I can almost touch it. And folks say there's a blankness in my eyes. Maybe it's so, 'cause I don't seem to have a feelin' anymore."

"That's normal, Jason. It's part of the healing process. Once you get through the mourning, you'll look back with wonder. Right now, it's hard to understand. Grief's a rugged path, but it's part of your way ahead. There's no neat trail to stay on. It's a lot messier than that, but there are milestones along the way."

"Yeah? Like what? What can I look ahead to?"

"As your numbness wears off, you'll still yearn for Denasha. That's expected. And you'll get angry, have regrets about things you two never shared or said. Even more sadness could follow."

"How long will these damned pleasantries last? Sorry, I just…"

"No need to apologize… There's no time table, Jason. After a while, your pain should lessen. Yet, bouts of gloom will come and go for the rest of your life. Don't fight them or bottle them up. They're natural. Down the road, you'll start to let go. And I didn't say forget. Your memories of Denasha will help pull your life back together.

"Just remember that others have travelled this road as well. You're not alone. Brighter days lay ahead. You'll never return to where you were, Jason, but you'll come to find joy in life in new ways, in ways that you invent."

"Thanks, Peter. I feel a little better already."

"I'm glad. Now, take this card. Keep it in your wallet. Whenever you're feeling down and out, just give it a scan. It's a quote from the laureate Tagore. He said, 'Death is not extinguishing the light; it's putting out the lamp because dawn has come.'"

"Thanks, but I don't know if I understand."

"You will, Jason… in time. You'll come to understand, appreciate and act on those words. Trust me, if you can."

—◊—

Andro cranks up Uncle Franjo's old VW for a Dubrovnik day trip to pick up Cousin Alcina. With Mara as copilot, the new aid worker couldn't be more at ease. Soon, the Beetle's zooming along, hugging the narrow, snake-like road while skirting its way down the Dalmatian Coast.

"Okay, Alcina's sailing in on a Greek patrol boat, but the Old City's a walking zone. How do we get there?"

"There's a parking lot on Iza Grada, the road that circles around town. My cousin's art gallery is there. He's arranged for a push cart to pick up Alcina's luggage from the dock. We just enjoy the city for a while."

"Walking around playing tourist, or sitting back and watching the world go by. It all sounds good to me."

"I think my cousins will opt for the latter, especially if wine's an option."

As they round a bend, countless white-washed and red-roofed stone structures jut from the water. They're a stark contrast to the sparkling azure sea. The medieval-era walled city is reminiscent of Venice, but on a smaller scale, with marble alleyways serving as surrogate canals. There are narrow, cobblestone streets lined with shops for bartering and buying, al fresco cafes for drinking and dining, as well as petite piazzas for sun soaking and people watching.

"Andelko! How are you?" Andro shouts as he hops from the car. The two strong, handsome men rush to each other, embrace, slap backs, press kisses, then burst into laughter, overjoyed at their reunion after so many years.

"This is my friend, Mara. She's now house-sitting while Baba Sofija rests."

"Welcome to the Pearl of the Adriatic. Let's hit the harbor and find our cousin."

As they meander through Old Town, a navy vessel docks. Its passengers begin clearing Customs. Andro and Andelko shout in unison, "Alcina! Alcina!" They wave handkerchiefs in hopes of catching her attention. Reunited, all share hugs, kisses and introductions, then set out on a Dubrovnik tour.

"I recommend we check out Gradska Kavana," Andelko proposes. "It's a great sidewalk café with waterfront views and tables on the plaza."

"And it serves a fine Dingac wine, no doubt?"

"But of course, Andro. It's known as the King of Croatian reds."

The foursome pass the time discussing Alcina's most recent eco-trek, Andelko's tribulations protecting his studio during the war, Mara's exploits in Belgrade and Andro's newfound nationality.

Andelko continues to brag on his city as the proudest feather in Croatia's tourist cap. "The repairs have already begun and people are returning in droves. Papa Thoma and Mama Sasha are back in Mostar. They've reopened the restaurant. So, all is good with this side of the Babich clan."

"And yet, there's so much to be done in Bosnia," Andro laments. "So many people lost everything in the war. They lost their homes, jobs and money."

"And what about the victims of unspeakable crimes?" Mara asks, "You expect them to work with those who abused them? A sane way ahead may not be in the cards."

"It's going to take lots of people and a lot of time. They must learn to talk all over again," Alcina points out. "That's not going to be easy, by any stretch."

"Enough trying to ruin a beautiful day," Andelko insists. "Besides, I think it's time you head back. I don't want Andro driving you fair damsels to Konjic in the dark."

⎯〰⎯

Back at her lodge in the Dinaric Alps, Dragana stands on the balcony watching the morning fog rise off the Neretva. The local cleric, Father Kraljić, steps into her realm of silent contemplation. "I hear tell you may be leaving us?"

"Yes, father, I've been called to serve a similar cause elsewhere."

"You're a strong creature of great moral obligation, Dragana, but please don't be remorseful. Admit it: You felt compelled to serve here, but in your heart, you knew you could leave at any time."

"Sure… And lose any chance of reward in the end. Why should I suffer those consequences? I've focused on hope to make this misery more tolerable. Regardless what you say, father, I had no choice but to stick it out."

"My poor child, as long as you feel like you have no choice, your suffering will only increase."

"I suppose you're right, but I don't feel forced to stay any longer. Who says Belgrade can always dictate what I do? Who says I have to obey them without question?"

"Well, that wasn't what I was inferring, but it seems to work for you."

"Dragana Kowalchuk is a winner and she know it. I'm a true eagle. I'm high-flying and successful. I can rise above this adversity. I can turn these bad-times into good. On to Kosovo and whatever lies beyond."

"Well, I guess my good work here is done," Father Kraljić mumbles as Dragana stomps off the porch. "That woman may be wise, but I fear she will never find what's needed to ripen her happiness. Lord, please help tend her fruitless garden… Amen."

—⁓—

As Mara shows Alcina to her room in back of the Babich farmhouse, Andro takes a seat by the hearth, next to Baba Sofija. Sharing glances, they bask in the warmth of the fire and their reunited lives.

"Andro, what's troubling you?"

"Is it that obvious, Baba? Okay, it's Bosnia, the war, the whole mess. I'm convinced, when people stand up against bias and hate, they'll find harmony in most everything they do. But the people of

this country need some kind of understanding about how we're going to live together. They need to change their feelings, if we're ever
going to solve the trials we face, but I can't get my arms around it.
At the same time, if we're not sure what caused this harm, maybe we
should put off trying to fix it so quickly."

"Don't try to rationalize this away, my boy. Accept it. Sometimes
things just come together. Don't spend so much time looking for the
cause. Don't ignore the option of just dealing with what's happened
and move on."

"This is why I come to you with my questions, wise lady."

"And that's what grand mammas are for, young man. None of us
have all the answers, but one should start by defining the problem. It's
time you do your homework by sifting the chaff from the grain. You
need to chart a map. Follow it down the road, even if you don't quite
know where it's leading you.

"But please, Andro, you're too young to be so serious all the time.
Lighten up. Be a little more like me. You should know by now I rarely
make the same mistake twice. Instead, I make it a little differently
each time… Now, pour us some wine so we can enjoy the fire and
hopefully, the silence it will bring."

—⁂—

"Five, six, seven, eight…" Anita counts, clapping her hands as a
cast of teenagers leaps through a Romantikeo fusion song. Denasha
choreographed the number. Its intent: Transport dancers and audience alike to a palm frond-covered Puerto Rican dancehall that's
swirling with tropical breezes. Today, the setting's a little less dreamy.
Rehearsal is in one of the Harlem Armory's gray-walled meeting
rooms.

As dancers work through the latest steps, a door opens and Major Stellwagon ushers in several followers. Anita claps her hands and shouts, "Okay, stop! Let's take a break. Ten minutes, please."

"Sorry to interrupt, but these folks need to speak with you."

"No problem. How can I help you?"

"We represent El Museo del Barrio," the group's spokesperson states. "The foundation has approved our request to send you on a sabbatical to San Juan. While there you can review your show ideas with performers from across the island. Yes, this is very quick, but we have only a small window of opportunity. The artists aren't available for long. Are you interested, Anita?"

"Interested? I'm ecstatic… You, the church, the entire community have put such faith in me. You sense my desire to bring Denasha's project to fruition and that drives me so. But now, with this, we can put it all to the test, fine-tune everything. We can transform hunch into concept. When do we go?"

"As soon as Friday, if that's possible? You should expect to be gone about a month. We ask that you select a dance troupe member as your assistant and translator. Room and board will be provided, along with a small stipend. We hope that meets with your approval?"

"Gracias," Anita replies, shaking the delegates' hands. "Muchas gracias. I'm mindful of what this means to everyone, to be so accepted without proof."

"We're more than confident you're suited to the task, but we also want you to take a little time to love Borinquen. We're sure our island will enrich you, your songs and your dance."

"Gracias a Dios. You won't regret your decision. Viva la emoción!"

———∽∽∽———

The late winter night brings forward a mountain chill. Alcina and Mara huddle with Baba Sofija near the fireplace in her Konjic home.

"What are you creating?" Alcina asks Sofija. "It looks so intricate, so beautiful."

"Thank you, dear. It's called šlinga, a kind of Croat embroidery. You stitch white thread on white fabric around little cloth cutouts."

"Amazing."

"It's almost a lost art," Mara points out. "You can't find such skills on a factory floor, or in some Asian sweatshop."

"You should sell your work, Sofija," Alcina suggests, "not only because it's unique, but the quality is priceless. What about other women in this village? Do they make crafts just as rare?"

"Certainly. The Balkans has a rich needlecraft tradition."

"Embroidery, tatting lace and hand-loomed rugs, to mention a few," Mara adds.

"I think we're on to something here, ladies. Try looking at arts and crafts as a way of lifting women out of grief while putting some money in their pockets."

"But the local market for crafts has been shrinking for years. People are turning to mass-produced stuff. Like our men in the war, our legacy is dying out. It's left to old women like me, but I'd love to pass it on."

"Andro tells me almost half the people in Bosnia are now out of work," Mara says. "And women have been hit the hardest."

"Okay, think about it," Alcina explains. "With a few crochet hooks, some yarn and a little hard work, we have the makings of a real cottage industry here. And we can offer relief, especially to those widowed by war."

"Every mother should have the chance to do something more than just be depressed and cry all the time," Sofija adds. "This could bring us together in a very special way."

"Yes!" Mara exclaims. "Bosnian, Croat and Serb women crafting a bit of harmony."

"I'm sure, with Andro's help, we can find ways to promote and sell such work," Alcina notes, "at home and abroad."

"It's a chance to forget the past for just a moment," Sofija suggests. "Through mingling together, we'll all grow stronger, helping women who've lost most everything. And like you said, earn a bit of cash along the way."

"Mara, would you take some notes?" Alcina asks. "We can share them with Andro and see what he thinks."

"Good idea," Sofija says, "but we need some rules about what we're going to make, like using traditional skills. No mass production and no machines."

"And we can't forget the environment," Alcina insists. "Everything should be made with natural products."

"Okay, but let's not limit ourselves. We should have a mix of traditional and modern designs. The work should stand for all our ethnic backgrounds," Mara notes.

Sofija tosses more wood on the fire while the three continue stoking their creative ideas. The brainstorming continues late into the night as Mara scribbles, trying to capture their mountain of dreams.

—m—

A few days after the women's inspired assembly, Andro stops by the farmhouse. "I presented your craft gild idea at staff meeting," he tells the three, "and they loved it. We're pretty sure USAID can help promote it, but that's going to take some time. If you're eager to start, you'll need to find your own resources."

"I'll talk to Father Malinko and Mara can check with the imam."

"If I draw up a flyer, will you make us some copies at work?" Alcina asks. "I'll post them around town."

"Sure, and that's all good, ladies, but what about a place to work?"

"Well, I haven't been back in my house since the war started, but I understand it was pretty well ransacked. I'm okay with clearing it out and making it our crafts center. It doesn't appear papa and my brother will be coming back any time soon."

"Speaking of that," Andro interjects, "I met a talib from the madrasa while walking up the lane. He gave me this letter for you."

Mara takes the note. Her hands begin to tremble as she opens it.

"Mara, dear, maybe you should take that aside."

"No, Sofija. We have no secrets any more. Besides, I may need you even closer to me." Mara begins to read aloud.

>*Selam, my sad and tarnished one,*
>
>*Tears still flow, although my loving son now rests in heaven. I was told of your mother's death and your dreadful shame.*
>
>*With nothing left for me, I have joined the Black Swan fighters. Al-Qaeda from Mohammad's homeland are now training us and will lead our jihad.*
>
>*Ask Allah for mercy and pray for me, retched creature.*
>
>*Your father—now and forever*

Mara crumples the letter and shakes her head in disbelief. Her eyes are void of tears. Andro steps closer in an effort to lend comfort, but Mara gestures for him to stop.

"Papa, the great mujahid… Let him have his struggle. My protests be damned!"

Never has Baba Sofija seen Mara express her emotions with such forcefulness and animation. "Gently, my child, your father's hurting too."

"No! You must be Muslim to read the anger and disappointment between these lines. Brother Aadil was favored in everything. Abbi only laments the loss of a son who's supposed to care for him in old age. Daughters, and their troubles, are married away. A son brings honor to a family. Daughters can only bring shame."

"Mara," Andro inquires, "You don't really believe that, do you?"

"I believe family should be at the center of everything, but must men always have the first and last word? Honor is important… Ask my father. Honor must always be protected and defended. Shame must be avoided at all costs."

"Regardless our beliefs," Sofija notes, "age and wisdom deserve some tribute. Your father feels most things in life are controlled by the will of God, rather than by human beings. Faith is his guide."

"I understand that you're upset, Mara," Alcina adds, "but be careful of insults and criticism. More people than just your father listen and take them seriously."

"I hear you, all of you, but must pride and honor always march ahead of respect? Above all, when violence is scrawled on the wall. Okay, that's enough. From now on, I will keep such thoughts to myself. Let it be settled. I'm going home to build a new life. My house is now ours. And yes, we will make our fortunes together. So, let's get working… Now!"

Before anyone can respond, Mara storms out, slamming the door behind her and stomping down the lane toward the family dwelling next door. "May Allah watch over and reward my strained journey to peace of mind," she mumbles as she marches.

—⚮—

Heath holds a string of dark foil shamrocks against the rail above Barrymore's main bar as Susie-Q stretches on a stool, securing the strand with tape. Glitter-covered *Lucky* signs cover the corner post. "Alright, that's enough St. Paddy's crap. Time you get back to the important work of pouring me another damn beer."

"No luck of Irish for you, mister."

"Right… The only potato famine you know about is when we run short of rot-gut vodka."

"Why you so grumpy, Mr. Newsman?"

"Oh, I'm sorry, Susie. The bigwigs at the *Times* want me back in Bosnia again, just when I thought I'd be able to kick back here for a while."

"Look on bright side, Heath. Andro there now. You drink beer together—good beer. No more light stuff. That cool, right?"

"Yes, ma'am. And thank you, as always, for putting things in perspective. It'll be good to see Andro again and report on what he's doing. It's not like they're going to be shooting at me this time, I hope."

"Here! Here!" a couple bar flies down the way shout out.

"Besides, it'll be interesting to see if Bosnia's on a path to reconciliation or headed down a road of revenge."

"What you mean, Heath?" the bartenderess asks.

"Like that *Boston Globe* reporter wrote, 'Once you put a human face to evil, it won't let you go.' And in Bosnia, it's like there's this crazy damn need for a reckoning. People are demanding some type of an accounting over there. Everyone is looking to lessen their guilt, answer their fears, or just kick someone's ass."

"Okay, big boy, that too deep for me. Time we switch you to hard liquor."

"Here! Here!" the bar fly acknowledgement is heard loud and clear once again.

—m—

A late-March sunrise breaks across the Frankfurt runway as TWA Flight 121 lands. After gathering his bags and clearing Customs, Heath steps into the Terminal E reception area where Sergeant Webb awaits. "Well, it's déjà vu all over again. How's my favorite chauffer sergeant?"

"Very good, sir. Here are your orders. I'll drive you to Rhein-Main where your C-130 chariot awaits. Your destination: IFOR Mission-Sarajevo."

*Notebook entry: Implementation Force (IFOR)—
NATO-led multi-national peacekeepers sent to BiH...
Part of a 1-year mandate... Codename: Operation Joint
Endeavour... Mission: Implement Dayton accord &
relieve U.N. forces*

By great coincidence, Heath's met at base ops by his burley crew chief buddy, Sergeant Green, still wearing what looks like the same drab flight suit. They exchange handshakes and paperwork, then head for the tarmac.

"Will we be making that corkscrew landing again?" Heath asks.

"I know how much you enjoy those," Green jokes, "but I'm afraid we're stuck with a peacetime touchdown this trip."

About three hours later, as the gray Hercules begins its final approach to Bosnia's capital, Green signals Heath to join him at the porthole. They gaze out the side window as the plane descends, following the majestic Miljacka River into the main valley. Shortly after landing, the aerial workhorse taxies close to Sarajevo's drab terminal.

Heath's greeted by Andro's Uncle Franjo who's still the airport's cargo manager. "Welcome back. Let's step inside. There's someone who wants to meet you."

"Andro, you son-of-a-bitch. Oops, there I go with the vernacular, again."

"We expect nothing less," Andro laughs as they hug, slap backs and kiss cheeks. "Heath, you look like you could use a beer."

"Franjo, can you join us? It's time we make a full frontal assault on Eoghan and the lounge."

"To the Holiday Inn for war stories," Franjo shouts, "as well as whiskey and whatever else… in no particular order."

—∽—

"What's a guy have to do for a beer around here?" Heath yells as he, Andro and Franjo enter the Inn's bar.

"Don't waste time waltzin' around. Just take a seat," Eoghan barks. "You might want to display an air of civility, not unlike the gentlemen who mistakenly joined you."

"I've missed you too, you arrogant Irish bastard."

"And the rest of the day to ya, Mr. Winslow. Beers all around, I presume?"

The four extend greetings and toast their good fortunes. "So, Heath, me boy, I thought your Balkan sojourn was over?"

"As did I, Eoghan, but the editor wants me to dig up some more dirt. Something about bootleg booze running through the tunnels of Sarajevo. You wouldn't know anything about such goings on now would you, my friend?"

"Like you taught me, Heath, I just tell 'em, I don't explain 'em. How about your cohorts in crime? They must have plenty of interestin' stories for ya."

"Oh, I'll get to the 'good deeds' stuff a bit later. Right now, I'm more intrigued by the graft and corruption that seems to be flowing all around."

"Sorry, sir. I fear the battery in me hearin' aid's gone bad. Me good Lord, the beer's stopped flowin' too."

"Then it's time to go upstairs, is it not?"

They all burst into laughter as Eoghan ices up four rock glasses. "It's good ta have ya back, me boy. And you lads as well."

"The pleasure's ours," Heath states. "I can assure you of that."

"Then assure me there's money in your pockets and we'll continue this conversation for all the wrong reasons."

—∽—

CHAPTER 23:
SARAJEVO ROSE BLOSSOMS

ANDRO ENTERS THE Holiday Inn-Sarajevo conference room to scope out the venue. He's greeted by a stern-looking suit in his mid-40s. The bureaucrat asks for Andro's passport, tells him to sign in, then suggests he find a seat. "There's coffee, juice and pastries against the far wall," the man grumbles.

After about three dozen more filter in, the room's double doors are closed. The G-man crosses to the podium and taps the microphone, not so much as a test, but more as a matter of routine.

"Morning… I'm Special Agent Trent. Due to increased incidents of carjacking in the Sarajevo area, I'm here to give you a safety briefing. There is no need to take notes. I will provide a pocket-size pamphlet with all the information covered today. Let's begin."

Boring briefing complete, Andro steps out of the hall. He spots Heath and Mara chatting in the sitting area near the reception desk. "Why don't we visit a café or cake shop nearby? I'm not comfortable with all the prying ears infesting this hotel."

"Is that a jab at journalists?" Heath jokes.

"If the gum-shoe fits…"

"Okay, gentlemen," Mara interjects. "Espresso and a crescent cookie will get us on track." The three stroll to a modern coffee bar just down the street where they claim a table abutting a large picture window facing the sidewalk.

"I wish I could stay, but I have a planning session this afternoon with your fellow newsman, Mr. Ackov, in Belgrade."

"Oh, please give Adrijan my love. Tell him I think of him often and hope to see him soon."

As Andro departs, Mara asks, "A little cynical this morning are we, Mr. Winslow?"

"No more than usual, Ms. Cesarec, but this shouldn't be about me. Andro told me what a strong woman you are and the stories you may want to reveal. I can write about them, if you're willing to share."

"Andro said you're a good and fair man, Mr. Winslow. My tale isn't easy to tell, but I'm willing to try. And it's not for me, but for all the women who suffer in shame."

"I understand, and if I say something you find uncomfortable, just tell me. First off, please call me Heath. And I'd like to call you Mara. So, when did this all start?"

"The nightmare began with the first rounds of cannon fire. Men were being blackmailed and women abused. The rebels were great at spreading hate and ruin. The war mongers drew lines on maps, then slashed corridors of death across the country."

"But I've heard of such atrocities on all sides. What do you think made Bosnia and Herzegovina unique?"

"The degree of insanity, Heath. The choice was made to wipe us out, rather than living with someone different, like we'd all done for decades before the war."

"But, Mara, it's said many Serbians rose up in protest."

"Sure, in Belgrade. They had anti-war groups, set up crisis lines, sheltered women and children, but none of those good works reached us here. Instead, we were trapped and humiliated from the beginning. They weren't under attack like we were. When Bosnian cities were shelled, maternity wards were made targets. Rape camps were set up to prostitute women—Croat, Roma and Bosniaks alike. This wasn't a one-time thing. It went on for months and months.

"If the rebels weren't enough, gangsters soon barged into the fight. We had a new state alright. It was a state of fear. They created it and we were its captives. Paranoia should have been the motto sewn on our new nation's flag."

"And what about the women who were attacked?"

"Yes, the women… What were they to do? Go back to their parents? And where might they be? Do they leave the country? And where do they go? They should find work, people say. How? Who will hire them? They're soiled goods.

"And what about the war babies? Do mothers keep them or give them up for adoption? Adoption by whom? Address those questions, Mr. Reporter. Answer them for me and the thousands still waiting for any kind of response.

"Oh, and don't forget the fighters coming back from the war—their heads all messed up. They continue the battle at home, beating their women and children for no reason. They snooze with their rifles like they're on the front lines. They rape their wives in their sleep and bust up the furniture. They scream and swear about the least little thing. When does this new war end?"

"I hear you, Mara. I do. So, are you willing to testify at the trials?"

"I don't know. So many crimes, so many women, so few answers. I'll do what I can to help those hurt the most. I want to help them be brave. I feel stronger being around these women. We have a special bond. But you can help too, Heath, by telling our story so that everyone knows. The court of world opinion. That's where I want our testimony heard. And I want it heard loud and clear!"

"You find me women willing to tell their stories and I'll do the rest. And if they're afraid of me, or ashamed to do so, I'll get a tape recorder and train you."

"Thank you, Heath. I'm willing to work with you on this, but for now, I must go. I'm exhausted and upset. I need to rest. We can talk more soon."

"Take your time, Mara, but remember: The longer we wait, the more such behavior is tolerated. There'll only be more violence, in the home and on the streets. This is the good fight. This is a battle all women must win."

—⚊—

Later that afternoon, Alcina steps into Baba Sofija's farmhouse. She hears sobbing from the far room. The door's ajar. Alcina steps in, finding Mara weeping on the bed.

"Are you alright?" Alcina whispers as she perches bedside, stroking Mara's hair.

"No, no I'm not. I had an interview with Andro's reporter friend this morning about women hurt in the war. All it did was hurt me more."

"You didn't tell him about your rape… your miscarriage, did you?"

"No, nor do I plan to. It's our secret. Okay, Alcina?"

"Of course, Mara. Now give me a hug. Let me help dry those tears."

The two are soon entwined in a comforting, supportive embrace. Without speaking, they hold each other close. Separating, they lock eyes and smile. Little by little, Alcina leans in. Their lips touch as Alcina cups Mara's cheeks in her hands.

Mara's spellbound. A series of freeze frame moments flash through her mind as she tries to discern fantasy from reality. Mara never imagined how God-forsakenly fantastic it would feel to kiss another woman. She then senses how Alcina is holding her. It's different than she's ever been held before. And oh, how right it feels.

Her hand is caressing my neck, Mara senses. *How softly she's descended on me, not just getting on top like Andro, or those thugs before. And now her lips are kissing my shoulder. Her teeth brush my skin with delight. This is so much better than I ever dreamed it could be.*

Mara's amazed by this series of sensual surprises. As she pulls back, she blushes and looks away. "What are we doing, Alcina?"

"What do you think is going on, Mara? I'm feeling something. Are you not?

"I don't know. I'm still angry, still frustrated and now confused, but I'm feeling warm inside and tingly all over. How crazy is that? Can you be drawn to someone and never realize it? Are you trying to give me that nudge?"

"Don't over-analyze a tender instant. It doesn't have to be some big heavy moment where you're forced to process every word and nuance that confronts you."

"So, now I'm a lesbian? Is that it? It just happens, like that?"

"Relax a little, Mara. Don't go bimbo on me. It takes all of us time to realize who we are. The world's too diverse to put labels on every-thing we come upon. And if you just want to be friends, don't despair. You're not losing anything here. I still want to be your comrade… regardless."

"And I want to be yours, but I think I want to rest now, if that's okay, Alcina?"

"It's more than okay, Mara. I understand. We'll talk more later. And if you still have questions, know I'm here, just like Sofija and the others. Sweet dreams princess."

—⚊—

Alcina steps into the kitchen, putting the tea pot on the front burn-er. She looks out the window to see a tall, slender man in forest-green fatigues trudging up the lane. "My God it is," she gasps, swinging the side door open. "Uncle Petar! Uncle Petar!" she screams. "You've come home… Praise God you're home."

"Alcina!" Petar exclaims. "What a joy and surprise to see you. Where's Baba Sofija? Is she alright?"

"She's fine, uncle. Sofija's next door with the craft gild ladies. Take my hand and follow me. Sofija! Baba Sofija!" Alcina yells as they near the old Cesarec house.

Responding to the calls and commotion, Sofija steps into the courtyard as Petar and Alcina round the corner. "God, there is a heaven. Petar, Petar, Petar! My son has come back to me," she cries as they fall into each other's arms, pressing on hair, cheeks and lips. "But where's my grandson? Please tell me he's okay."

"Alen's fine, mama. He just had surgery on his knee at a hospital in Selce. He tore it up a while back, but the operation went well. He'll be coming home next week."

"Thank God. So, turn around. Turn around… Everything attached? Everything working?"

"Yes, ma'am. Everything's in order. And you?"

"Who can hurt this tough old woman? Good Lord, I almost forgot. Andro is here—in Sarajevo. He's working for the Americans and visits on weekends. Chapeka and Suzana are safe and sound with Franjo and Florica. Alcina's been with us about three weeks now.

"And here comes Mara," Sofija notes, pointing up the street. "She's staying with us too, watching over me. No, son, it's not all been good, but at least the war's over and my family's home once again… Praise the Lord."

"Amen, mama," Petar says as he kisses her forehead. "Amen."

—⟋⟍—

"Might I see your stamped carjacking brochure, sir?" the motor pool mechanic asks Andro before handing him keys to the gray Opel. "Very good. There's a full tank of gas, but just in case, this NATO card is accepted at Esso and BP. Please bring back any receipts."

Andro plops inside, adjusts the seat and mirrors, then sets out for TV Belgrade.

Since his return, he's become obsessed not only with thwarting Ackov's propaganda campaign, but the impact it's having on his homeland. Just as Andro uses the media to measure the Balkan nightmare effect, Dragana spends countless hours assessing its cause. Their counterpoints have been reduced to a strange cat and mouse game with Kowalchuk trying to stay one step ahead of the American crusader. She struggles to avoid identification and confrontation at all cost.

Okay, that's just too much stuff rattling around in my head; not while I'm driving, Andro scolds himself. *Focus on the moment. Steer your way to Adrian's office. Deal with those other things later.*

No sooner had Andro put his brain game on hold than a dinged-up green Yugo, with a couple scraggly young men inside, taps his rear bumper. Both the driver and passenger share a contrite smile, then gesture for Andro to pull over. Assuming they want to apologize and maybe exchange license info, he stops and steps from the car.

In a flash, the driver leaps out with pistol pulled, flicking it in Andro's face. The gesture needs no translation. It clearly means "Step aside." At the same time, his disheveled accomplice dashes around back of the clunker, jumps in, grinds it into gear and speeds away.

"Okay, you can have my sedan, but please, please, put down the gun. Nobody needs to get hurt here."

"Just shut up and get away from the car!" the punk shouts. "Over there, on the grass. Kneel down… Now!"

There's a strange zip-like sound, as if something had been spit in Andro's direction with amazing speed. The assailant is struck in the back of his leg. He yells out, and then crumples to the pavement, writhing in pain.

A stout Black man in blue jeans and ski sweater rushes to Andro's side. "Are you alright, sir?"

"Yes, yes, I'm fine, but what about him?"

"Damn good shot with a silencer, if I say so myself. Don't worry about him. They're rubber bullets. No lethal damage, but it'll leave one hell of a mark."

"But how? How did you know? You came upon us so fast."

"Consulate security," the man quips as he pulls up his sweater to expose a shiny badge clipped to his belt. "We follow everyone on their first motor pool ride. There's a trackin' device in all our fleet vehicles now. That GPS is pretty cool stuff, eh?"

"Absolutely, but I'm more concerned about the story you'll be telling back at the office."

"First time's a pass, sir. That is, if you're inclined to buy a lowly civil servant a beer on some occasion."

"Drinks are on me, good man. Here's my card. You name the time and place. So, you just take him away and I continue on? It's that simple?"

"Pretty much. You might wanna scan that carjackin' pamphlet one more time. We don't print 'em for nothin' ya know. And be a bit more careful about playin' the Good Samaritan next time. Have a safe trip."

—m—

As Dragana's bright red MGB races through Alpine switchbacks near her mountain retreat, she cranks the radio. Wagner's *Ride of the Valkyries* blares across the valley. Dragana brushes back her hair, relishing this private moment of passion and power only she can feel by incessantly living on the edge.

"We interrupt this program for a breaking news story," barks the announcer. "The International Criminal Tribunal for the Former Yugoslavia has issued a warrant for the arrest of Dragana Kowalchuk for possible war crimes. Ms. Kowalchuk is being charged with…"

Dragana snaps off the radio and slings her sports car into a nearby pullout. The wheels spit gravel and a massive cloud of gray dust as the racer slides to a halt. "Damn it!" she screams, pounding on the dashboard. "How can this be? How could those righteous bastards make such charges?

Okay, just think for a moment. What's my next step? You need a plan. State the objective and map the way ahead. Get it together, Dragana!

The devil woman's mind continues to race, not unlike the heated engine of her sports car. Although she's not the bloody architect of Balkan ethnic cleansing, she knows full well her blueprints are all over the campaign's execution. Dragana casts aside further introspection and self-criticism. In their place, she starts responding to a wave of paranoia and the need for self-preservation knocking on her brain's door.

I accepted this role in exchange for favors. Prosecution was never in the bargain.

"Okay, there's no going to the lodge," she reasons aloud. "Those back-stabbing, spineless fools will be waiting like hungry wolves.

There's but one option: It's time I move on. Why pack when I can shop on the way. I hear medieval Serbia calling... Kosovo, here I come."

—⚏—

It's the first of May and time, the Greek government says, for Alcina's return to Piraeus. Mara stands facing the morning sun, basking in its warm glow as she leans against the Aegean Odyssey's lido deck rail. This small cruiser sails the Dalmatian Archipelago between Athens and Dubrovnik, revealing a myriad of coastal treasures larger ships could never explore.

"Why am I not surprised to find you here?" Alcina asks, stepping close to her friend and gazing at the shoreline.

"Just look. The water's how many shades of blue? Mix in the sunny sky, red-tiled roofs and all the plants. It's a feast for all the senses, but I still can't believe you're going home."

"As hard as it was to say to goodbye to Baba Sofija, Uncle Petar and Andro, I think we owe Andelko a special thanks for getting us on board this amazing ship."

"What connection doesn't that man have? Never mind. I don't think I want to know."

Alcina grasps Mara's forearm. "I'm so glad you could join me for a visit. You'll love my crazy family and the food. My mother is such an incredible cook."

"I've always dreamed of a Greek vacation. Now I'm having it with my own tour guide. I couldn't be happier," Mara replies, placing her hand on top of Alcina's and starring back at the sea. "I've thought a lot about what you said, about being proud of who I am. I'm starting to feel comfortable with myself again."

"That's fantastic. Your frustration and confusion was normal. You must accept yourself for the way you are and everyone will love you so."

"Easier said than done. I still have plenty of doubts."

"Yes, but one step at a time. When someone else's heart touches yours, you'll know. Exploring your womanhood shows you're confident and have strong character. It isn't easy to own your identity, or share it with others. Just be proud of who you are."

"I'm trying, but every now and then the anger, the hate and disgust. They rush over me with no warning."

"It's going to take time, Mara, but don't take that journey without love. Love is something we all should be proud of, with no apologies required. The way we feel love is part of that adventure. Your gift of giving and accepting love makes you what you are."

"It's all about strength, isn't it? Women can't lift as much as some men, but we make up for it in willpower. Allah knows. Women can take a lot of pain."

"That's most insightful, Ms. Cesarec. I know how you like to write. So, if you note what you're feeling now, I'm sure you'll find lots of things you can take pride in later.

"Okay, enough of all that. We have a cruise to enjoy. Soon we dock in Mljet. It's one of the most beautiful islands in the Adriatic. There's this ancient monastery that's a must see. And the great lake castle is a Renaissance jewel."

"Sounds captivating, Alcina.

"Speaking of captivating, we have a couple hours left before the boat docks. Let's head back to our cabin for a while. You can help me pick out a sun dress, put sunscreen on my back, or any other deed that might interest you."

Mara takes Alcina's hand. "Just show me the way. I'm willing to follow."

Bluebonnets and Indian Paintbrushes lead the wildflower parade carpeting the rolling hills of southeast Oklahoma. Trout dance in Mountain Fork River. Spring's beauty is again celebrated across the Choctaw Nation, but nowhere more intensely than in Beavers Bend State Park.

Wearing an eye patch, and with his right arm in a sling, Cashton approaches the information desk at Broken Bow Casino. "Excuse me. Where are the Red Earth Women meeting?" He's directed to a small room just beyond the Blue Moon Café.

"… is enough. We have the power to stop war and we must use it!" a middle-aged Indian woman dressed in faded blue jeans and a Dallas Cowboys sweatshirt exclaims.

"Yes! Yes we do!" several other Hacha Hatak shout. Then the tribal women turn, almost in unison, toward the just opened door. They stare, looking to discern who's entered their inner circle.

"Cashton, you've come… Ladies, this is my son. He's back from that big Army hospital in Washington. Thanks to your prayers, he's mending well. The evil spirits have been kept at bay."

"Really, mother, evil spirits? Anyway, I too thank you for your thoughts and prayers… and the moccasins you made for me with Mother Earth sewn inside. They helped keep the evil spirits away as well," Cashton notes as he winks at his mother.

"Excuse us, there's someone my son must meet. You moccasin makers and war breakers keep the good talk going. I'll be back soon."

"Who are those anarchists?" Cashton chuckles as they walk the hallway.

"Well, your mother now leads this new group of care givers, wives and lovers. We've heard the call. It's the call for a new world direction. We're duty-bound to act. We're united for peace. We practice team-work and harmony. They're the very essence of an Indian woman's soul."

"Right on, mom," Cashton says with enthusiasm as he kisses her forehead. "How cool and refreshing, but I fear I may not be welcome any more."

"Fear not, my loving son. We can protest war, but we'll never turn our backs on the brave men—our husbands, sons and brothers—who volunteer to fight. And we'll always honor them, however they come home. But we'll speak more of this later," Cashton's mother says as they step into the casino manager's reception room. "We're the Steels. Here to see Councilman Jefferson."

A smoked glass door swings open. The tribal elder, dressed in a light gray suit and sporting a turquoise-covered arrowhead bolo, invites Cashton and his mother in.

"I must get back to my working group, but Cashton, please go ahead. I'm sure Chief Jefferson has much he wants to share with you."

"Halito," the slender, middle-aged man states as he extends his hand in greeting. "Ant chukoa. Come in, Sergeant Steel. Yokoke. Thank you for your service to America and our nation, as well. Please, have a seat.

"I'll cut to the chase, Cashton. As I wrote your mother while you were at Walter Reed, we now have grant money to help soldiers transition back to tribal life. Yes, our vets group is doing great things, but we think more can be done. All on the council agree. Yet, we need someone like you to pull it together."

"I'm willing, sir, but I don't quite understand what ya'll are looking for."

"There's no sugar-coating it. Things are rough across our tribal lands. Drugs and violence attack us everywhere. Crime runs the gambit from stealing cigarettes to rape. Our young people need a role model who's name isn't Jack Daniels.

"The council wants to focus on homeless vets. We need to explore ways to battle unemployment and alcohol abuse. We're looking for ideas, as well as answers. How do we partner with the VA, Indian Affairs and business? You and other warriors have the skills, the devotion to duty we need. The Army's trained and tested you. Help us, Cashton. Bring all those talents to the fight. Help us make our nation strong again."

"That's a big order, sir, but I'm willing to try."

"Good. I was hoping you'd say that. In honor of this moment, I'm asking that you take the Choctaw name *Nashoba Nowa* as a symbol of your strength and determination in the great task ahead."

"Walking Wolf it is, sir."

"May the Okla Humma spirit, the Red People's mettle, be your guide, Cashton. I'm sure you'll do great things, Walking Wolf. Now, let's tell your mother and the others about our pact. Maybe then, we can all link arms in a new life circle pow-wow."

—⁓—

C H A P T E R   2 4 :

FORGING A FOURTH ESTATE

LIGHT BEAMS STREAK between curtain panels, sliding into Heath's hotel suite and intensifying his late-May wakeup call. He sits up slowly and starts massaging a swollen right knee. This is followed by a crude attempt to fire up the coffee maker while stumbling toward the shower.

"Shit," Heath grumbles as he dumps the small wicker basket where multiple coffee packets should be sequestered. "Sticks, creamer, sugar and that blue crap… Not even decaf."

Heath dons a pair of sweats and tennis shoes before trudging down the hallway to the elevator. "Why me, Lord? Why me?" he mumbles.

Aggravating interruptions like this don't bode well for Heath making deadline. A month has passed since his talk with Mara. In that time, he's conducted more than a dozen battered women interviews. As a result, Heath's amassed a stack of cards highlighting those exchanges. Each is cross-referenced to a mini-cassette stashed in his nightstand. His intended morning tasks include sorting those piles and making sense out of what he's collected. Instead, Heath's shuffling through the lobby in search of a java jolt.

"Excuse me, Mr. Winslow," the clerk at the counter says. "There's a Telex for you, sir. Sign here, please."

"Shit. What's up now? A call back to the concrete canyons? Thanks… And send up a couple boxes—boxes, not packs—of regu-

319

lar coffee, please. The maid seems to have overlooked me the last few days."

> DATE: 16 May 1996
> FROM: U.S. Embassy, The Hague, Netherlands
> SUBJECT: Notice of Possible Summons
> TO: Mr. Heath Winslow c/o Holliday Inn-Sarajevo
>
> *Under Hague Service Convention authority, you are being considered for summons before the International Criminal Tribunal for the Former Yugoslavia to provide documentation, or possible testimony, in the matter of state-directed propaganda campaigns during the Balkan Conflict intended as weapons of war against the peoples of Serbia, Croatia, Bosnia & Herzegovina.*
>
> *Reporting details and requirements will be provided through an in-country U.S. State Department representative once determination is made by the ICTY. You are not required to acknowledge or respond to this notification.*
>
> *SIGNED:*
> *For the Chargé d'Affaires T: +31 70 310-2209*

"Shit… Make my day," Heath snarls with a Clint Eastwood-esque grovel. "Make that a double espresso. It's going to be a beautiful morning. I can tell already."

—⚏—

Andro's uncle, Franjo, steps into the base ops reception area and hands off two fresh cups of coffee. Andro appreciates the simple gesture, especially in light of his 0-dark-30 arrival at the Sarajevo airport. "You add the cream and sugar. I'll check the milk run manifest."

"The what?" Andro asks.

"Passenger and crew list for today's flight to Athens," Franjo states. "Hate to see you up this early and not get on the plane."

"Funny, uncle. I'm the courier. Besides, I thought this was a weekly down and back with hardly anyone on board?"

"It is, my bureaucratic buddy, but the U.S. Air Force is flying this mission, so we've got to do all the proper paperwork in triplicate."

As Franjo completes his morning rounds and the aircrew finishes its pre-flight checklist, Andro scans the *Herald Tribune* left folded on the counter. A front page headline declares *Bosnian Serb President Karadžić Resigns*.

"My God… He's out of office. And they're indicting the bastard for war crimes."

Unbelievable, Andro ponders. *I wonder what Heath thinks about this? Is this a step toward reunion, or setting the stage for revenge? And what about the battles inside people's heads? Are we finally coming to terms with our past?*

"Babich?" the C-130 crewman walks up and asks. Before Andro can answer, the airman continues, "Good. Grab your bags and follow me. The fog's lifting. It's time we kick tires and punch a hole in the sky. We're wheels up in 15."

"Uncle Franjo, thanks… Check out the *Tribune*, then go buy some champagne. We'll celebrate when I get back. Ciao!"

About two hours later, the Herculean cargo plane begins its final approach on Eleftherios Venizelos, Athens' international airport. Once Andro transfers the diplomatic pouch and clears Customs, he steps into the arrival lounge. There he's met by an exuberant welcoming committee made up of his aunt, uncle, Alcina, Mara and several family friends. They share hugs and kisses, then sweep the young man toward the awaiting caravan of cars. Next stop: Taverna Poseidon.

Upon entering the beachside bistro, tunes playing on the local Euro-rock station are cranked and everyone's told to grab a shot of ouzo. Andro's Uncle Abeiron bellows, "Στην Υγεια σου!"

"And to your health as well!" Andro shouts back.

With the anise-flavored aperitif downed, the kitchen doors burst open. Silver serving trays appear in mass. They're covered with an assortment of hummus, tzatziki, spanakopita and chicken kabobs. Abeiron insists everyone pour copious amounts of retsina, beer or soda to wash it all down.

The welcome party rolls on with an endless staging of music, food and drink, as well as the obligatory plate smashing session initiated by Alcina. Andro's overwhelmed by the intensity of it all. He takes a moment, steps out to the patio and stares at the twinkling lagoon. He's soon joined by Mara and his cousin.

"You've had a good vacation, I hope?" Andro asks Mara.

"The best… Everyone's rolled out the red carpet at every stop."

"And it's fun playing tour guide," Alcina notes. "You show your guests the neat stuff you've been meaning to see, but never quite got around to. We're both wiser for it."

"Ready to go home? Baba Sofija misses you," Andro hints.

"Right. She misses the pot holes I dig in her road to wherever."

"Okay, Baba can be a bit controlling," Andro says, "but she longs for the spirited way you change stuff around all the time. I know she'd never say that, but you sense the fun in it too. I know you do. The way you two play off each other is special. Isn't it?"

"Yes, you're right. Maybe it's time to go back."

"Besides, she may be the craftswoman," Andro adds, "but no one knows the marketing or managing end of it like you."

"He's got you there, Mara. Saving the art and raising women up are important, but if there are no coins in the cash register, how will the business grow?"

"Okay… Your tag-teaming is a success. I'll head north soon. Sure, Sofija and I have issues, but Andro can help us work through them.

It's just that I tend to focus on process while Sofija is always zeroing in on results."

"Come on. One can't function without the other," Alcina says. "Here we have Mara, the mechanic that leads us to an outcome. And then there's Sofija, the very product of those actions."

"Absolutely… It's a match made in heaven. And with that settled, what are you ladies going to show this vacationer in the week ahead?"

—m—

Yielding to an exhausted brain and sore feet on day four of his visit, Andro insists they return to Uncle Abeiron's watering hole for adult beverages and a stool on which to rest his rubbery legs. At the taverna, Andro, Mara and Alcina grab cocktails and head for beach hammocks.

"Cheers… And thank you for the sightseeing extravaganza, but we're done and I insist we don't move an inch for at least a day."

"On your feet, sailor!" an almost larger than life silhouette yells from the patio. "When Jason Banks says jump, you snap to."

"My God, it is. It's Jason, but why, when, how, where?"

"Still with a million and one questions," Jason chuckles as he jumps the steps and stomps through the sand. "Like the great sea god, Oceanus, circlin' the globe, I seek safe harbor in a storm. Might I drop anchor here, sir?"

"But of course," Andro says as tears well up and they share a massive bear hug. Stepping back from the embrace, Andro says, "Jason, you know Alcina, but please let me introduce my friend, Mara from Konjic. Mara, this is my comrade and mentor, Mr. Jason Banks."

"Andro didn't send me a picture, but his simple words could never have described your true beauty, my lady."

"Thank you, Jason, I've heard so…"

"You still know how to spread honey on a roll, don't you?" Alcina pipes in. "Come on everyone; let's hit the bar. We might as well declare this reunion week."

Throughout the afternoon and into the evening, the whole Constantinides extended family stops by. They join in welcoming Jason back into the fold while expressing selfish sadness at hearing his sailing days may be numbered. All agree another seaside celebration should be launched to honor him, Mara and Andro before they cast off.

—⋙—

The next morning finds Andro leaning against the Poseidon's patio rail, sipping a café latte. He gazes at the ships in the harbor. Memories wash over him like gentle waves caressing the nearby beach.

"It's been almost four years since we met here," a voice from behind him states.

"That's the memory I was savoring. And that of the villain Karadžić stepping down. Now it's Kowalchuk's time to pay the piper. I will make her bear the cost of her actions, if it's the last thing I do."

"I hear you, Andro, but put it aside for a few days, alright? Here we are in the heart of the Med. Let's just soak it in, sip it up and slurp it down, my man."

"You're right. The mess at home isn't going anywhere. There's one other thing, though, Jason. You know how sorry we all are about your incredible loss. So, I have to ask: What brings you to Greece at such a troubling time?"

"I guess you could call it my farewell cruise, Andro. I wanted to see everyone one more time before droppin' anchor in New York for good."

"And what will you do there?"

"Losin' Denasha was, well… Let's just say I want to set it right. Her death can't be an ending. Rather, I've gotta start somethin' that's unending. I have real hope and I feel Denasha's support as well. The gang violence will be answered, in time.

"And the priest you sent me to; he's quite the character. His readin' list was spot on. He told me to study that Bengali guy, Tagore. It's as if the dude knew Denasha. Take a look at this part right here," Jason says, creasing open a dog-eared paperback just pulled from his pocket. Pointing to a key passage, Jason says, "It finally makes sense to me…"

> *The flower is exhausted after giving its beauty to this world. It brightened the day for us. It soothed our eyes when they wanted relief from the painful sight of agony. It charmed us with its marvelous color. Now it's dying, but it has accomplished its journey. It has fulfilled its purpose.*

…from the writings of Rabindranath Tagore

"You're right, Jason, and we should get that kid priest canonized one of these days," Andro says as a comforting jest.

"First we've gotta get you and Mara back to Bosnia where you both can do some good, now that the storm clouds have started to clear. And might I be sensin' more than just a friendship with Ms. Mara, my man?"

"I think not. Yes, we're close, but I don't feel any kind of spark. Mara's been through so much… so much hurt. I just don't know where her heart lies, nor does she, I'm afraid."

"Okay, we'll leave that sit where it is. We've got a few days before I sail, or you fly. So, like I said, let's make the most of it."

"I'm game, but beware of Alcina. She's a licensed tourist killer."

—⁂—

"What's the story, bud?" Eoghan shouts to Andro as he enters the Ballygoan. He's recently returned to Sarajevo and is now well rested from his Grecian retreat.

"We thought you got lost, young man," Heath chides.

"Good God, do you two live in this bar?"

"Pretty much this be it for me," Eoghan replies.

"And your point is?" Heath asks.

"Yesterday was Tuesday, the 28th of May. It was the 750th anniversary of the Feast of Corpus Christi."

"Wow… Was I supposed to buy a gift?" Heath scoffs.

"No, you heathen. Anyway, I spent the last few days with my family in Konjic. John Paul sent a memo to all parish priests saying they should redouble efforts teaching the Holy Eucharist. Well, Baba Sofija took that as a personal letter from the Pope and drilled us, along with the congregation, on spiritual growth for three days straight."

"Well then, Andro, you shouldn't have to do penance for a month of Sundays." Following that sarcastic remark, Eoghan starts back-peddling down the bar, away from Heath. "And where the hell are you going, Mr. Barkeep?"

"No need for both of us bein' struck by lightenin', now is there? Let's drop the Bible banter and get back to important matters. Like, did ya get laid in Athens or not, me boy?"

"You two are incorrigible," Andro concedes as he plops on the stool next to Heath, "but when you meet Baba Sofija, that will be a good thing. Her story is a Pulitzer in the rough. In this bloody conflict alone, she's gone from protester, to prisoner, to craft mistress. And all for the sake of her beloved Yugoslavia."

"She meets herself comin' back," Eoghan adds. "That be for sure."

"Okay," Andro adds, "she's intense and she may live a bit in the past, but that's her way. The craft gild she and Mara started will be selling wears across Europe soon."

"It's quite the story, Heath. Baba's been through the mill, but she's still a hard-chargin' lass. Ms. Sofija takes the biscuit in my book."

"Alright, guys!" Heath declares. "You had me sold at the prison break. So, Andro, set up a meeting and join us, if you like."

"I'm rather busy the next couple weeks, but Mara's back and I'm sure she'd be glad to help. Thank you, Heath. You'll find Baba Sofija is like a tree in the forest, an anchor for a mighty ship, or…"

"Or someone who hired P.T. Barnum as her promoter. I get it Andro and I look forward to meeting her. I do. Just bring it down a notch so we can get the bloody Irishman back over here to serve us a couple more beers."

"Now that's a different kettle o' fish, Mr. Winslow. Although me feelings be crushed, I'll see what I can do to put a little sustenance on the counter."

"And a little less drama behind it, if you would be so kind." Heath's cutting remark is followed by an extended silence. Then, all three blokes break into laughter, quick to toast their latest non-occasion.

"Not a bother. And tanks, laddy," Eoghan chuckles as he draws another round.

⸺ ⁂ ⸺

"… a government spokesman says talks will begin soon in Northern Ireland, without Sinn Féin at the table," the radio announcer states. "And that's the news for June 10, 1996 on B.H. 1 Radio."

"Sounds like the Brits are having as much luck waging peace as we are," Baba Sofija grumbles as she reaches toward the bookshelf in the spic and span living room of her Konjic farmhouse. She pushes a button, shutting off the stereo.

"Enough of the politics, Sofija," Mara insists. "We have a business to run and you have a visitor coming up the lane. It's Andro's reporter friend."

"How's the place look? You put on a fresh pot of coffee, right? And these doilies, are they okay here?"

"Stop fluttering about. The man doesn't write for *Europa Style*. He's a journalist coming to hear about you. Just relax and enjoy the moment."

"Easy for you to say. He sent you home in tears, did he not?"

Before she can offer a rebuttal, there's a knock at the door. Mara opens it wide. "Heath, how good to see you again. Please, come inside. It's my pleasure to introduce the family matriarch and my adopted grandmother, Mrs. Sofija Babich. Baba, this is Mr. Winslow."

"Dobro dan," Baba Sofija says, extending her hand to welcome the seasoned writer.

"And a good day to you, ma'am, but please call me Heath." He presents a small bouquet and a bottle of brandy. "Flowers to compliment the lady's beauty and a little slivovitz to warm a chilly night."

Sofija rolls her eyes, then looks to Mara, murmuring, "And you said this is the nasty man who made you cry? No, no, Heath, Žao mi je. I'm just kidding. Have a seat please. Mara, would you serve the coffee and pastries?"

Pleasantries exchanged, the battery acid poured and dusty cookies served, Heath launches into a series of questions about Sofija's long and intriguing life. In response, she shares a string of clever and poignant recollections. To this day Sofija remembers, as if it were yesterday, how the Nazis practiced genocide against Jews, Roma and Serbs in the Balkans. This memory isn't lost on those struggling through recent upheavals.

"Mara, how about a little plum brandy, a mineral water and a slice of your baklava for our guest?"

"Oh, I couldn't."

"But I insist," Sofija says as she glances over her shoulder toward the kitchen, then leans in to whisper, "Besides, it will give me a moment to share these." Baba pulls an old attaché from under the sofa. Inside the satchel are dozens of letters postmarked New York, Piraeus, Sarajevo, Zagreb and who knows where else.

"This was our church-on-church connection. They're notes from Andro, my sons and priests across Europe. They kept us in touch during the dark days. They're the glue that held the Babich clan together. This is the real tale, Mr. Winslow, not me. I want you to take and read these. The story will come to you. You'll see."

"Hvala, Ms. Sofija. I'd like to copy them, if that's alright? I can get the originals back to you faster that way."

"Of course, but now, Zivjeli... To your writing success," Sofija proposes as they take two cut crystal schnapps glasses from the tray Mara has delivered. Eyes sparkle and smiles broaden as Sofija and Heath toast Babich peace and prosperity.

—⁂—

About a week later, Heath is sitting outside Adrijan's Belgrade office, scanning the *Herald Tribune's* June 16th edition. The day before, a massive IRA bomb injured more than 200 and devastated a large part of Manchester city center. *Sure as hell hope England's not my next assignment,* Heath wishes. *I'm ready to pass the Edward R. Morrow monocle to a younger bloke.*

A buzzer sounds at the receptionist's desk. Adrijan's buxom brunette assistant half giggles and says, with a blank gaze, "Mr. Ackov will see you now."

"Heath, please come in. I hope I didn't keep you waiting long?"

"No problem, ol' boy, but I don't think my wait time is what you should be focusing on. Oh, Adrijan, you may think you know what's happening, but I can assure you, I now know more of the truth. And it's not pretty.

"Your way ahead is limited by what needs to be done right now. So, let's get to the point. You saw my note about The Hague summons. Beyond having my ethics questioned, I have no desire serving as a lackey to their Balkan witch hunt. Yes, you're square in their crosshairs, but I argue they have far bigger fish to fry than one, each Adrijan Ackov.

"There's no question one of the first casualties of this damn war was the truth. Using PR tricks and propaganda campaigns like the crap you and Dragana cooked up was not only reckless, it was dangerous and deadly. So, something must be done, and done quickly, to salvage what's left of the Fourth Estate here. To that end, I have a proposal. I think it's about the only option left to pull your ass out of this quagmire."

"You'd do that for me, Heath?"

"Screw you, Adrijan. You're just a pudgy little piece in the bigger scheme of things. The U.N. and NATO brass missed a lot of chances to help journalists during the war, but letting a bunch of bureaucrats launch new outlets carries its own risks. It may sound hokey to you, but Americans are here to promote democracy through awareness. You can interpret that as the sound of honesty via the airways.

"With that said, I've come across some concrete info about a young Muslim girl whose family was ripped apart back in '92. Later, disguised as a Gypsy, she went through hell to gather info on rebel ops up and down the valley. She was almost caught in the process. Today she's helping run a craft gild for war widows. That's the kind of story you should be telling. Do you hear me, Adrijan? Do you understand?"

"Truth and reconciliation… Yes, it will be our greatest aspiration, Heath."

"I hope you believe that. As you've been told, Andro Babich will be monitoring your work like a hawk. He tells me you've already met. Accept it, Adrijan: You're going to be held accountable like never before. There's no other option, if you want to stay on this side of a prison cell.

"So, here's how it'll go down: Her name is Mara Cesarec. She lives and works in Konjic. Mr. Babich will escort her to your Sarajevo station. The TV staff will coordinate with Andro on the story line while he monitors production. In the meantime, I'm encouraging you to seek out as many similar stories as possible, if you expect any kind of longevity on your media career path."

Flipping through his reporter's notebook, Heath says, "Well, that's pretty much it, Adrijan. Now, I hope you don't think I've tried boxing you into a corner. I've always felt people should have options. You can either get on board with this, or wave the train goodbye as you're hauled off to the pokey. It's your choice."

—⁂—

DEATH IN ALL THE WRONG PLACES

It's a brisk, mid-June morning along Bosnia's Neretva River. Andro tightens his boot laces, straps on an extra canteen, then grabs grandpa's walking stick while scrunching his loose-knit tuque. This trekker is setting out from the Babich farmhouse to hike the Herzegovinian Himalayas. He's hoping the ramble will clear his muddled mind, while helping strengthen body and soul.

"Leaving early to avoid Baba Sofija's lecture?" Andro's brother whispers as he hobbles into the kitchen. "Do watch out for land mines. Rebels threw the damn things everywhere. And the military maps are garbage."

"Then I'll have to be extra careful, won't I? I promise not to go on any path that hasn't been cleared. And give me a break, Alen. I've done this hike how many times? At least there shouldn't be avalanches today."

"Okay, I hear you… I'm jealous, I guess. I could do with a climb as well, let alone a plate of Aunt Sasha's musaka. And please call before Uncle Thoma pulls out the rakia."

"I will. I've got some time off, so I plan to stay a couple days. Andelko may drive up. If not, I'll head for Dubrovnik. You should take the bus down and join us."

"Sounds good. I'll see how this damn knee feels after my workout. Have a good ramble and keep your eyes open."

It's late afternoon when Andro finishes his mountain decent into Mostar. He's struck and saddened by the wonton destruction that's been heaped upon this ancient town. The city now smolders in the cross-hairs of devastation piled on from all directions. Andro makes his way past the crater-pocked football field to Sasha's restaurant.

"Andro! Dobro vece!" a lady shrieks as she looks up from wiping down a small sidewalk bench in front of the café.

"Good afternoon, Aunt Sasha."

"Thoma, come quickly."

"What is it?" Thoma grumbles as he steps on to the patio. "Oh, it's another one of those Americans. Are you looking for a bridge to far, sir?"

"Such a loving uncle. How can I ever be worthy?"

"No, Andelko!" Thoma yells back toward the kitchen. "Put the hors d'oeuvre down. Just bring that cheap wine. It's not President Clinton after all."

Andro falls into Thoma's arms. An intense embrace follows. It's chased by similar squeezes and kisses with Sasha and Andelko. The chiding and teasing continue as the three men screech metal chairs around a wrought iron table on the veranda.

"Andelko's shared your stories," Sasha says, returning with several small plates of appetizers. "So many exploits in such a short time."

"Andro, we're so very proud of you," Thoma says with selfless delight. "And now you come home to help put things right. That's amazing. You don't buy from my son's art studio, but you can tell people what to play on radio and TV. That's amazing."

"Thank you, uncle, but it's not that impressive. First off, I don't think anything Andelko had for sale would have fit in Franjo's Beetle. Secondly, I'm way down the employee totem pole. I supervise radio and TV production. If it helps them tell the truth, than it's a good thing."

"It got you back with us," Andelko points out. "That's even better."

"And it gives us reason to open the fine wine," Thoma boasts. "That's the best." With that, Sasha places a bottle each of Blatina red and Zilavka white. Andelko begins the uncorking process.

Glasses filled and held high, Thoma says, "Sasha and I have always been a little smug when it comes to you go-getters. You both spot a challenge, then follow it like blood hounds. And once you settle on what's needed, you go on point for it."

"But all the time they care for the people around them," Sasha adds. "That's what makes Andelko and Andro so special."

"Of course… They're from the loins of the Babich clan. We should expect nothing less."

Glasses clink and wine is quaffed, then Thoma looks to the street. A taxi is pulling up. "It's Alen… Boys, help him from the car. Bring that wounded warrior this way, but be gentle now."

"Alen, your timing couldn't be better," Sasha states. "Let's move inside where there's more room. Places are set for dinner. You still like musaka, yes?"

Settled at the oversized Beachwood table in the main dining room, Thoma inquires, "So, nephew, tell us about your war wound."

"Actually, uncle, it's not. I tripped and fell down a ravine, firing up an old football injury. I just had surgery to put it right. It's working well, but it'll take time."

"You and papa saw some awful things while you were away," Andro says.

"And we'll not speak of them today," Sasha insists.

"Then what should we talk about?" Andro asks.

"Drugs, sex, rock and roll!" Andelko shouts. "Just kidding, but it's what the announcers say on Armed Forces Radio when they talk about some American bloke called 'Slick Willy.'"

"Actually, there is something I was thinking about. Andro, could you go through those hand-loomed rugs from Baba Sofija's craft guild? I can put some on consignment. I'm sure the cruise shippers will scarf them up in no time."

"And all three of you can help get the word out on Cousin Sasha," their aunt states. "With the war over, he's putting his band back together. *The Yugos* are now six guys doing folk music that crosses all the ethnic divides. They're singing at the Sarajevo Music Fest next month."

"And if you're still looking for something to do, you can help me as well," Thoma adds. "The premier league wants me as a color commentator, but I need to hone my play-by-play skills."

"What a coincidence," Alen chimes in. "The Hrvatski športski Klub has offered me a coaching job. I'm sure they have miles of game tape you can screen."

"You see," Sasha insists as she refills everyone's glass and lifts hers to propose a toast. "This is why we must get together more often. Such good things can only happen when we make our minds one. As you say, Thoma, our clan is firm… Živjeli!"

—⁂—

A couple weeks later, Andro finds himself on a lazy afternoon drive back to Sarajevo. A short distance outside Belgrade, he spots a car with the bonnet popped. A stranded motorist appears bent over the engine. With a renewed degree of caution, Andro pulls alongside the marooned traveler and asks, "Might you need a hand?"

A tall, slender forty-something woman in a stylish sweat suit ensemble looks back. "The radiator hose has come loose. I can't seem to hold it in place and tighten the coupling at the same time. If you could…"

"Certainly," Andro acknowledges as he parks his gray staff car in front of the bright red roadster. He reaches under the driver's seat and slides the Colt .45 semi-automatic out of its metal travel holster. Holding the gun low to the floorboard, he pulls a magazine from the glove box and slaps it in the stock. Swinging the door open, Andro takes a wide step on to the pavement, turns and points toward the unsuspecting day tripper. "Hands on the fender, facing the car," he states.

"Excuse me, sir," Dragana says as she throws her hands in the air. "The car's broke. If you want it so badly, at least let me get it started."

"Where you are is just fine, ma'am. Hands on the vehicle… Now! I'm going to frisk you for weapons."

"Whatever gets you off, young man."

Andro steps forward and begins patting down the woman. He glances under the hood and sees a flashlight, tools and a couple cleaning rags. "Wow, you really are broken down."

"No. It's a just a ruse to lure studs like you into slapping my ass for no apparent reason."

"I'm sorry. I'm so sorry," Andro says, stepping back from the woman while popping the magazine from the revolver. "I was carjacked the other week and, well, I guess I over-reacted. I'm so, so sorry. Can I still offer a hand?"

"If it doesn't have a gun in it."

Andro slides the magazine in his right pocket and the pistol in his left. He then stands to, awaiting further instruction.

"You hold the hose in place and I'll tighten the clamp."

Once the connection is secured and the two wipe most of the grease from their hands, he extends his and says, "I'm Andro Babich with USAID. And you are?"

"Ah… Michelle Nice, monsieur," Dragana stammers with an over-drawn French accent. "Perhaps you have heard of my aunt, Hellé

Nice, the famous sports car driver. She was known as La Bugatti Queen of motorsport."

"No, I can't say I do. What part of France are you from?"

"Le petite village du Sainte-Mesme. Ah… north-central, Île-de-France region. You ask many questions. Are you a reporter or something?"

"No, just curious. This is such a beautiful driving machine. Do you race?

"Ah, no, no… I buy and sell classics. I'm on my way to Zagreb with this one. MGBs bring a good price. Well, merci. I'm running late, so I must go."

"I have a couple jugs in the boot. I'll get them while you check the water level."

As soon as Andro starts walking toward the sedan, Dragana jumps in the coupe, starts the engine, slaps it in gear and launches down the highway. Years of slalom racing and autocross help her grease today's exit. She looks in the rear view to see a befuddled Andro rotating midst a cloud of freshly spun-up dust. He's raising a plastic jug in each hand as if to question her quick departure and need for liquids.

"Poor Andro. Your ignorance is my bliss. You've never been so close, yet so far away."

—❧—

"Mara, must you go?" Baba Sofija asks as the young woman prepares her backpack for a Sarajevo hike. "This morning Hezbollah blew up a tower in Saudi Arabia. Two dozen Americans were killed. It's a bad omen. I can feel it."

"Soldiers in harm's way. Yes, that's a tragic thing Sofija, but we have our own demons to fight. And if my doing this documentary will help, then I must be there. Besides, I need the exercise. Now, don't worry. I'll be fine."

A couple hours later, Mara catches sight of a narrow, wooden suspension bridge that joins two ridges high above the river. A tall man in ragged military garb approaches the near end. Mara waits for him pass. He casts a cold stare while sauntering by. The pock-faced former fighter brandishes a row of half-rotten yellow teeth as he tips his hat. Disgusted and concerned by his motives, Mara grabs the bridge rope lines and begins walking toward the other side with a newfound briskness in her step.

"Wait! Wait! You, you wait… You're that Muslim wench from Konjic. We pushed a couple big 'Thank yous' your way," the brute snorts as he stomps his legs apart and grabs his crotch. "You want another warm welcome, bitch?"

Mara's knees quiver. Her stomach twists into a knot as her chest tightens. The hideous creature is now storming her way. Mara picks up the pace in a desperate lunge to reach the far side. The passage begins to sway as the mad man carries his charge to the bridge's center. Mara continues her sprint, but realizes she won't reach the bluff before he's upon her. She drops her shoulder. The backpack strap falls free. Smelling his rotten closeness, Mara whirls the satchel with all her might, striking the animal broadside his face and chest. He falls back against the rope which does little to break his continued fall into the ravine. The landing site far below is brimming with jagged boulders and frothy-white mountain waters.

Mara's shocked by the rapid chain of uncontrolled events. Without looking down, she slips on the rucksack and continues her trudge across the wooden pathway. Moments later, Mara enters Rakitnica Canyon with the suspended tragedy no longer in sight. She stops to rest on a moss-covered bolder. The shaken soul cups her face with trembling hands and begins to weep. Soon, Mara's kneeling near the rock and retching. Once the heaving ends, she pulls a wet wipe from her knapsack and cleans up as best she can. Somewhat composed, Mara takes out and begins eating a nutrition bar while sipping a small bottle of mineral water in silent repose.

Several hours of hiking pass. Mara descends the Mount Igman foothills, soon to be in a familiar Sarajevo suburb. It's home to Franjo, Florica and the children. She can only pray today's nightmare has now come to an end.

—⟆—

"No, no, I'm sorry. I should have called earlier," Florica explains to Baba Sofija. "Mara was worn out when she got here. I made her take a shower while I warmed some soup. When I checked on her, she was cuddled up, asleep on the bed. So, I pulled up the comforter and shut off the light. Yes, yes, I'm sure our little Gypsy's okay. She's just tired. It's alright. I'll have her ring you in the morning. Good night, Sofija… We love you too."

—⟆—

Mara wakes early. Darkness cloaks the neighborhood as dim white light from a nearby street lamp struggles to pierce the morning fog. She slips on her jogging suit, then laces tight her tennis shoes. Tiptoeing down the hallway into the kitchen, Mara mounts a step stool next to the refrigerator. She swings open the cabinet above and gropes inside. Grasping a cold metal shape, she extracts it from the family hiding place. Mara then flips back the kitchen door lock and slips outside.

As the morning's mist begins to lift, Mara advances on Vrelo Bosne. Outside the park's entrance, the costumed carriage driver finishes pouring a cup of steaming java from his metal thermos. Glimpsing Mara's approach, he tips his hat and smiles. She dips a quick curtsey. The whole time, his mare grazes on the lush grass made heavy with morning dew.

Moments later, a piercing pistol pop breaks the dawn's silence. The buggy handler snaps tight the reins as his steed makes a startled lurch to the right. His cup tumbles, spilling hot coffee down the wagoner's leg. "Osuditi!" he yells, then looks toward the entrance, wondering if fowl play might be afoot.

The driver brings the horse about, clip-clopping down the cobblestone path into the commons. In the distance he can barely make out a shape draped against a park bench.

"Whoa," the man whispers to his charge. He pulls back on the buggy's brake handle, ties off the harness straps and dismounts. As he approaches the form, it becomes clear it's the young woman who entered the park earlier.

"My God," he sighs as he steps closer. He spots a limp, out-stretched arm. The dainty hand is clutching a blood-smeared letter. For some inexplicable reason, he feels compelled to remove the crimpled paper and read the note:

> *I can suffer in silence no more. My mind-numbing terror has been relentless. It never truly ends. I want to feel worthless no longer. The time has come to make my escape from this Hell on Earth. So, I am ending it today. Papa's damaged goods will be no more.*
>
> *May Allah forgive my sin and stop my spirit's journey toward the eternal Fire.*

Slowly, almost reverently, the coachman kneels and slides the memo back in Mara's curled palm. He begins blowing his metal pea whistle in hopes of alerting security. Having heard the gun discharge, a policeman can be seen running in their direction. Approaching the horse and carriage, the lawman shouts, "Is she…"

"…as a doornail."

"Do you know who she is?" the officer asks.

"No, no I don't," the driver mumbles, unaware he's slipping into shock. "She came to the park often, sometimes with children. She would meet with an older woman in a business suit. There was nothing strange about it, though." Soon, the horseman's vomiting near the pathway, using the gas lamp pole to steady himself.

"Are you going to be alright, sir?" the cop asks. "I'll need you to come down to the station to make a statement."

"Well, she certainly made a statement, didn't she?"

—⚒—

"Where in the hell can she be?" Adrijan asks Andro as he paces around the cavernous Federalna TV studio in downtown Sarajevo. "We only have this space for a couple hours."

"Mara will be here soon," Andro says in a confident tone. "Fretting about won't make her show any sooner. Might I see your interview questions? If you have b-roll cued up, maybe we could review that as well."

"Excuse me, gentlemen," one of the news producers gasps, rushing into the studio. "A young lady's shot herself in the park. I'm short on crew today. I'll have to take your camera and sound man on scene."

"We understand," Andro states. "I have experience covering such events. I'll go with you. Adrijan, tell Mara we'll have to reschedule. I'm sure she'll empathize with what's going on. That should give you time for more fact checking as well. I'll call your Belgrade office tomorrow."

Andro, the producer and two technicians grab equipment and run out the side door. They leap into a white utility van and roar off. Adrijan is now left alone on set. "I script the shoot, schedule this place and now I'm holding the bag? Who the hell's producing this puff piece anyway?"

Damn, Adrijan complains. *Too much serious thinking. It's giving me another one of those nasty headaches. This one's weird, though. It aches all down my neck and arm this time, too. I'd better catch the Olympic Express back to Belgrade before the dizziness gets any worse.*

A few hours later, as the train pulls into Prokop Centre, Sasha Kovasevic, the train's conductor, slides open the compartment's glass door and announces their arrival in the Serbian capital. "Time to wake up, sir," Sasha states as he nudges the man. "This is the end station. Everyone must exit."

The trainman then shakes Adrijan more firmly, at which point he slides out of the coach seat and slumps on to the linoleum floor. "Wow… I guess he's been drinking. Well, that's what porters are for. My work here is done."

—⁓—

"Na zdorovje!" Eoghan yells as Heath enters the Holiday Inn lounge.

"You know drunken Soviets don't say 'Cheers' that way."

"Well, that's what California commies holler in those Hollywood movies, eh?"

"Point well taken. So, what are we toasting today? No that I give a damn."

"Yeltsin won the election. Here's to good ol' Boris, the Russian bear. Hey, that beats any shout out in your direction. Ya gotta admit, Heath, it's bleedin' rapid the way your friends and enemies are droppin' and desertin'. I'm about the only drinkin' partner ya got left nowadays."

"Makes you wonder why I'm here at all, doesn't it?"

"Well, at least, with Ackov kickin' the bucket, you shouldn't be summoned to The Hague any time soon."

"Hopefully, you're right. I'm relieved about not having to contrast ethics against war crimes before that group. Now, I've tried to be fair in my reporting, but not knowing how those damn judges might interpret my work… well, that was a big concern of mine."

Notebook entry: Limitation of Harm—When a journalist withholds submission details, i.e.: names of children, crime victims, info not related to a news report… Release might harm reputation, put people in danger

"But Mara's suicide. Damn… I don't know how to step out with that one."

"You've gotta drive on, Heath. You may scrape the road in spots, but her sacrifice should be your signal to tell the whole bloody tale as best ya can."

"I hear you, Eoghan, and I don't mean to sound like a pompous ass, but if I'm to cover the bullshit in the Balkans, I need to write more than just rape, plunder and pillage pieces. I need to interview leaders from all the warring factions. Kowalchuk's one of them, but she's been so damn afraid of capture. She refuses to cooperate. That crazy broad has made every kind of rendezvous I try next to impossible."

"What I hear on the bar room channel is you'll need your passport and a visa for Kosovo, if you're gonna question the Devil Woman again."

"That may be. I'm still fascinated by her fixation with restoring Serbian supremacy… You heard me. I said fascinated, not sympathetic. So, I plan to follow her for as long as I can."

"What makes you think these cat-and-mouse shenanigans ain't just a game Dragana's playin'?"

"What? You think she's trying to manipulate me?"

"Isn't it obvious, Mr. H? She wants ya to be coverin' all her exploits. It's both self-servin' and vainglorious."

"As if that'll ever happen. So, Eoghan, you think I'm that gullible? Sure, I'll go along and gather up as much as I can. And yes, I've slept with the devil before, but…"

"Damnú!" Eoghan shouts an interruption, followed by slamming a stein on the wash counter for emphasis. It shatters and shards explode in all directions. "You're soundin' like your dead buddy Ackov now. He was a flippin' eejit. Idiot I say… Okay?

"What's all this for?" Eoghan bellers as he throws a bar rag in the sink, splashing suds that cover much of the splintered glass. "Or, do ya want to be more like that bitseach Dragana? Thar she blows! Steppin' 'round shite 'cause she don't wanna get her boots dirty and you sniffin' right close behind. Just wait. She'll be on ya like a ton of bricks. Mark me words."

"Damn strong stuff from someone who's pissing off a regular… And don't expect me to pay extra for your latest bad acting lesson."

"Everyone's givin' ya the bull's rush. For Christ's sake, Heath, why can't ya see it?"

"Alright, let's both chill out for a minute. Where's this piss and vinegar of yours coming from, anyway?"

"Sorry, buddy, but I care about ya… one hell of a lot. I don't wanna be losin' ya," Eoghan says with striking honesty and humility. "Ya gotta admit most everyone you've met with isn't with us any longer. I say what I say 'cause I wanna make sure your playin' your cards right, me man. Knowin' when to hold 'em and fold 'em."

"I appreciate your concern, Eoghan. I do, but I've learned over the years that a lot of this baggage just comes with the territory."

"And I want ya ta know I'm givin' me eye tooth to be there for ya. You know that, don't ya, Heath?"

"Of course I do, man. I just wish everything didn't have to be so damn intense all the time, to include a cold beer with my buddy."

"You can't have your bread buttered on both sides, ya know. It just don't work that a way."

"You're right, Eoghan. Again, my apologies. And yours accepted. At the same time, I guess we should take a moment to think about those who have, indeed, left us. Since some of them have gone upstairs, it's time I do the same."

"Cute, you cynical bastard… Will that be gin or vodka?"

—ᴍ—

PART IV

CHAPTER 26

A GATHERING OF THE CLAN

ACCORDING TO THE Sahat Kula clock tower, it's just past 5 p.m. on Monday, June 30, 1997 in Old Town Sarajevo. In Asia, it's one minute after midnight, July 1st. Heath finds himself standing spellbound in the Holiday Inn lobby. He's fixated, like so many other reporters around him, on live TV coverage of the Hong Kong handover.

Who could have imagined? he ponders, as hundreds of high-stepping soldiers in starched uniforms parade through a pageant-filled ceremony. Their solemn precision and the crisp martial music signal far more than China's resumed sovereignty over a colony of free-wheeling capitalists. It marks the end of 156 years of proper British rule.

In snow-white tunics, the Hong Kong Police Band stands at ramrod attention, awaiting their turn to perform inside the packed convention center. *God Save the Queen* is heralded by the Scots Guards, complete in their tall, black, bearskin hats. The Union Jack descends for the final time. The moment British cymbals stop vibrating, the Chinese national anthem is trumpeted throughout the chamber. A giant red banner with five gold stars is hoisted alongside a new Hong Kong flag.

Half-a-dozen officers of the Royal Police Training School snap through a choreographed rifle drill, then turn and perform a slow-step salute to the governor. A lone bugler sounds *Last Post* as the British contingent departs the stage. A drizzle brushes the ceremonial courtyard. It turns into a shower, then a downpour, drenching Hong Kong's harbor with sheets of monsoon-borne rain.

"Amazing," Heath whispers. "One minute it's British, the next, it belongs to Red China… such a painless, yet poignant, execution."

—⁂—

Simultaneously, but far less ceremoniously, Dragana Kowalchuk relinquishes the role of outlandish Balkan rebel leader to a bunch of bungling lieutenants barely capable of reading a road map. No herald-trumpet fanfare or heal-clicking honor guard at her non-event. But then, a little less pomposity and a bit more humility seem appropriate, all things considered. The only element the two observances have in common is the onslaught of bad weather. As sprinkles arrive in Belgrade, Dragana scurries about in a desperate attempt to raise her roadster's canvas roof before the driving rain hits.

Hong Kong is now serine, but the ongoing crisis in the Balkans has shifted focus to the Yugoslav province of Kosovo. After years of perceived Serb abuse, Kosovars, and their Albanian allies, are busy planting seeds of rebellion. While Milošević makes plans to send in the army, he calls on Kowalchuk to begin uprooting the discontent. The Bitch of Bosnia is flattered to be considered a cultivator. Bowing to the country's leader, Dragana reaffirms her loyalty before the Belgrade brass. She's now ready to face the Kosovo Liberation Army on the ancient fields of Slavic battle.

At the same time, this wench is still bitter about the recent turn of events. As she slips into her sports car, Dragana spouts an old military axiom, addressing that very angst: "War doesn't determine who is right, only who's left."

With the Serb capital in her rear-view mirror, Dragana steers south through the country's heartland. She stops at the Ravanica monastery, a tribute to its founder, Prince Lazar. Its five-domed Church of the Ascension houses the gallant one's relics. Killed during the battle of Kosovo in 1389, he's pretty much the trumped-up reason for all the bloody battles that have decimated so much of this region over the last half-dozen years.

Respects paid, Dragana floors it, intent on completing her one-woman road rally before the sun sets on the city of Niš, the birthplace of Constantine the Great. Dust-covered history books refer to this site as the gateway from East to West, or vice versa. Keeping to an ancient Roman highway, Dragana ends up in front of the Joca i Nena restaurant on the town's north side.

"Are you Zoran?" she asks the clean-cut, well-built man dressed in army fatigues, relaxing near the door.

"Yes, ma'am," the rich-voiced baritone replies, "and that beautiful red MG tells me you're Dragana Kowalchuk."

"Guilty as charged."

"I booked you a room in the guesthouse across the street. My aunt runs it. Besides, she'll make you a great breakfast."

"Thanks, Zoran, but I'm hungry now. I'm hoping we rendezvous here because the food's good."

"As is the wine, Dragana. Our table awaits."

"Good. We have much to talk about, as I'm sure those in Belgrade briefed you."

"Yes, but food and drink come first. The night is young."

As Heath ambles up the lane toward the Babich family farmhouse, his right knee gives way. He tumbles to the ground, half on the sidewalk, half in the gutter. A father and son, walking toward him, rush to help Heath back on his feet.

"Jeste li dobro?" the young man asks.

"Da, da. Yes, I'm okay. Hvala... Thank you much."

As the two Samaritans continue on, Heath brushes himself off and mumbles, "It's the third time this week that's happened. I should have brought that damn cane after all."

Well, at least none of the bottles were broken, Heath observes as he adjusts the cloth wine satchel and rearranges several small American flags. *It is the 4th of July, after all.*

Even with the kraut-rock music blaring off the back patio, boisterous conversations and raucous laughter can be heard resounding from the Babich manor.

Andro steps on the front porch and yells, "Heath, welcome! Come meet the family… You know my Uncle Franjo from Sarajevo, but I don't believe you've met his wife, Florica. Their kids are running wild in the back yard. This is my father, Petar, and my brother, Alen."

"I've heard so much about you two. And I'm sure Baba Sofija's glad to have you home again."

"Well, I know the cows are," Petar kids. "Alen, please get Mr. Winslow a beer."

"Thanks and it's Heath, please, everyone."

"What? I get no introduction?" Uncle Thoma shouts.

"You need none!" Heath roars back. "Nor does your wife's cooking. And where might that lovely lady be?"

"Sasha's in the kitchen with mama; where else?"

"And this is my Uncle Abeiron and his loving wife, my Aunt Jadranka."

"So, did Andro ever learn to cast a net or fillet a fish while in civilization's cradle? I'm sure he broke his share of plates," Heath jokes with the couple from Greece.

"Continuing on," Andro interjects, "my cousins: Alcina, Andelko and Sasha."

"The table's ready," Baba Sofija announces from the kitchen. "We set a buffet on the patio. Please serve yourselves, then find a seat. And don't worry, there's plenty more where that came from."

"Ah, I find the lady of the house yet again dusted in flour," Heath chides. "Sofija, what a joy to see you. I bring wine and America flags for the celebration. Did you bake Uncle Sam a cake?"

"Da, da. Just grab a plate you silly man. Get some food before you starve," Sofija chuckles, poking his pot belly. In response, she and Heath fall into a tender embrace, followed by loud, smacking kisses to both cheeks.

"Ah, Father, so glad you could join us," Sofija says looking around Heath's shoulder to see the parish priest stepping through the doorway. "We're just plating up. Come this way. Father Malinko's arrived. Say hello, everyone.

"Saints alive, let's eat!" the priest declares.

The boisterous clan attacks the food display with a vengeance, then set their plates, thus securing seats in the outdoor arena. Drinks are refreshed. Everyone sits for a culinary feast spanning the gastronomy of Southeast Europe.

Before dining commences, Baba Sofija claps her hands several times to gain everyone's attention. "Since this is the USA's birthday, and Heath is our special guest, might there be something you'd like to share, sir?"

"First of all, thank you, Sofija. And thank you all for inviting me. As the oldest American here, I would like to suggest one of my family's traditions. On special occasions like this, everyone shares something they've gained or learned since we were last together. Seeing as it's the 4th of July, I'd like to start with one of our newest Americans, Andro."

"Thank you, Heath. And yes, I too am proud to be an American, but I'm even more blessed to be part of the Babich clan. With a lot of help from so many people these last few years, I've become far more comfortable with my inner and outer worlds, but the best is our family. We're back together again."

"Here, here, Andro," Heath calls out. "Baba Sofija, is there something you'd like to share?"

"First, I ask that we take a moment to remember Mara, praying for her and her family's souls. Amen. And as the Babich matriarch, I hereby order we meet like this every year to celebrate America's birthday."

"Živjeli! Υγεία! Fenékig! Cheers!" The salutations ring out around the table as glasses clink and everyone sips in agreement.

"Willpower is the heartbeat of this family," Petar says after he rises. "As Andro said, we're again together as one. Once more we have proven our strength is greater than the sum of our parts."

Glass clink again and Alen stands. The strong young man finds it hard to speak, then says, "Da… and double what papa just said." Everyone chuckles. Alen blushes, then takes his seat.

The remembrances, affirmations and toasts continue to flow. Thoma and Sasha insist next year's reunion be at their Mostar restaurant. Abeiron and Jadranka vow to top it a year later with a sunset buffet on the Poseidon's patio. Franjo and Florica announce they're setting up a center in Sarajevo for kids with special needs.

"You've all seen the artwork above the buffet," Andelko notes. "I had one of Andro's photos blown up. From it, a painter friend did the abstract. Baba Sofija knows the artist who wove the tapestry. This is the first of many sets I plan to hang in my gallery, with the proceeds going to help run your childcare center."

Shouts of, "Bravo! Hurrah! Hooray!" echo across the patio.

"And now, Father Malinko," Sofija states as the padre rises for the occasion.

"Let us pray. Dear Lord, continue to bless this stoic clan. This family was torn apart by war and is now reunited in peace. Help them maintain a balance between the material and spiritual that make up our daily lives. May their actions today be useful to others come the morrow. Amen."

"Amen," is whispered several times. Everyone begins eating. As large as the group is, quiet reflections continue uninterrupted. This is their food for thought moment, with several absorbing large portions of renewed vitality. This is the Babich cornucopia of beliefs and experiences spread upon a table of awareness. It's the banquet they trust others will peruse and consume. The hope is no one gets heartburn in the process.

—◆—

"A warm summer's eve, excellent food and a private balcony," Dragana notes. "You've pretty much thought of everything, Zoran. Thank you."

"You're welcome, Dragana, but don't forget the wine, which I'm convinced we should continue sharing," he states while refilling both their cut crystal goblets.

"Okay, but it's time we talk about why I'm here. I know what's going on in Kosovo, but what's behind these troubles? How do we get them under control?"

"Is finding out the 'who and what' that important? Why waste time looking for a cause? I've got a better idea: Deal with what's at hand."

"That may be easy for you, Zoran, so why not make it even simpler? I solve problems by opposing them, as well as the bastards behind them. I say we need a plan to detract from our detractors."

"And how did that approach work for you in Bosnia?"

"Careful how you speak, sir. Knowing my enemy is critical. It helps me better understand the task at hand. That way, I can form a strategy to attack…"

"According to your commandos, that approach wore thin quickly. While you revised and revised, Dragana, your troops stayed tangled in their trenches."

"Excuse me… You weren't the one trying to lead a mob of inept thugs through the Alps. You weren't there in those thorny times."

"No, I wasn't, but you're here now and this is my neck of the woods. You have a long history of arguing against anyone or anything that opposes you. I haven't time for that crap. Let me make something clear: You were sent here so that we might build a team. And I'm willing to play full partner. But if push comes to shove, let there be no doubt whose ass will be made bloody and tossed on the next boxcar back to Belgrade."

"Alright, Zoran, I get it. Bosnian lesson learned. But you must understand: My dedication is what drives me. It's why I haven't quit, regardless what's thrown down in front of me."

"I don't think dedication's the issue, Dragana. I question your focus. It's not enough just listening to your ego. You must follow your dictates. Devotion must be to the real truth. In our case, that's a Greater Serbia. That must be what drives us. It's a given. It doesn't have to be legislated, or always enforced at the point of a sword. It must beat in our hearts."

"Okay, I think we've had plenty of wine and waxed philosophical long enough. Let's talk again when more sober heads prevail. No hard feelings, Zoran? I'm just passionate about everything I do. You had no problem seeing that. Tomorrow we can thrash out how to deal with this gang of brutes."

"Agreed. I'm calling a time out on the playing field. Now, let me escort you to your room."

"And I was afraid you'd never offer," Dragana quips as she winks at her potential bedroom partner. At the same time, she thinks, *The last thing I want, Zoran, is to hurt you, but it's staying on my list of things I probably will need to do.*

—⁓—

"Sofija, I'm so glad you could join me on this pilgrimage," Father Malinko says as the two step off the bus from Mostar. Before them unfolds a fairytale town nestled in the alpine forests and lush vineyards of the Hertzegovian Mountains. This is the Slavic version of a hand-colored Currier and Ives print.

"I've never attended the Feast of St. James and it's been a long time since I've prayed at the feet of Our Lady of Međugorje, but I'm eager to make a day of it, Father."

"Good. The visionaries tell us that no one comes here by chance. Rather, we're called by Our Lady. If you're ready, Sofija, we have a full schedule. After Mass, we'll lunch in the village. Then we can follow the same path up Apparition Hill as the young women who first encountered the Virgin Mary. Later in the day, we join the pilgrims to pray the Holy Rosary and offer a blessing for the sick."

"Excellent. I have but one request, Father: We rest in the Oasis of Peace near the hilltop. It's an island of tranquility for me. I have some things I'd like to discuss with you there."

"In the peace garden, or by Kravice Falls, whichever pleases you."

Baba Sofija and Father Malinko complete the obligatory elements of their religious trek, then enter the oasis to sit on a stone bench overlooking the parish. Both pilgrims stare in silence at the pristine valley. Time passes, then Sofija speaks.

"What's with all the chaos in my life, Father?"

"Is chaos the right word, Sofija? Certainly, a lot of changes have been made to the patterns of your life. And yes, you're concerned about keeping things organized. That's clear. But you're a strong woman and change has never been a problem for you before, as long as you kept it orderly."

"I fear you know me too well, sir. But I also feel like I can't get there from here anymore. It's as if my whole world has to be taken apart and rebuilt from the ground up."

"And maybe you're right. At your family banquet, didn't Alcina announce plans to help your gild do just that? You should remember that sometimes a little chaos needs to reign so that a log jam can be broken. You're an organizational fiend, Mrs. Babich. That's a given.

Maybe it's time you step back from your garden a little so that new plants can find room to grow."

After another pause, Sofija looks skyward and asks, "Tell me then, Father, beyond me and my family, why have so many people all around us been made to suffer so?"

"I think it's time you reread the Book of Job, Sofija. That glorious poem of the Old Testament answers the very question you ask. You must believe that God cares about people who suffer troubles. And God will help them, although, sometimes they must be patient."

"I hear what you're saying, but I fear the anger that's raging inside me."

"It's normal, Sofija, especially after what we've all been through. We're only human. In part, it's why I asked you to join me today. Like you, I too need to refocus on how to live a compassionate life. As children, we all learned the Golden Rule. Many can recite it, but few put it into practice. To me, it means we must draw the violence out of our lives. Step back from the abyss. We must learn to love our enemies all over again."

"That's been a struggle for me my entire life, Father."

"Yes, but we must never stop making room for others in our minds."

"Isn't that a whole lot easier for someone like you? Someone who's married to the Church."

"I would argue religion is part of the problem, not the solution. Going to church doesn't make you a Christian any more than standing in a garage would make me a car.

"And we don't hear priests, pastors, rabbis and imams talking about empathy enough, either. Caring must be at the forefront of all we say and do. The world's calling for us to act as never before. Compassion reminds us daily that belittling others, even those we may see as our enemies, means we're rejecting the very humanity we all must share."

"That's profound, Father, but I'm not sure I understand."

"Let me put it another way, Sofija. We all have bad habits we need to break, right? So, how do we do that? We need to be honest with ourselves and aware of what we're doing. Then we can split from the routine. Yes, we may stumble on occasion. That'll happen, but we don't need to beat ourselves up over it. Just get back up and try again.

"And then there's the matter of love, unqualified love, be it from God or mankind. We can't just seek it out. We have to live it each and every day. Then it'll come to us naturally. And we need to be open, not judging how it comes our way.

"Sofija, you know how to love and be loved. And with the creative ladies you've brought close, I can see you love very much what you're doing. We all can sense your passion. You're inspired. That, in turn, stirs others to further action."

"But these old bones don't feel as lively as they use to, Padre."

"Then it's time you embrace your age. Look at it as God's blessing. It means you're still vibrant."

"You're right. It is all about the Golden Rule… If we have faith in ourselves…"

"and practice what we preach,"

"then living with a good spirit,"

"filled with love and civility,"

"will become the center of God's life cycle for all of us," Sofija surmises. "As the old church saying goes, 'We all must learn to live simply, love generously, care deeply, speak kindly and leave the rest to God.'"

"I couldn't have said it up better. So, how about a scoop of ice cream with chocolate sauce?"

"And crushed pistachios on top?" Sofija asks.

"Absolutely… I know this great little kiosk in town," the priest says. "And Lord knows we've earned it."

—w—

FAREWELL EVIL QUEEN & HANDSOME PRINCE

"Ando, please come in. Have a seat," his USAID supervisor urges. "Here we are in sunny Sarajevo. It's mid-July, 1997. As I'm sure you're aware, it's time for your annual performance review. Can you believe it's been over a year since you joined the agency?"

"Time flies when you're having fun. Although, mind you, I don't consider such reviews a joke, Ms. Stapleton."

"Relax, Andro. You're a rising star around here, but there are always things we can improve. That's what these sessions are for. We discuss coaching, training and other things. It's a chance to make sure your goals align with our team objectives, as well as laying the foundation for growth. So, shall we start?"

"Yes, ma'am. I'm all ears."

"As you know, our media efforts in country are intense and I think we're making great progress, but more can always be done. You, Andro, like the others on staff, need to continue focusing on the effects you're having."

"I like to think I am."

"Yes, but you may need to charge harder at immediate problems. I realize this is your homeland and that brings many pluses to the table. At the same time, your swipes at tracking down rebel leaders, intimidating media bosses and pushing your own news agenda can run counter to what we're trying to achieve overall."

"I hear what you're saying, but it's difficult to restrain myself at times."

"That's understandable, especially when one considers what your family's been through, but let's not bring it back to the office. I want you to ask yourself ever day: What's been the outcome of my work so far? Conversely, don't spend too much time debating all the pros and cons. In other words, don't beat a dead horse."

"Point well taken, ma'am."

"Andro, you're doing great things. Heck, in the time you've been here, you've done a superb job gathering intel. Now's the time to do the analysis. Ask yourself: What are the positives and negatives of all the things you've dealt with so far?"

"Okay, Ms. Stapleton, how would you like me to proceed?"

"Well, Andro, I think it's time for you to share what you've learned. It's time for the student to become the teacher. I've talked with a journalist friend of yours—a Mr. Winslow, I believe?"

"Yes, Heath. He writes for the *Times* and the *Herald Tribune*."

"Right. Well, he's been talking up an idea with his cohorts and folks at the Journalism Center in New York. They think we should host a reporters' seminar. We haven't nailed down any kind of agenda yet, but I'd like you to speak on the agency's role in reconstruction. Are you interested?"

"Yes, but what would you like me to talk about?"

"You and Mr. Winslow will come up with a topic. Just don't fall back on some staid mission brief. We already have the ability to PowerPoint people to death. We need something fresh. It'll come to you. Trust me… Alright?"

"Yes, ma'am. I'll get together with Heath right away and report back as soon as I can. But what about my performance report? Did I make the grade?"

"Andro, you passed with flying colors. I'm also recommending you for a monetary award. I was in the military too. Money beats medals every time. Well, don't just sit there. Get to work. Time's a wastin.'"

"Very good and thank you Ms. Stapleton. Hvala."

—⁂—

There's a knock at Heath's Holiday Inn suite. Its hobbled tenant is scurrying about inside. "Be right there… Andro, welcome," Heath says as he swings open the door. "I'm just gathering my stuff. The weather's so great, let's head down the boulevard to a coffee house."

As they walk the hallway toward the elevator, Heath asks, "What's so urgent, Andro? What did you have to see me about right away?"

As the lift doors swish open and the two step in, Andro tells Heath about his recent evaluation meeting and Ms. Stapleton's support of the reporters' conference.

"Yes, she called me to say the same. Oh, the Institute for War & Peace Reporting is on board now as well. And yes, I'll help you develop your presentation. Café Tito sound good? It's just a block away. So, any idea what you want to talk about?"

"Too many. The more I think on it, the more overwhelmed I become."

"I don't find that the least bit surprising. For Andro Babich, gathering info is synonymous with gaining knowledge. But I argue, sometimes we can learn new things just by looking through old data with a fresh approach."

"Okay, but how do we address that in the here and now?"

Their discussion is interrupted as the maître d' greets them at the coffee house door. "Two on the patio, please," Heath instructs. Once seated, the conversation continues.

"Look, Andro, I think it's obvious to you, as it is to me, the BiH is going to slide back into the same ethno-nationalist bullshit if something isn't done and done soon. I'm talking about this country's Fourth Estate. Public discourse is now so damn infused with bigotry it's disgusting. And so many in the media just feed the beast, knowingly or not. People don't realize it, but the effect on this country, and the whole democratic process, will be huge.

"This crazy amplified anger is spreading through the media like wildfire. It's wiping out any kind of dialogue. The independent press is being undermined. Hell, Nazi-like rhetoric is front page fodder now. It leads the six-o'clock news. This super-patriot journalism crap has got to stop!"

"Wow, Heath, I think you've just written opening remarks for the conference, or at least the program's back cover."

"Alright, I'm on my third cup of coffee, but you get my point. So, is there anything in that clap-trap you want to zero in on?"

"As you've said before, training reporters will be the key to breaking the county's propaganda cycle, especially as they move ahead with the war crimes trials."

"Yes, but that's a given, Andro. That's what you're agency is here for. Dig deeper, my man. I know you can. I think we've identified the cause. Now, what are the tools needed to achieve the desired effect?"

"I don't know the answer yet, Heath, but I think you've pointed me in the right direction. Thanks. It's time I get back to the office. I've got my work cut out for me."

"One more thing," Heath says as he grabs Andro's arm and stares into his eyes. "This is all about the truth, all the history and all the facts. I sense the future of this country's at stake. If reporters perpetuate the myths of war, the people here will be taking up arms again in no time… And on that pleasant note, I bid you ado."

—∞—

It's a sumptuous Sarajevo summer morning as Heath strolls into Vrelo Bosne. This time he's walking with the aid of a cane. The park is resplendent with bed after bed of multi-colored flowers. A light breeze wafts with the smell of freshly-mowed grass. Most pleased with his bucolic surroundings, Heath plops on a bench and opens the July 20th edition of *The Stars & Stripes* to the sports section.

"That Tiger Woods is one amazing golfer," says a woman approaching from behind his perch.

"The first Black man and the youngest player to win Augusta," Heath replies as he turns and looks over his shoulder to see whose approaching. "Are you Jasna? Franjo said I should expect you."

"Yes and you must be Mr. Winslow, the intrepid American reporter."

"Call me Heath."

Jasna takes a seat on the bench as they continue the sports banter about the many records Tiger set at the Masters.

"Okay, you know your sports, Jasna. Now, what can I do for you?"

"Seeing as you asked, Heath, there's someone I'm interested in contacting… a Dragana Kowalchuk."

"Me too, but for significantly different reasons, I'm sure. So, NATO, CIA, Interpol? Who punches your ticket?"

"Well, isn't that just a little presumptuous?"

"Oh, I don't know. Put yourself in my position. A stranger approaches you and asks for info on the whereabouts of a war criminal that's been called before The Hague. You don't find that the least bit intriguing?"

"There should never come a time when the United States can't ask its citizens to assist in combating a threat to national security. Do you not agree, Heath?"

"So, Jasna, while you twist the Law of Unintended Consequence, I'm expected to compromise my professional integrity, impede my ability to function and put my life in jeopardy just to help you? Where's the tit-for-tat in that spy-verses-spy cartoon?"

Notebook entry: Operation Mockingbird — CIA campaign to influence news media… Began in the '50s… Activities, extent & project's existence remain in dispute… Media recruited & infiltrated by CIA for propaganda purposes

"A simple 'No' would have been sufficient."

"The hell it would… I thought our government banned such practices years ago. But then, I'm gullible enough to think the CIA has a code of conduct. So, what? If recruiting a reporter doesn't work, you go for their credentials so that some clever agent has a cover? I'm sure Walter Cronkite and the Council on Foreign Relations would love to hear about your current state of affairs."

"Please calm down, Mr. Winslow. You have a function and we have a function to…"

"But it's oil and vinegar, Jasna, and we're not tossing a salad here. We're talking about real dangers. So, is this one of The Company's smoke and mirror tricks, or yours?"

"Heath, I understand. I just thought we could discuss…"

"The discussion's over, damn it. The fact that we're even talking casts a cloud over my credibility. If I wasn't tainted before, I sure as hell am now. Thank you very much!" Heath barks as he starts to storm away. He trips and falls onto the cobblestone pathway. He tries several times to get up, but is unsuccessful. "Shit… My damn knee is really messed up this time."

"Heath, let me help you. Those sprinklers have tripped me up as well. There's a clinic nearby. I'll take you there."

"No thanks, no clinic. Just call me a taxi."

"That will take a while. I'll have the horseman come around. You might as well ride in style."

"Alright, Jasna, but get me to Franjo's office at the airport. Understood? No tricks."

"Please. This isn't some James Bond movie gone bad, Mr. Winslow."

"Oh, no? I'd argue the contrary. I feel like Dean Martin without a parachute in a damn Matt Helm movie. And you're 'America's loaded weapon.' So, roll the credits."

—⚊—

Zoran's bronzed, chiseled physique is silhouetted on the guest-house balcony as the sun rises over Kosovo's ancient city of Niš. He stands a proud 185 centimeters with but a towel synching his slender waist. Dragana approaches, placing her hands on his shoulders and glancing down the small of his back. "My goodness, I'm so sorry." she says.

"About what? You find a need to apologize for last night?"

"No, not at all, but it appears I left several scratches on your backside."

"I consider them trophies," Zoran says in a strange, cocky manner. "Besides, if I didn't want you taking part in those games, there'd be no marks on the playground."

There's a light tap, tap, tap on the door. "Coffee and a moment of your time, sir" a voice is heard saying. Zoran charges across the bedroom and into the hallway, slamming the door behind him. Dragana grabs her overnight bag and steps into the bath.

"Finish your shower now!" Zoran yells as he strides back into the room. "We've got to move out."

"What's up?" Dragana asks as she slips into the room, towel drying her long, thick, jet-black hair and flopping onto the bed. "We have time for a little morning delight, do we not?"

"I wish, but my lieutenants tell me otherwise. The Kosovars are coming to kidnap you for sale to the highest bidder."

"How do they even know I'm here?"

"That damn fire-engine red MGB of yours. It's like a beacon in the night. Who in the hell else drives a mint-conditioned, vintage sports car in Kosovo for Christ's sake?"

"Well, jump my ass, why don't you?"

"Hey, I didn't say it was your fault… I'm just blaming you. Now, put some clothes on and grab your shit. We're getting the hell out of here while we still can."

"Okay, I can drive us to…"

"No, Dragana. That's just too obvious. You take the train back to the capitol. I'll follow with the car. I know these country roads like the back of my hand. I'll lose them in no time. So, decision made… Let's move!"

—m—

As Dragana alights in the train compartment, she looks to the station's far parking lot. She can barely see Zoran mounting her roadster. Out of her right eye, she notices a flash of some type. Before Dragana can discern what's happening, the rocket-propelled grenade strikes the MGB, igniting an intense, gold and red-streaked fireball. The blast's percussion soon strikes the railcar's side. Not unlike a startled steed, the train lurches forward. With all the horsepower it can muster, the locomotive is soon galloping down the tracks, in route to Belgrade.

"Damn! There goes my car and one of the strangest, hottest studs I've ever put to bed."

Well, Zoran, life's a bitch and this one's glad she took your advice. Now, where's that drink cart? Dragana muses. *I never did get my morning coffee.*

—m—

"Horse and carriage?" Franjo chuckles as the coachman reigns in at the cargo ops building. "A little pretentious, Heath. Don't you think?"

"Funny, ha-ha. Give me a hand into your office. My knee's all messed up and I need to get my ass stateside, pronto."

"Sure. What can I do to help?"

"Is Sergeant Green flying in or out? If so, I want on the next manifest to Rheine-Main. First, though, give Andro a call and tell him to come over here immediately. There's no time for lollygagging… Oh, and get me a couple of aspirin. Thanks."

By coincidence, as Franjo sets Heath's requests in motion, Dr. Besich steps into the ops center. "Doc! It's Heath, Heath Winslow, the reporter. We met in Goma, Zaire when my Army buddies were injured. Remember?"

"Of course, Heath. How are you?"

"Not well, I'm afraid. I think I blew out my knee. I'd appreciate it if you could take a look and maybe give me a couple pain pills for the flight home."

"I can do much better than that. We've got a Nightingale med-evac flying in late tonight. I'll make sure you're a patient shipping out to Landsthul in the morning."

"You'd do that for me, doc? Really?"

"Absolutely, Heath. Those features you wrote about my team in Africa were all over the *Herald Tribune* and *Stars & Stripes*. *Time* magazine even did a photo spread. And CNN shot all kinds of footage. Heck, the PAO in Frankfurt still calls me Doc Hollywood."

As Heath thanks the medical officer, Andro bursts through the side door. "Heath, I got here as fast as I could. Are you okay? What happened? How can I help?"

"First, take a chill pill, partner. Thanks to the good doctor, my medical concerns have been addressed. Now, I need your help with another situation."

As Heath explains the bizarre encounter with Jasna in the park, he urges Andro rush to the hotel. His mission: Secure all of Heath's papers and cassette tapes.

"Here's my room key. Take a box and just throw everything that's not clothes into it. Don't forget to check the nightstand. Park in back and use the fire escape. You know how the place is covered with cameras. We'll worry about my clothes later."

"Sure. I can bring the stuff back to Franjo, or mail it to you, if you like."

"No, Andro, no! Sorry, but no. Take it to Eoghan. Ask him to put it away until I write with instructions. Alright? I've just got to know those things are safe."

"Sure, Heath, but what is all of this? You auditioning for a remake of *Live and Let Die*?"

"This is no joke, Andro. I fear spying eyes are everywhere. Just humor me. And I'm sorry, but the James Bond reference has been used… So, move out, Green Card Soldier!"

—m—

Aug. 15, 1997… It's day two of the Balkan Media Symposium. More than 200 attendees funnel into the Holiday Inn-Sarajevo main conference room to hear the afternoon session's final speaker. An event coordinator approaches the podium.

"Without further ado, it's my pleasure to introduce a member of the U.S. Agency for International Development. He's a Bosnian-American who earned his citizenship through a special U.S. Army program. Ladies and gentlemen, please welcome Mr. Andro Babich to the microphone."

"Thank you. And first off, I fully acknowledge you're the journalists and I'm not. So, please don't hesitate shouting out questions, comments or concerns as we go along. And yes, there are a couple other things I'm not. I'm not here to bore you with a mission briefing. And I'm not here to speculate about the Fourth Estate's future, especially with the Internet launching us all into cyberspace." A light applause and several supportive mumbles follow Andro's qualifiers.

"But I am here to challenge you, all of you, to become more involved in your work by celebrating diversity." That comment's followed by several groans and a significant amount of paper rustling.

"I know many of you balk at the idea of adding under-represented voices to the news equation. You see it as pandering, or some type of distortion. In response, I argue what's off the mark now is how news coverage is being conducted in this country. It's all about one group's ideas or opinions, verses exposing all the facts and telling the whole truth."

"So, what about certain groups always getting blamed when there are reports about crime or poverty?" someone in the middle of the hall shouts out.

"Yes, the flip-side can be skewed as well. So, if you're not checking a number of sources, chances are your story will have a lot of holes in it. That's why I say knowledge should be everyone's synonym for broadmindedness in these challenging times."

Some eyes roll, but many others feed the diversity discussion's growth. As things heat up, Andro becomes animated and excited. In response, reporters, writers and talk show hosts throw out a spectrum of questions and comments, further enlivening the debate.

"So, how should we proceed?" a naive, but eager journalism student asks.

"Attend events like this. Network. Look around. See what others are doing. You'll gain a new perspective. I'm living proof of that. And trust me; all good things don't happen in a lecture hall. Elbow up to a bar, or ask a seasoned reporter to join you for coffee. Seek a mentor outside the walls of academia, or beyond your job."

"It sounds like you're preaching about nothing more than respect," another says.

"And that's a bad thing? We're all human beings. We're all equal; are we not? Like my Baba Sofija taught me, 'Do onto others as you would have them do onto you.'"

"Beyond the Golden Rule, what else can we as journalists do?" a woman in the back of the room asks.

"Through your truthful work, teach others how to recognize and challenge biases. Let them know how to question unjust things. How they can be a part of the process."

"You really think, Mr. Babich, all the different ethnic and religious factions in the Balkans can work together?"

"I'm no more a pie-in-the-sky Pollyanna than you are, but we need to make a connection and we need to do it now. We're much more alike than you might think. We all have hearts and dreams. Just keep an open mind. Try listening to what others have to say. Trust me. You're bound to learn something new that way."

The back and forth continues. Andro realizes his allotted time has well passed.

"I must wrap this up, but again I want to confront you: Be proud of your heritage, but reach out to others and continue building the peace. You're special. Don't hide that. Share your culture while you get to know someone different. I'm convinced tolerance and trust are the keys to your success as great communicators. Good luck and thank you."

Andro's exit is accompanied by a solid applause. An energized buzz charges through the audience. The first-time lecturer feels good about the intercourse, but heads straight to the lounge in hopes Eoghan can offer a shot of fortitude, as well as a stool upon which to sit and drink it.

—⚍—

As Andro sips a beer at the end of the bar, his boss approaches and gives him a firm slap on the back. "I think you nailed it, kid," Ms. Stapleton states. "If nothing else, you sure got a lot of folks thinking. And that's a good thing."

"Well, thank you ma'am, but I'll be the first to admit I'm glad it's over."

"Ah, but your speaking tour's just begun, Andro. As you head stateside for your Army Guard training, you should plan on giving a status update to our Washington bosses, as well as addressing the upcoming Army Public Affairs Symposium. I'd planned on going, but they need to hear a fresh voice, someone who's been on the front lines of our work. I'll give you my outline and we can discuss details later. Again, congratulations on doing us proud."

"Thank you, ma'am. I'm flattered and honored, but are you sure?"

"Couldn't be more so. I do have one question, though: What drives Andro Babich?"

"It all goes back to my Army recruiter, I guess. He helped me become a Green Card Soldier and a proud American. We were battle buddies and always will be. Cashton's a lot like my homeland, if that makes any sense. As I often say, Bosnia may not be perfect, but I'll hold her hand until she gets well again."

—w—

CHAPTER 28:

A TRAIN TO SOMEWHERE

It's mid-July, 1999… a beautiful Bosnian farewell afternoon for Mr. Heath Winslow. As he flits around the Sarajevo flat, gathering the last of his belongings, Heath carries on yet another snarly tête-à-tête with himself, trying to discern why he came back to Sarajevo in the first place.

That's at least twenty pounds of diddly-squat smashed into a ten-pound bag, Devilish Heath quips as his master finishes grouping spiral notepads and cassette tapes.

And bless that crusty milk carton for serving your filing needs so well, Angelic Heath muses.

Excuse me, sir, Devilish asks. *Why was it so damn important to build this cross-referenced paper scrap heap in the first place?*

That's a good question, Angelic notes. *Did it ever provide any real direction?*

Hell, I don't know, Heath thinks. *I guess I should have published this refuse from my teeming shores ages ago.*

So, it stands as a mighty chronicle to your lack of wisdom in general. Is that what you're saying? The devilish one asks.

Or, at least something like that, the angelic one injects. *Think about it… All this stuff was meant to bring clarity to vagueness. And how well did that work out, Mr. Winslow?*

"Okay, you two, enough of the condescending self-talk!" Heath shouts, trying to bring his mind back into a singular reality. "It's better to focus on the task at hand… for it's time to blow this popcorn stand."

And what part of the Fort Knox gold reserve will you borrow in order to ship all this garbage home? Devilish asks.

How about Danvor's wife having the FedEx man take it away, Angelic suggests.

"For once, you two might be on to something," Heath declares. "I ask Tasha to dispatch this stuff, then I send her a check. Done."

With the self-deprecation complete, Heath steps out of his classy Old Town bungalow, locking the door one last time. "Damn, I'll miss the smell of Sarajevo roses while sipping coffee on that patio," he sighs. Readjusting his shoulder bag, Heath begins dragging a scuffed-up roller case down the alley. His destination: The Ballygoan.

—⚬—

"Well, if it isn't Mr. Happy Face," Eoghan remarks as Heath shuffles into the pub. "One for the road, I reckon?"

"Make it a double."

"And where ya be off to, sir?"

"Oh, the *Times* editor sent me a fax asking a favor. He wants me to cover some 21st century meeting, since I'm flying out of Budapest. They'll put me up and pay for the flight home. Penny-pincher that I am, I can't say no."

"Ta hell with the new millennium… So what? Do folks actually believe the world's comin' to an end at midnight?"

Notebook entry: Millennium bug— '60s & '70s software programs dropped first 2 digits of each year… saved expensive & limited memory… Can't distinguish 2000 from 1900… Leap year algorithms & computations could run amuck

"Be careful, Eoghan. Those sky-is-falling crazies are convinced the New Year's Eve Y-2-K bogyman's going to get us all. Computers are destine to crash the world over. There'll be water outages, no gas, heat or electricity. People will be panic-struck. So, why, I ask, are we welcoming the dawn of the Information Age?"

"Doesn't that pretty well describe the shite we've been livin' here for most of the '90s? Hell, I'll be glad to see this century gone."

"Oh, yes. We can't forget our indiscriminate war. No good guys and no bad guys, just a shitload of ugliness on all sides—in the trenches and on the streets. And what's Bosnia left with? A bunch of simple-minded folk intent on branding every last victim and villain. Why in the hell did any of this happen in the first place? Every explanation's an insult to someone. A bunch of hotheads who turned healthy de-bate into a holocaust."

> *Notebook entry: Archbishop Tutu: Reconciliation is not about being cozy; it is not about pretending that things were other than they were... Reconciliation based on falsehood, on not facing up to reality, is not reconciliation at all*

"Like they say, Heath, 'History's written in blood. Only the signa-tures are in ink.'"

"Don't be getting bartender philosophical on me, Irishman. You said my debt's settled, right? I don't want to leave this fine establish-ment in arrears."

"Me five cent foolishness aside, Mr. Winslow, did ya accomplish what you'd set out to do on this trip?"

"Oh, I'm still processing all of that, Eoghan. Sure, I reconnected with a lot of people. And that was good, very good."

"Well, I'd say that calls for a trip upstairs, sir."

"I'm right behind you, mate. And what do you have there?"

"Let us worship at Saint Magdalene's alter," Eoghan says as he dusts and uncorks a special bottle of scotch. "At nineteen years, she's the perfect single malt for toastin' such a moment."

Heath and Eoghan sip scotch in silence, knowing full well this will be their last call for who knows how long. Refreshments knocked back, Eoghan steps out from behind the bar to give Heath a goodbye bear hug. "Remember the ol' sayin', 'Don't argue with an idiot. He'll drag you down to his level and beat you with experience.' And as any good Irishman would say: Slán agus beannacht leat, me friend."

"Goodbye and God's blessings be with you as well, my sweet Eoghan."

—w—

Heath exits the behemoth labeled Tram No. 1 and saunters into Sarajevo's massively drab train station. Ticket in hand, he heads to Platform 6 where the Budapest IC awaits.

"Gospodin! Mr. Heath," Sasha shouts, stepping from a nearby rail-car. "How great for to see you. So good to catch before you go," he says, reaching into his backpack and pulling out a cassette. "*Sevda-linka: Folk, Love & Blues*. It be the new *Yugos* album. A bunch of wild and crazy guys strumming tunes over Dinaric Alps. Please to listen often and us remember."

"How could I ever forget, Sasha, but I'll be back to hear you sing live… I promise."

"And not so worry, Heath. Hard feelings here now start to fade. Young peoples no looking back. We now free to go forward. Soon, maybe, Yugoslavs all united again."

"I so want to believe you," Heath whispers as the two fall into a farewell embrace. They grab shoulders, then boldly kiss each other's cheeks. "Now get out of here you light-hearted lummox. I have a train to catch."

As the young man ambles down the platform, Heath turns and yells, "Journalist to musician: Don't you worry, either. This reporter has his notepads. I'll be sending you all the extra adjectives and dangling participles I can spare."

"Svi na brodu!" a conductor shouts from afar.

Board the train, yes, but to who knows where? Heath ponders.

For who knows what reason? The hidden hellish one asks.

Or to do what when we get there? An angelic voice adds.

"All aboard, indeed," Heath mumbles as he embarks.

ABOUT THE AUTHOR

For almost 40 years, Bruce Zielsdorf worked as a military journalist, newspaper editor and Army civilian public relations practitioner at locations around the globe. From drafting feature stories during the Vietnam era through coverage of the Lake Placid Olympics, he's documented airmen at work worldwide through his writing, editing and photographic skills—an Air Force career that spanned 23 years. Today, Bruce lives in Killeen, Central Texas. He retired a few years ago as the civilian public affairs director at Fort Hood. That was after serving 11 years as the Army's spokesperson in the "media capital of the world"—New York City. Zielsdorf describes himself as a freelance writer and quality management consultant, pursuing a creative writing future in both fiction and non-fiction.

EDITOR'S NOTE

It is common convention within the *Chicago Manual of Style* to italicize foreign phrases when they appear as spoken dialog. However, for this book we have opted not to do so, to avoid confusion with the italicized inner dialog of the book's protagonist. We felt it would be less confusing to keep the foreign phrases in Roman style. We hope this adds to the reader's understanding and enjoyment of the story.

CPSIA information can be obtained at www.ICGtesting.com
Printed in the USA
LVOW13s1118240114

370832LV00003B/5/P